LUCY

SPEAK OUT!

Other *Peanuts* Kids' Collections

Snoopy: Cowabunga!

Charlie Brown and Friends

Charlie Brown: Pow!

Woodstock: Master of Disguise

Snoopy: Contact!

Snoopy: Party Animal

Charlie Brown: Here We Go Again

Snoopy to the Rescue

Snoopy: What's Wrong with Dog Lips?

I'm Not Your Sweet Babboo!

Snoopy: Boogie Down!

LUCY
SPEAK OUT!

A **PEANUTS**™ Collection

CHARLES M. SCHULZ

Andrews McMeel
PUBLISHING®

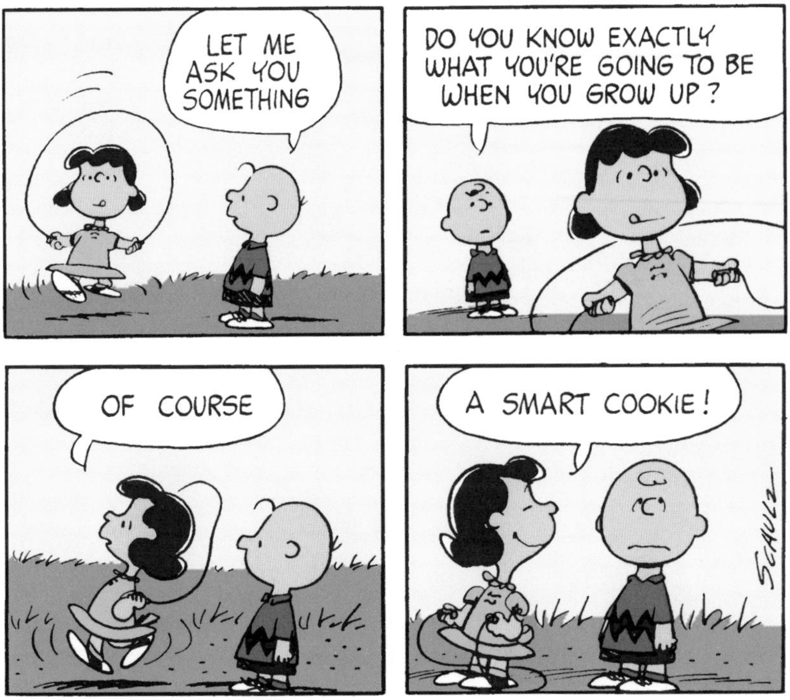
LET ME ASK YOU SOMETHING
DO YOU KNOW EXACTLY WHAT YOU'RE GOING TO BE WHEN YOU GROW UP?
OF COURSE
A SMART COOKIE!
SCHULZ

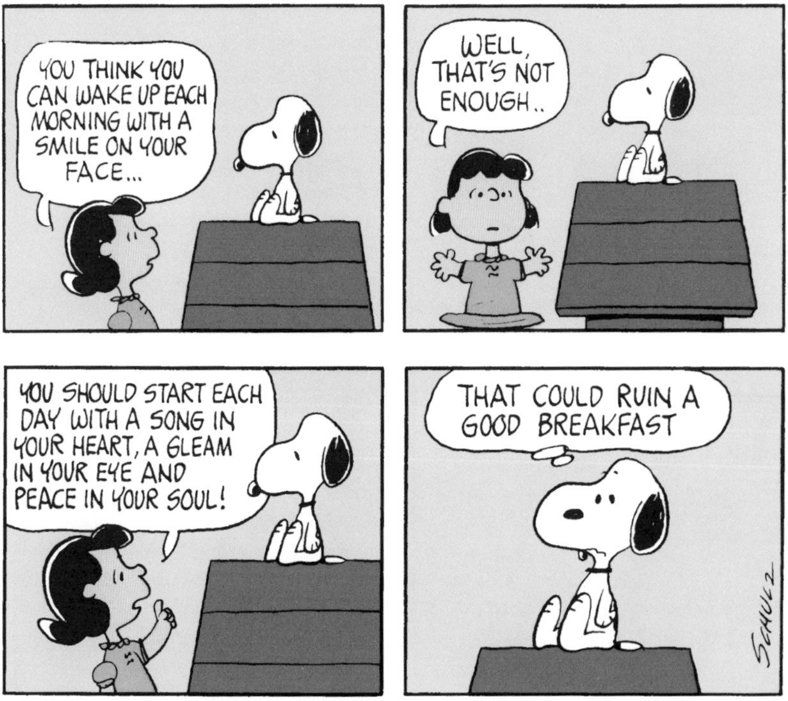
YOU THINK YOU CAN WAKE UP EACH MORNING WITH A SMILE ON YOUR FACE...
WELL, THAT'S NOT ENOUGH..
YOU SHOULD START EACH DAY WITH A SONG IN YOUR HEART, A GLEAM IN YOUR EYE AND PEACE IN YOUR SOUL!
THAT COULD RUIN A GOOD BREAKFAST
SCHULZ

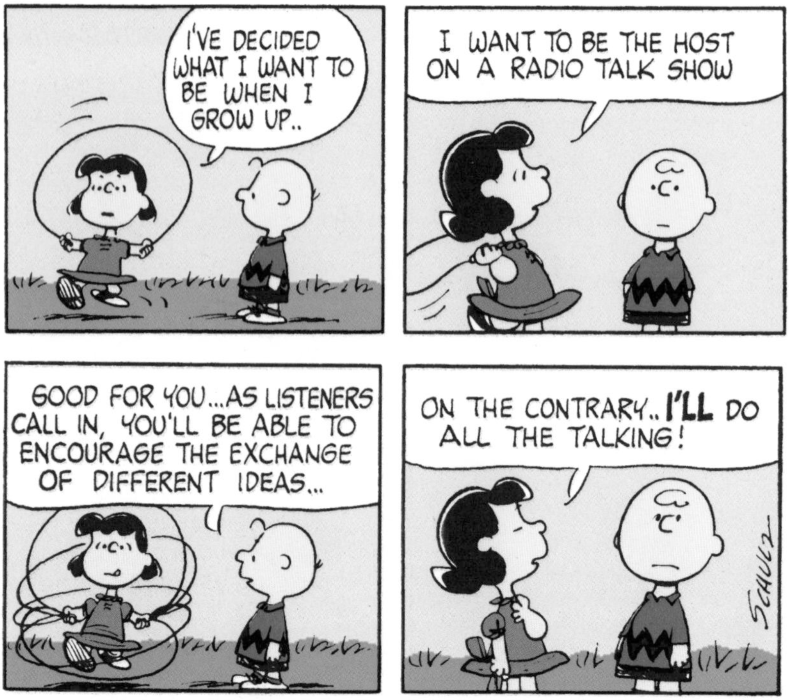
I'VE DECIDED WHAT I WANT TO BE WHEN I GROW UP..
I WANT TO BE THE HOST ON A RADIO TALK SHOW
GOOD FOR YOU...AS LISTENERS CALL IN, YOU'LL BE ABLE TO ENCOURAGE THE EXCHANGE OF DIFFERENT IDEAS...
ON THE CONTRARY.. **I'LL** DO ALL THE TALKING!
SCHULZ

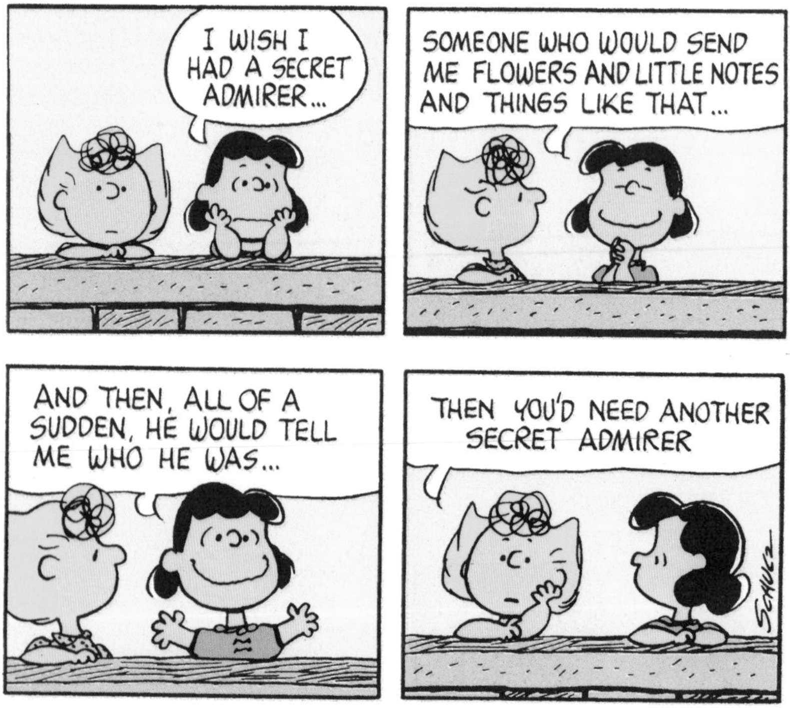
I WISH I HAD A SECRET ADMIRER...
SOMEONE WHO WOULD SEND ME FLOWERS AND LITTLE NOTES AND THINGS LIKE THAT...
AND THEN, ALL OF A SUDDEN, HE WOULD TELL ME WHO HE WAS...
THEN YOU'D NEED ANOTHER SECRET ADMIRER
SCHULZ

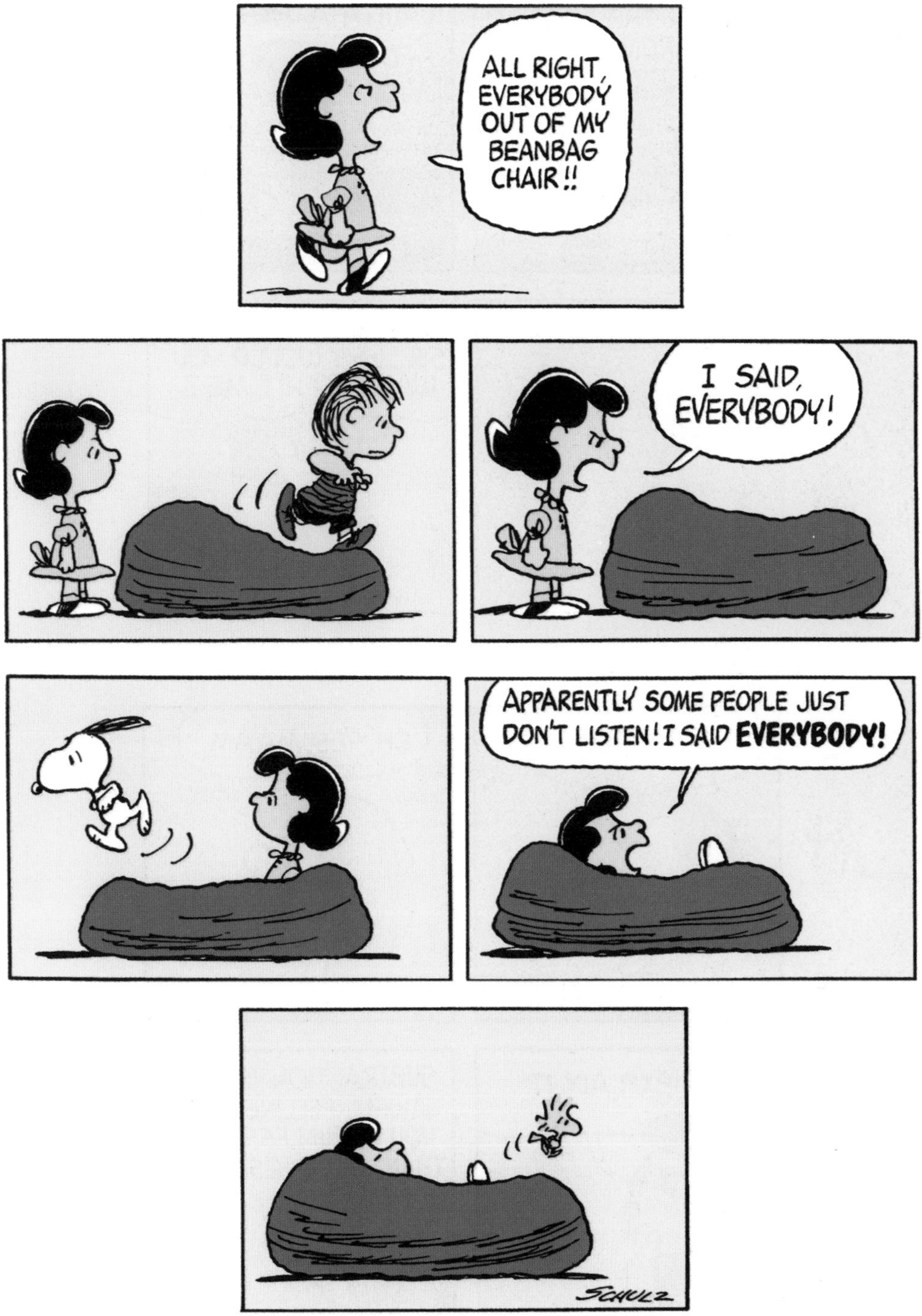
ALL RIGHT, EVERYBODY OUT OF MY BEANBAG CHAIR!!
I SAID, EVERYBODY!
APPARENTLY SOME PEOPLE JUST DON'T LISTEN! I SAID **EVERYBODY!**
SCHULZ

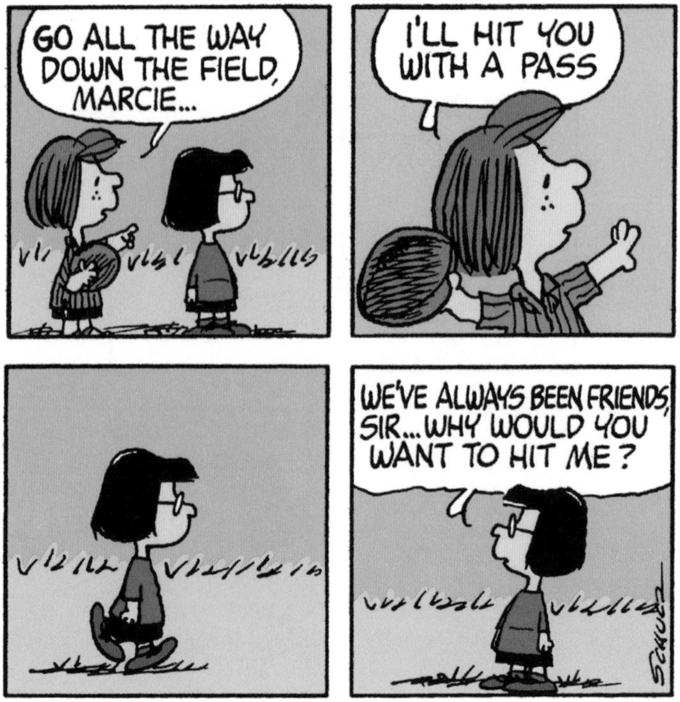
GO ALL THE WAY DOWN THE FIELD, MARCIE...
I'LL HIT YOU WITH A PASS
WE'VE ALWAYS BEEN FRIENDS, SIR...WHY WOULD YOU WANT TO HIT ME?
SCHULZ

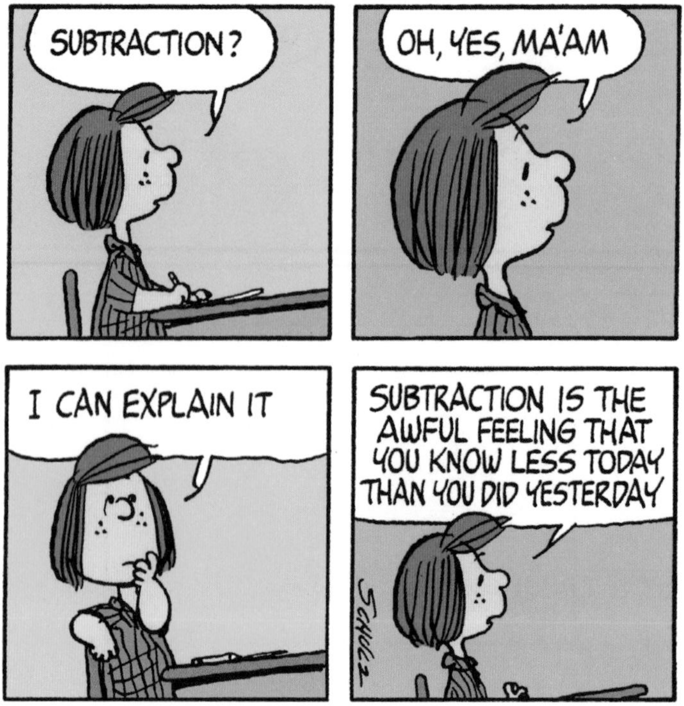
SUBTRACTION?
OH, YES, MA'AM
I CAN EXPLAIN IT
SUBTRACTION IS THE AWFUL FEELING THAT YOU KNOW LESS TODAY THAN YOU DID YESTERDAY
SCHULZ

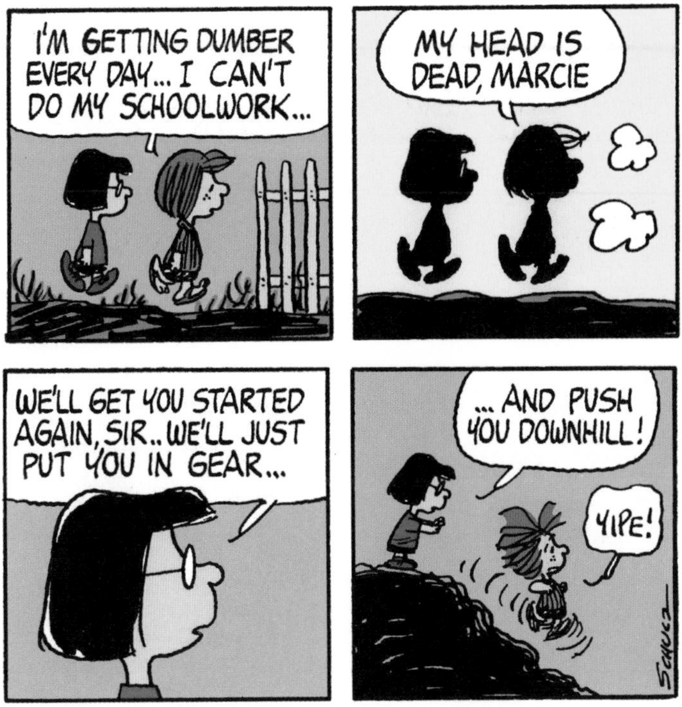
I'M GETTING DUMBER EVERY DAY... I CAN'T DO MY SCHOOLWORK...
MY HEAD IS DEAD, MARCIE
WE'LL GET YOU STARTED AGAIN, SIR.. WE'LL JUST PUT YOU IN GEAR...
... AND PUSH YOU DOWNHILL!
YIPE!

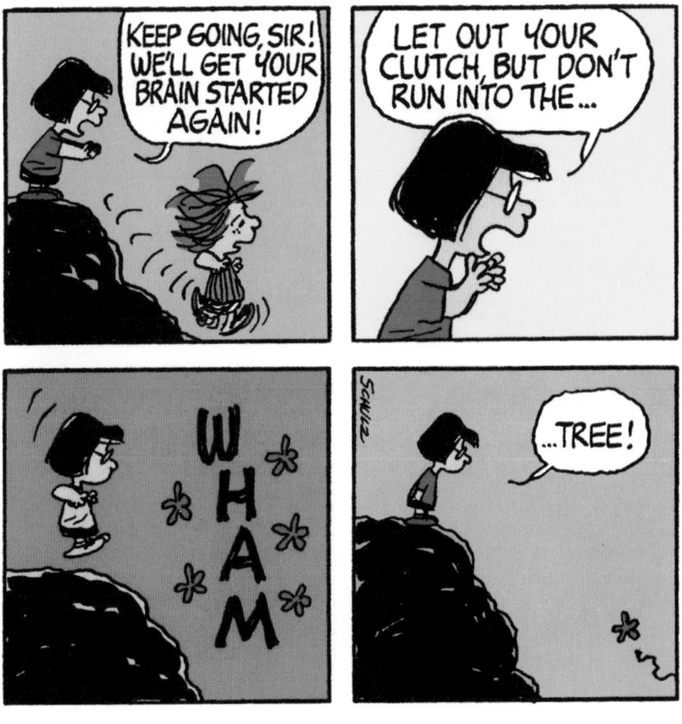
KEEP GOING, SIR! WE'LL GET YOUR BRAIN STARTED AGAIN!
LET OUT YOUR CLUTCH, BUT DON'T RUN INTO THE...
WHAM
...TREE!

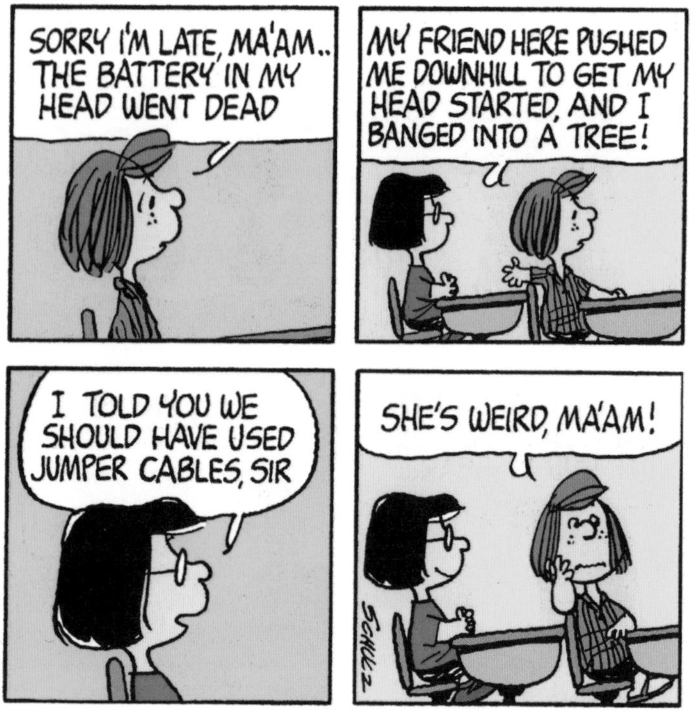
SORRY I'M LATE, MA'AM.. THE BATTERY IN MY HEAD WENT DEAD
MY FRIEND HERE PUSHED ME DOWNHILL TO GET MY HEAD STARTED, AND I BANGED INTO A TREE!
I TOLD YOU WE SHOULD HAVE USED JUMPER CABLES, SIR
SHE'S WEIRD, MA'AM!
SCHULZ

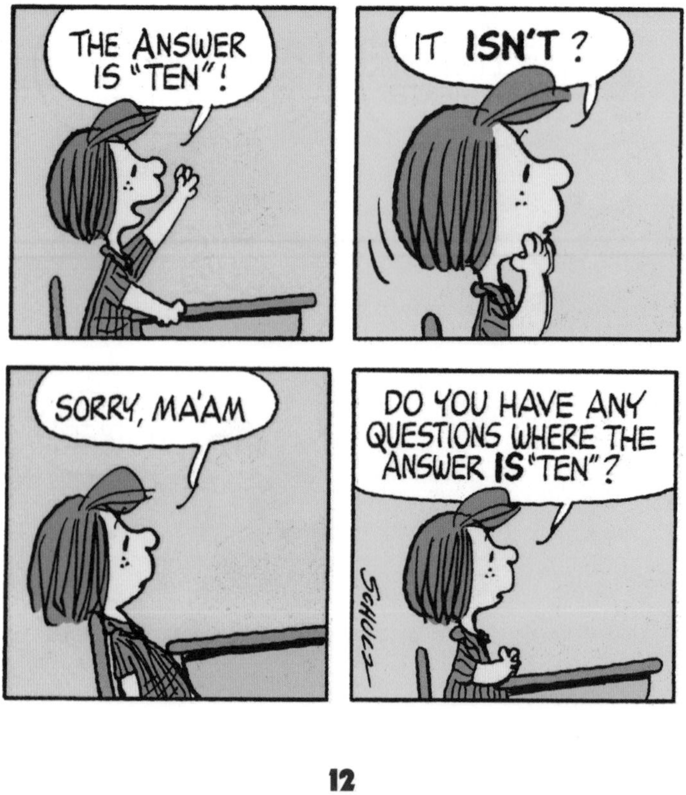
THE ANSWER IS "TEN"!
IT ISN'T ?
SORRY, MA'AM
DO YOU HAVE ANY QUESTIONS WHERE THE ANSWER IS "TEN"?
SCHULZ

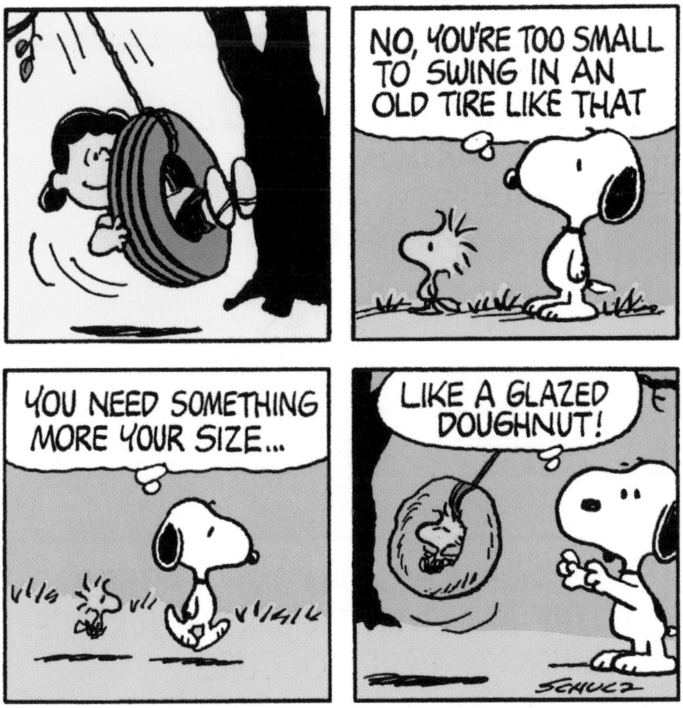
NO, YOU'RE TOO SMALL TO SWING IN AN OLD TIRE LIKE THAT
YOU NEED SOMETHING MORE YOUR SIZE...
LIKE A GLAZED DOUGHNUT!
SCHULZ

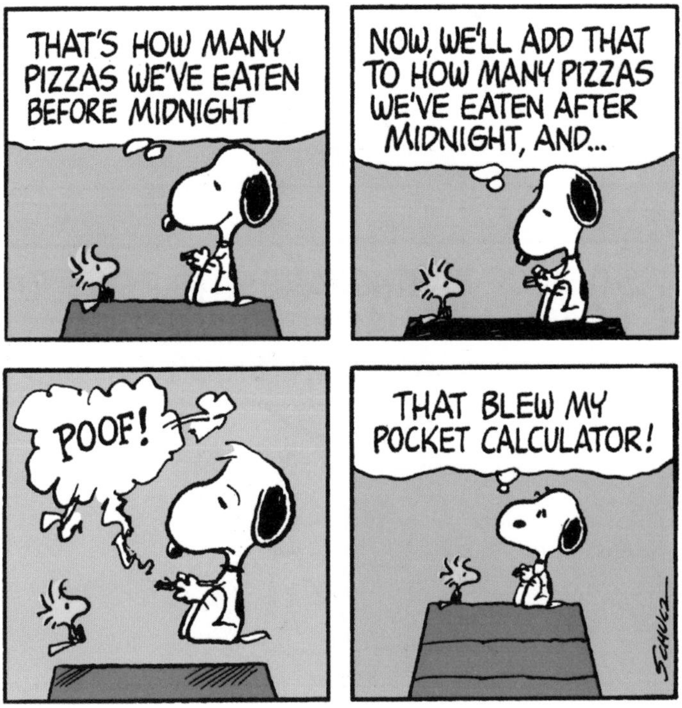
THAT'S HOW MANY PIZZAS WE'VE EATEN BEFORE MIDNIGHT
NOW, WE'LL ADD THAT TO HOW MANY PIZZAS WE'VE EATEN AFTER MIDNIGHT, AND...
POOF!
THAT BLEW MY POCKET CALCULATOR!
SCHULZ

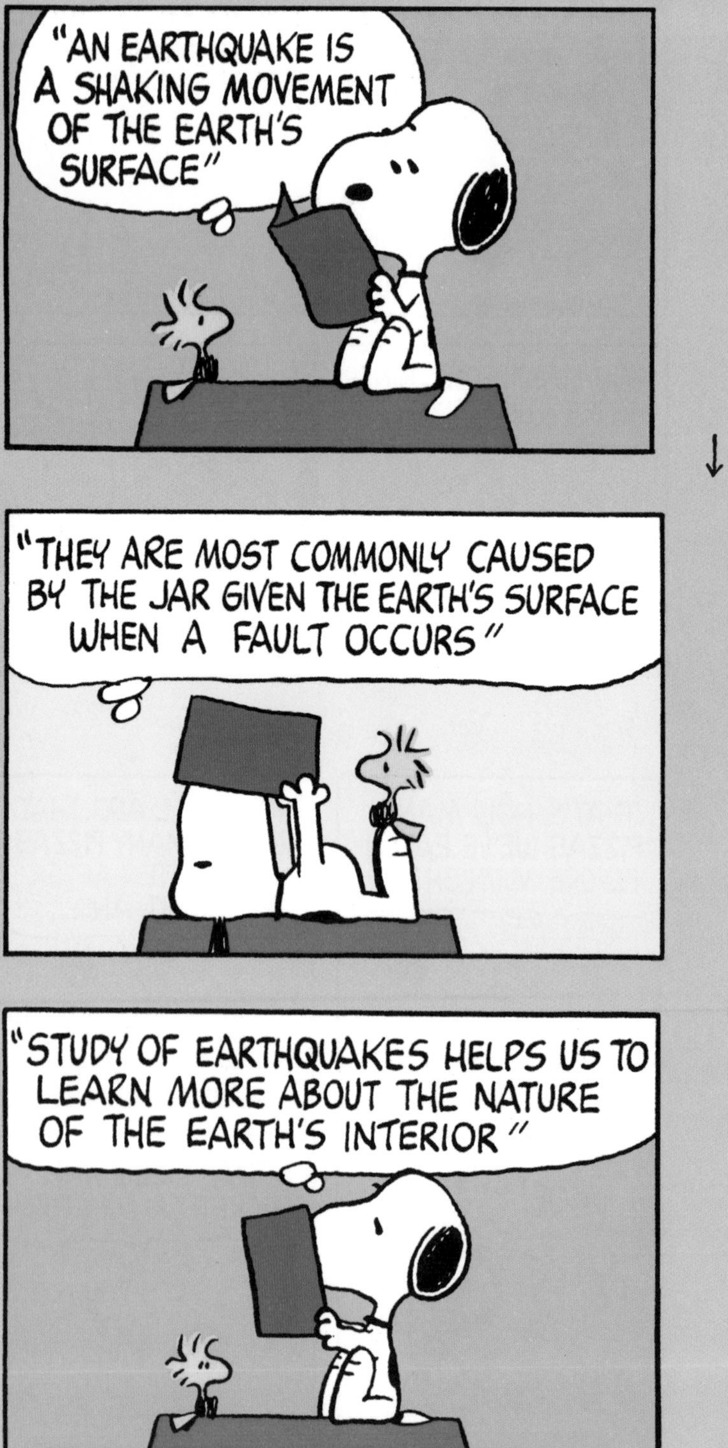
"AN EARTHQUAKE IS A SHAKING MOVEMENT OF THE EARTH'S SURFACE"
"THEY ARE MOST COMMONLY CAUSED BY THE JAR GIVEN THE EARTH'S SURFACE WHEN A FAULT OCCURS"
"STUDY OF EARTHQUAKES HELPS US TO LEARN MORE ABOUT THE NATURE OF THE EARTH'S INTERIOR"

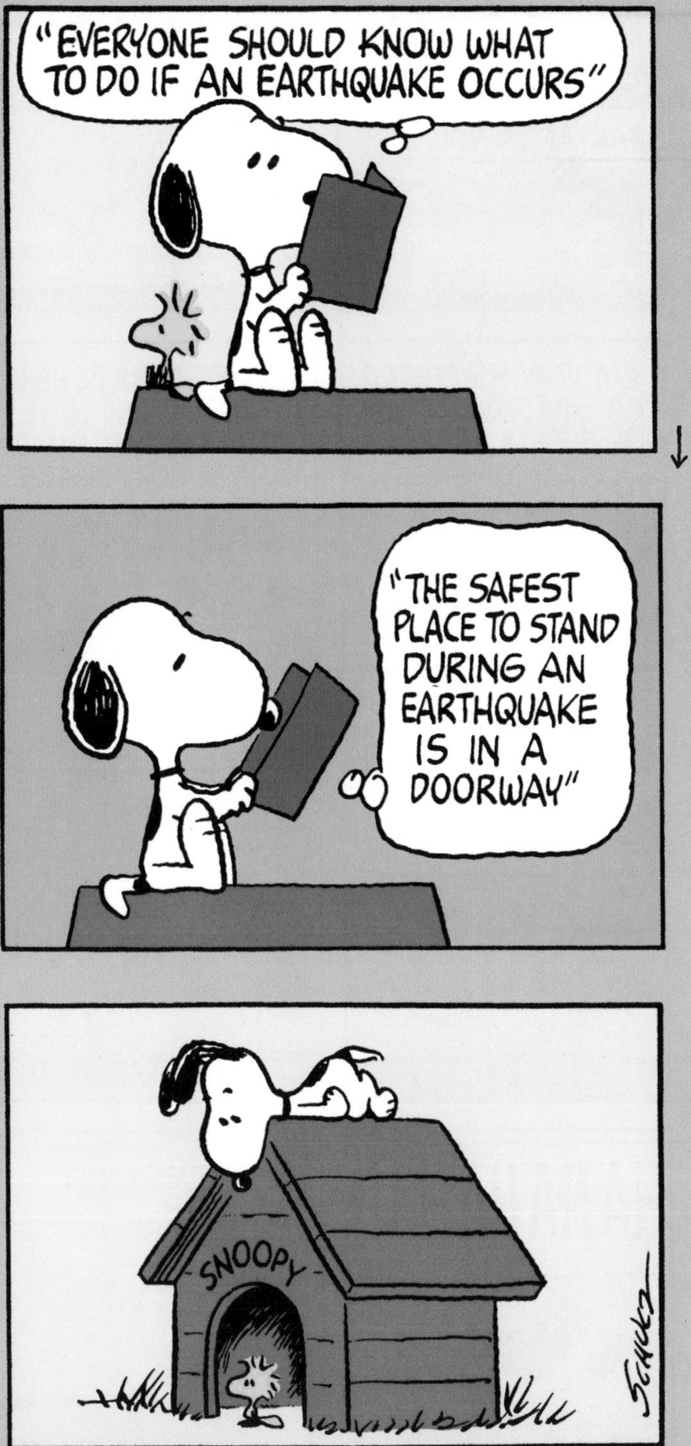
"EVERYONE SHOULD KNOW WHAT TO DO IF AN EARTHQUAKE OCCURS"
"THE SAFEST PLACE TO STAND DURING AN EARTHQUAKE IS IN A DOORWAY"
SNOOPY
SCHULZ

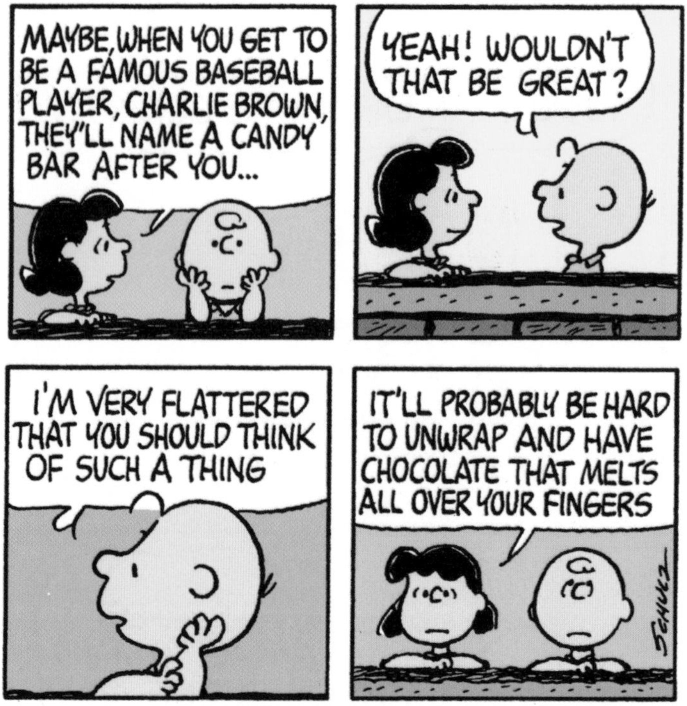
MAYBE, WHEN YOU GET TO BE A FAMOUS BASEBALL PLAYER, CHARLIE BROWN, THEY'LL NAME A CANDY BAR AFTER YOU...
YEAH! WOULDN'T THAT BE GREAT?
I'M VERY FLATTERED THAT YOU SHOULD THINK OF SUCH A THING
IT'LL PROBABLY BE HARD TO UNWRAP AND HAVE CHOCOLATE THAT MELTS ALL OVER YOUR FINGERS
SCHULZ

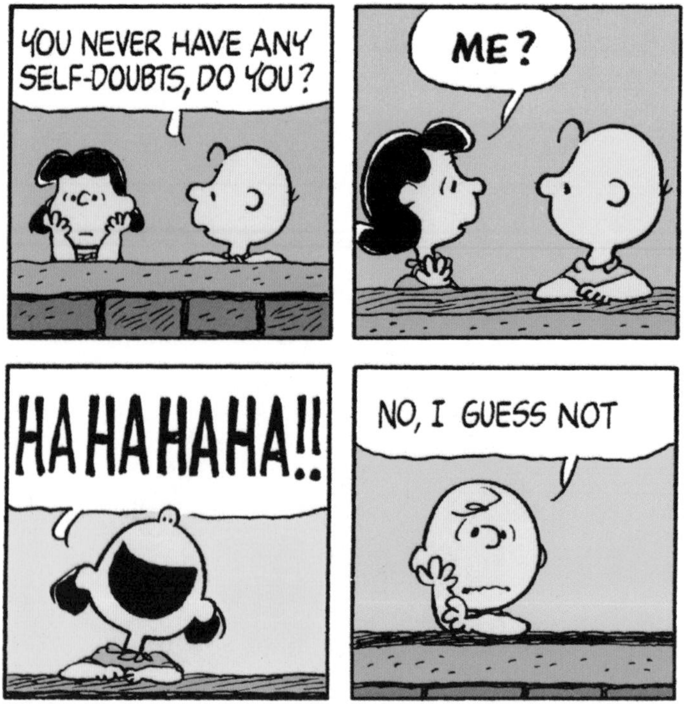
YOU NEVER HAVE ANY SELF-DOUBTS, DO YOU?
ME?
HAHAHAHA!!
NO, I GUESS NOT

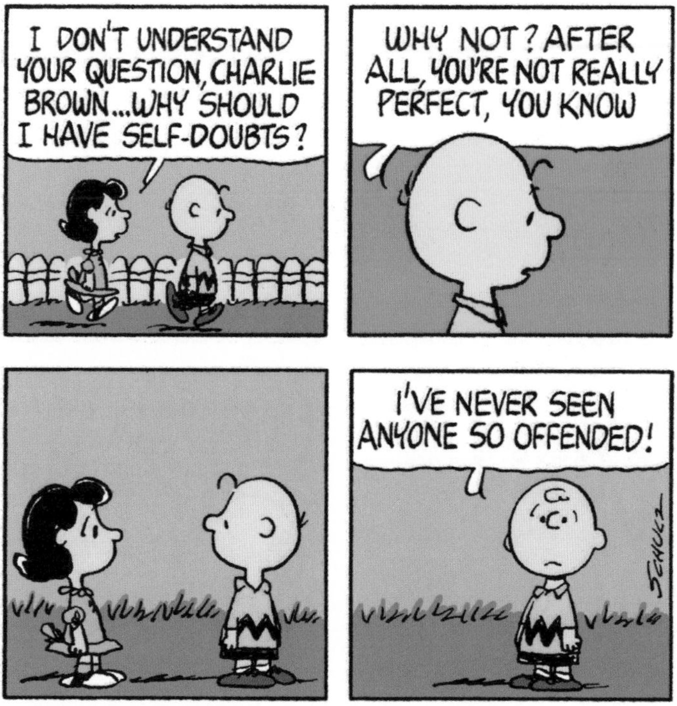
I DON'T UNDERSTAND YOUR QUESTION, CHARLIE BROWN...WHY SHOULD I HAVE SELF-DOUBTS?
WHY NOT? AFTER ALL, YOU'RE NOT REALLY PERFECT, YOU KNOW
I'VE NEVER SEEN ANYONE SO OFFENDED!
SCHULZ

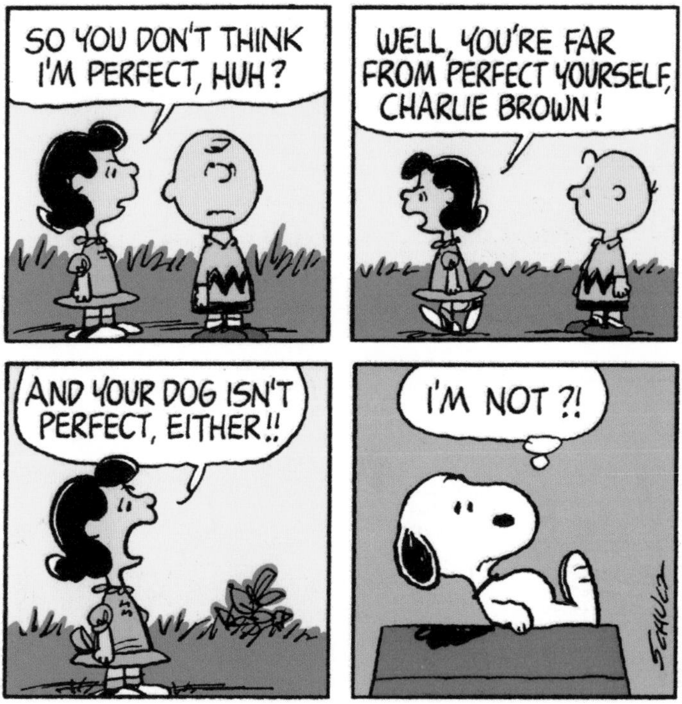
SO YOU DON'T THINK I'M PERFECT, HUH?
WELL, YOU'RE FAR FROM PERFECT YOURSELF, CHARLIE BROWN!
AND YOUR DOG ISN'T PERFECT, EITHER!!
I'M NOT?!
SCHULZ

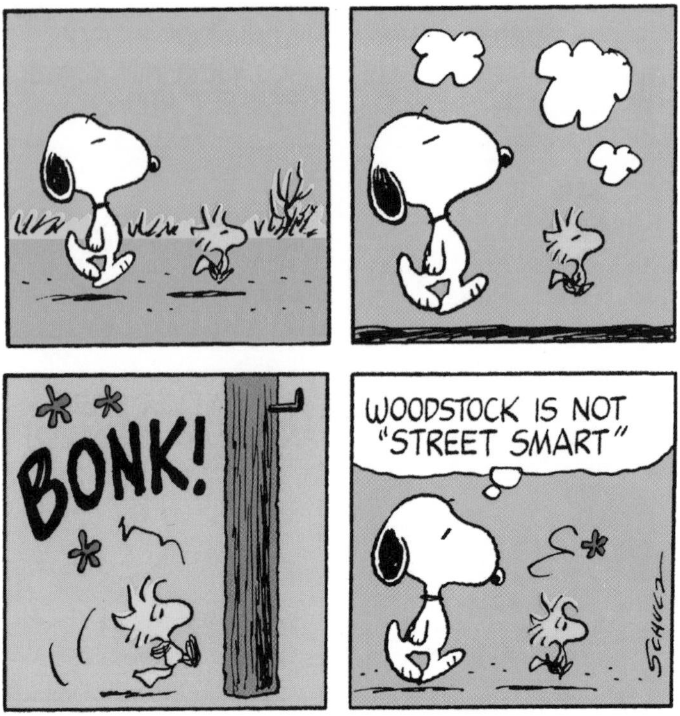
BONK!
WOODSTOCK IS NOT "STREET SMART"
SCHULZ

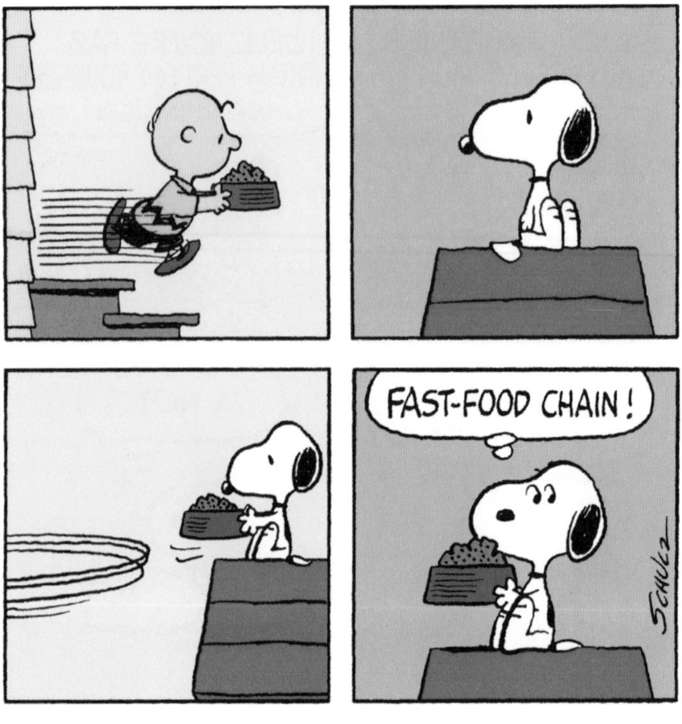
FAST-FOOD CHAIN!
SCHULZ

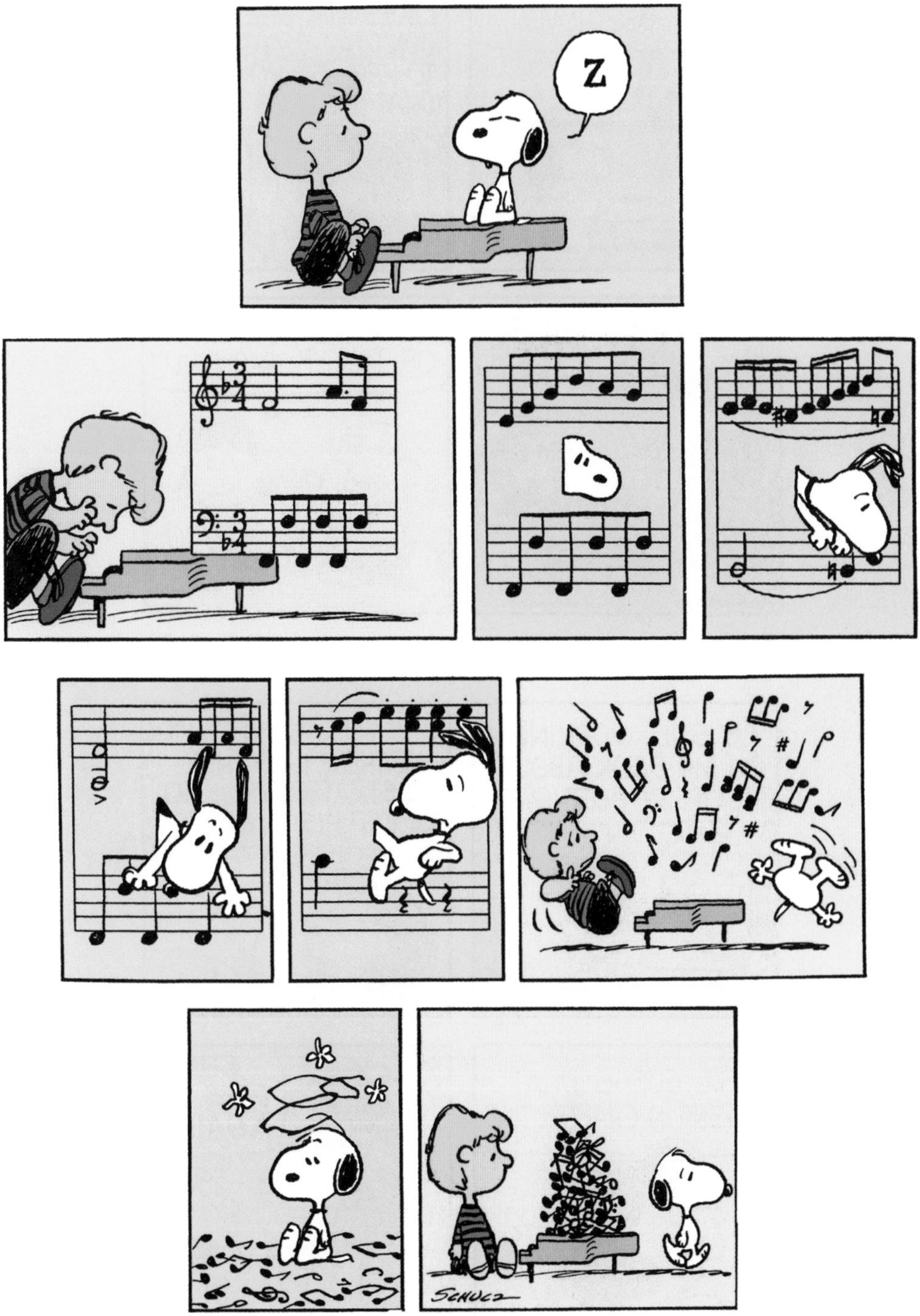
Z
SCHULZ

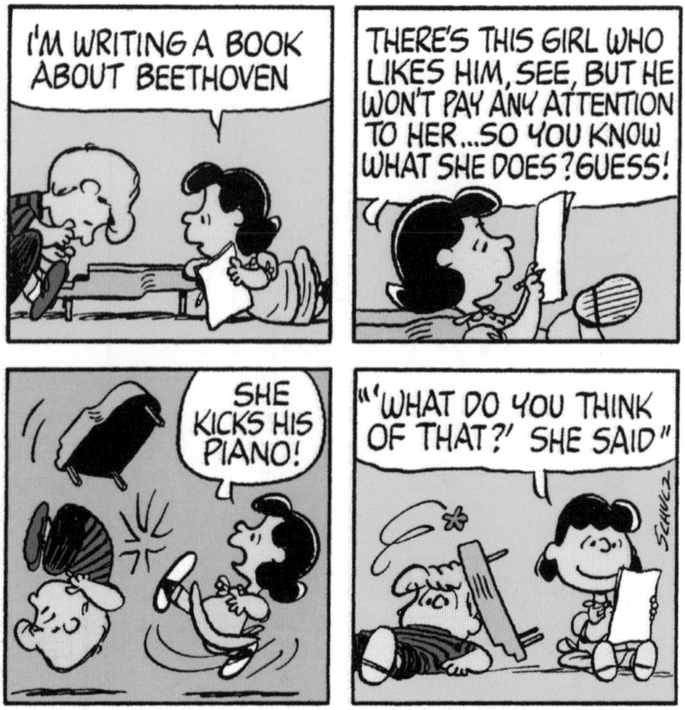
I'M WRITING A BOOK ABOUT BEETHOVEN
THERE'S THIS GIRL WHO LIKES HIM, SEE, BUT HE WON'T PAY ANY ATTENTION TO HER...SO YOU KNOW WHAT SHE DOES? GUESS!
SHE KICKS HIS PIANO!
"'WHAT DO YOU THINK OF THAT?' SHE SAID"

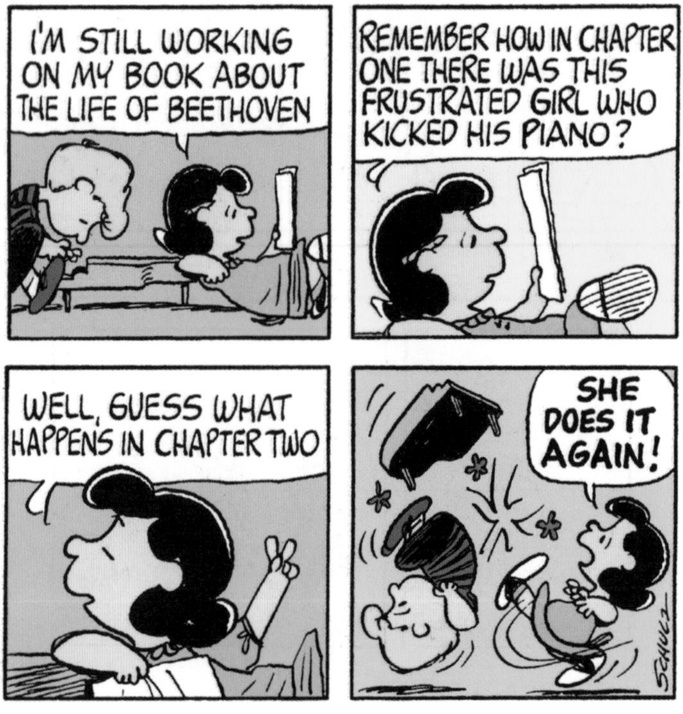
I'M STILL WORKING ON MY BOOK ABOUT THE LIFE OF BEETHOVEN
REMEMBER HOW IN CHAPTER ONE THERE WAS THIS FRUSTRATED GIRL WHO KICKED HIS PIANO?
WELL, GUESS WHAT HAPPENS IN CHAPTER TWO
SHE DOES IT AGAIN!

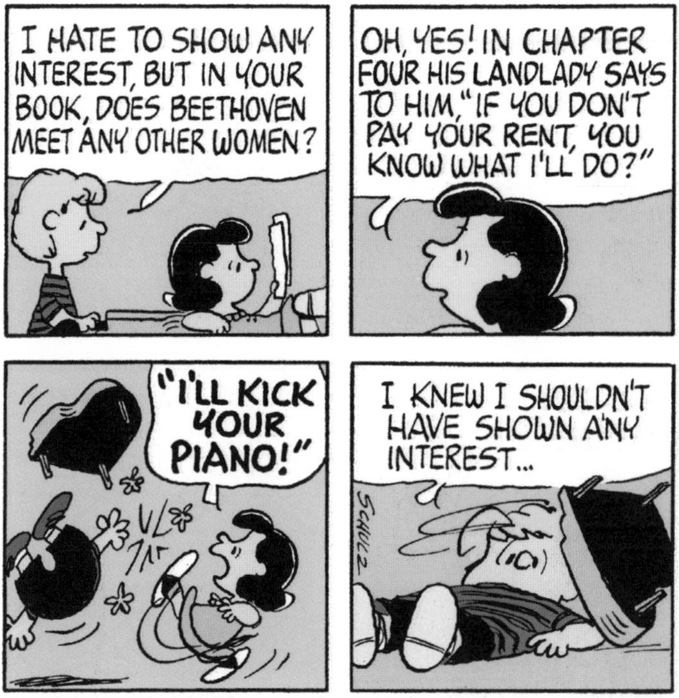
I HATE TO SHOW ANY INTEREST, BUT IN YOUR BOOK, DOES BEETHOVEN MEET ANY OTHER WOMEN?
OH, YES! IN CHAPTER FOUR HIS LANDLADY SAYS TO HIM, "IF YOU DON'T PAY YOUR RENT, YOU KNOW WHAT I'LL DO?"
"I'LL KICK YOUR PIANO!"
I KNEW I SHOULDN'T HAVE SHOWN ANY INTEREST...
SCHULZ

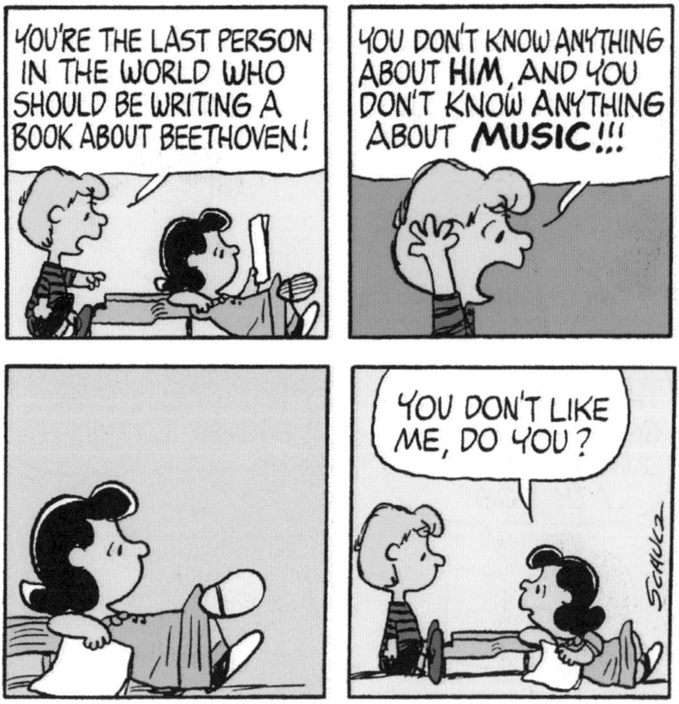
YOU'RE THE LAST PERSON IN THE WORLD WHO SHOULD BE WRITING A BOOK ABOUT BEETHOVEN!
YOU DON'T KNOW ANYTHING ABOUT HIM, AND YOU DON'T KNOW ANYTHING ABOUT MUSIC!!!
YOU DON'T LIKE ME, DO YOU?
SCHULZ

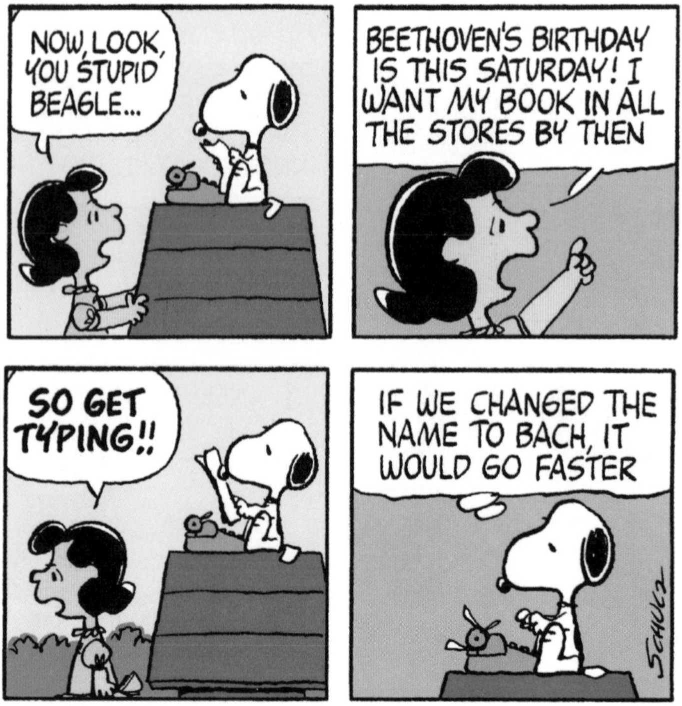
NOW, LOOK, YOU STUPID BEAGLE...
BEETHOVEN'S BIRTHDAY IS THIS SATURDAY! I WANT MY BOOK IN ALL THE STORES BY THEN
SO GET TYPING!!
IF WE CHANGED THE NAME TO BACH, IT WOULD GO FASTER
SCHULZ

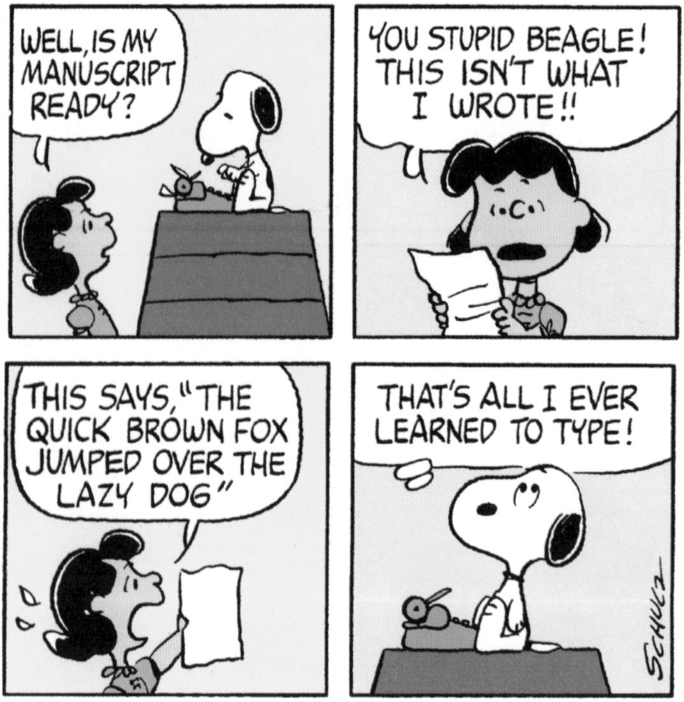
WELL, IS MY MANUSCRIPT READY?
YOU STUPID BEAGLE! THIS ISN'T WHAT I WROTE!!
THIS SAYS, "THE QUICK BROWN FOX JUMPED OVER THE LAZY DOG"
THAT'S ALL I EVER LEARNED TO TYPE!
SCHULZ

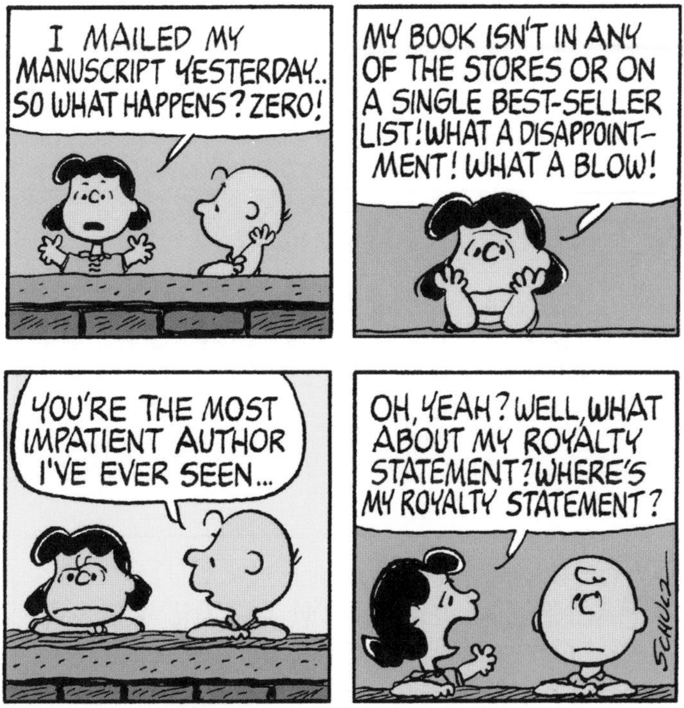
I MAILED MY MANUSCRIPT YESTERDAY.. SO WHAT HAPPENS? ZERO!
MY BOOK ISN'T IN ANY OF THE STORES OR ON A SINGLE BEST-SELLER LIST! WHAT A DISAPPOINTMENT! WHAT A BLOW!
YOU'RE THE MOST IMPATIENT AUTHOR I'VE EVER SEEN...
OH, YEAH? WELL, WHAT ABOUT MY ROYALTY STATEMENT? WHERE'S MY ROYALTY STATEMENT?
SCHULZ

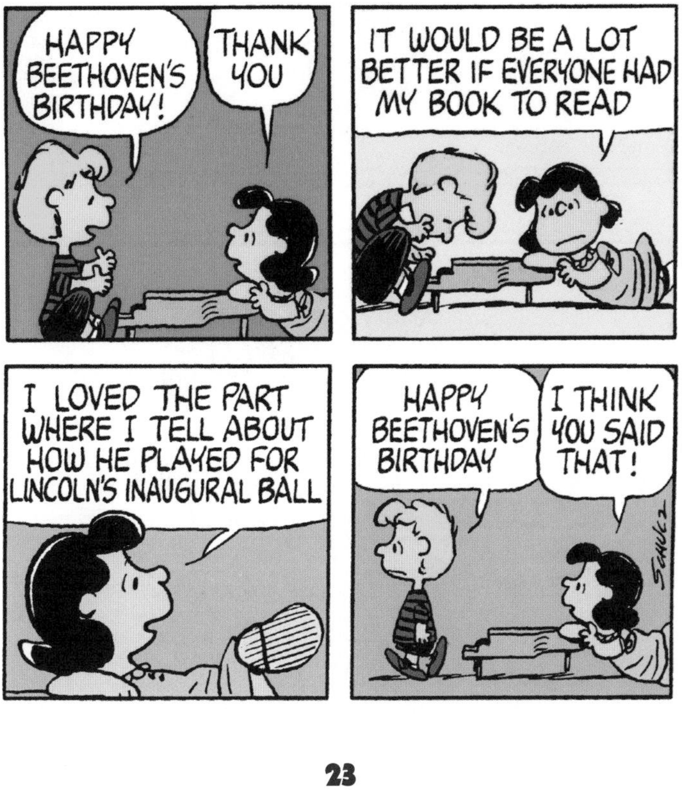
HAPPY BEETHOVEN'S BIRTHDAY!
THANK YOU
IT WOULD BE A LOT BETTER IF EVERYONE HAD MY BOOK TO READ
I LOVED THE PART WHERE I TELL ABOUT HOW HE PLAYED FOR LINCOLN'S INAUGURAL BALL
HAPPY BEETHOVEN'S BIRTHDAY
I THINK YOU SAID THAT!
SCHULZ

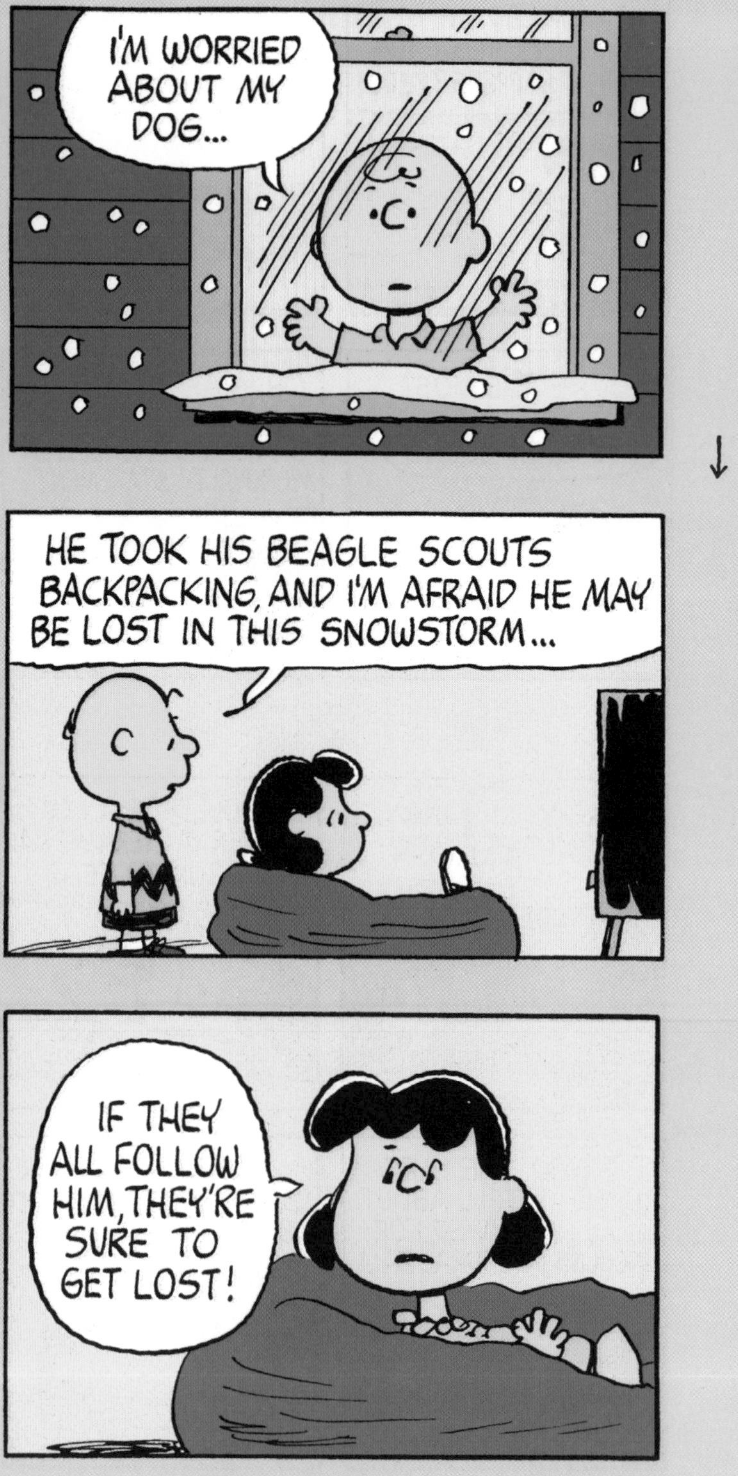
I'M WORRIED ABOUT MY DOG...
HE TOOK HIS BEAGLE SCOUTS BACKPACKING, AND I'M AFRAID HE MAY BE LOST IN THIS SNOWSTORM...
IF THEY ALL FOLLOW HIM, THEY'RE SURE TO GET LOST!

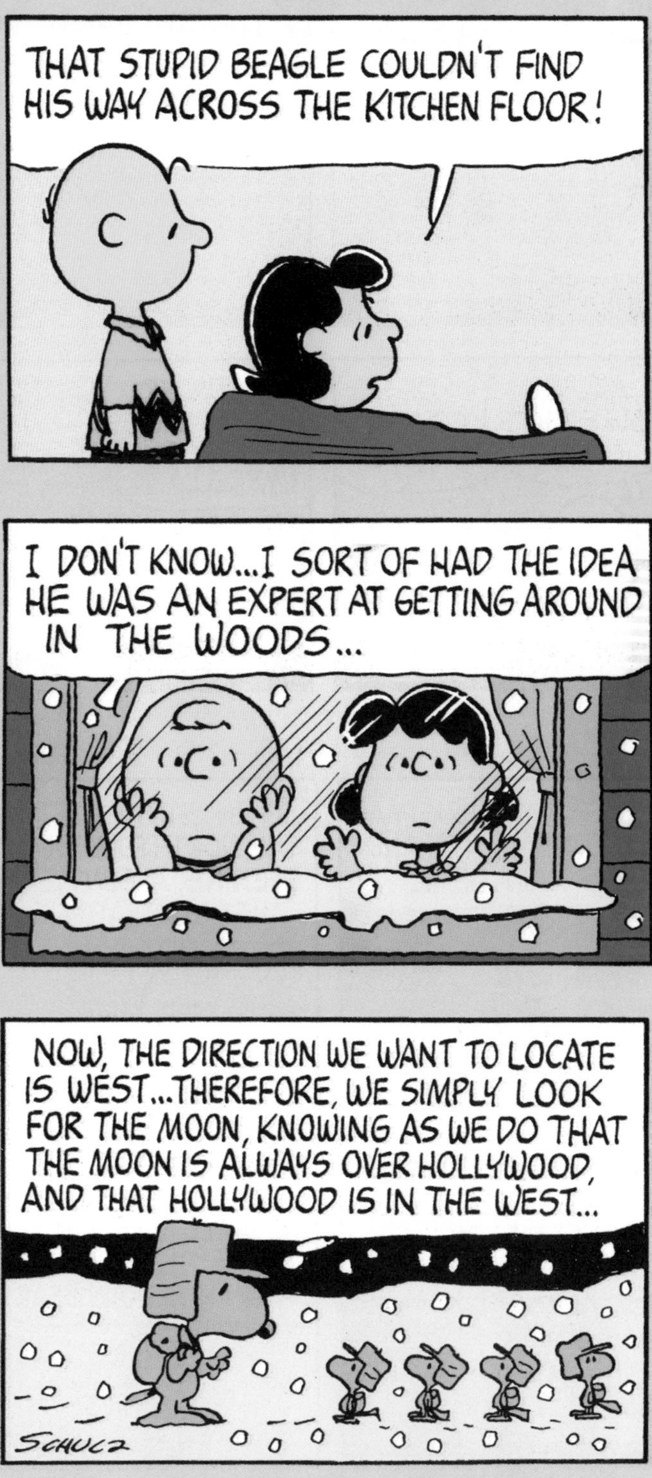
THAT STUPID BEAGLE COULDN'T FIND HIS WAY ACROSS THE KITCHEN FLOOR!
I DON'T KNOW...I SORT OF HAD THE IDEA HE WAS AN EXPERT AT GETTING AROUND IN THE WOODS...
NOW, THE DIRECTION WE WANT TO LOCATE IS WEST...THEREFORE, WE SIMPLY LOOK FOR THE MOON, KNOWING AS WE DO THAT THE MOON IS ALWAYS OVER HOLLYWOOD, AND THAT HOLLYWOOD IS IN THE WEST...
SCHULZ

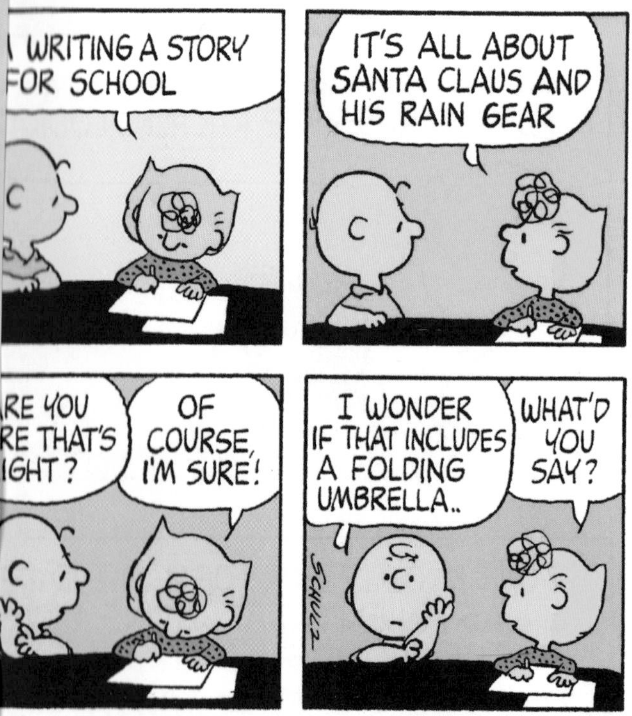
WRITING A STORY FOR SCHOOL
IT'S ALL ABOUT SANTA CLAUS AND HIS RAIN GEAR
RE YOU RE THAT'S IGHT?
OF COURSE, I'M SURE!
I WONDER IF THAT INCLUDES A FOLDING UMBRELLA..
WHAT'D YOU SAY?
SCHULZ

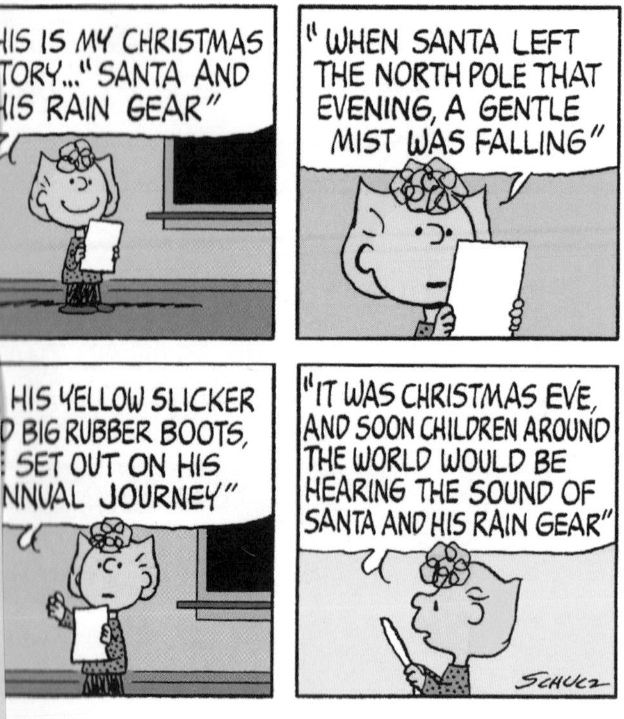
HIS IS MY CHRISTMAS TORY..."SANTA AND HIS RAIN GEAR"
"WHEN SANTA LEFT THE NORTH POLE THAT EVENING, A GENTLE MIST WAS FALLING"
HIS YELLOW SLICKER BIG RUBBER BOOTS, SET OUT ON HIS NNUAL JOURNEY"
"IT WAS CHRISTMAS EVE, AND SOON CHILDREN AROUND THE WORLD WOULD BE HEARING THE SOUND OF SANTA AND HIS RAIN GEAR"
SCHULZ

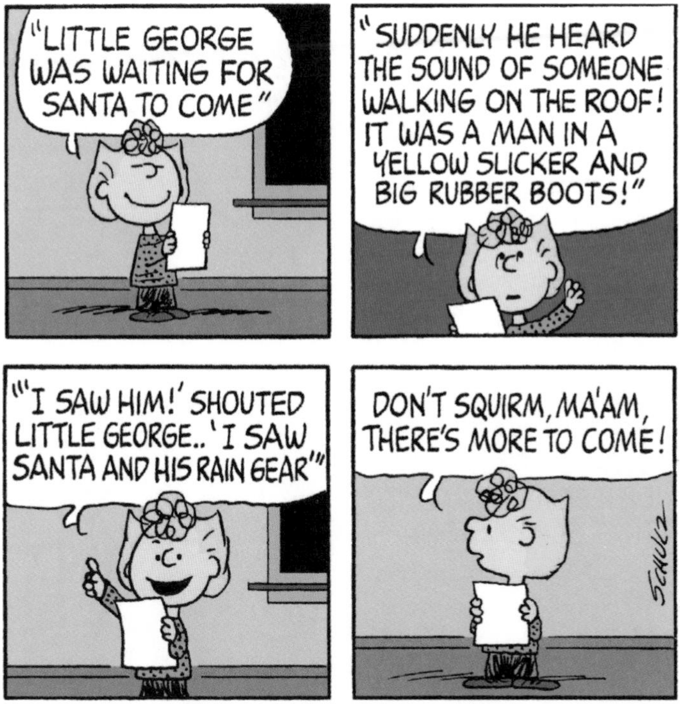
"LITTLE GEORGE WAS WAITING FOR SANTA TO COME"
"SUDDENLY HE HEARD THE SOUND OF SOMEONE WALKING ON THE ROOF! IT WAS A MAN IN A YELLOW SLICKER AND BIG RUBBER BOOTS!"
"'I SAW HIM!' SHOUTED LITTLE GEORGE.. 'I SAW SANTA AND HIS RAIN GEAR'"
DON'T SQUIRM, MA'AM, THERE'S MORE TO COME!
SCHULZ

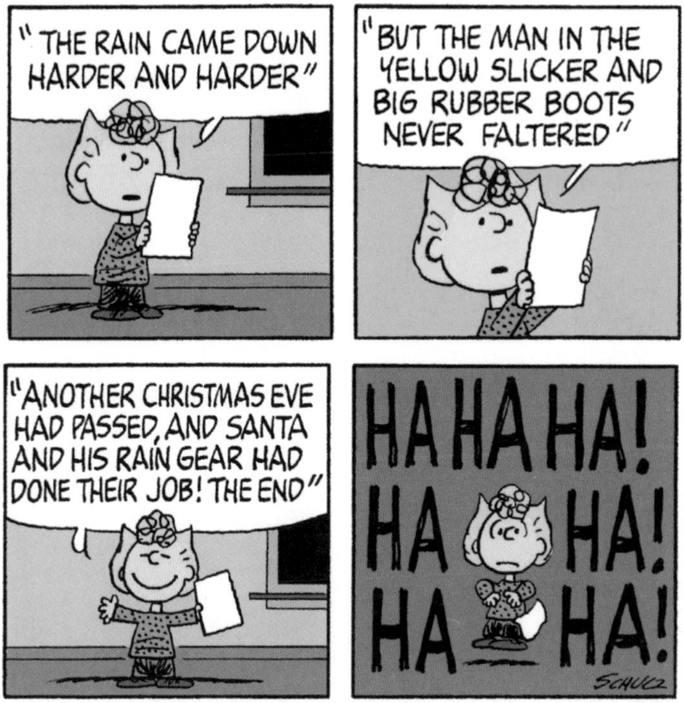
"THE RAIN CAME DOWN HARDER AND HARDER"
"BUT THE MAN IN THE YELLOW SLICKER AND BIG RUBBER BOOTS NEVER FALTERED"
"ANOTHER CHRISTMAS EVE HAD PASSED, AND SANTA AND HIS RAIN GEAR HAD DONE THEIR JOB! THE END"
HA HA HA HA! HA HA! HA HA!
SCHULZ

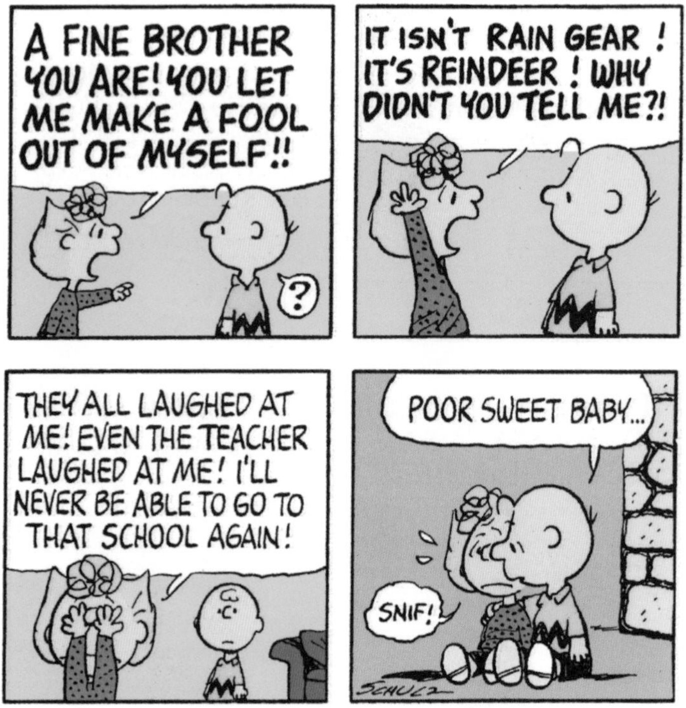
A FINE BROTHER YOU ARE! YOU LET ME MAKE A FOOL OUT OF MYSELF!!
?
IT ISN'T RAIN GEAR! IT'S REINDEER! WHY DIDN'T YOU TELL ME?!
THEY ALL LAUGHED AT ME! EVEN THE TEACHER LAUGHED AT ME! I'LL NEVER BE ABLE TO GO TO THAT SCHOOL AGAIN!
POOR SWEET BABY...
SNIF!
SCHULZ

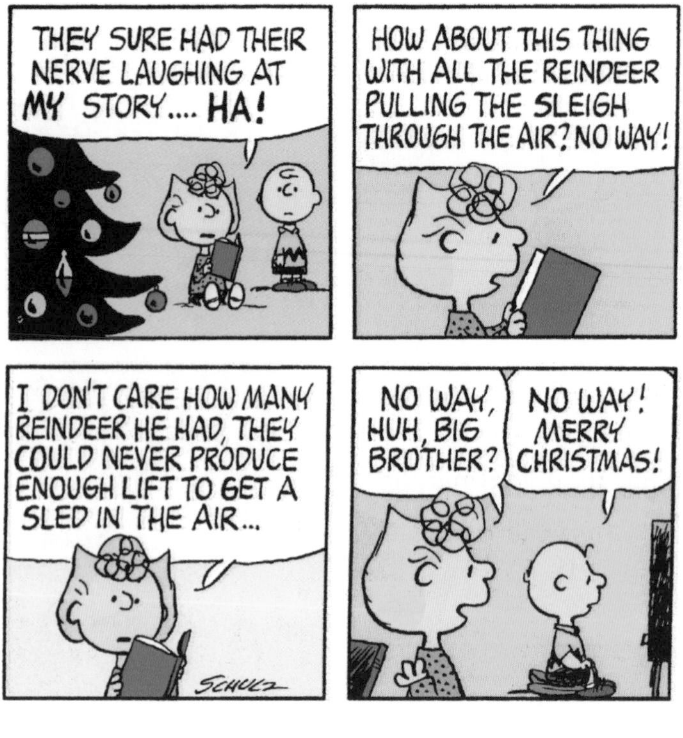
THEY SURE HAD THEIR NERVE LAUGHING AT MY STORY.... HA!
HOW ABOUT THIS THING WITH ALL THE REINDEER PULLING THE SLEIGH THROUGH THE AIR? NO WAY!
I DON'T CARE HOW MANY REINDEER HE HAD, THEY COULD NEVER PRODUCE ENOUGH LIFT TO GET A SLED IN THE AIR...
SCHULZ
NO WAY, HUH, BIG BROTHER?
NO WAY! MERRY CHRISTMAS!

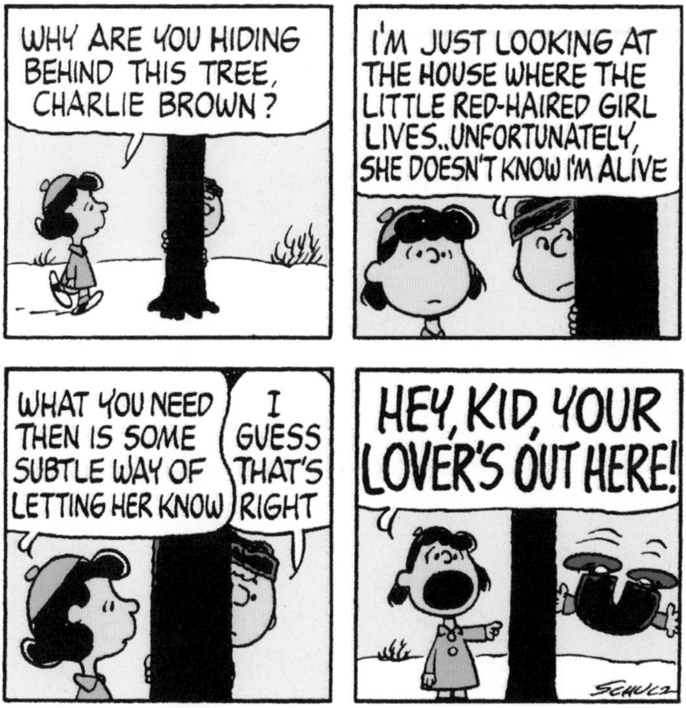
WHY ARE YOU HIDING BEHIND THIS TREE, CHARLIE BROWN?
I'M JUST LOOKING AT THE HOUSE WHERE THE LITTLE RED-HAIRED GIRL LIVES..UNFORTUNATELY, SHE DOESN'T KNOW I'M ALIVE
WHAT YOU NEED THEN IS SOME SUBTLE WAY OF LETTING HER KNOW
I GUESS THAT'S RIGHT
HEY, KID, YOUR LOVER'S OUT HERE!
SCHULZ

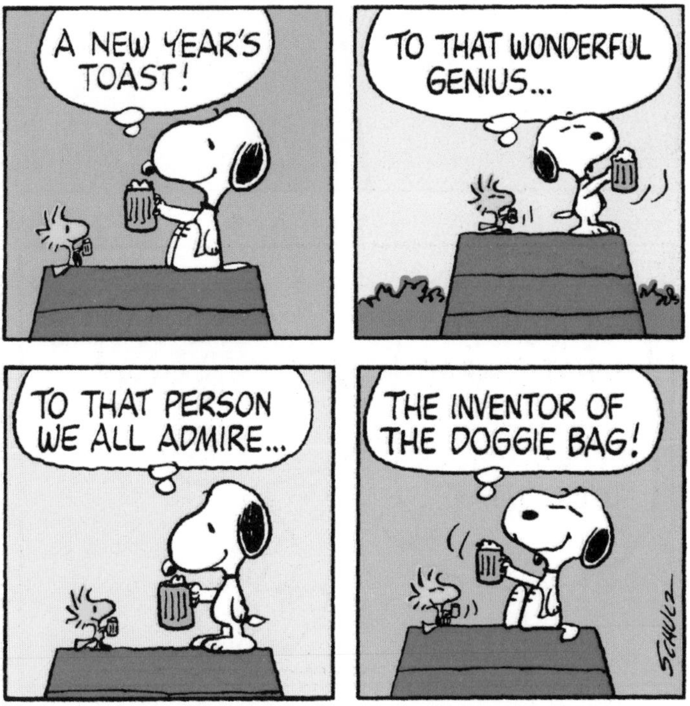
A NEW YEAR'S TOAST!
TO THAT WONDERFUL GENIUS...
TO THAT PERSON WE ALL ADMIRE...
THE INVENTOR OF THE DOGGIE BAG!
SCHULZ

AH!
WHAT A GREAT HAT!
I LOVE NEW YEAR'S PARTIES
I WONDER WHAT CONRAD, BILL, OLIVIER AND WOODSTOCK WILL WEAR...

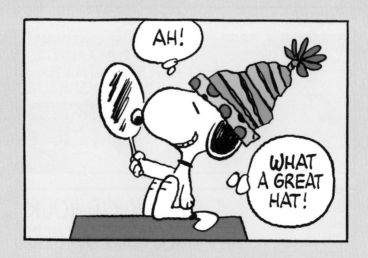

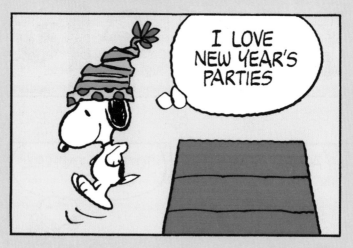

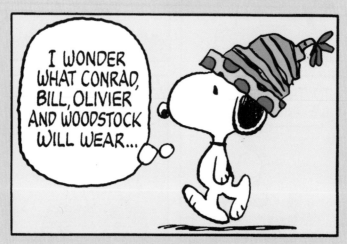

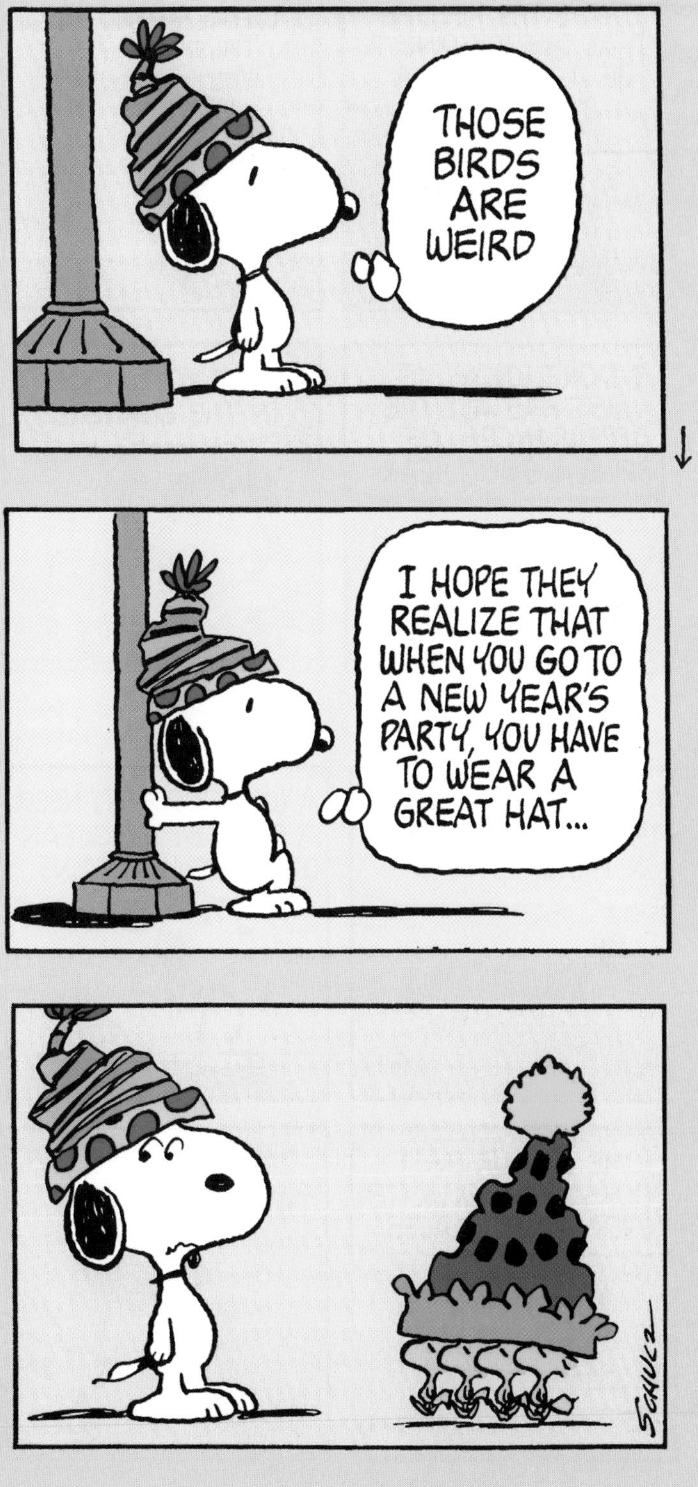
THOSE BIRDS ARE WEIRD
I HOPE THEY REALIZE THAT WHEN YOU GO TO A NEW YEAR'S PARTY, YOU HAVE TO WEAR A GREAT HAT...
SCHULZ

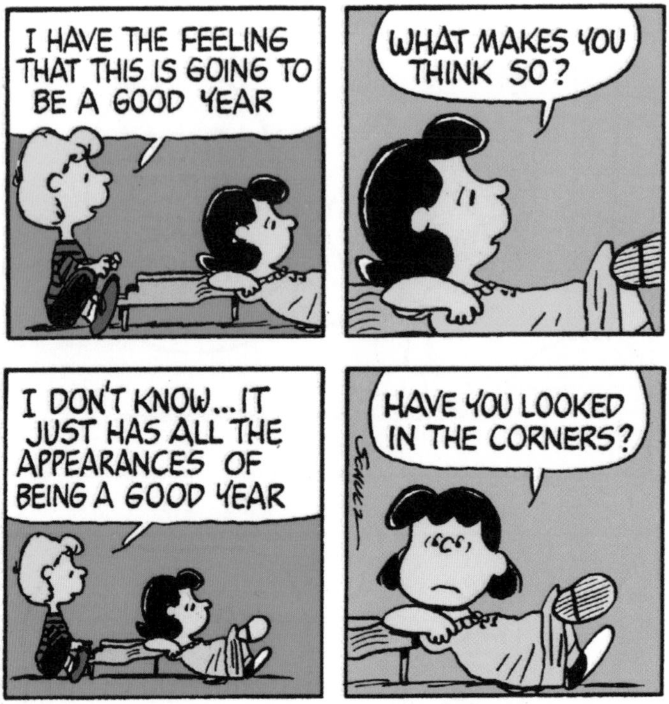
I HAVE THE FEELING THAT THIS IS GOING TO BE A GOOD YEAR
WHAT MAKES YOU THINK SO?
I DON'T KNOW... IT JUST HAS ALL THE APPEARANCES OF BEING A GOOD YEAR
HAVE YOU LOOKED IN THE CORNERS?

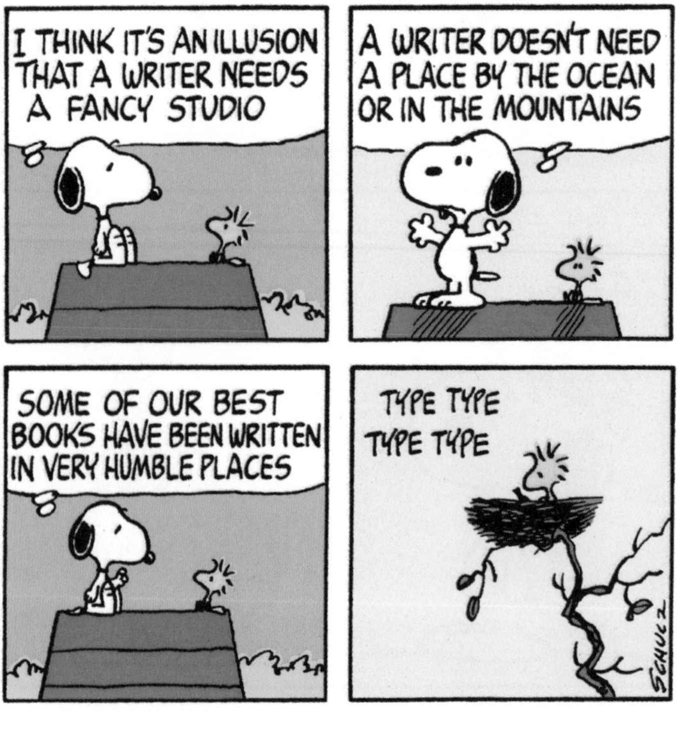
I THINK IT'S AN ILLUSION THAT A WRITER NEEDS A FANCY STUDIO
A WRITER DOESN'T NEED A PLACE BY THE OCEAN OR IN THE MOUNTAINS
SOME OF OUR BEST BOOKS HAVE BEEN WRITTEN IN VERY HUMBLE PLACES
TYPE TYPE
TYPE TYPE

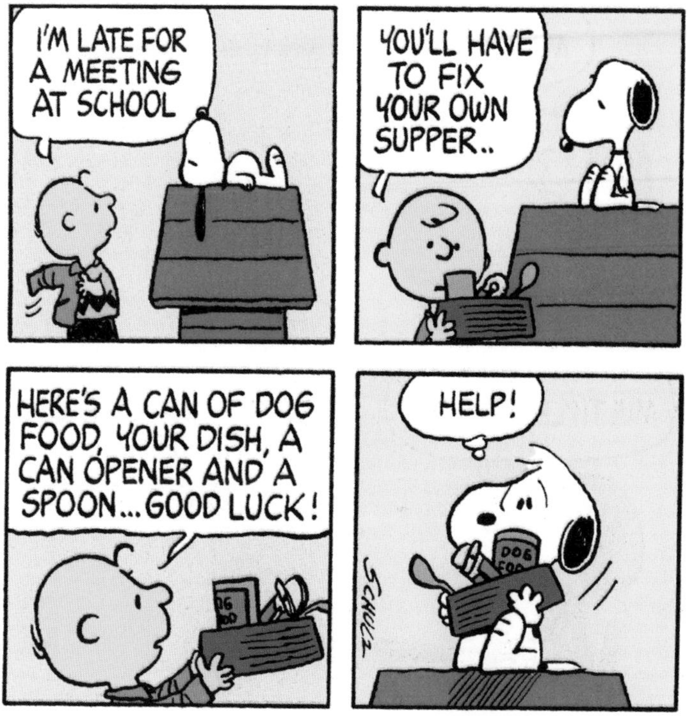
I'M LATE FOR A MEETING AT SCHOOL
YOU'LL HAVE TO FIX YOUR OWN SUPPER..
HERE'S A CAN OF DOG FOOD, YOUR DISH, A CAN OPENER AND A SPOON...GOOD LUCK!
HELP!
DOG FOOD
SCHULZ

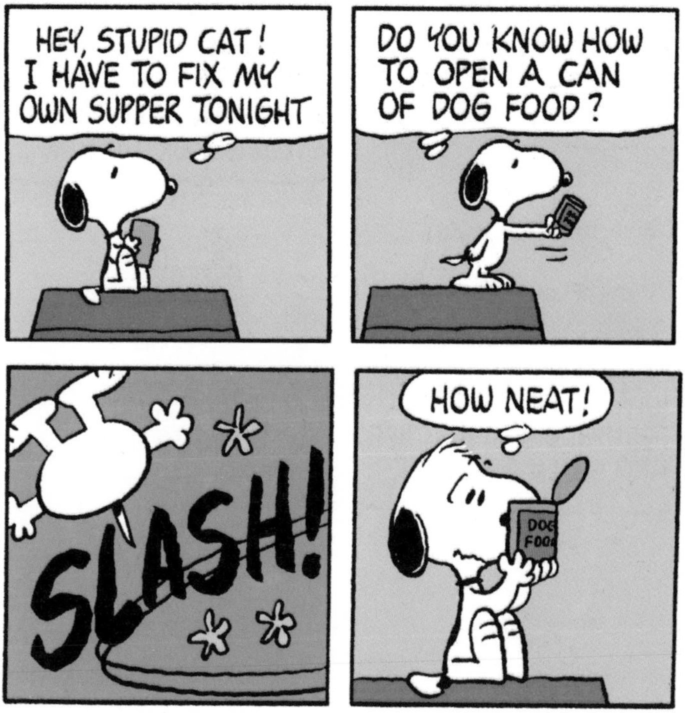
HEY, STUPID CAT! I HAVE TO FIX MY OWN SUPPER TONIGHT
DO YOU KNOW HOW TO OPEN A CAN OF DOG FOOD?
SLASH!
HOW NEAT!
DOG FOOD

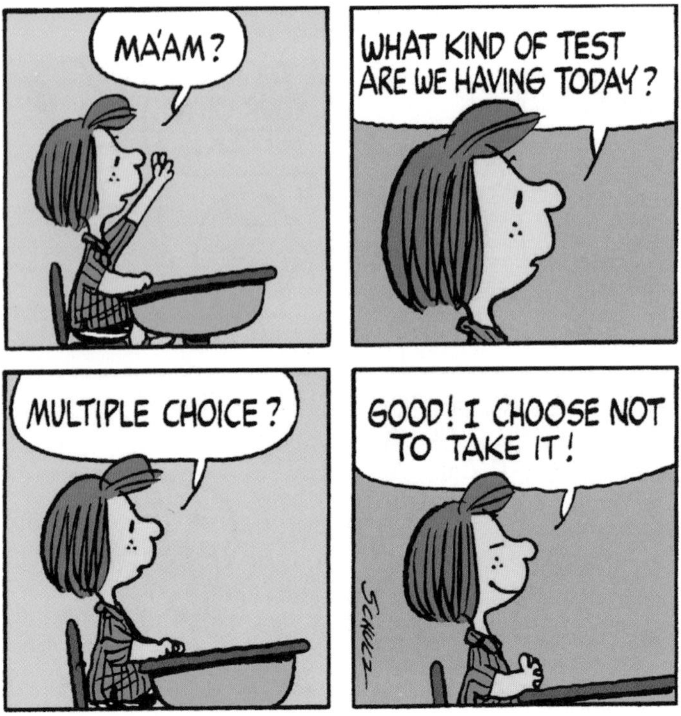
MA'AM?
WHAT KIND OF TEST ARE WE HAVING TODAY?
MULTIPLE CHOICE?
GOOD! I CHOOSE NOT TO TAKE IT!
SCHULZ

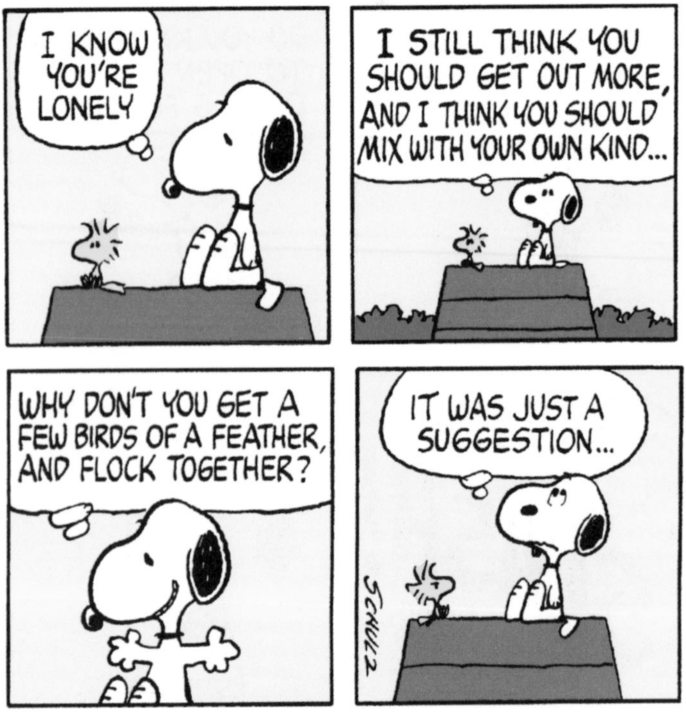
I KNOW YOU'RE LONELY
I STILL THINK YOU SHOULD GET OUT MORE, AND I THINK YOU SHOULD MIX WITH YOUR OWN KIND...
WHY DON'T YOU GET A FEW BIRDS OF A FEATHER, AND FLOCK TOGETHER?
IT WAS JUST A SUGGESTION...
SCHULZ

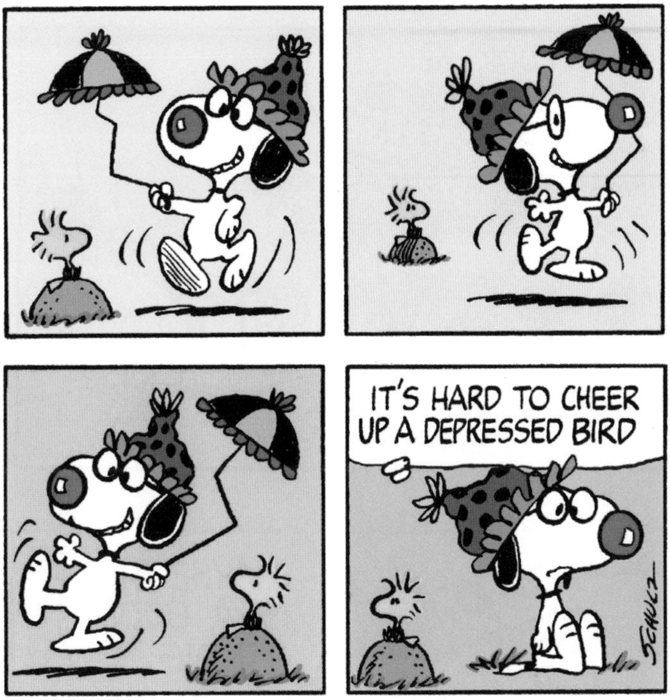
IT'S HARD TO CHEER UP A DEPRESSED BIRD

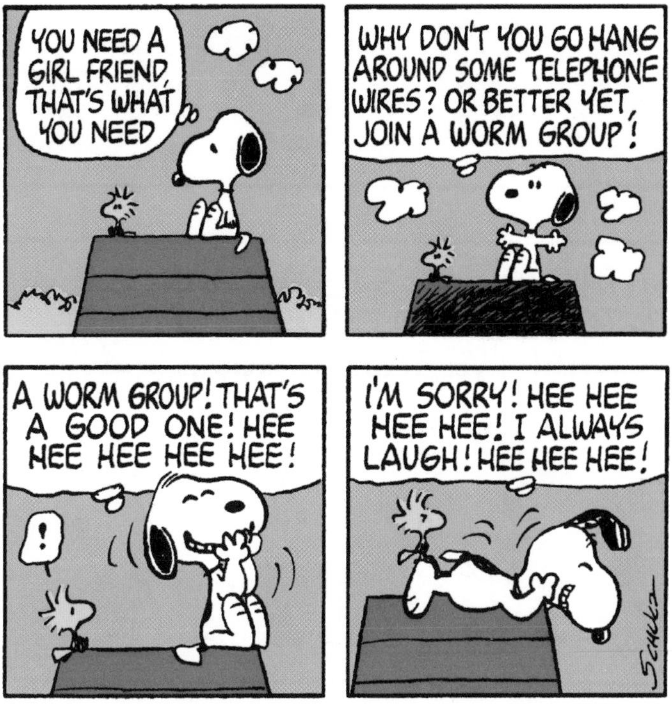
YOU NEED A GIRL FRIEND, THAT'S WHAT YOU NEED
WHY DON'T YOU GO HANG AROUND SOME TELEPHONE WIRES? OR BETTER YET, JOIN A WORM GROUP!
A WORM GROUP! THAT'S A GOOD ONE! HEE HEE HEE HEE HEE!
!
I'M SORRY! HEE HEE HEE HEE! I ALWAYS LAUGH! HEE HEE HEE!

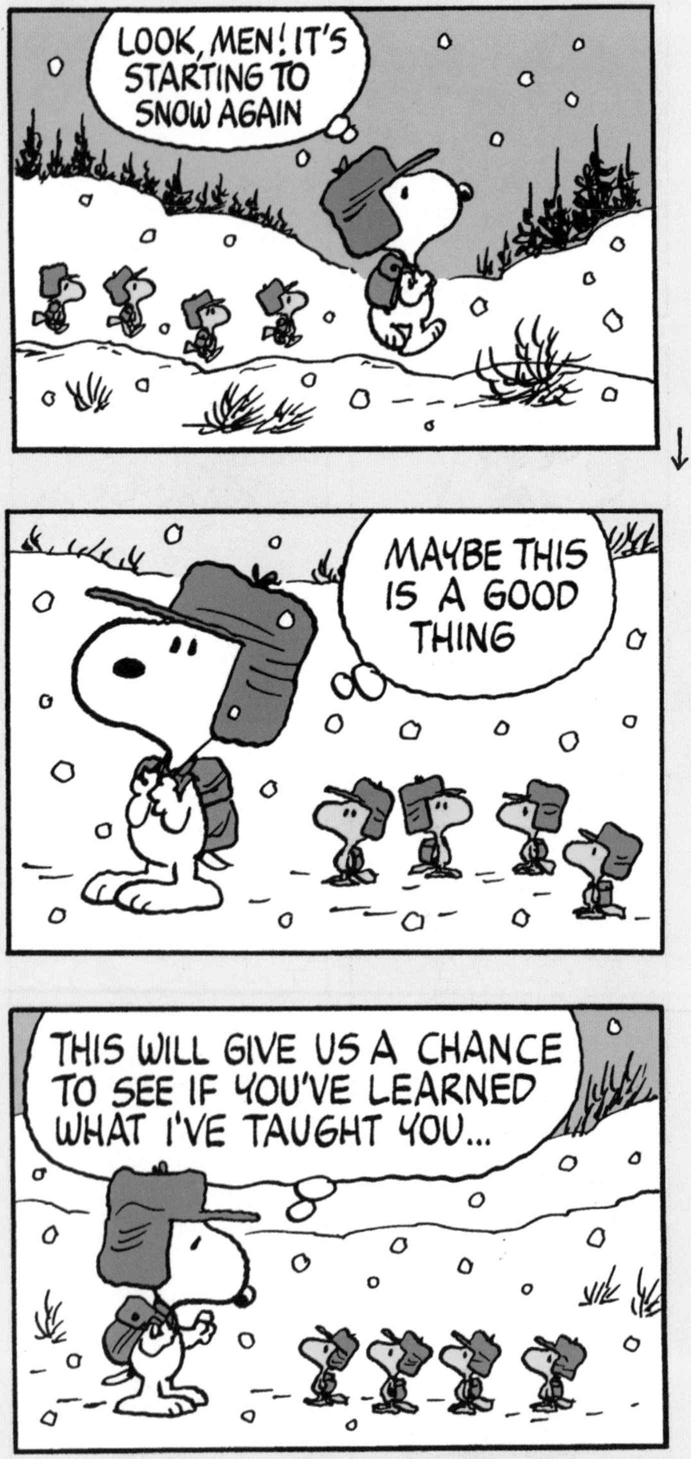

LOOK, MEN! IT'S STARTING TO SNOW AGAIN
MAYBE THIS IS A GOOD THING
THIS WILL GIVE US A CHANCE TO SEE IF YOU'VE LEARNED WHAT I'VE TAUGHT YOU...

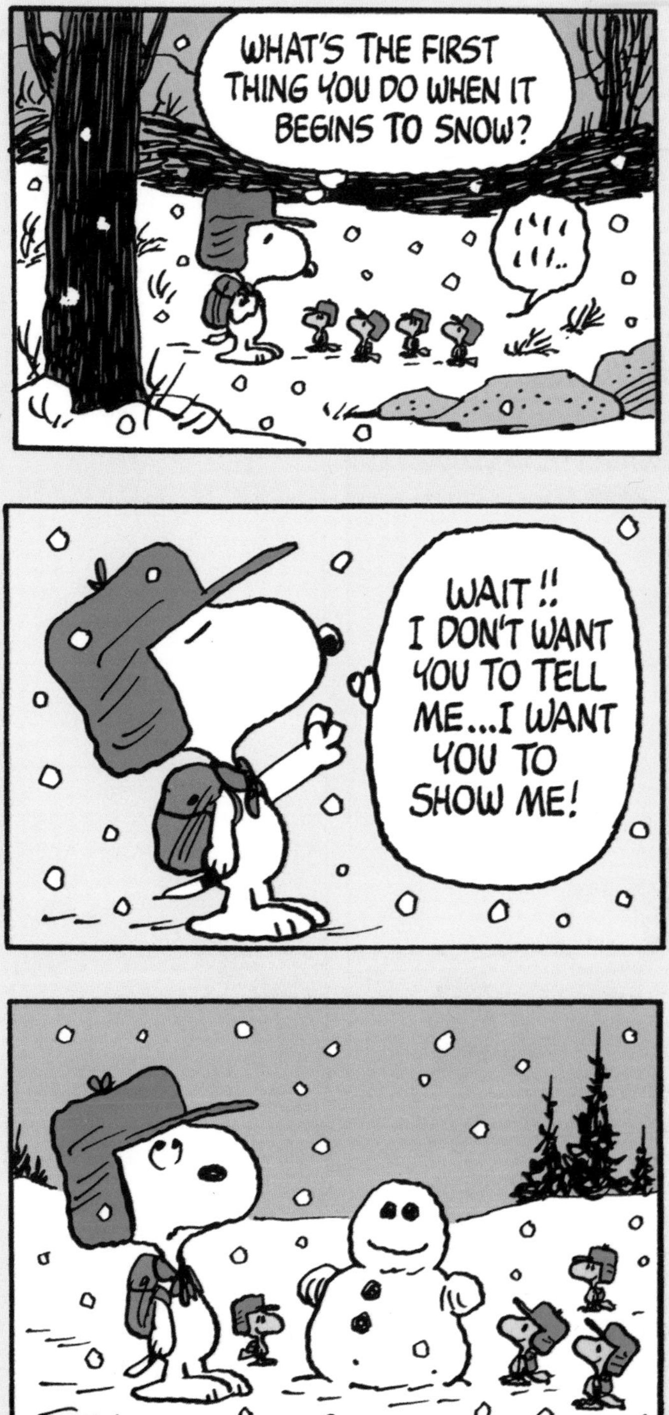
WHAT'S THE FIRST THING YOU DO WHEN IT BEGINS TO SNOW?
WAIT !! I DON'T WANT YOU TO TELL ME...I WANT YOU TO SHOW ME!
SCHULZ

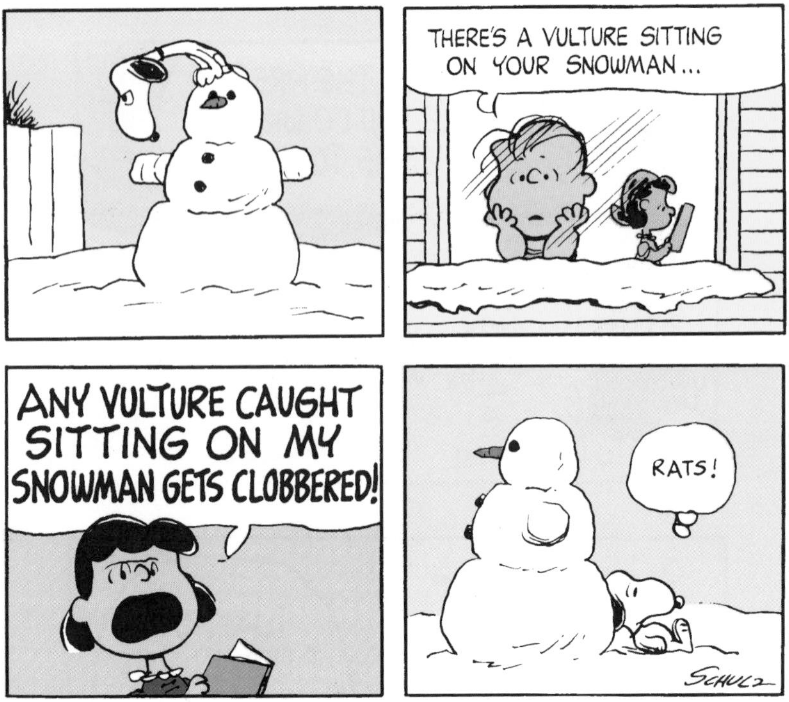
THERE'S A VULTURE SITTING ON YOUR SNOWMAN...
ANY VULTURE CAUGHT SITTING ON MY SNOWMAN GETS CLOBBERED!
RATS!
SCHULZ

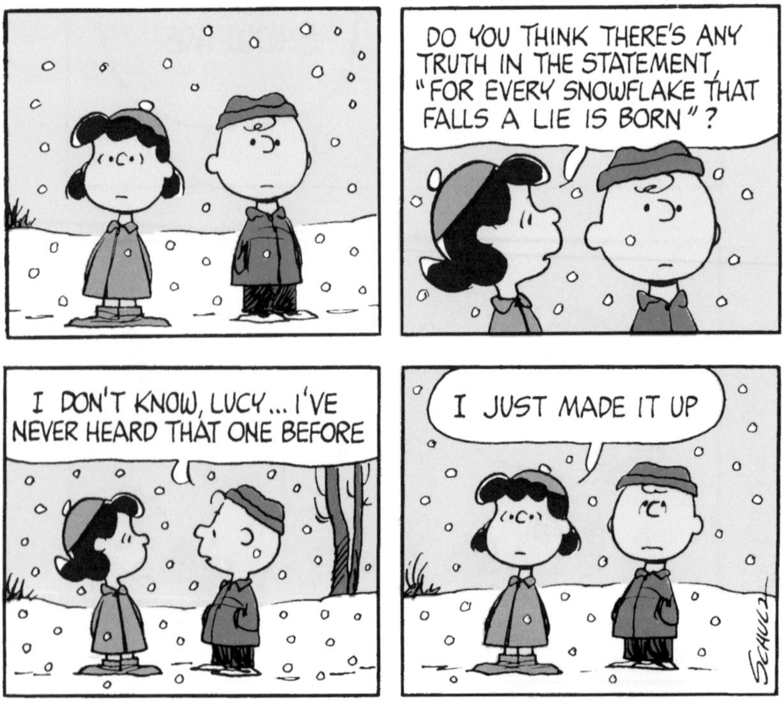
DO YOU THINK THERE'S ANY TRUTH IN THE STATEMENT, "FOR EVERY SNOWFLAKE THAT FALLS A LIE IS BORN"?
I DON'T KNOW, LUCY... I'VE NEVER HEARD THAT ONE BEFORE
I JUST MADE IT UP
SCHULZ

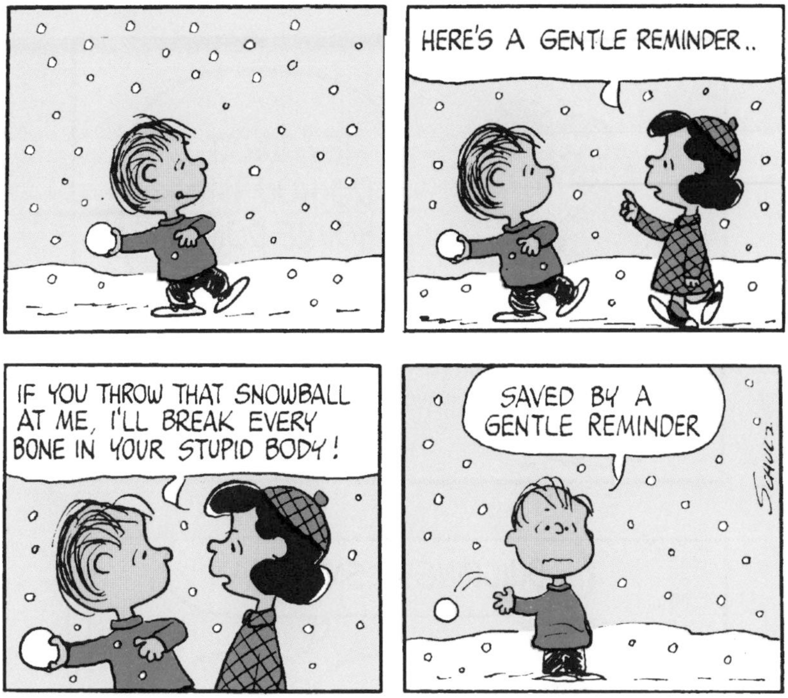
HERE'S A GENTLE REMINDER..
IF YOU THROW THAT SNOWBALL AT ME, I'LL BREAK EVERY BONE IN YOUR STUPID BODY!
SAVED BY A GENTLE REMINDER
SCHULZ

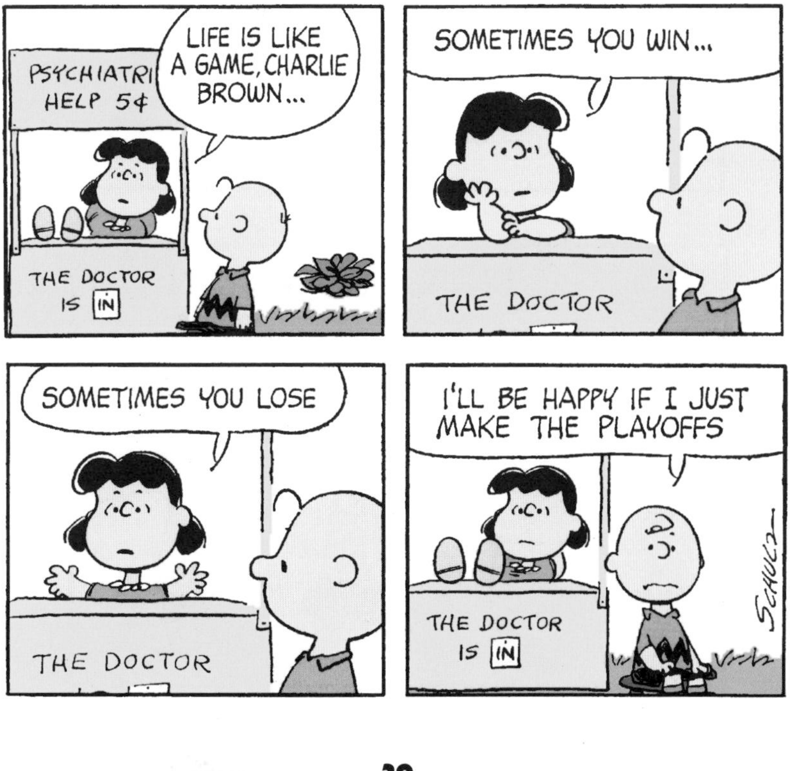
PSYCHIATRI HELP 5¢
LIFE IS LIKE A GAME, CHARLIE BROWN...
THE DOCTOR IS IN
SOMETIMES YOU WIN...
THE DOCTOR
SOMETIMES YOU LOSE
THE DOCTOR
I'LL BE HAPPY IF I JUST MAKE THE PLAYOFFS
THE DOCTOR IS IN
SCHULZ

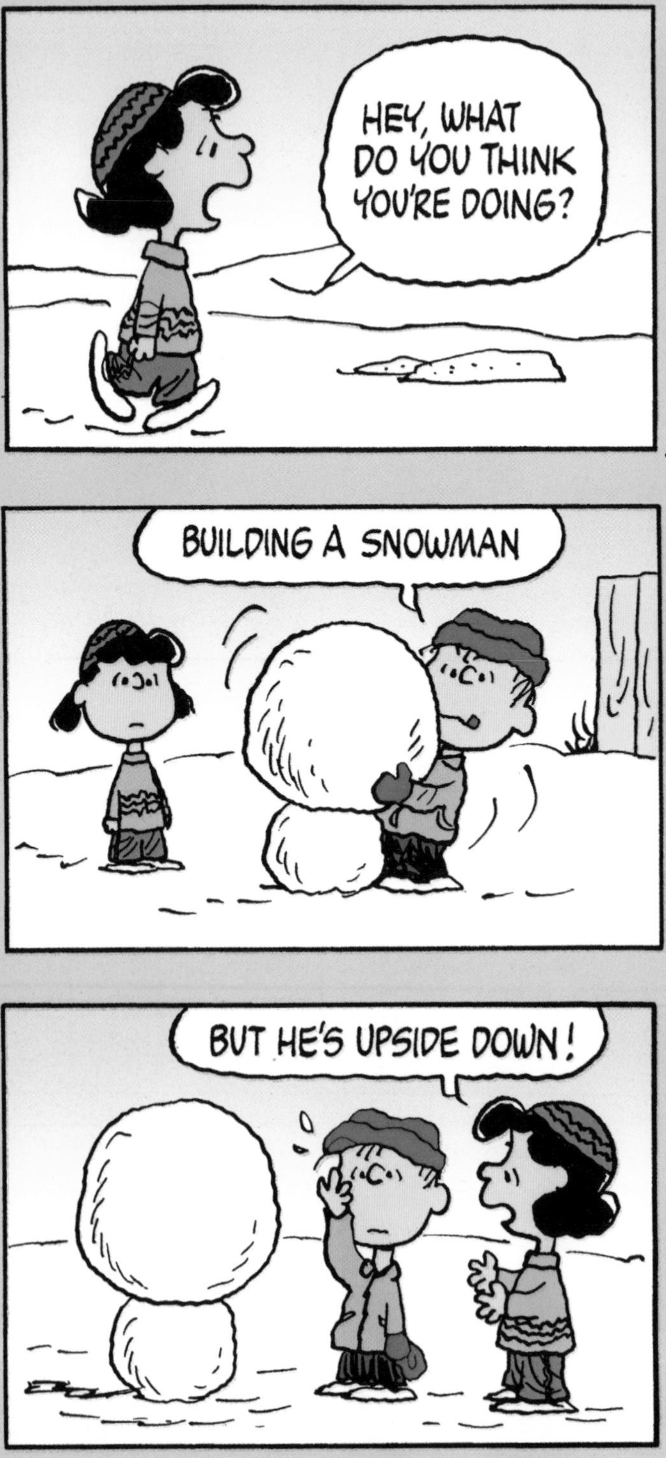
HEY, WHAT DO YOU THINK YOU'RE DOING?
BUILDING A SNOWMAN
BUT HE'S UPSIDE DOWN!

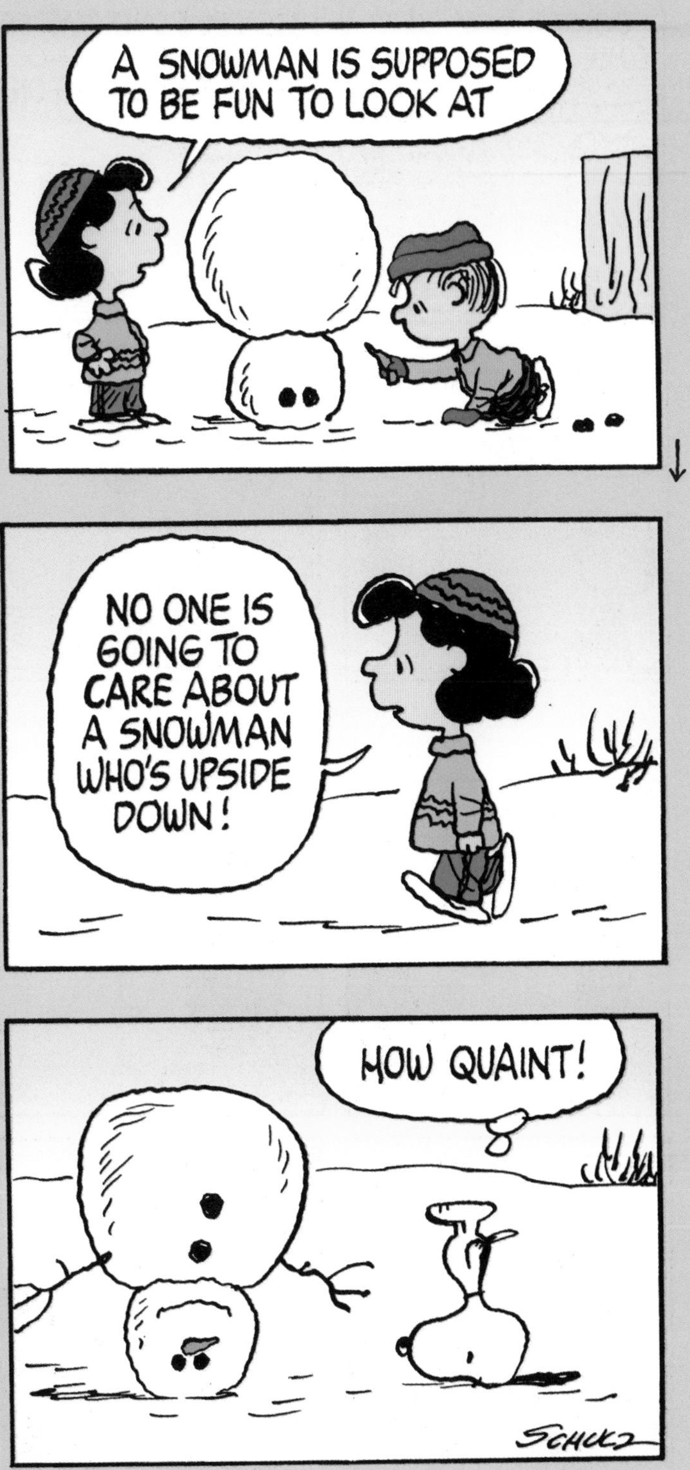
A SNOWMAN IS SUPPOSED TO BE FUN TO LOOK AT
NO ONE IS GOING TO CARE ABOUT A SNOWMAN WHO'S UPSIDE DOWN!
HOW QUAINT!
SCHULZ

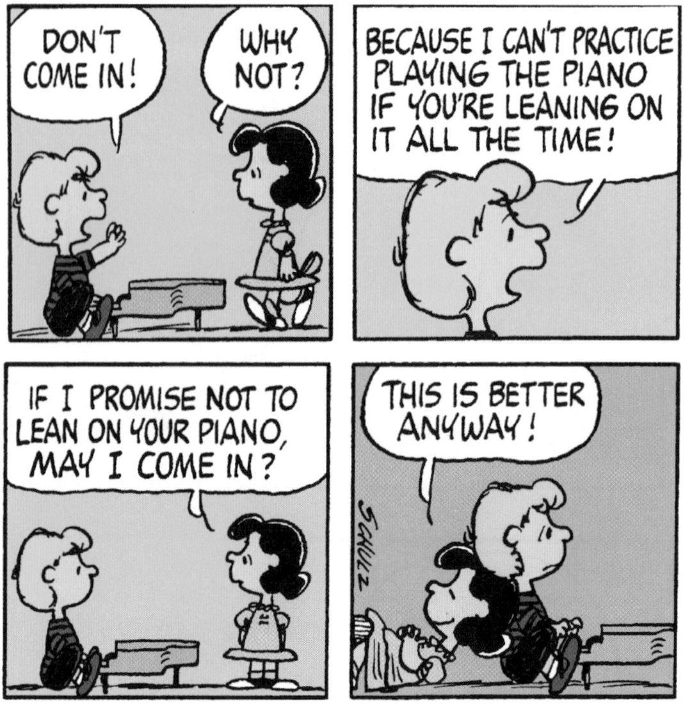
DON'T COME IN!
WHY NOT?
BECAUSE I CAN'T PRACTICE PLAYING THE PIANO IF YOU'RE LEANING ON IT ALL THE TIME!
IF I PROMISE NOT TO LEAN ON YOUR PIANO, MAY I COME IN?
THIS IS BETTER ANYWAY!
SCHULZ

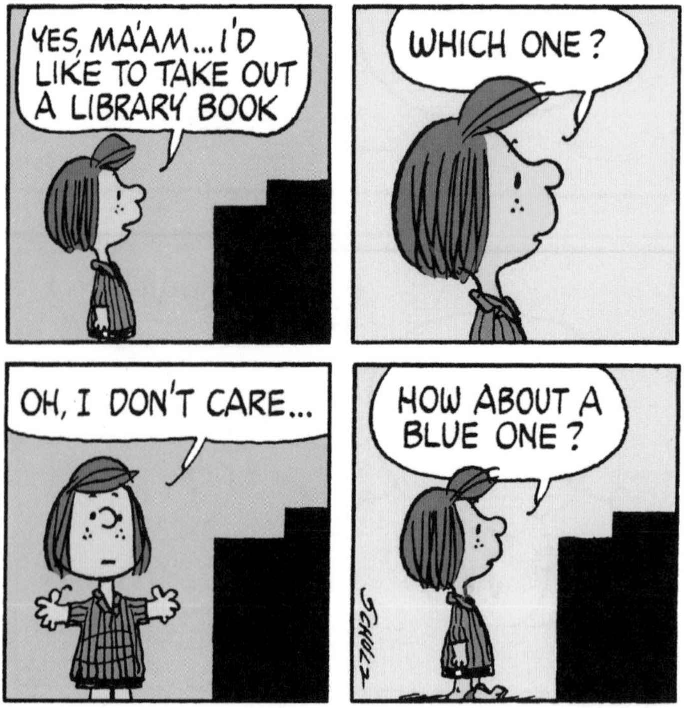
YES, MA'AM...I'D LIKE TO TAKE OUT A LIBRARY BOOK
WHICH ONE?
OH, I DON'T CARE...
HOW ABOUT A BLUE ONE?
SCHULZ

HERE'S A BOOK ABOUT PIRATES, SIR
YOU MEAN GUYS WHO STEAL OTHER PEOPLE'S RECORDINGS?
I WONDER IF THEY MAKE TREASURE MAPS TELLING WHERE THE RECORDINGS ARE BURIED...
YOU'RE HOPELESS, SIR!

"KISS ME ONCE AND KISS ME TWICE..THEN KISS ME ONCE AGAIN... IT'S BEEN A LONG LONG TIME..."
SHH!! YOU HAVE TO BE QUIET IN A LIBRARY, SIR!
JUST SINGING AN OLD WORLD WAR II SONG, MARCIE...
BET IT BROUGHT BACK A FLOOD OF MEMORIES, HUH, MA'AM?

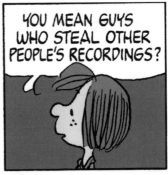

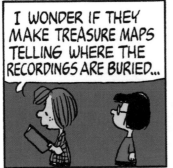

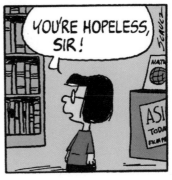

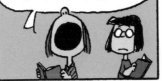

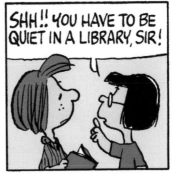

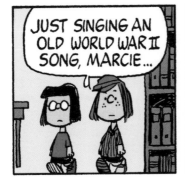

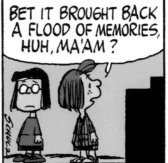

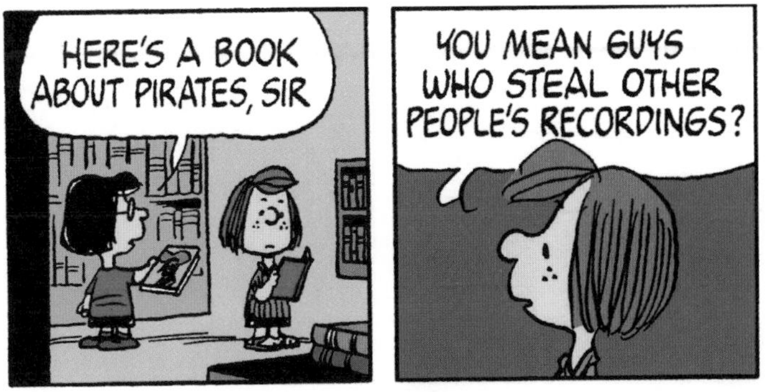

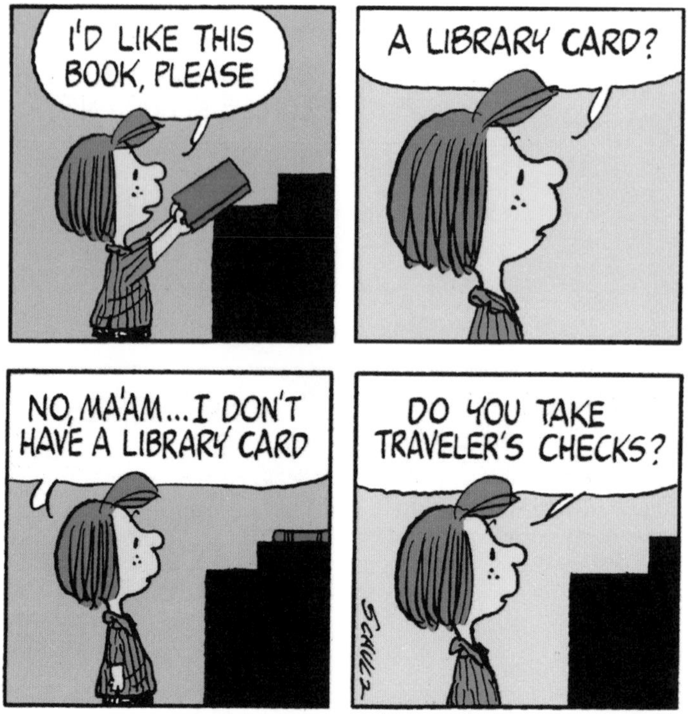
I'D LIKE THIS BOOK, PLEASE
A LIBRARY CARD?
NO, MA'AM...I DON'T HAVE A LIBRARY CARD
DO YOU TAKE TRAVELER'S CHECKS?
SCHULZ

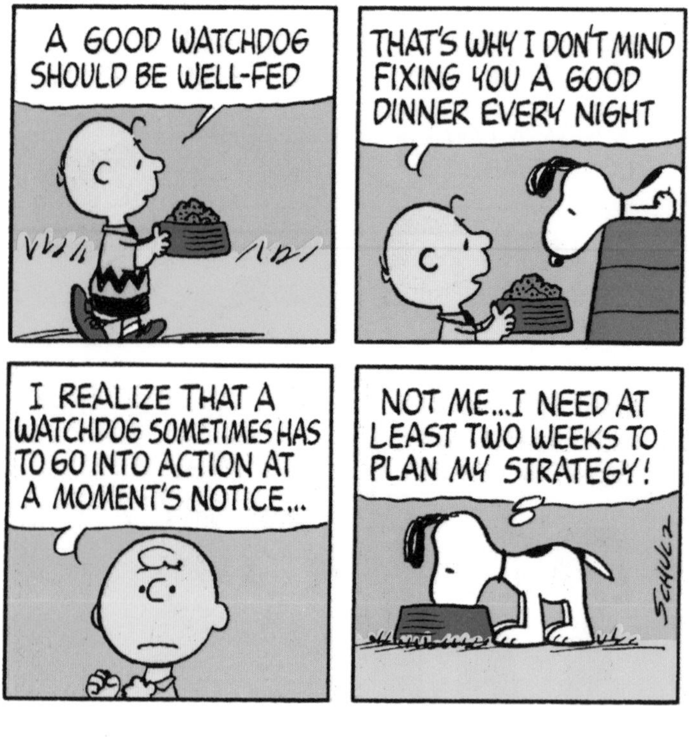
A GOOD WATCHDOG SHOULD BE WELL-FED
THAT'S WHY I DON'T MIND FIXING YOU A GOOD DINNER EVERY NIGHT
I REALIZE THAT A WATCHDOG SOMETIMES HAS TO GO INTO ACTION AT A MOMENT'S NOTICE...
NOT ME...I NEED AT LEAST TWO WEEKS TO PLAN MY STRATEGY!
SCHULZ

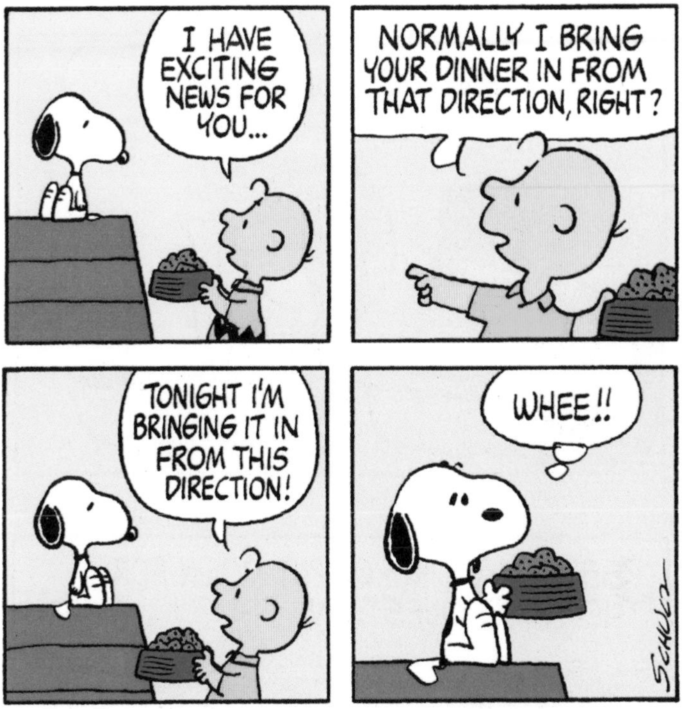
I HAVE EXCITING NEWS FOR YOU...
NORMALLY I BRING YOUR DINNER IN FROM THAT DIRECTION, RIGHT?
TONIGHT I'M BRINGING IT IN FROM THIS DIRECTION!
WHEE!!

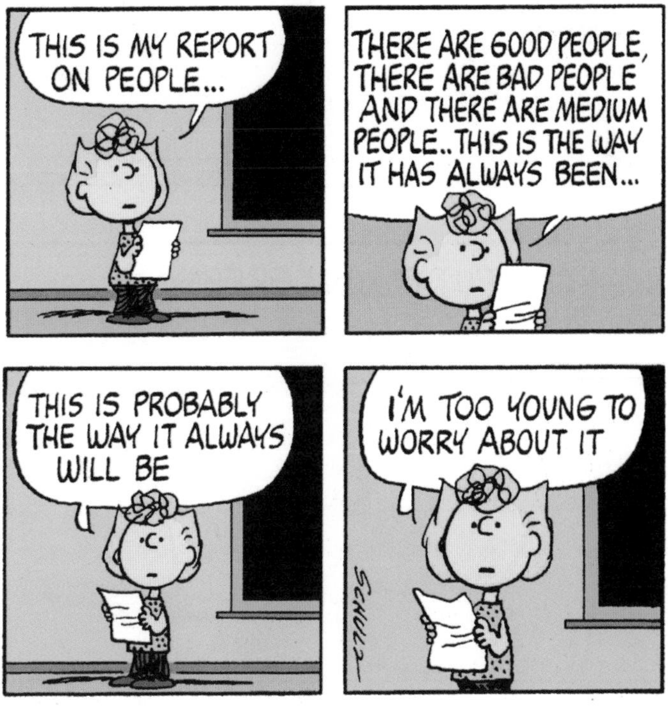
THIS IS MY REPORT ON PEOPLE...
THERE ARE GOOD PEOPLE, THERE ARE BAD PEOPLE AND THERE ARE MEDIUM PEOPLE..THIS IS THE WAY IT HAS ALWAYS BEEN...
THIS IS PROBABLY THE WAY IT ALWAYS WILL BE
I'M TOO YOUNG TO WORRY ABOUT IT

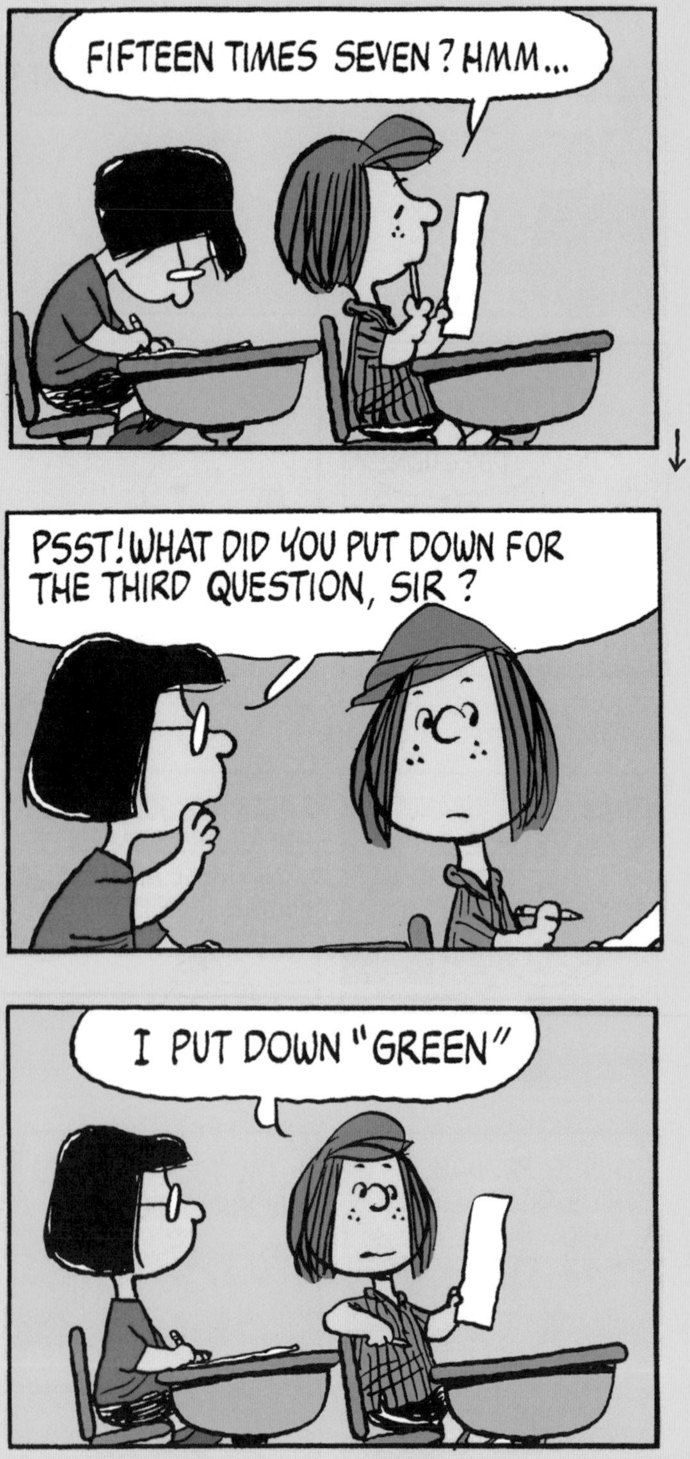
FIFTEEN TIMES SEVEN? HMM...
PSST! WHAT DID YOU PUT DOWN FOR THE THIRD QUESTION, SIR?
I PUT DOWN "GREEN"

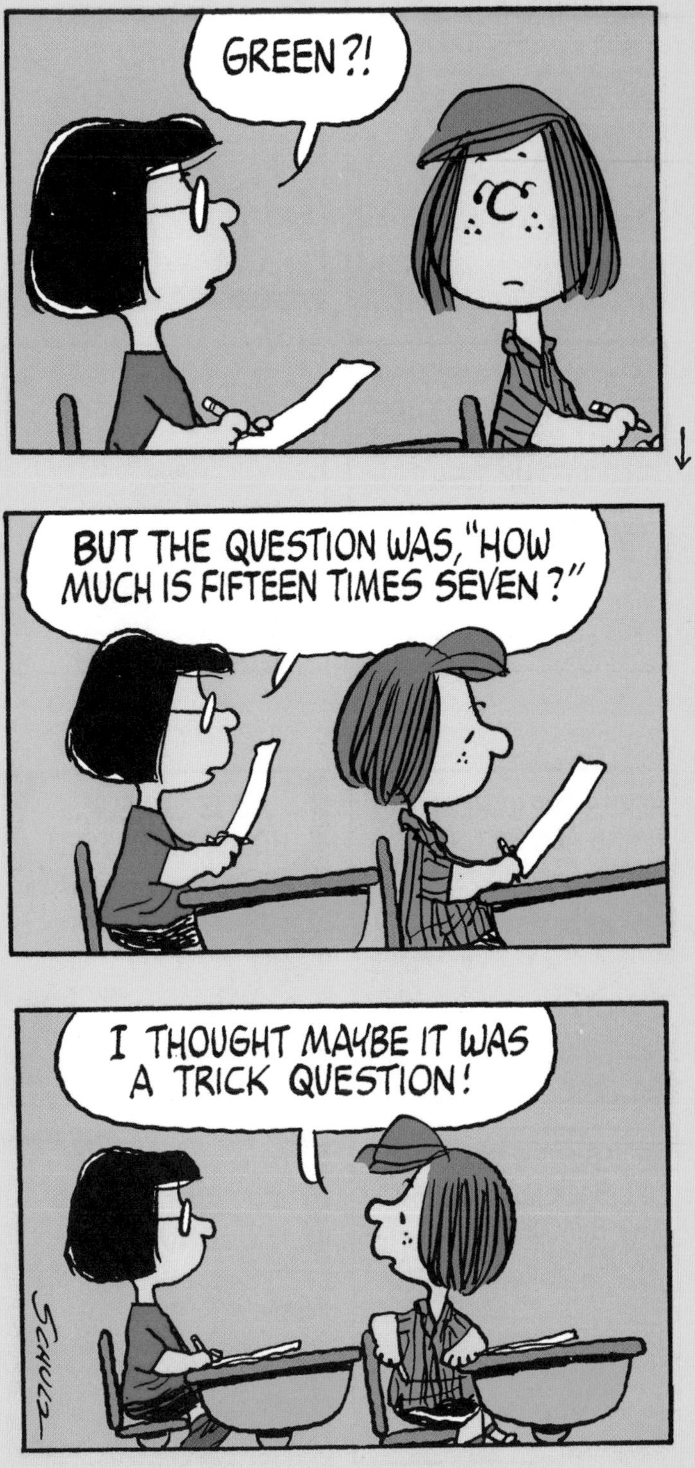
GREEN?!
BUT THE QUESTION WAS, "HOW MUCH IS FIFTEEN TIMES SEVEN?"
I THOUGHT MAYBE IT WAS A TRICK QUESTION!
SCHULZ

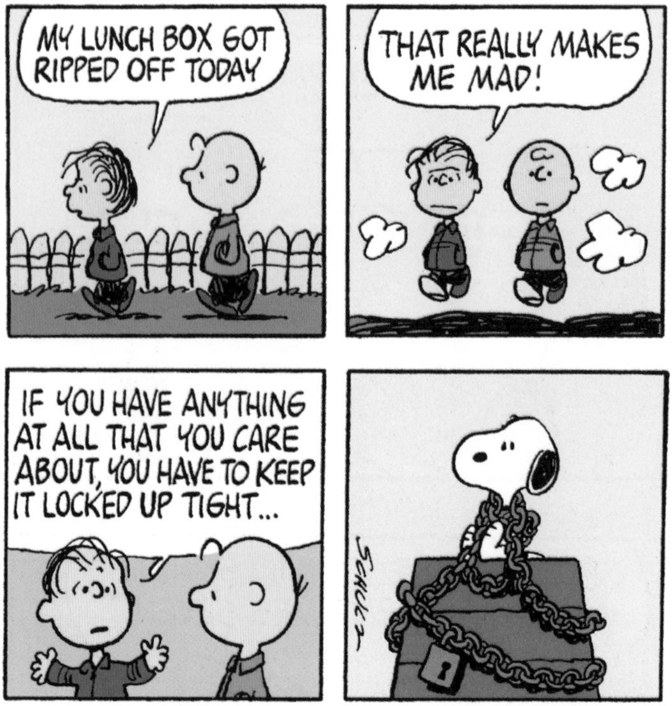
MY LUNCH BOX GOT RIPPED OFF TODAY
THAT REALLY MAKES ME MAD!
IF YOU HAVE ANYTHING AT ALL THAT YOU CARE ABOUT, YOU HAVE TO KEEP IT LOCKED UP TIGHT...
SCHULZ

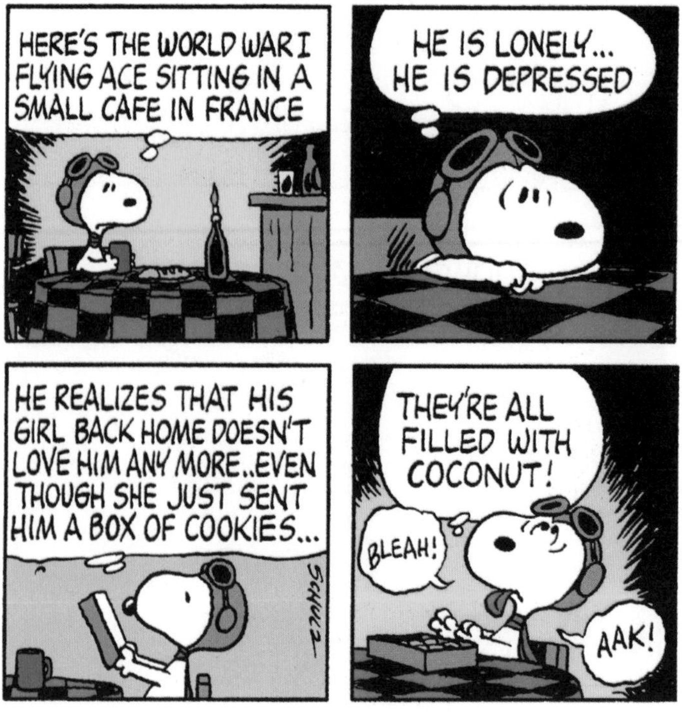
HERE'S THE WORLD WAR I FLYING ACE SITTING IN A SMALL CAFE IN FRANCE
HE IS LONELY... HE IS DEPRESSED
HE REALIZES THAT HIS GIRL BACK HOME DOESN'T LOVE HIM ANY MORE..EVEN THOUGH SHE JUST SENT HIM A BOX OF COOKIES...
SCHULZ
THEY'RE ALL FILLED WITH COCONUT!
BLEAH!
AAK!

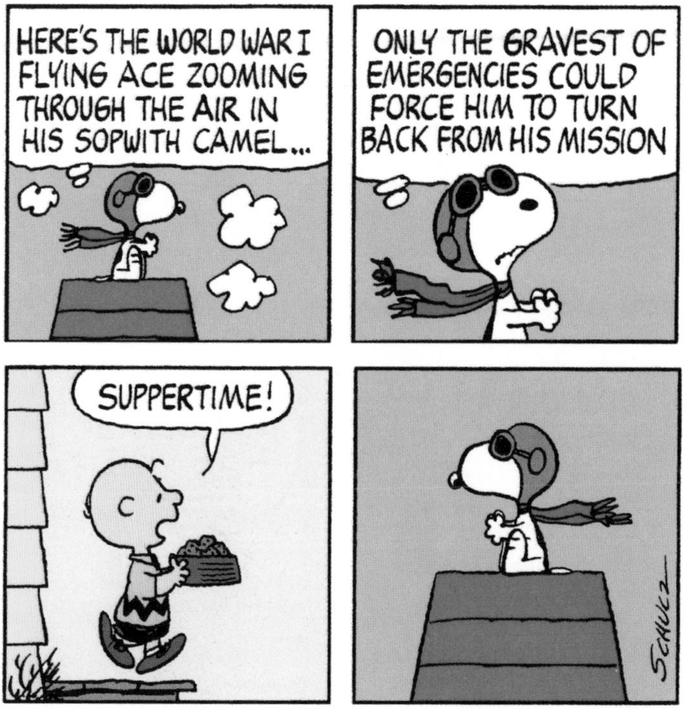
HERE'S THE WORLD WAR I FLYING ACE ZOOMING THROUGH THE AIR IN HIS SOPWITH CAMEL...
ONLY THE GRAVEST OF EMERGENCIES COULD FORCE HIM TO TURN BACK FROM HIS MISSION
SUPPERTIME!
SCHULZ

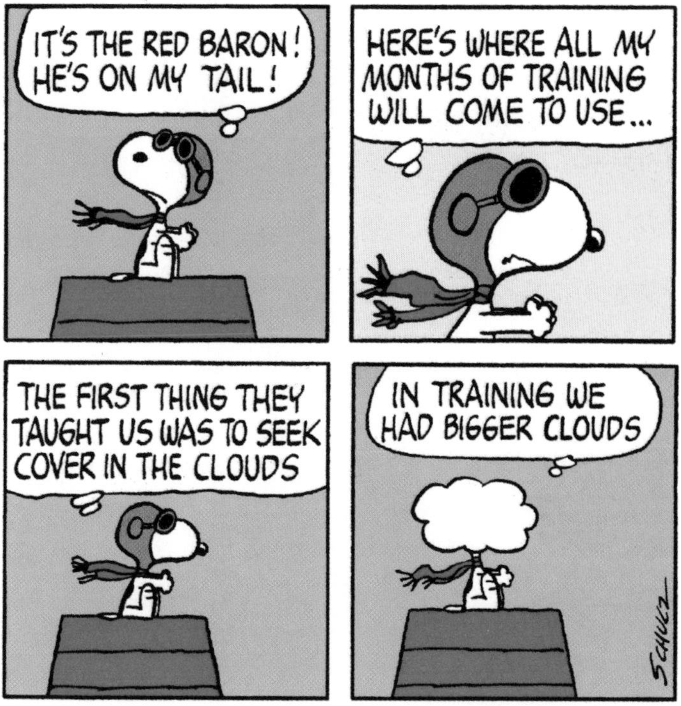
IT'S THE RED BARON! HE'S ON MY TAIL!
HERE'S WHERE ALL MY MONTHS OF TRAINING WILL COME TO USE...
THE FIRST THING THEY TAUGHT US WAS TO SEEK COVER IN THE CLOUDS
IN TRAINING WE HAD BIGGER CLOUDS
SCHULZ

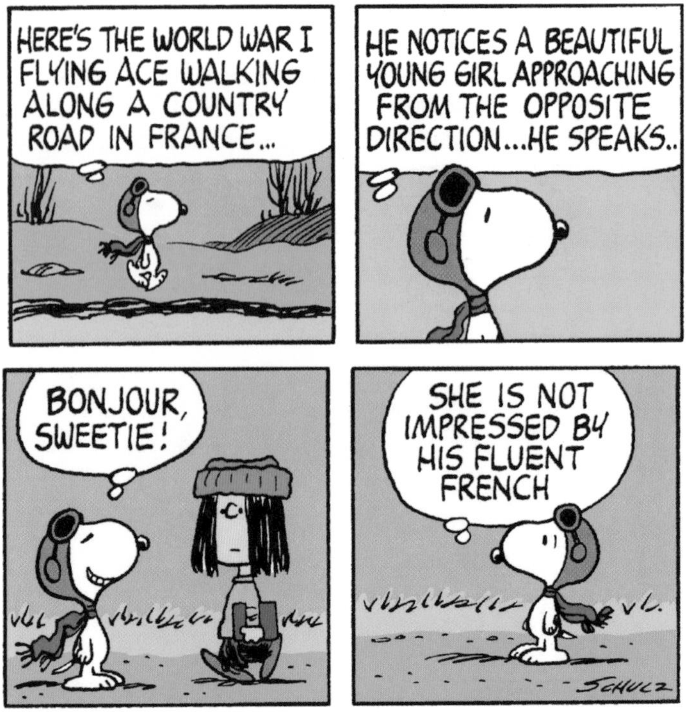
HERE'S THE WORLD WAR I FLYING ACE WALKING ALONG A COUNTRY ROAD IN FRANCE...
HE NOTICES A BEAUTIFUL YOUNG GIRL APPROACHING FROM THE OPPOSITE DIRECTION...HE SPEAKS..
BONJOUR, SWEETIE!
SHE IS NOT IMPRESSED BY HIS FLUENT FRENCH
SCHULZ

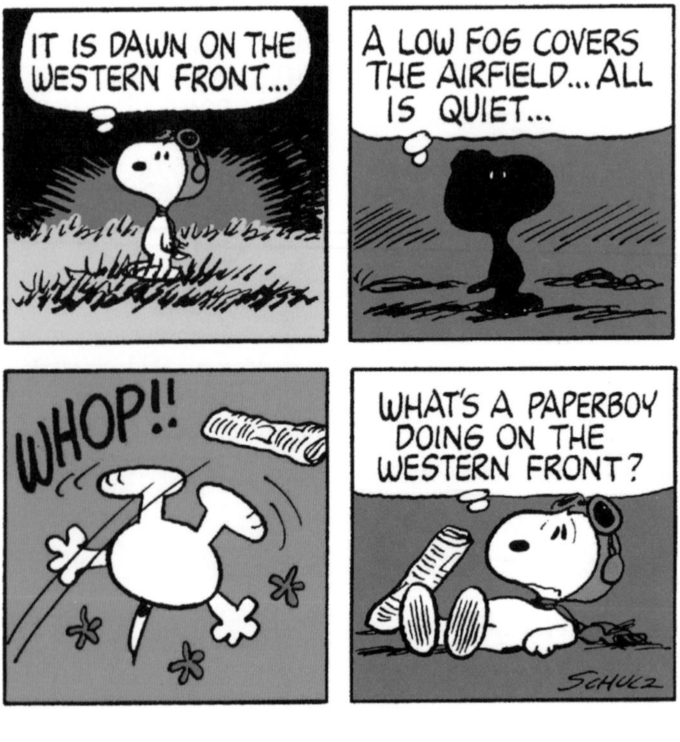
IT IS DAWN ON THE WESTERN FRONT...
A LOW FOG COVERS THE AIRFIELD...ALL IS QUIET...
WHOP!!
WHAT'S A PAPERBOY DOING ON THE WESTERN FRONT?
SCHULZ

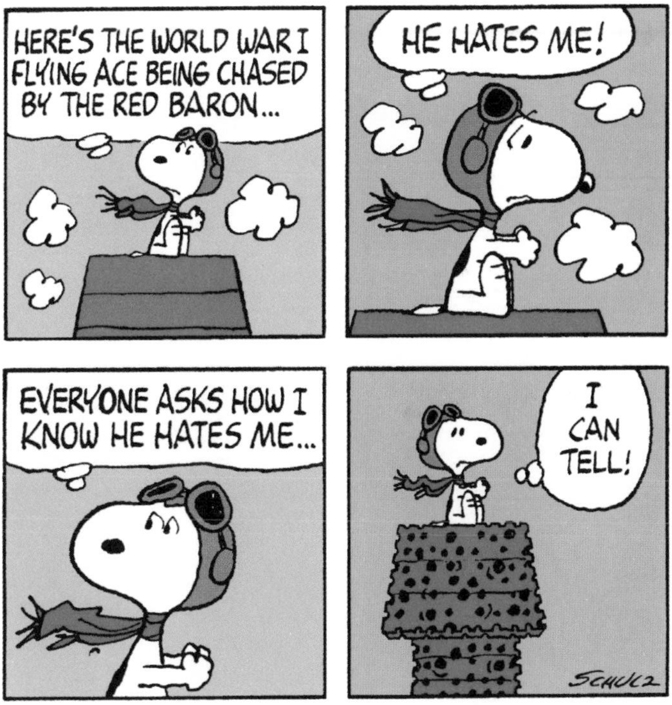
HERE'S THE WORLD WAR I FLYING ACE BEING CHASED BY THE RED BARON...
HE HATES ME!
EVERYONE ASKS HOW I KNOW HE HATES ME...
I CAN TELL!
SCHULZ

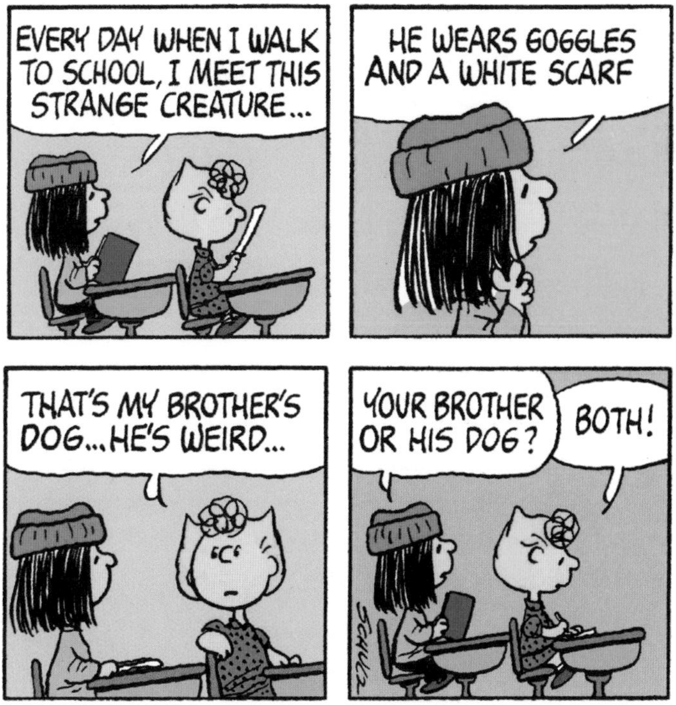
EVERY DAY WHEN I WALK TO SCHOOL, I MEET THIS STRANGE CREATURE...
HE WEARS GOGGLES AND A WHITE SCARF
THAT'S MY BROTHER'S DOG...HE'S WEIRD...
YOUR BROTHER OR HIS DOG?
BOTH!
SCHULZ

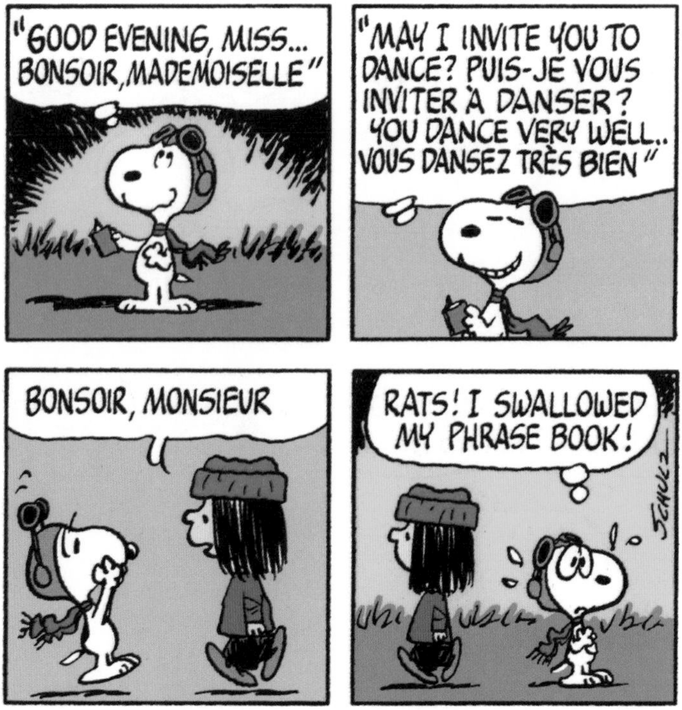
"GOOD EVENING, MISS... BONSOIR, MADEMOISELLE"
"MAY I INVITE YOU TO DANCE? PUIS-JE VOUS INVITER À DANSER? YOU DANCE VERY WELL.. VOUS DANSEZ TRÈS BIEN"
BONSOIR, MONSIEUR
RATS! I SWALLOWED MY PHRASE BOOK!

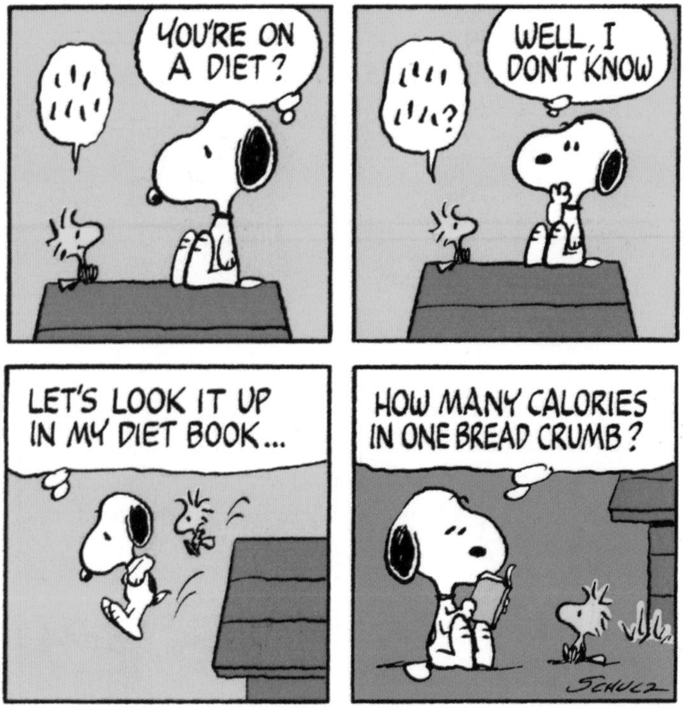
YOU'RE ON A DIET?
WELL, I DON'T KNOW
LET'S LOOK IT UP IN MY DIET BOOK...
HOW MANY CALORIES IN ONE BREAD CRUMB?

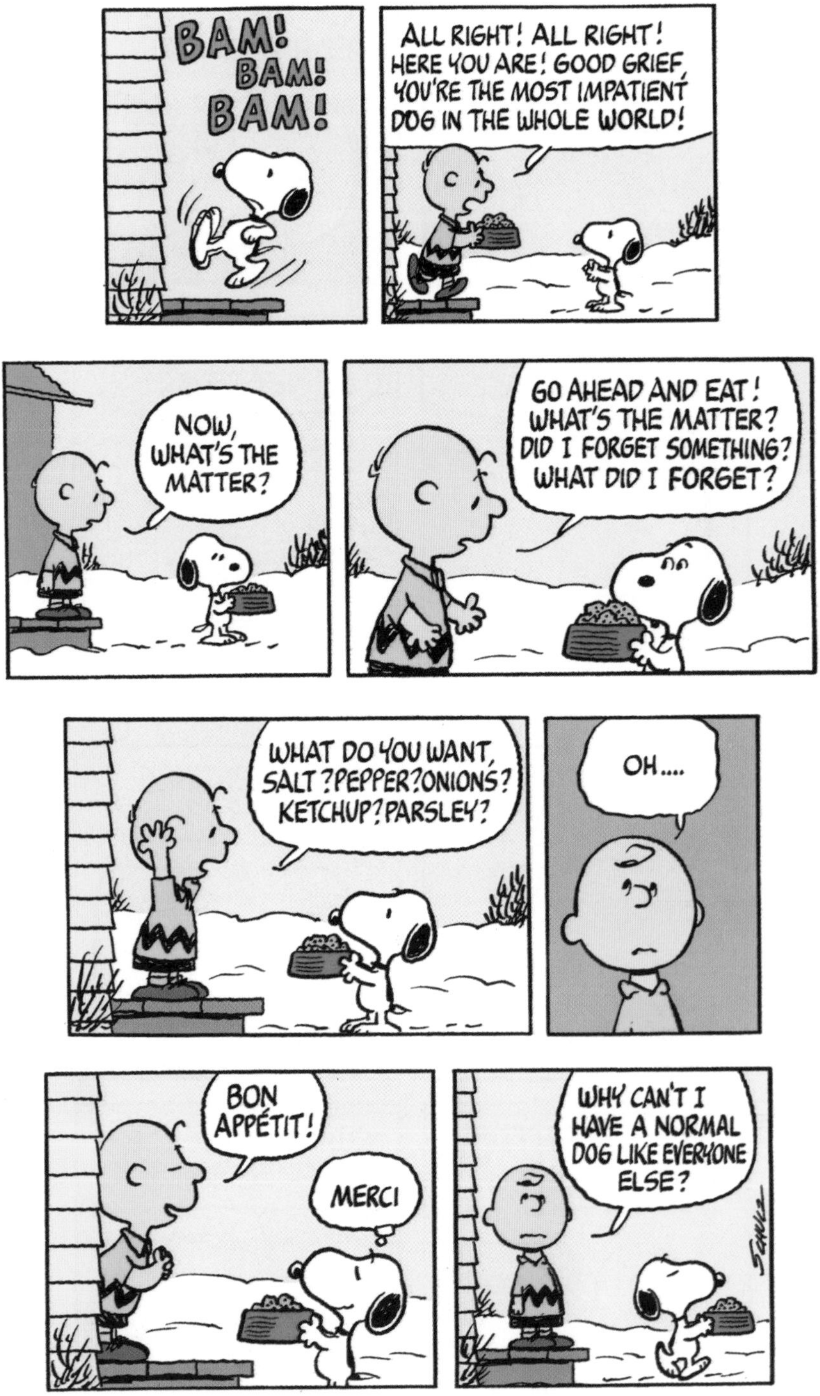
BAM! BAM! BAM!
ALL RIGHT! ALL RIGHT! HERE YOU ARE! GOOD GRIEF, YOU'RE THE MOST IMPATIENT DOG IN THE WHOLE WORLD!
NOW, WHAT'S THE MATTER?
GO AHEAD AND EAT! WHAT'S THE MATTER? DID I FORGET SOMETHING? WHAT DID I FORGET?
WHAT DO YOU WANT, SALT? PEPPER? ONIONS? KETCHUP? PARSLEY?
OH....
BON APPÉTIT!
MERCI
WHY CAN'T I HAVE A NORMAL DOG LIKE EVERYONE ELSE?
SCHULZ

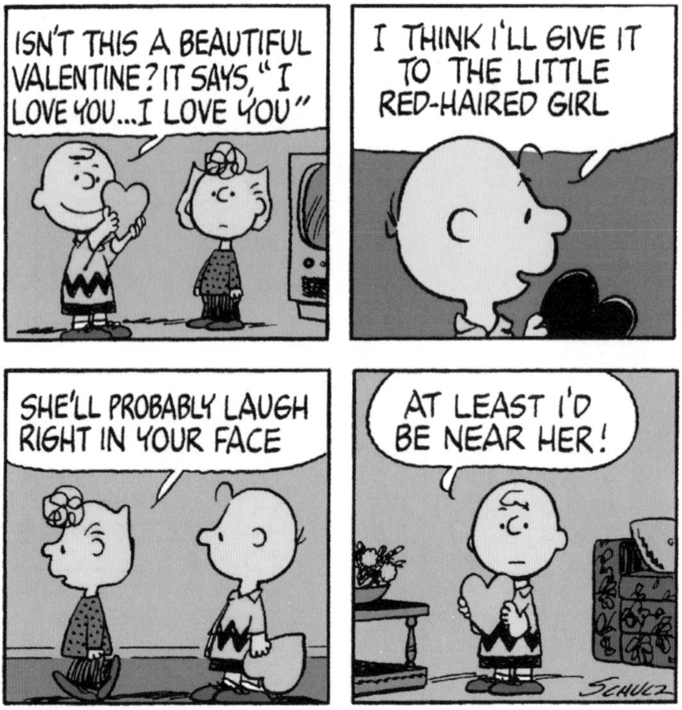
ISN'T THIS A BEAUTIFUL VALENTINE? IT SAYS, "I LOVE YOU...I LOVE YOU"
I THINK I'LL GIVE IT TO THE LITTLE RED-HAIRED GIRL
SHE'LL PROBABLY LAUGH RIGHT IN YOUR FACE
AT LEAST I'D BE NEAR HER!
SCHULZ

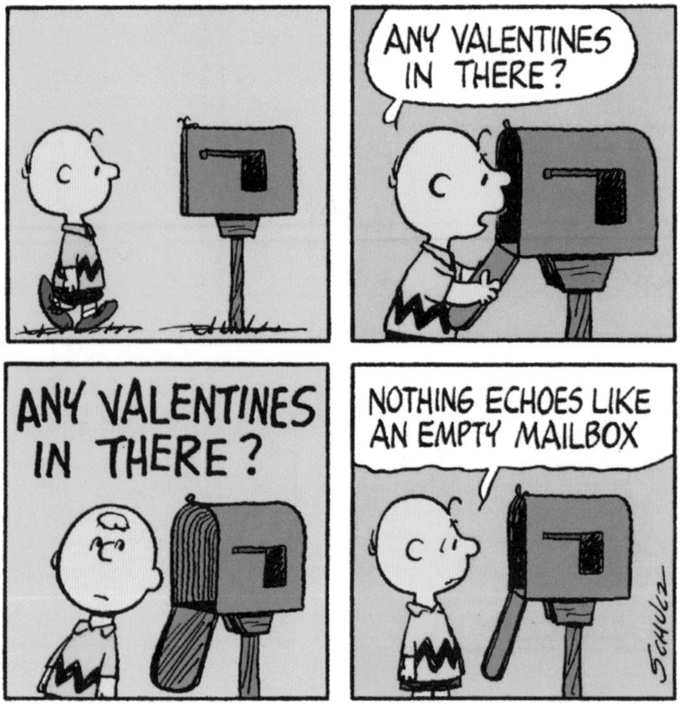
ANY VALENTINES IN THERE?
ANY VALENTINES IN THERE?
NOTHING ECHOES LIKE AN EMPTY MAILBOX
SCHULZ

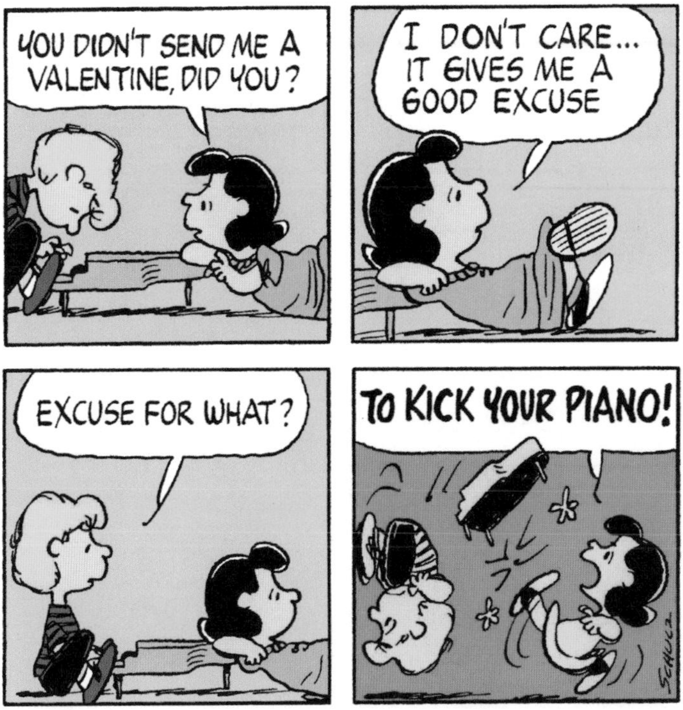
YOU DIDN'T SEND ME A VALENTINE, DID YOU?
I DON'T CARE... IT GIVES ME A GOOD EXCUSE
EXCUSE FOR WHAT?
TO KICK YOUR PIANO!

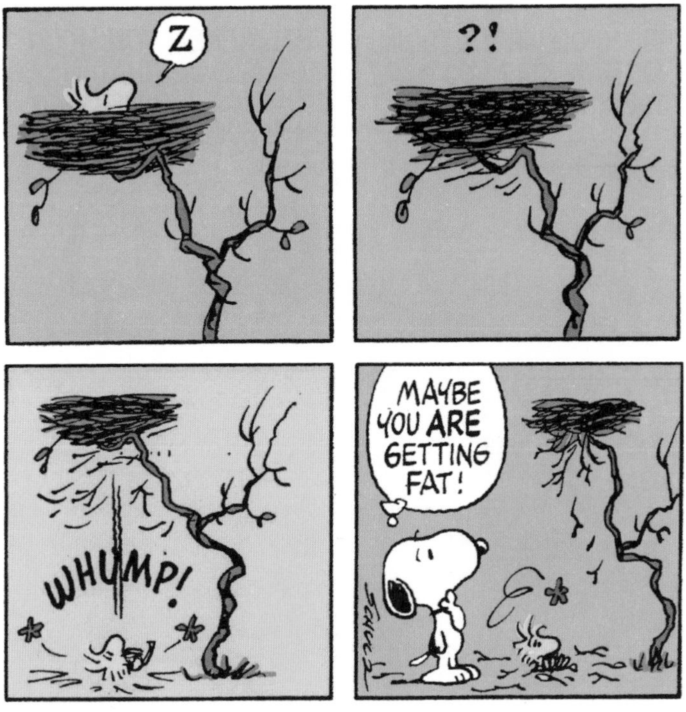
Z
?!
WHUMP!
MAYBE YOU ARE GETTING FAT!

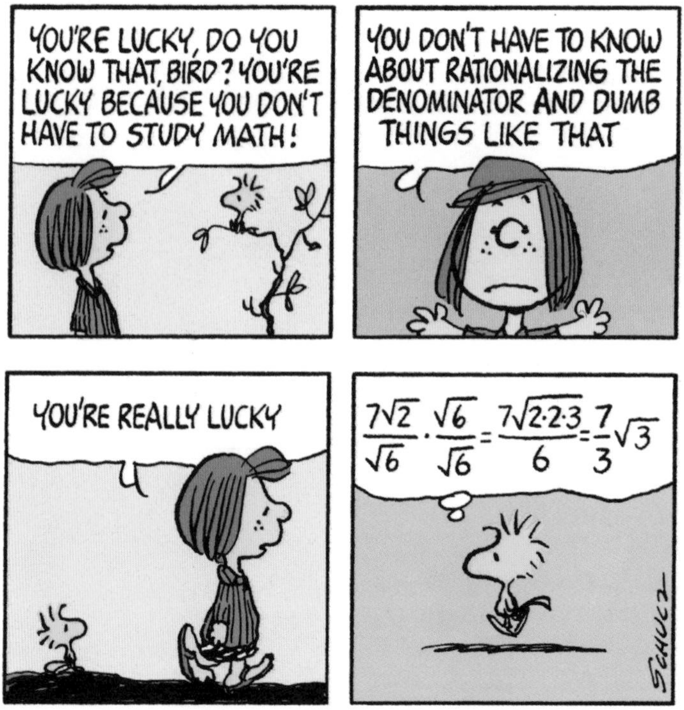
YOU'RE LUCKY, DO YOU KNOW THAT, BIRD? YOU'RE LUCKY BECAUSE YOU DON'T HAVE TO STUDY MATH!
YOU DON'T HAVE TO KNOW ABOUT RATIONALIZING THE DENOMINATOR AND DUMB THINGS LIKE THAT
YOU'RE REALLY LUCKY
$\frac{7\sqrt{2}}{\sqrt{6}} \cdot \frac{\sqrt{6}}{\sqrt{6}} = \frac{7\sqrt{2 \cdot 2 \cdot 3}}{6} = \frac{7}{3}\sqrt{3}$
SCHULZ

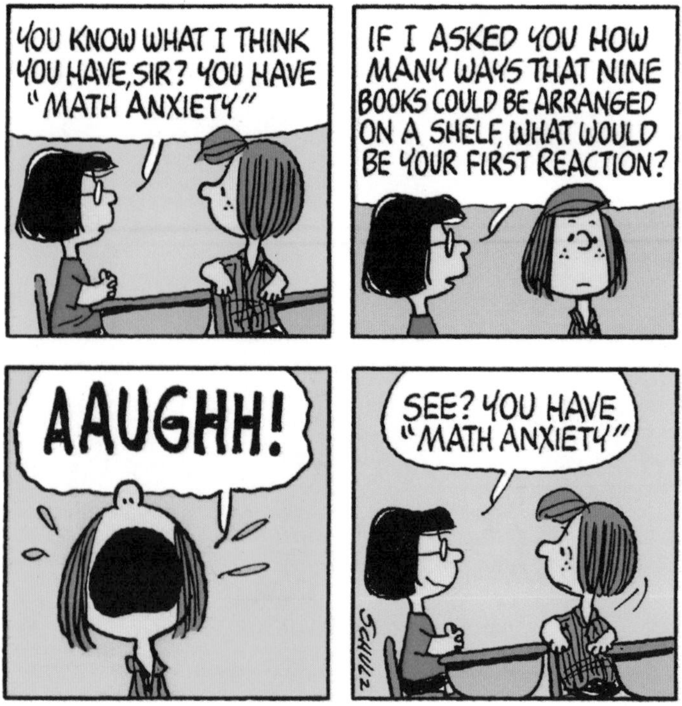
YOU KNOW WHAT I THINK YOU HAVE, SIR? YOU HAVE "MATH ANXIETY"
IF I ASKED YOU HOW MANY WAYS THAT NINE BOOKS COULD BE ARRANGED ON A SHELF, WHAT WOULD BE YOUR FIRST REACTION?
AAUGHH!
SEE? YOU HAVE "MATH ANXIETY"
SCHULZ

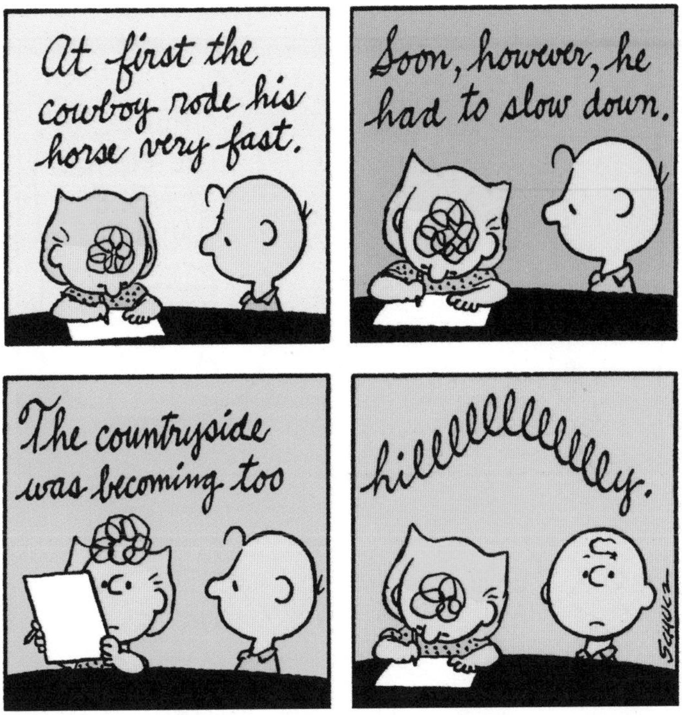
At first the cowboy rode his horse very fast.
Soon, however, he had to slow down.
The countryside was becoming too
hillllllllllllly.
SCHULZ

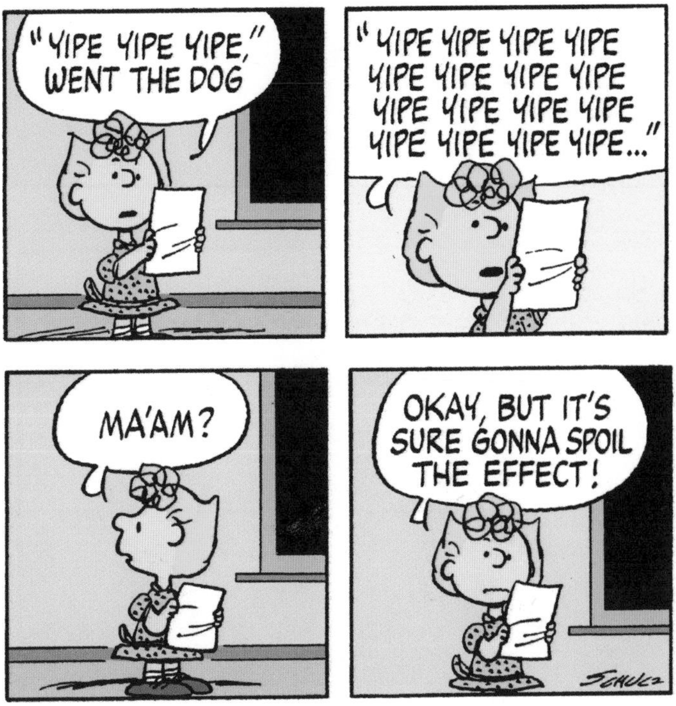
"YIPE YIPE YIPE," WENT THE DOG
"YIPE YIPE YIPE YIPE YIPE YIPE YIPE YIPE YIPE YIPE YIPE YIPE YIPE YIPE YIPE YIPE..."
MA'AM?
OKAY, BUT IT'S SURE GONNA SPOIL THE EFFECT!
SCHULZ

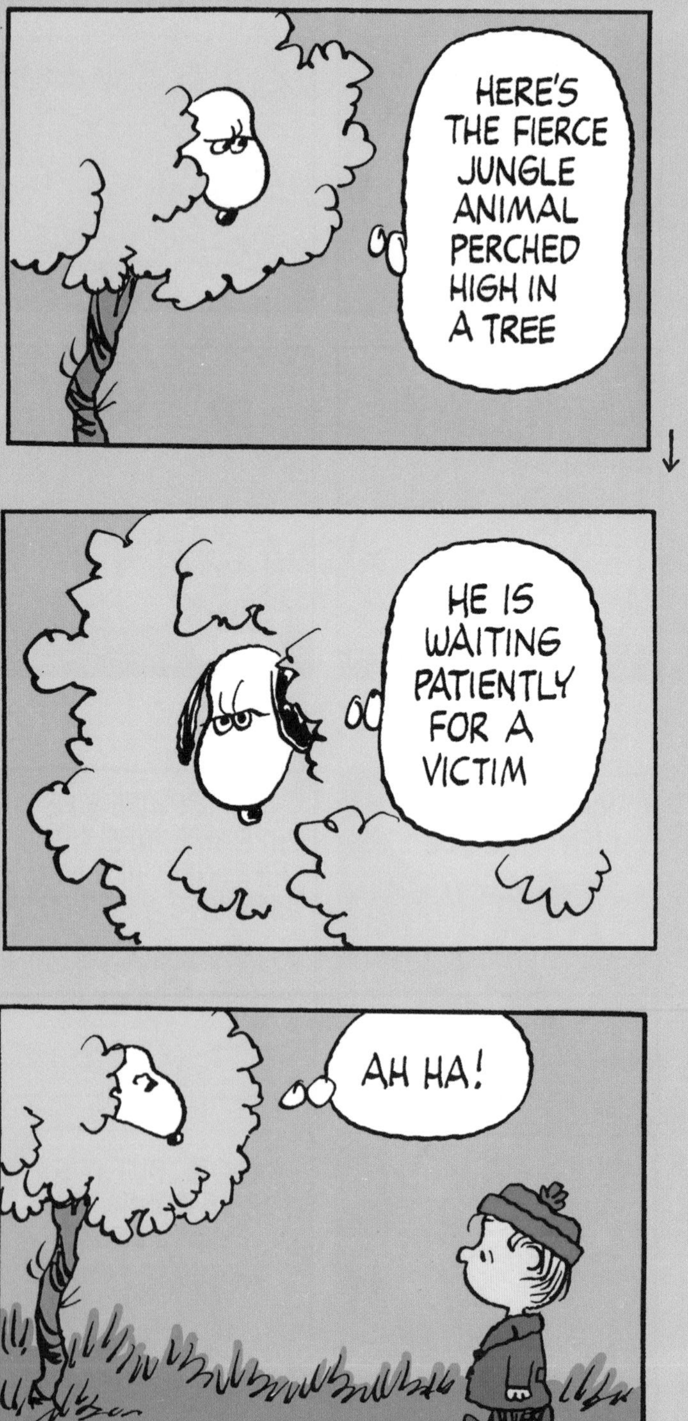
HERE'S THE FIERCE JUNGLE ANIMAL PERCHED HIGH IN A TREE
HE IS WAITING PATIENTLY FOR A VICTIM
AH HA!

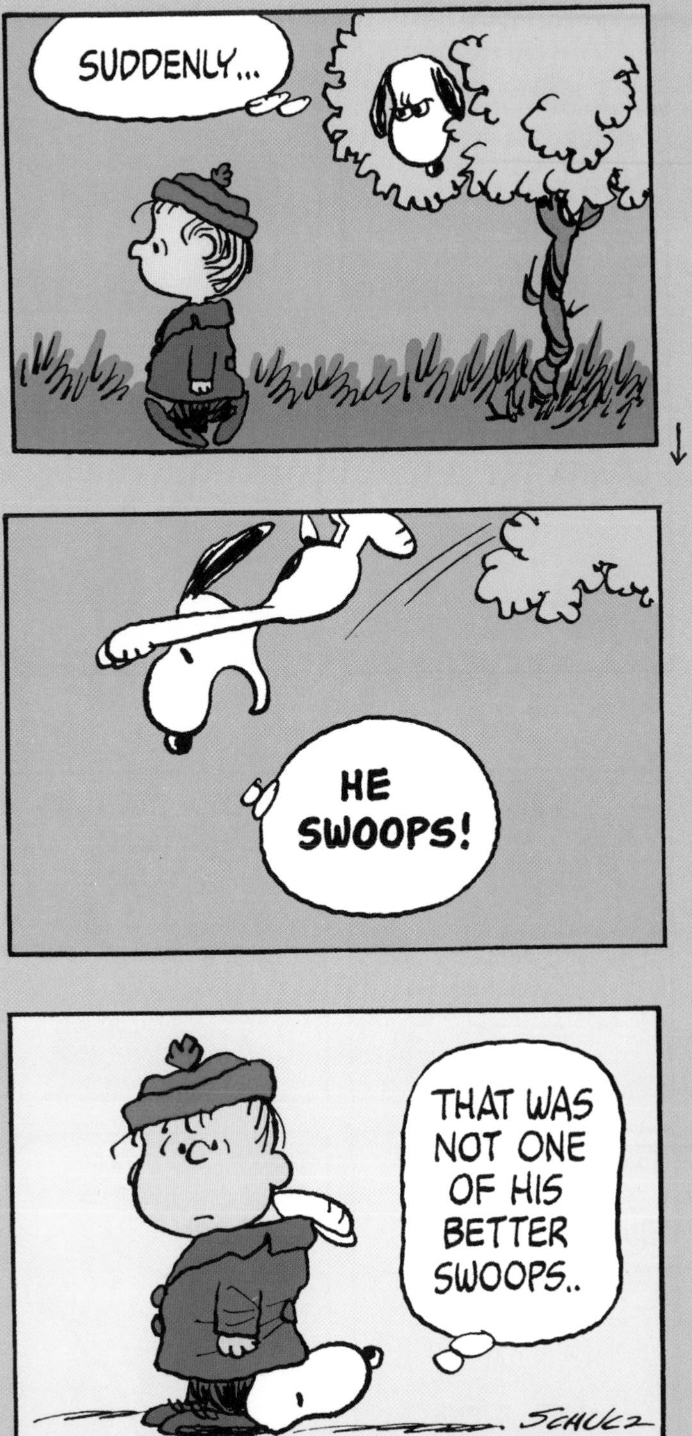
SUDDENLY...
HE SWOOPS!
THAT WAS NOT ONE OF HIS BETTER SWOOPS..
SCHULZ

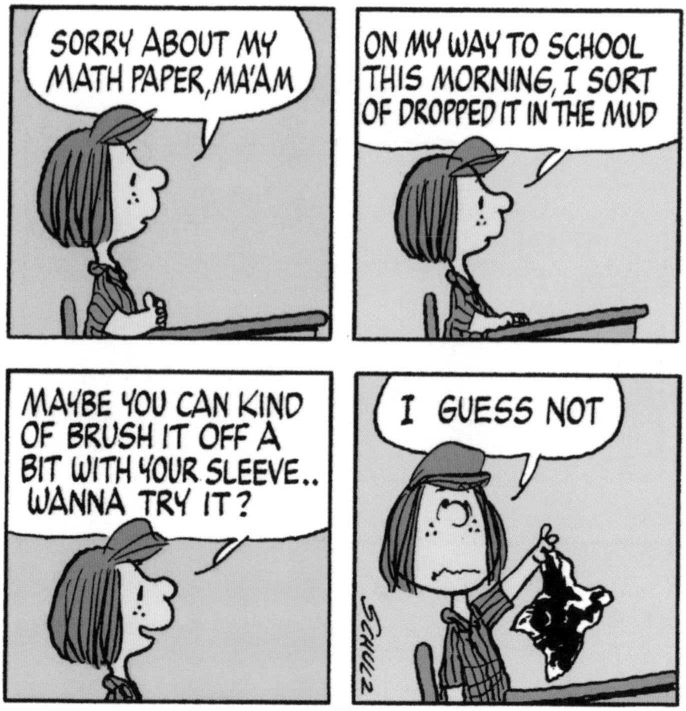
SORRY ABOUT MY MATH PAPER, MA'AM
ON MY WAY TO SCHOOL THIS MORNING, I SORT OF DROPPED IT IN THE MUD
MAYBE YOU CAN KIND OF BRUSH IT OFF A BIT WITH YOUR SLEEVE.. WANNA TRY IT?
I GUESS NOT

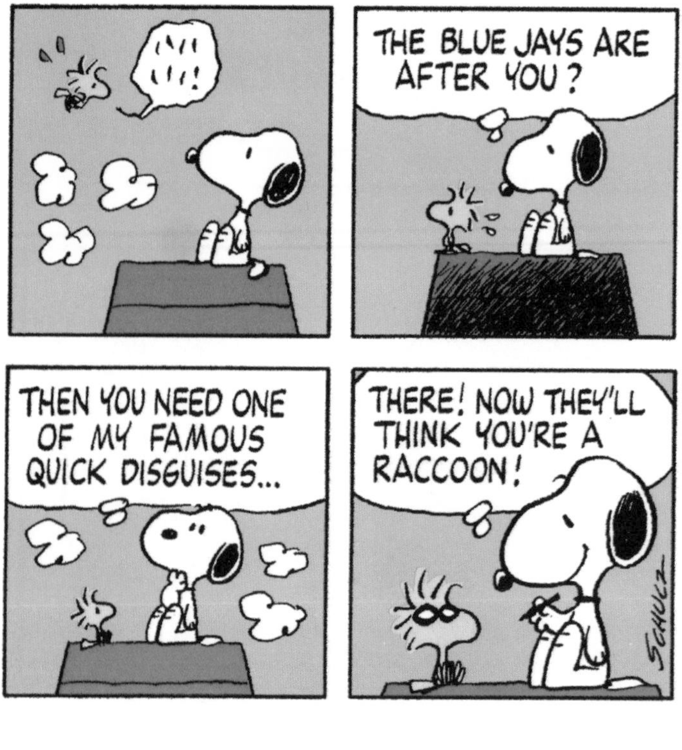
THE BLUE JAYS ARE AFTER YOU?
THEN YOU NEED ONE OF MY FAMOUS QUICK DISGUISES...
THERE! NOW THEY'LL THINK YOU'RE A RACCOON!

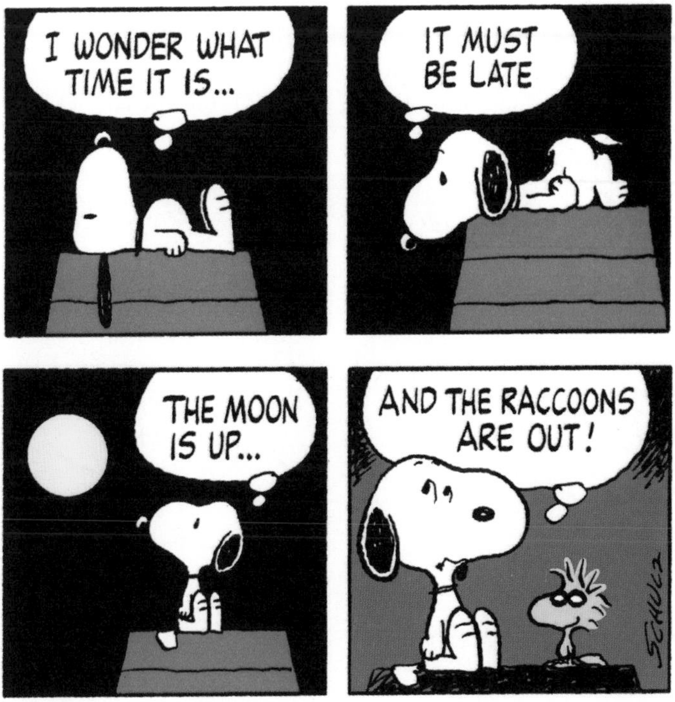
I WONDER WHAT TIME IT IS...
IT MUST BE LATE
THE MOON IS UP...
AND THE RACCOONS ARE OUT!
SCHULZ

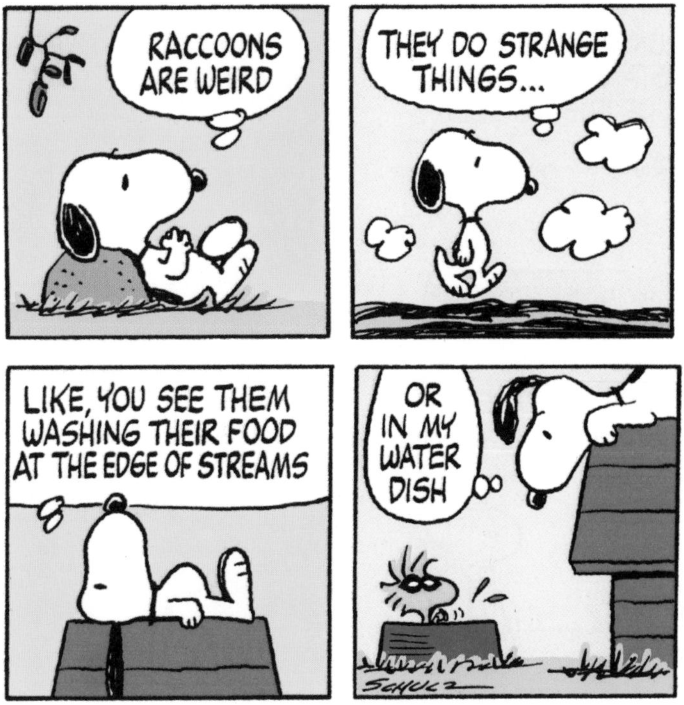
RACCOONS ARE WEIRD
THEY DO STRANGE THINGS...
LIKE, YOU SEE THEM WASHING THEIR FOOD AT THE EDGE OF STREAMS
OR IN MY WATER DISH
SCHULZ

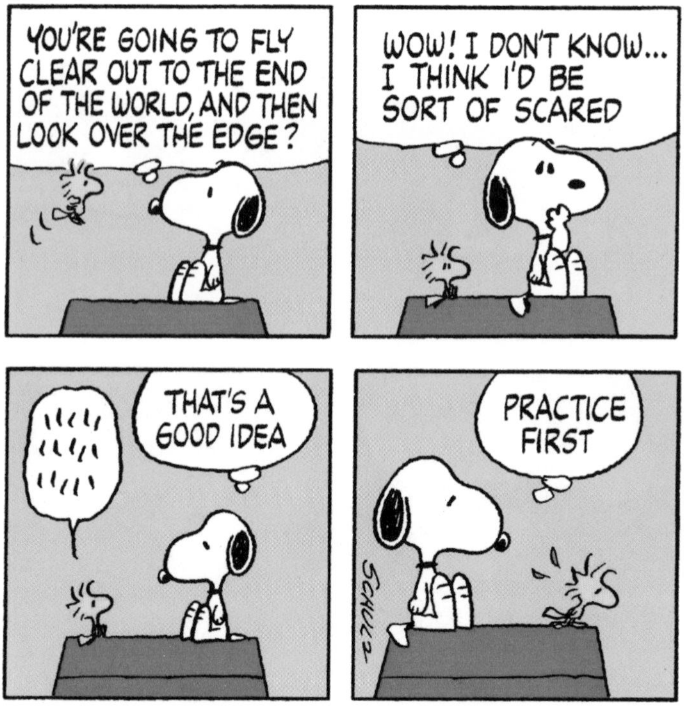
YOU'RE GOING TO FLY CLEAR OUT TO THE END OF THE WORLD, AND THEN LOOK OVER THE EDGE?
WOW! I DON'T KNOW... I THINK I'D BE SORT OF SCARED
THAT'S A GOOD IDEA
PRACTICE FIRST

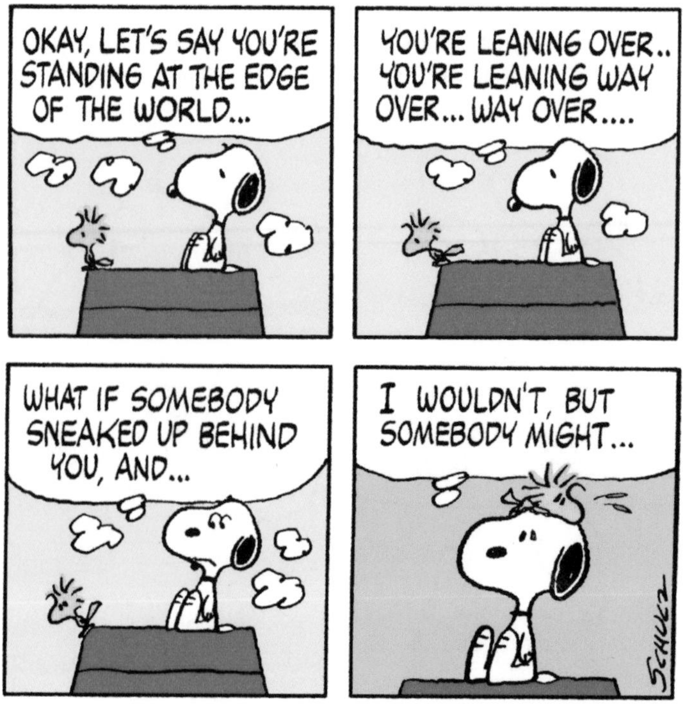
OKAY, LET'S SAY YOU'RE STANDING AT THE EDGE OF THE WORLD...
YOU'RE LEANING OVER.. YOU'RE LEANING WAY OVER... WAY OVER....
WHAT IF SOMEBODY SNEAKED UP BEHIND YOU, AND...
I WOULDN'T, BUT SOMEBODY MIGHT...

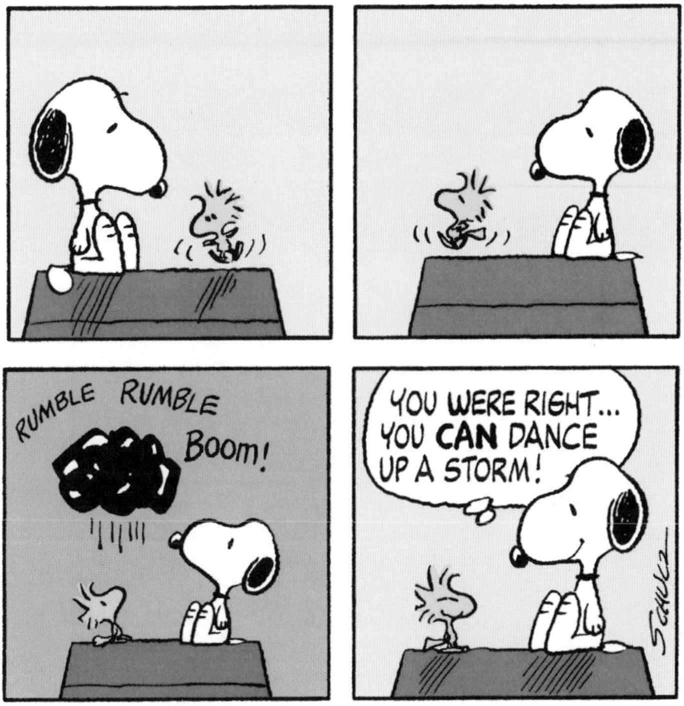
RUMBLE RUMBLE
Boom!
YOU WERE RIGHT... YOU **CAN** DANCE UP A STORM!

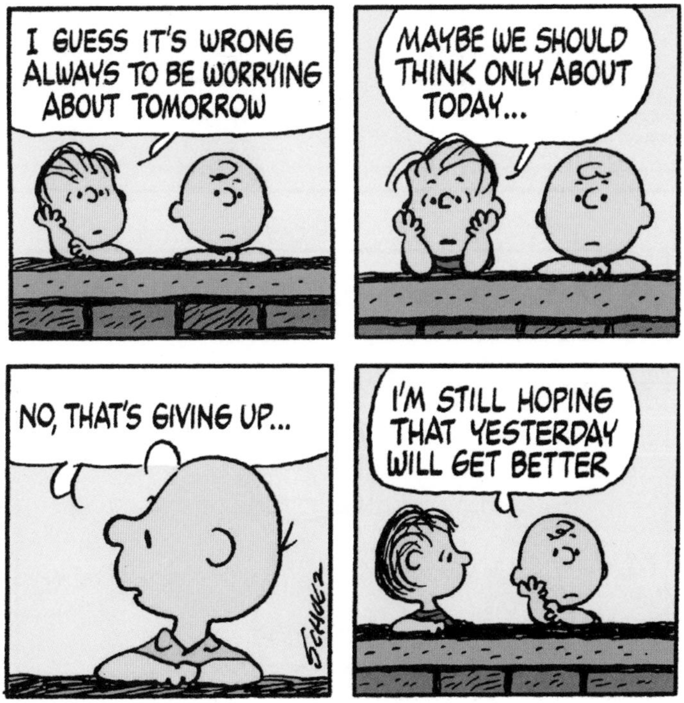
I GUESS IT'S WRONG ALWAYS TO BE WORRYING ABOUT TOMORROW
MAYBE WE SHOULD THINK ONLY ABOUT TODAY...
NO, THAT'S GIVING UP...
I'M STILL HOPING THAT YESTERDAY WILL GET BETTER

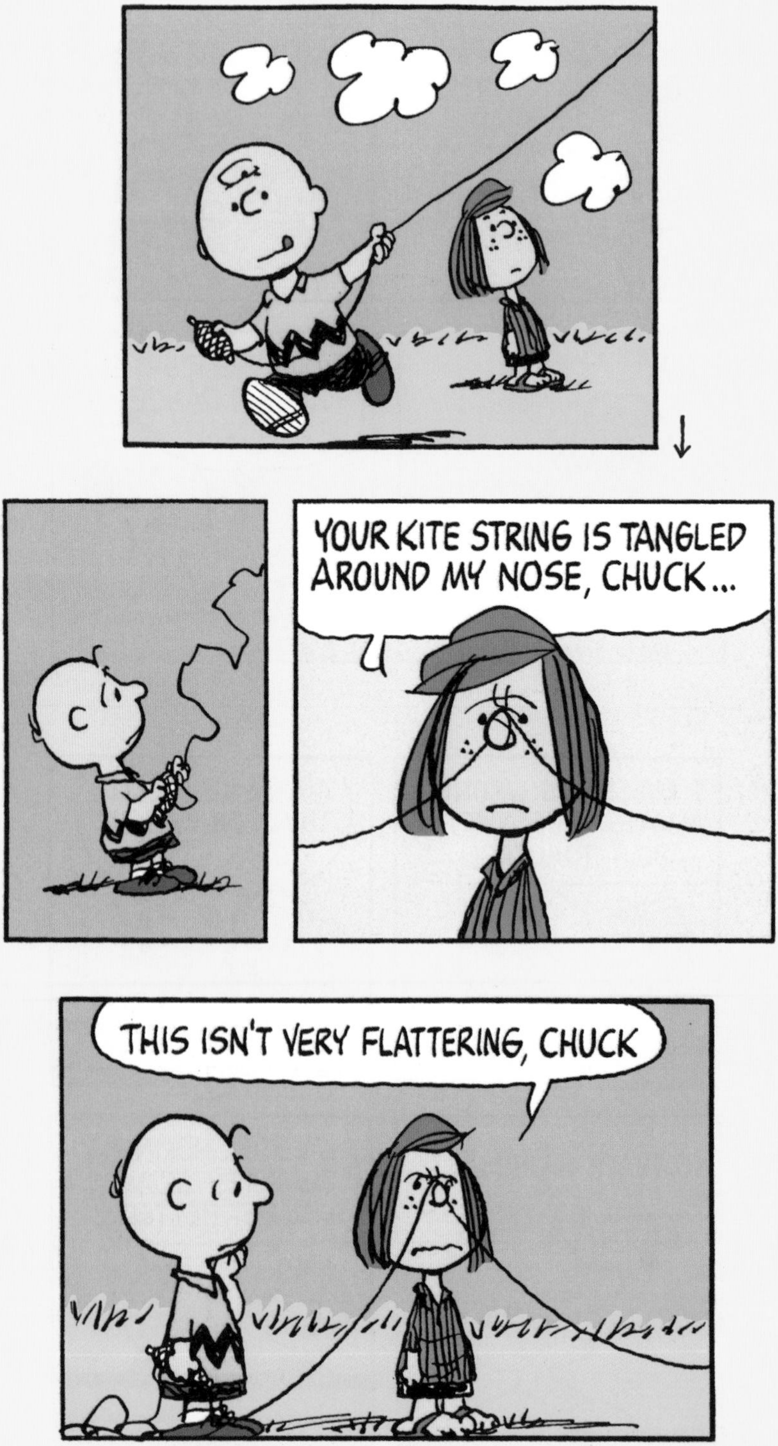
YOUR KITE STRING IS TANGLED AROUND MY NOSE, CHUCK...
THIS ISN'T VERY FLATTERING, CHUCK

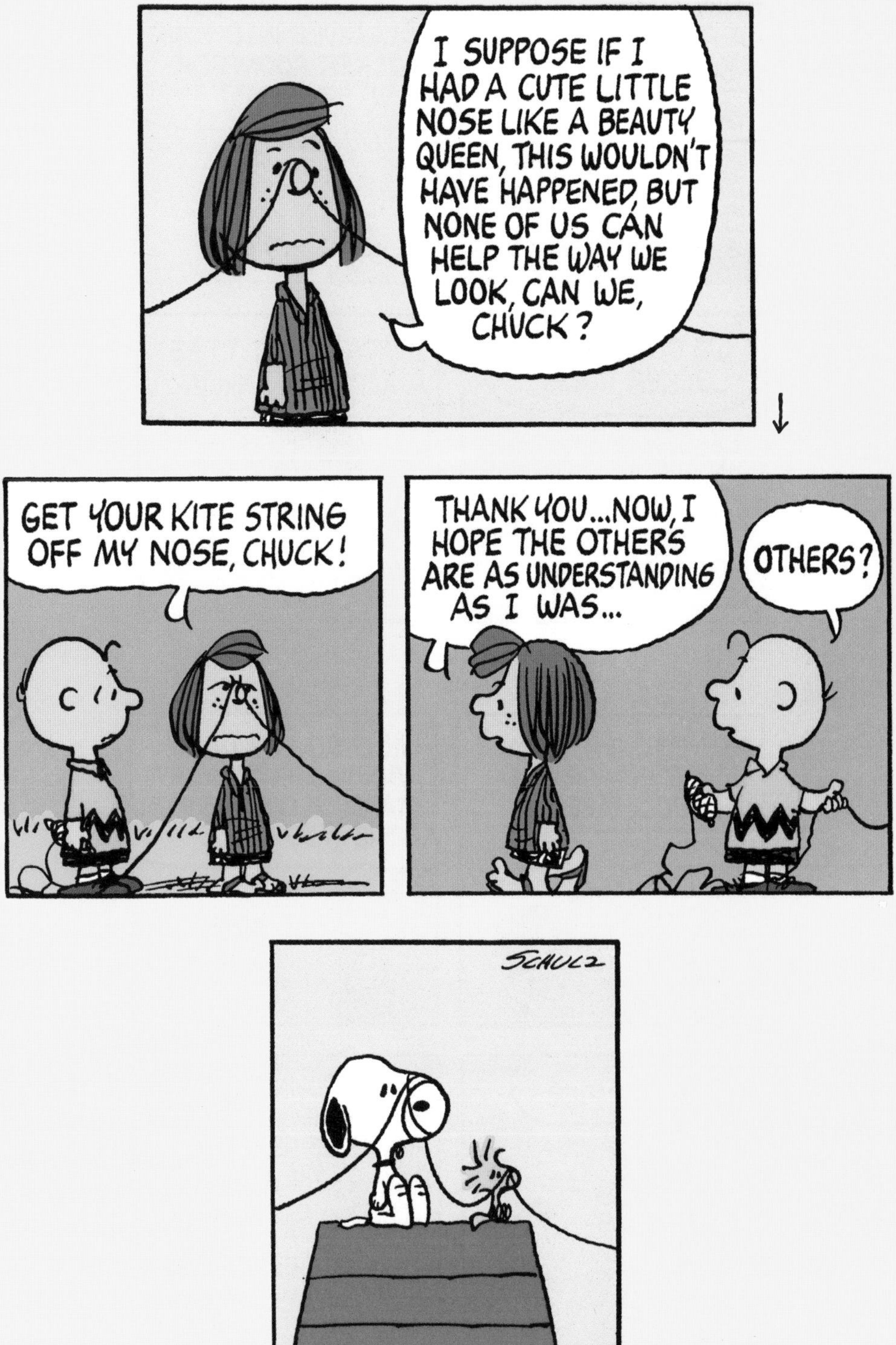
I SUPPOSE IF I HAD A CUTE LITTLE NOSE LIKE A BEAUTY QUEEN, THIS WOULDN'T HAVE HAPPENED, BUT NONE OF US CAN HELP THE WAY WE LOOK, CAN WE, CHUCK?
GET YOUR KITE STRING OFF MY NOSE, CHUCK!
THANK YOU...NOW, I HOPE THE OTHERS ARE AS UNDERSTANDING AS I WAS...
OTHERS?
SCHULZ

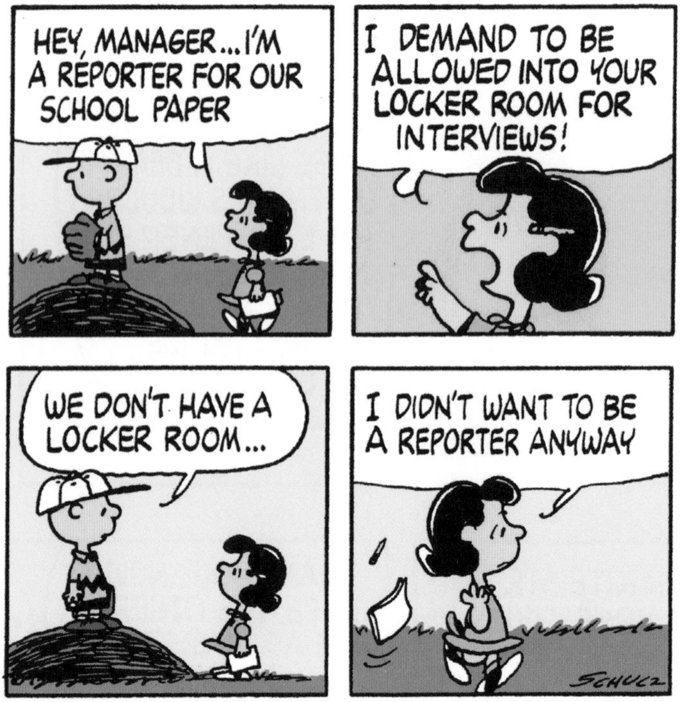
HEY, MANAGER...I'M A REPORTER FOR OUR SCHOOL PAPER
I DEMAND TO BE ALLOWED INTO YOUR LOCKER ROOM FOR INTERVIEWS!
WE DON'T HAVE A LOCKER ROOM...
I DIDN'T WANT TO BE A REPORTER ANYWAY
SCHULZ

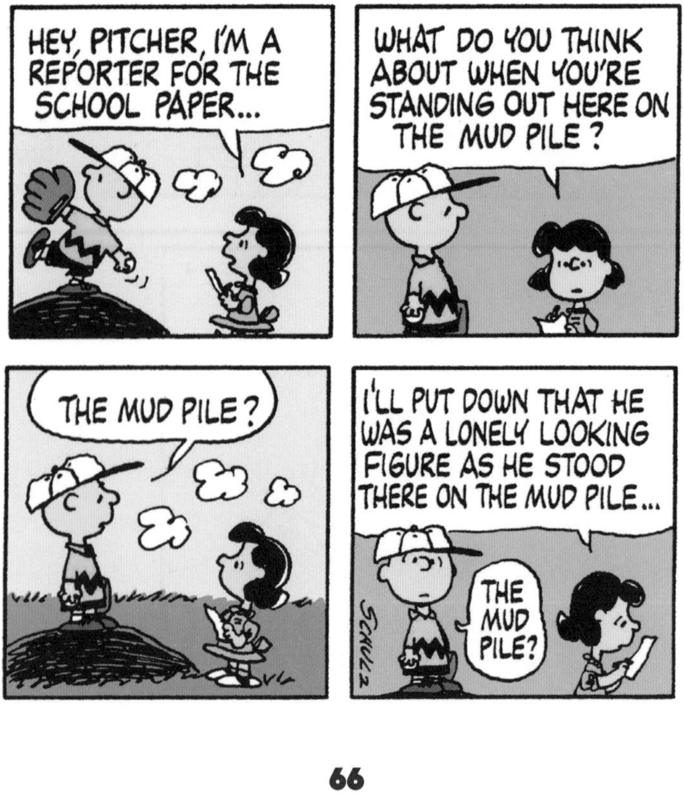
HEY, PITCHER, I'M A REPORTER FOR THE SCHOOL PAPER...
WHAT DO YOU THINK ABOUT WHEN YOU'RE STANDING OUT HERE ON THE MUD PILE?
THE MUD PILE?
I'LL PUT DOWN THAT HE WAS A LONELY LOOKING FIGURE AS HE STOOD THERE ON THE MUD PILE...
THE MUD PILE?
SCHULZ

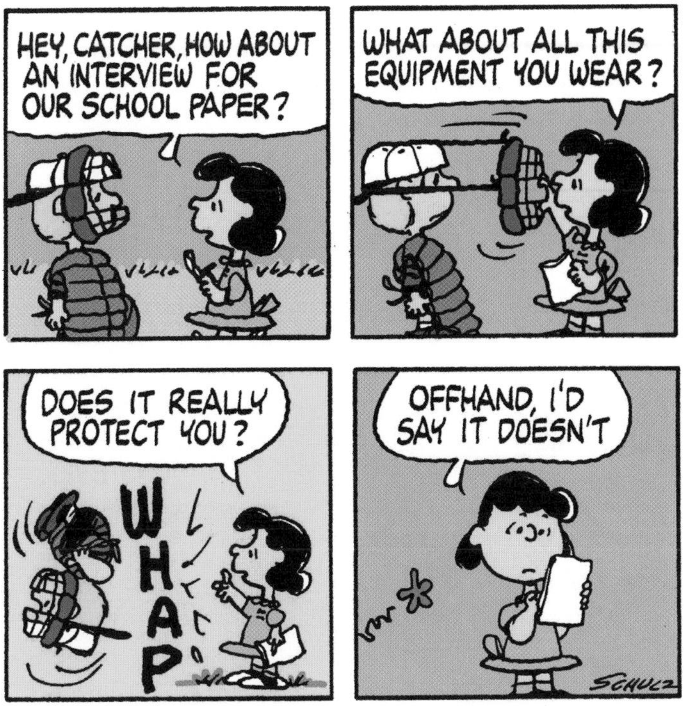
HEY, CATCHER, HOW ABOUT AN INTERVIEW FOR OUR SCHOOL PAPER?
WHAT ABOUT ALL THIS EQUIPMENT YOU WEAR?
DOES IT REALLY PROTECT YOU?
WHAP
OFFHAND, I'D SAY IT DOESN'T
SCHULZ

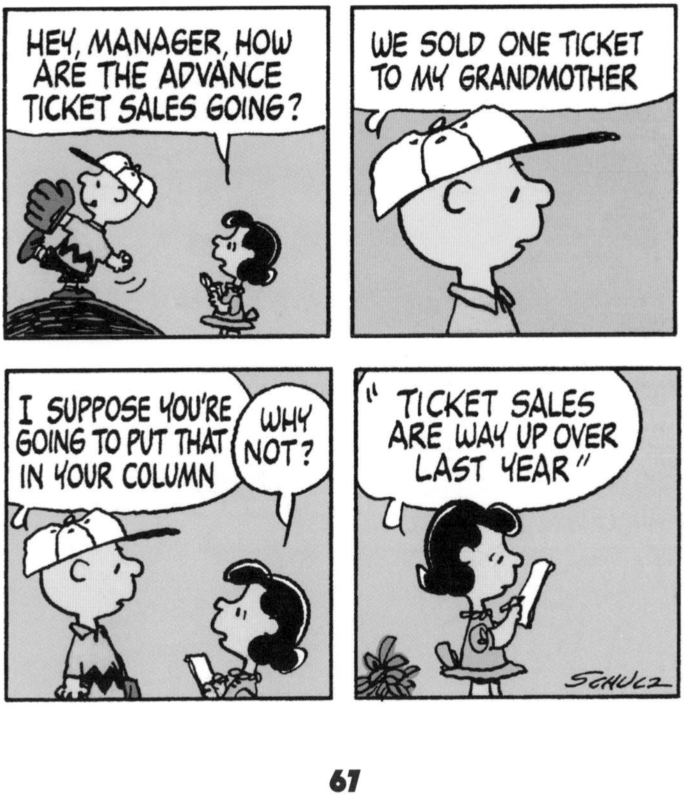
HEY, MANAGER, HOW ARE THE ADVANCE TICKET SALES GOING?
WE SOLD ONE TICKET TO MY GRANDMOTHER
I SUPPOSE YOU'RE GOING TO PUT THAT IN YOUR COLUMN
WHY NOT?
"TICKET SALES ARE WAY UP OVER LAST YEAR"
SCHULZ

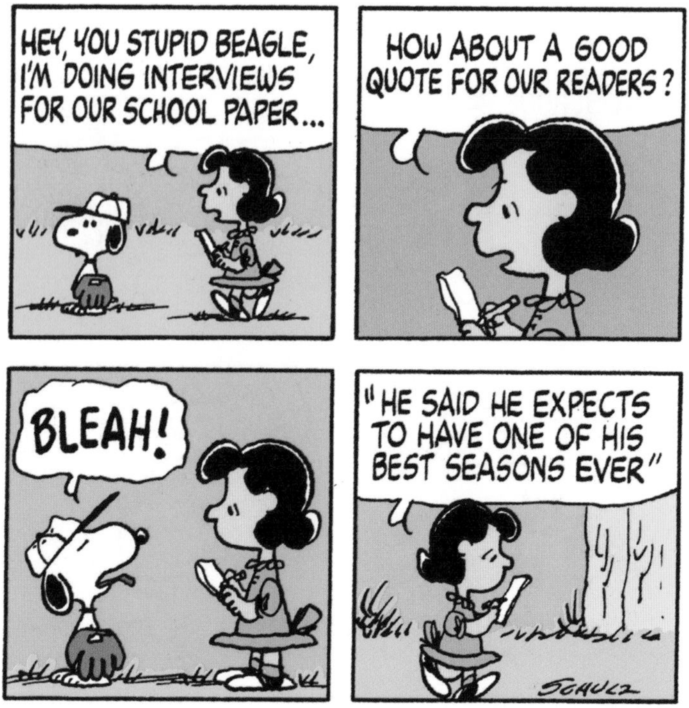
HEY, YOU STUPID BEAGLE, I'M DOING INTERVIEWS FOR OUR SCHOOL PAPER...
HOW ABOUT A GOOD QUOTE FOR OUR READERS ?
BLEAH!
"HE SAID HE EXPECTS TO HAVE ONE OF HIS BEST SEASONS EVER"

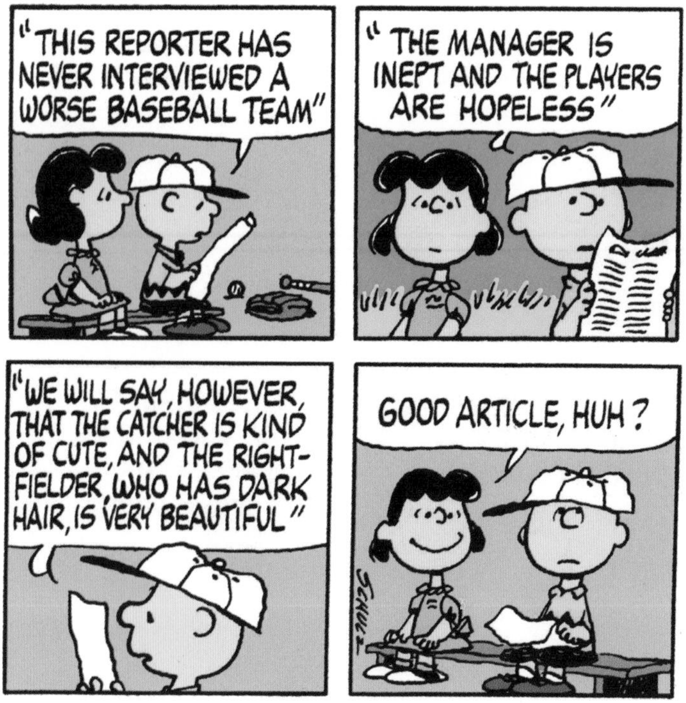
"THIS REPORTER HAS NEVER INTERVIEWED A WORSE BASEBALL TEAM"
"THE MANAGER IS INEPT AND THE PLAYERS ARE HOPELESS"
"WE WILL SAY, HOWEVER, THAT THE CATCHER IS KIND OF CUTE, AND THE RIGHT-FIELDER, WHO HAS DARK HAIR, IS VERY BEAUTIFUL"
GOOD ARTICLE, HUH ?

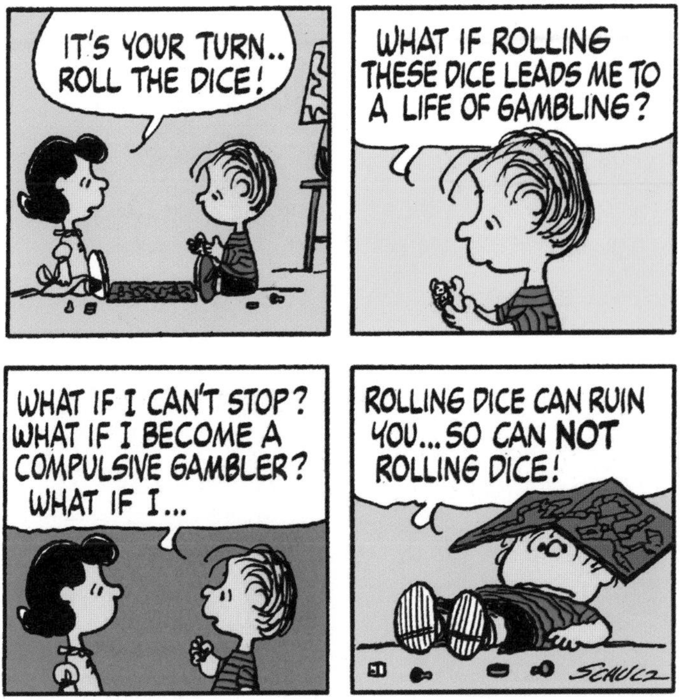
IT'S YOUR TURN.. ROLL THE DICE!
WHAT IF ROLLING THESE DICE LEADS ME TO A LIFE OF GAMBLING?
WHAT IF I CAN'T STOP? WHAT IF I BECOME A COMPULSIVE GAMBLER? WHAT IF I...
ROLLING DICE CAN RUIN YOU...SO CAN **NOT** ROLLING DICE!
SCHULZ

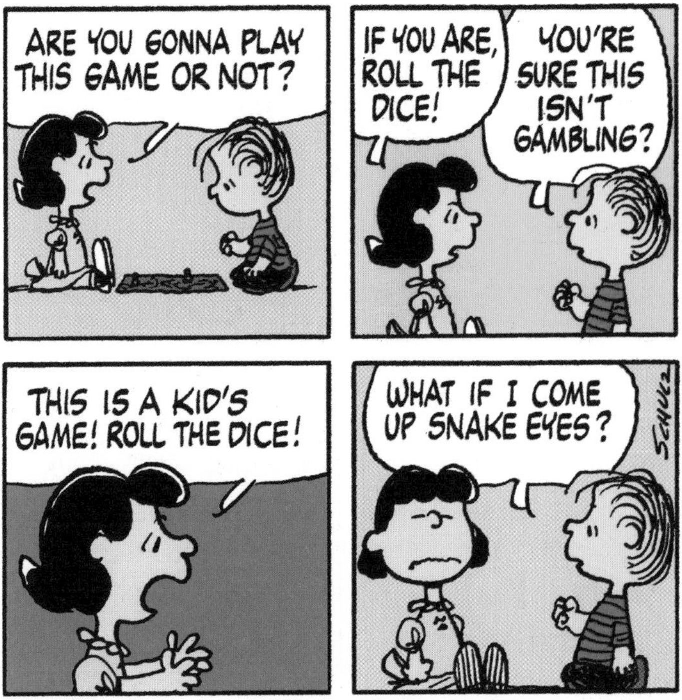
ARE YOU GONNA PLAY THIS GAME OR NOT?
IF YOU ARE, ROLL THE DICE!
YOU'RE SURE THIS ISN'T GAMBLING?
THIS IS A KID'S GAME! ROLL THE DICE!
WHAT IF I COME UP SNAKE EYES?
SCHULZ

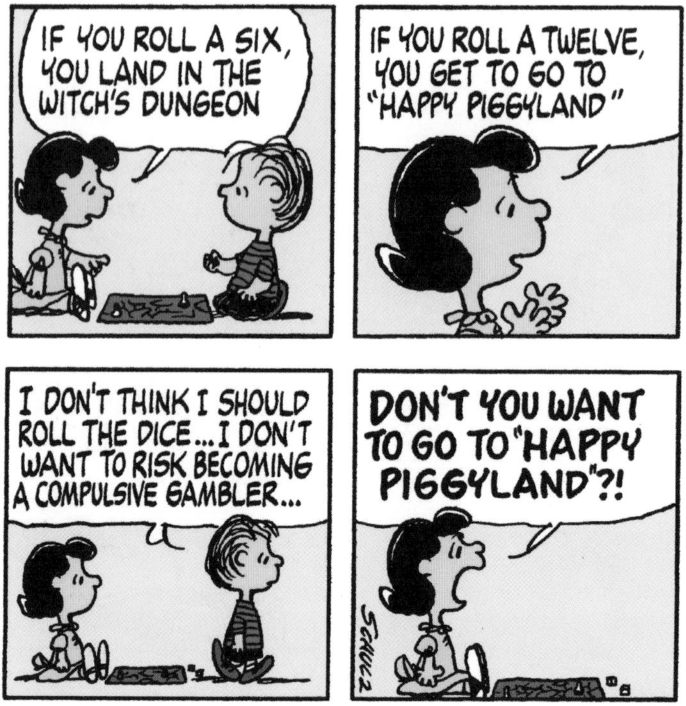
IF YOU ROLL A SIX, YOU LAND IN THE WITCH'S DUNGEON
IF YOU ROLL A TWELVE, YOU GET TO GO TO "HAPPY PIGGYLAND"
I DON'T THINK I SHOULD ROLL THE DICE...I DON'T WANT TO RISK BECOMING A COMPULSIVE GAMBLER...
DON'T YOU WANT TO GO TO "HAPPY PIGGYLAND"?!

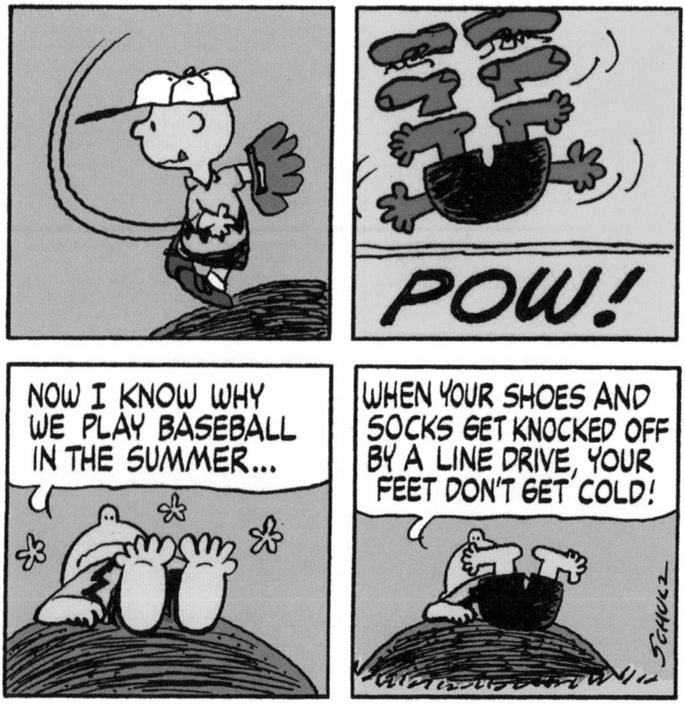
POW!
NOW I KNOW WHY WE PLAY BASEBALL IN THE SUMMER...
WHEN YOUR SHOES AND SOCKS GET KNOCKED OFF BY A LINE DRIVE, YOUR FEET DON'T GET COLD!

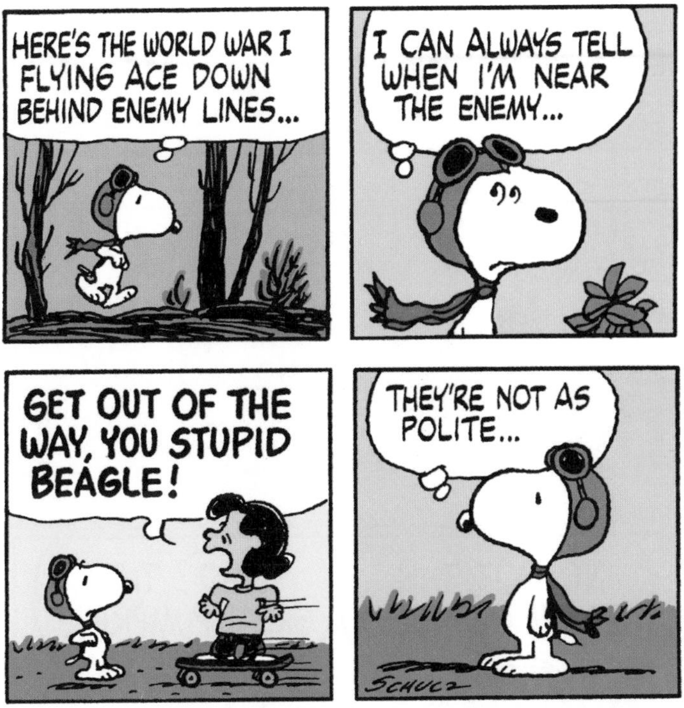
HERE'S THE WORLD WAR I FLYING ACE DOWN BEHIND ENEMY LINES...
I CAN ALWAYS TELL WHEN I'M NEAR THE ENEMY...
GET OUT OF THE WAY, YOU STUPID BEAGLE!
THEY'RE NOT AS POLITE...

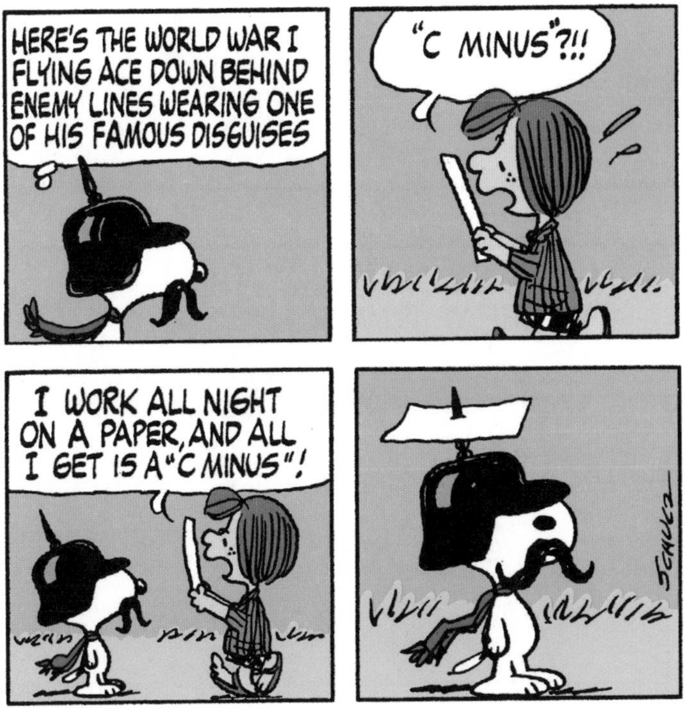
HERE'S THE WORLD WAR I FLYING ACE DOWN BEHIND ENEMY LINES WEARING ONE OF HIS FAMOUS DISGUISES
"C MINUS"?!!
I WORK ALL NIGHT ON A PAPER, AND ALL I GET IS A "C MINUS"!

HE'S COMING! HE'S COMING!
WHO? THE EASTER BEAGLE?
NO, NOT THE EASTER BEAGLE!
WHO? THE GREAT PUMPKIN?
NO, NO, NO!! NOT THE GREAT PUMPKIN!

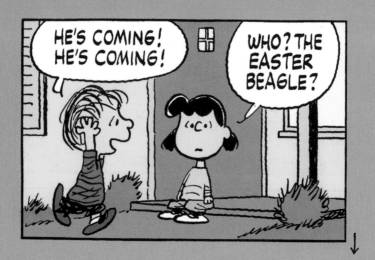

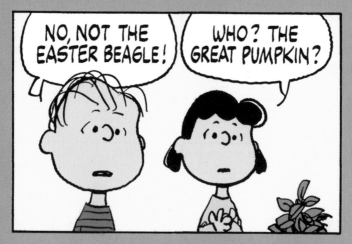

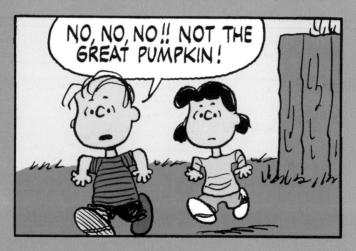

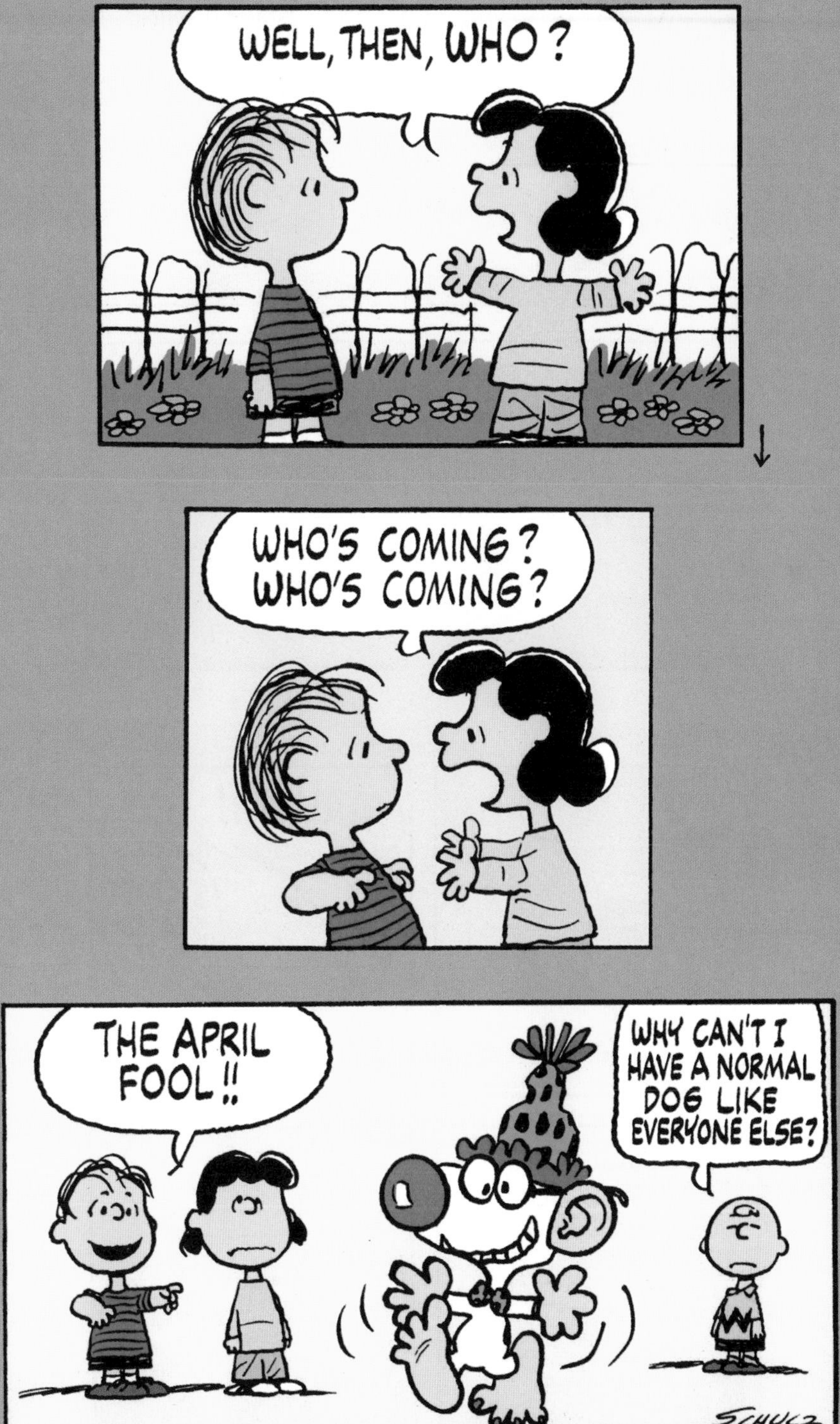
WELL, THEN, WHO?
WHO'S COMING? WHO'S COMING?
THE APRIL FOOL!!
WHY CAN'T I HAVE A NORMAL DOG LIKE EVERYONE ELSE?
SCHULZ

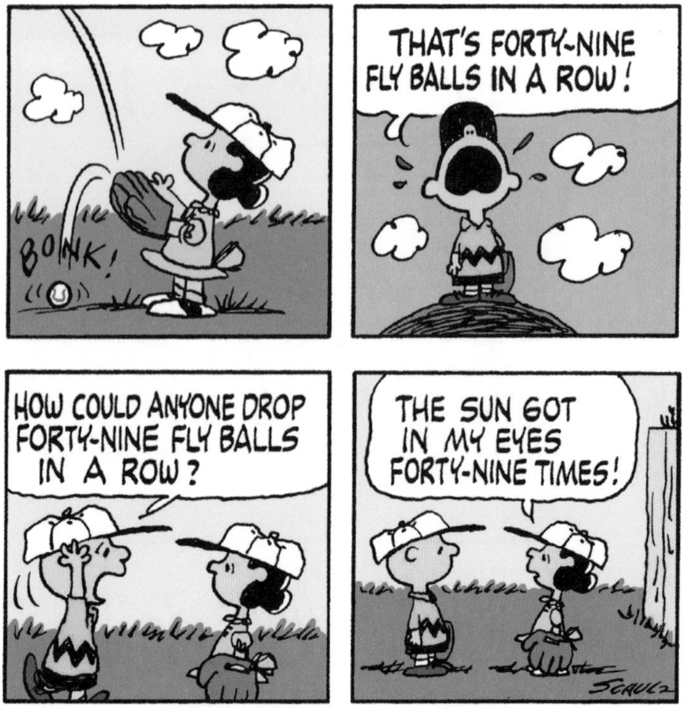
BONK!
THAT'S FORTY-NINE FLY BALLS IN A ROW!
HOW COULD ANYONE DROP FORTY-NINE FLY BALLS IN A ROW?
THE SUN GOT IN MY EYES FORTY-NINE TIMES!
SCHULZ

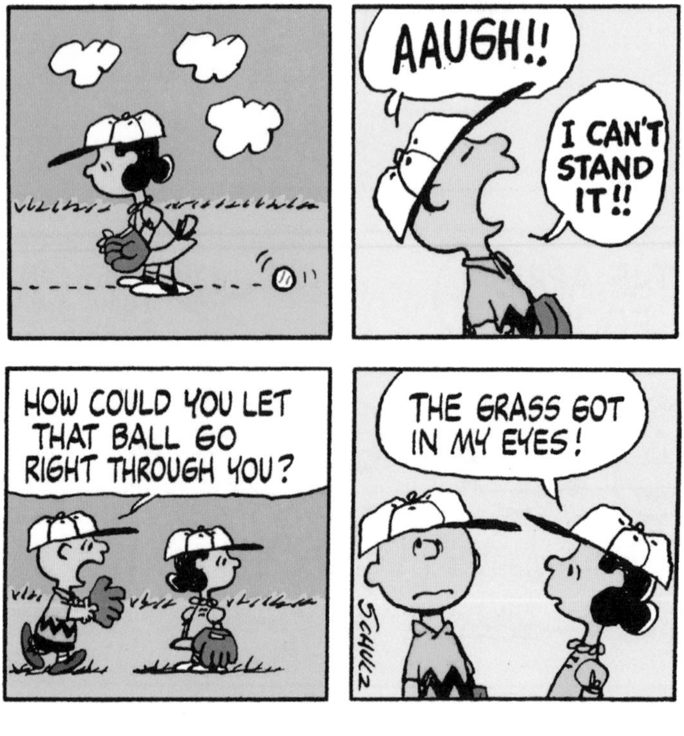
AAUGH!!
I CAN'T STAND IT!!
HOW COULD YOU LET THAT BALL GO RIGHT THROUGH YOU?
THE GRASS GOT IN MY EYES!
SCHULZ

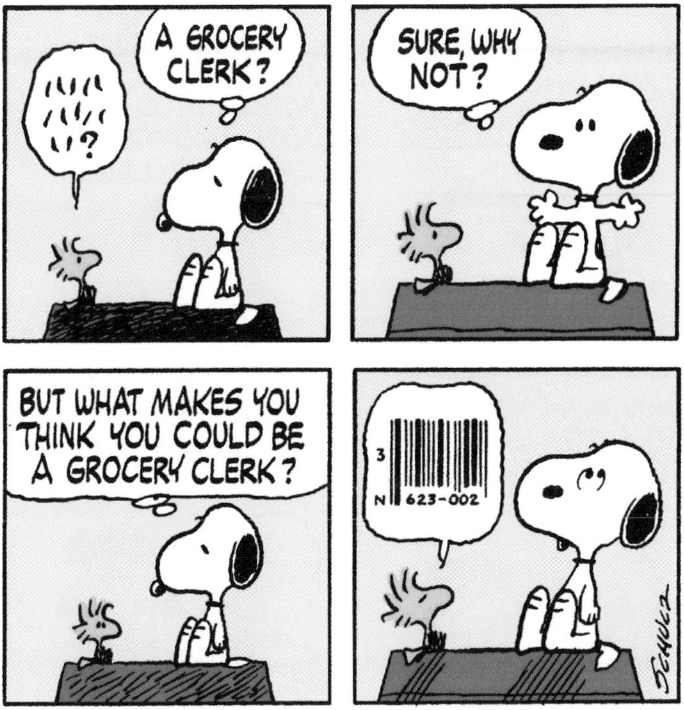
A GROCERY CLERK?
SURE, WHY NOT?
BUT WHAT MAKES YOU THINK YOU COULD BE A GROCERY CLERK?
3
N 623-002
SCHULZ

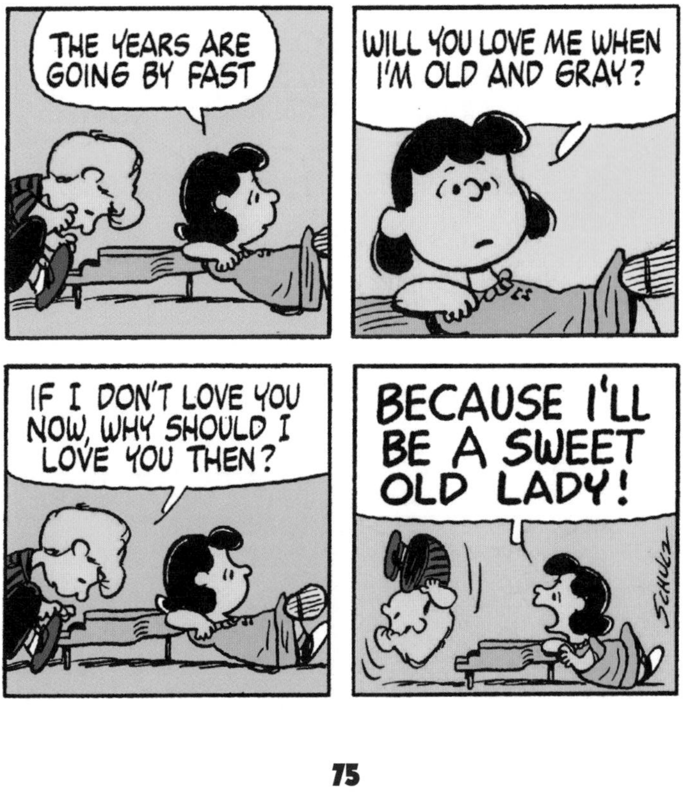
THE YEARS ARE GOING BY FAST
WILL YOU LOVE ME WHEN I'M OLD AND GRAY?
IF I DON'T LOVE YOU NOW, WHY SHOULD I LOVE YOU THEN?
BECAUSE I'LL BE A SWEET OLD LADY!
SCHULZ

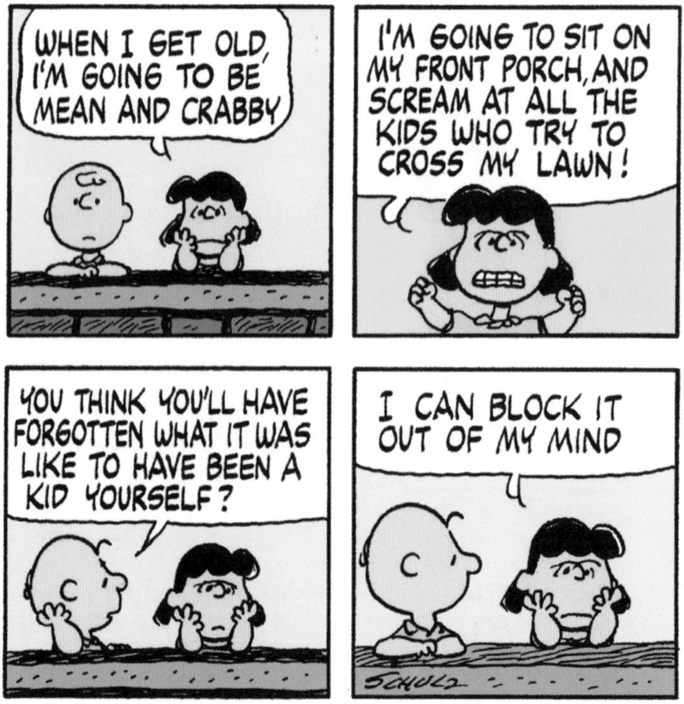
WHEN I GET OLD, I'M GOING TO BE MEAN AND CRABBY
I'M GOING TO SIT ON MY FRONT PORCH, AND SCREAM AT ALL THE KIDS WHO TRY TO CROSS MY LAWN!
YOU THINK YOU'LL HAVE FORGOTTEN WHAT IT WAS LIKE TO HAVE BEEN A KID YOURSELF?
I CAN BLOCK IT OUT OF MY MIND
SCHULZ

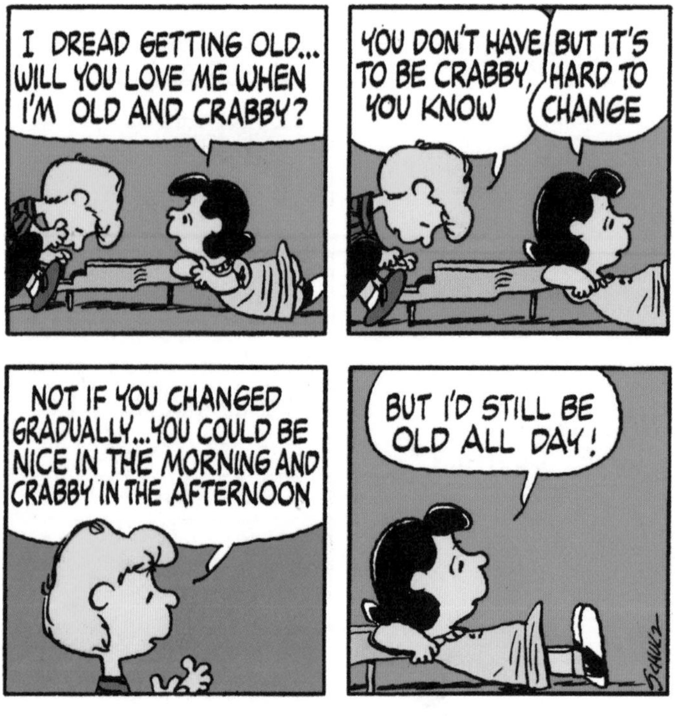
I DREAD GETTING OLD... WILL YOU LOVE ME WHEN I'M OLD AND CRABBY?
YOU DON'T HAVE TO BE CRABBY, YOU KNOW
BUT IT'S HARD TO CHANGE
NOT IF YOU CHANGED GRADUALLY...YOU COULD BE NICE IN THE MORNING AND CRABBY IN THE AFTERNOON
BUT I'D STILL BE OLD ALL DAY!
SCHULZ

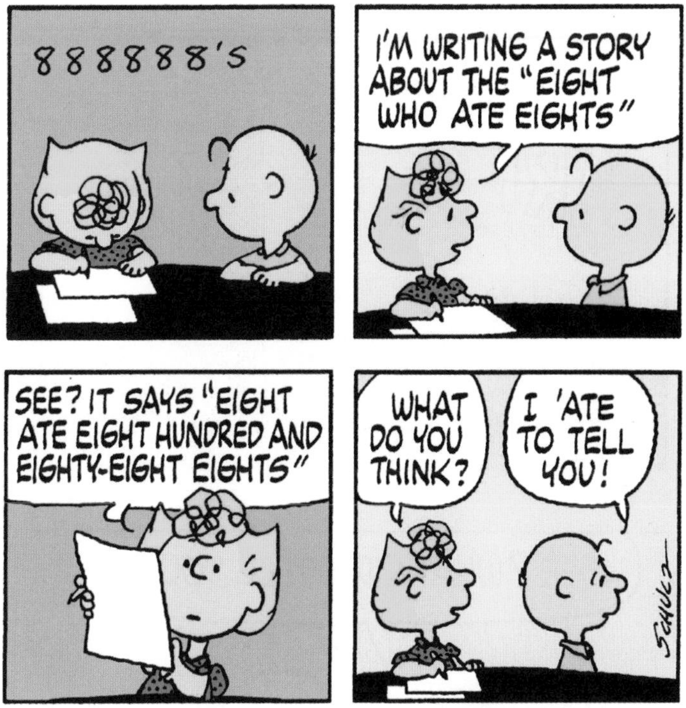
888888'S
I'M WRITING A STORY ABOUT THE "EIGHT WHO ATE EIGHTS"
SEE? IT SAYS, "EIGHT ATE EIGHT HUNDRED AND EIGHTY-EIGHT EIGHTS"
WHAT DO YOU THINK?
I 'ATE TO TELL YOU!
SCHULZ

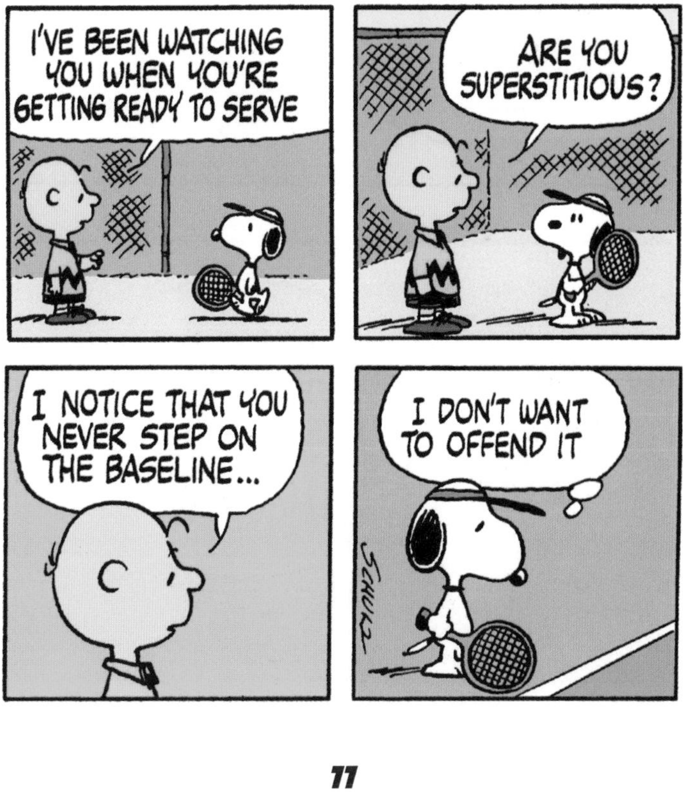
I'VE BEEN WATCHING YOU WHEN YOU'RE GETTING READY TO SERVE
ARE YOU SUPERSTITIOUS?
I NOTICE THAT YOU NEVER STEP ON THE BASELINE...
I DON'T WANT TO OFFEND IT
SCHULZ

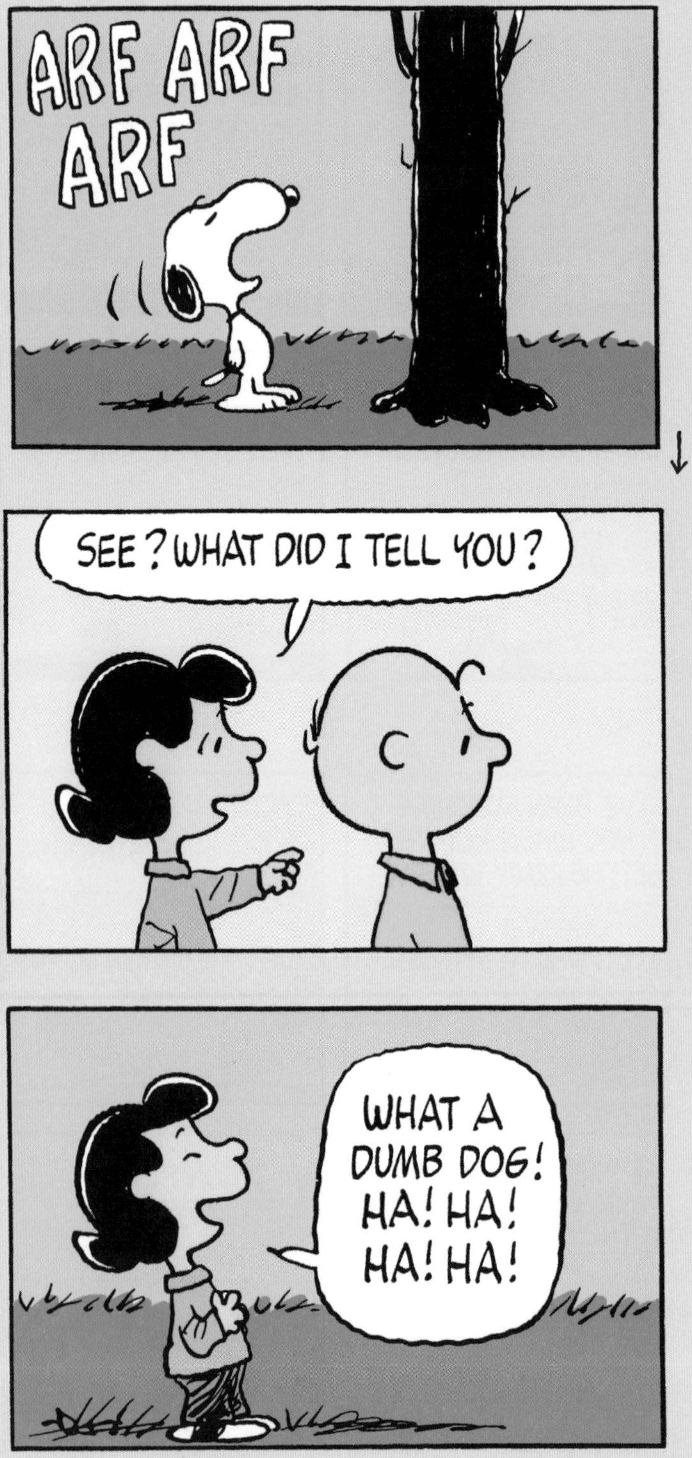
ARF ARF ARF
SEE? WHAT DID I TELL YOU?
WHAT A DUMB DOG! HA! HA! HA! HA!

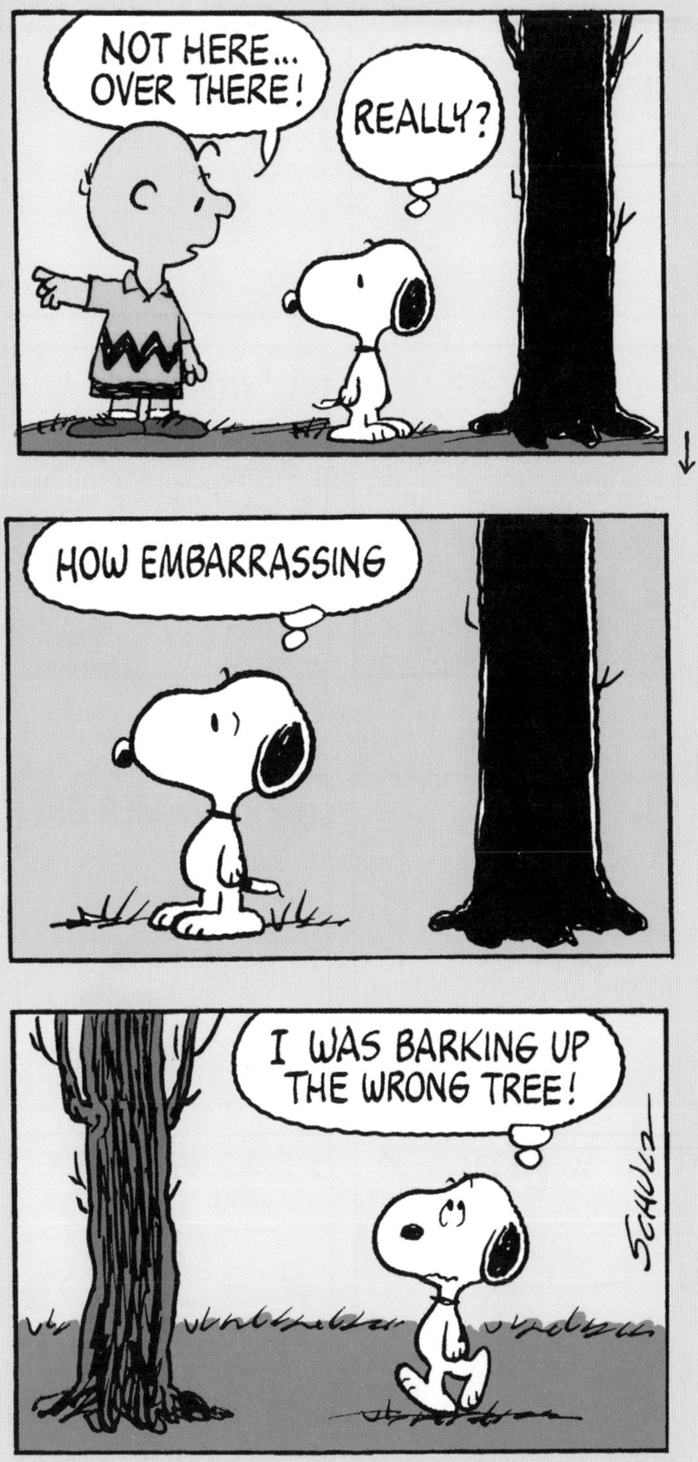
NOT HERE... OVER THERE!
REALLY?
HOW EMBARRASSING
I WAS BARKING UP THE WRONG TREE!
SCHULZ

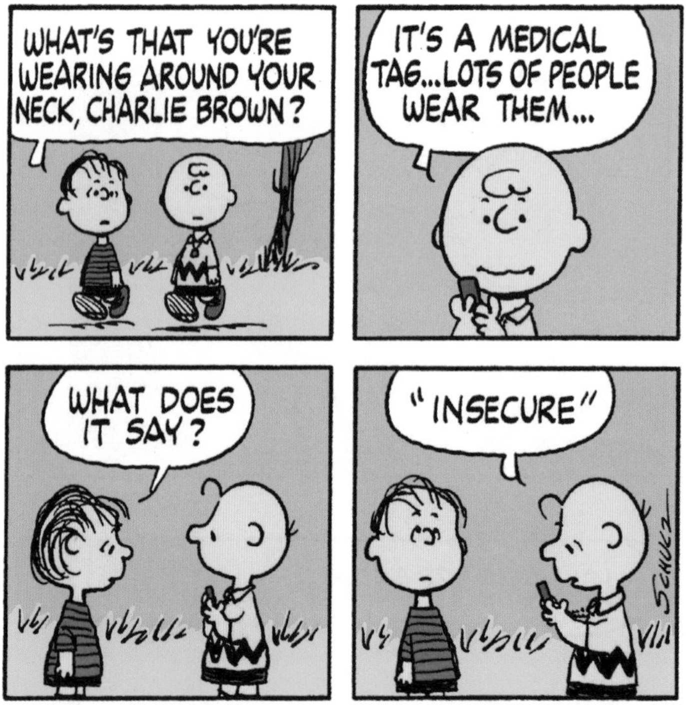
WHAT'S THAT YOU'RE WEARING AROUND YOUR NECK, CHARLIE BROWN?
IT'S A MEDICAL TAG...LOTS OF PEOPLE WEAR THEM...
WHAT DOES IT SAY?
"INSECURE"
SCHULZ

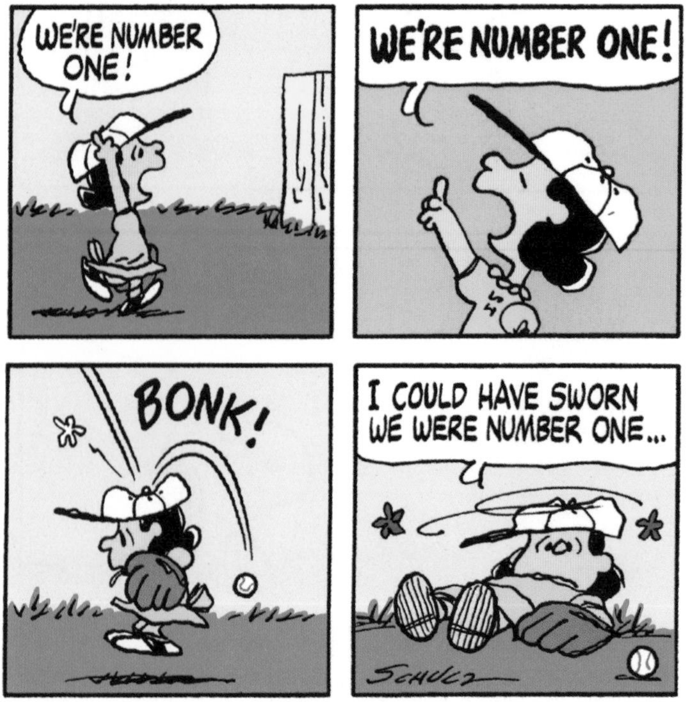
WE'RE NUMBER ONE!
WE'RE NUMBER ONE!
BONK!
I COULD HAVE SWORN WE WERE NUMBER ONE...
SCHULZ

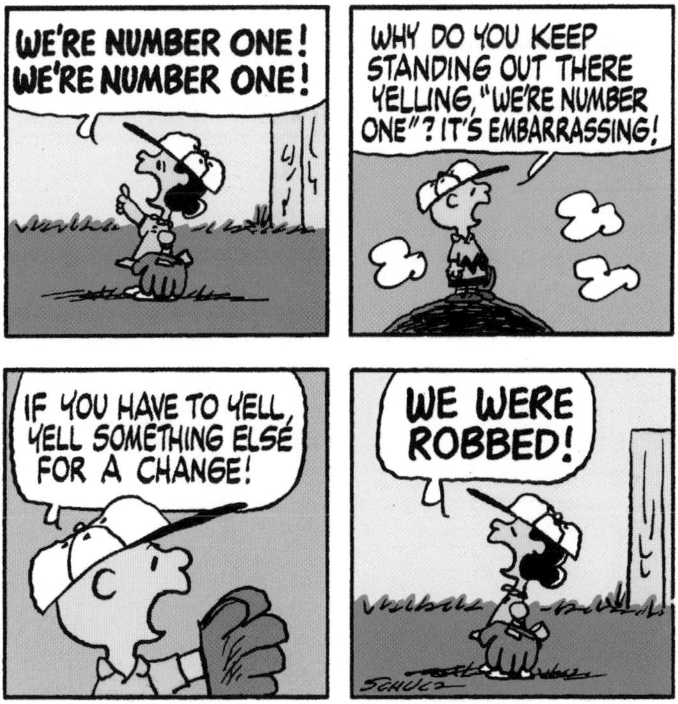
WE'RE NUMBER ONE! WE'RE NUMBER ONE!
WHY DO YOU KEEP STANDING OUT THERE YELLING, "WE'RE NUMBER ONE"? IT'S EMBARRASSING!
IF YOU HAVE TO YELL, YELL SOMETHING ELSE FOR A CHANGE!
WE WERE ROBBED!

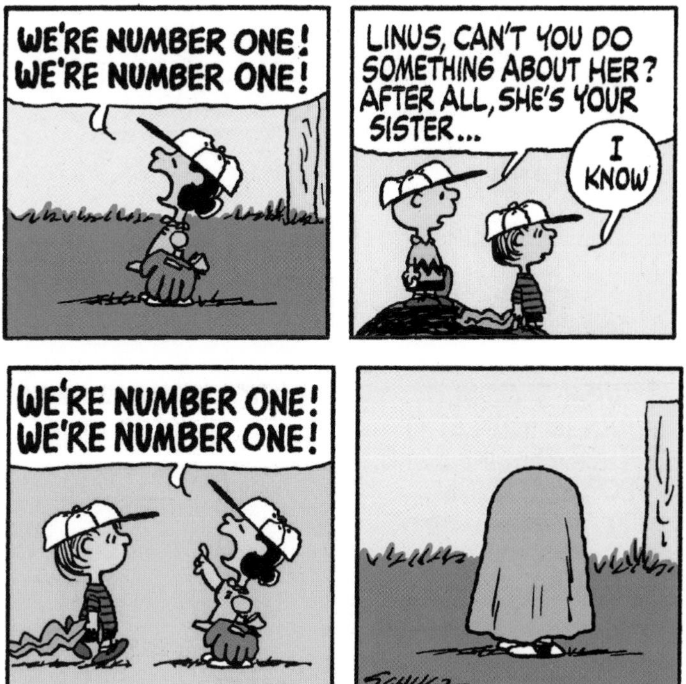
WE'RE NUMBER ONE! WE'RE NUMBER ONE!
LINUS, CAN'T YOU DO SOMETHING ABOUT HER? AFTER ALL, SHE'S YOUR SISTER...
I KNOW
WE'RE NUMBER ONE! WE'RE NUMBER ONE!

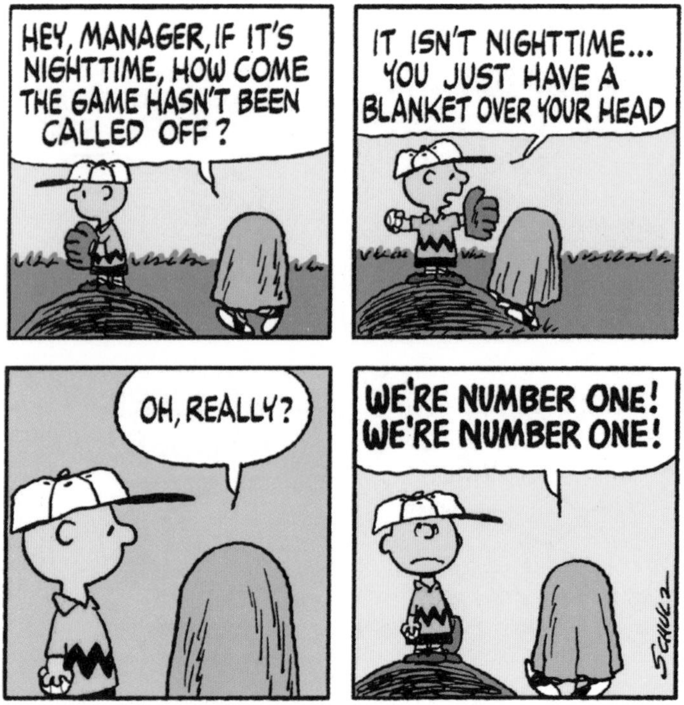
HEY, MANAGER, IF IT'S NIGHTTIME, HOW COME THE GAME HASN'T BEEN CALLED OFF ?
IT ISN'T NIGHTTIME... YOU JUST HAVE A BLANKET OVER YOUR HEAD
OH, REALLY?
WE'RE NUMBER ONE! WE'RE NUMBER ONE!
SCHULZ

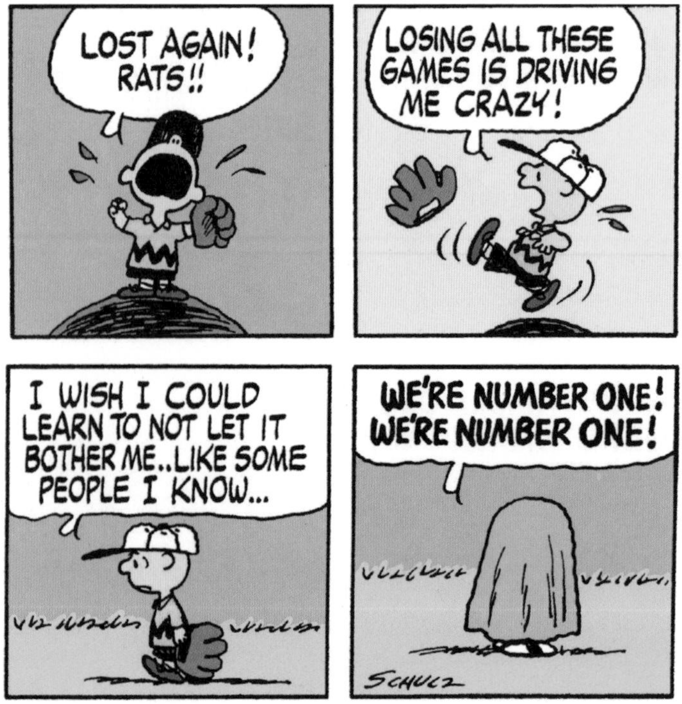
LOST AGAIN! RATS!!
LOSING ALL THESE GAMES IS DRIVING ME CRAZY!
I WISH I COULD LEARN TO NOT LET IT BOTHER ME..LIKE SOME PEOPLE I KNOW...
WE'RE NUMBER ONE! WE'RE NUMBER ONE!
SCHULZ

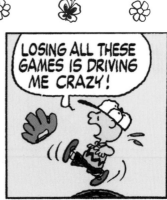

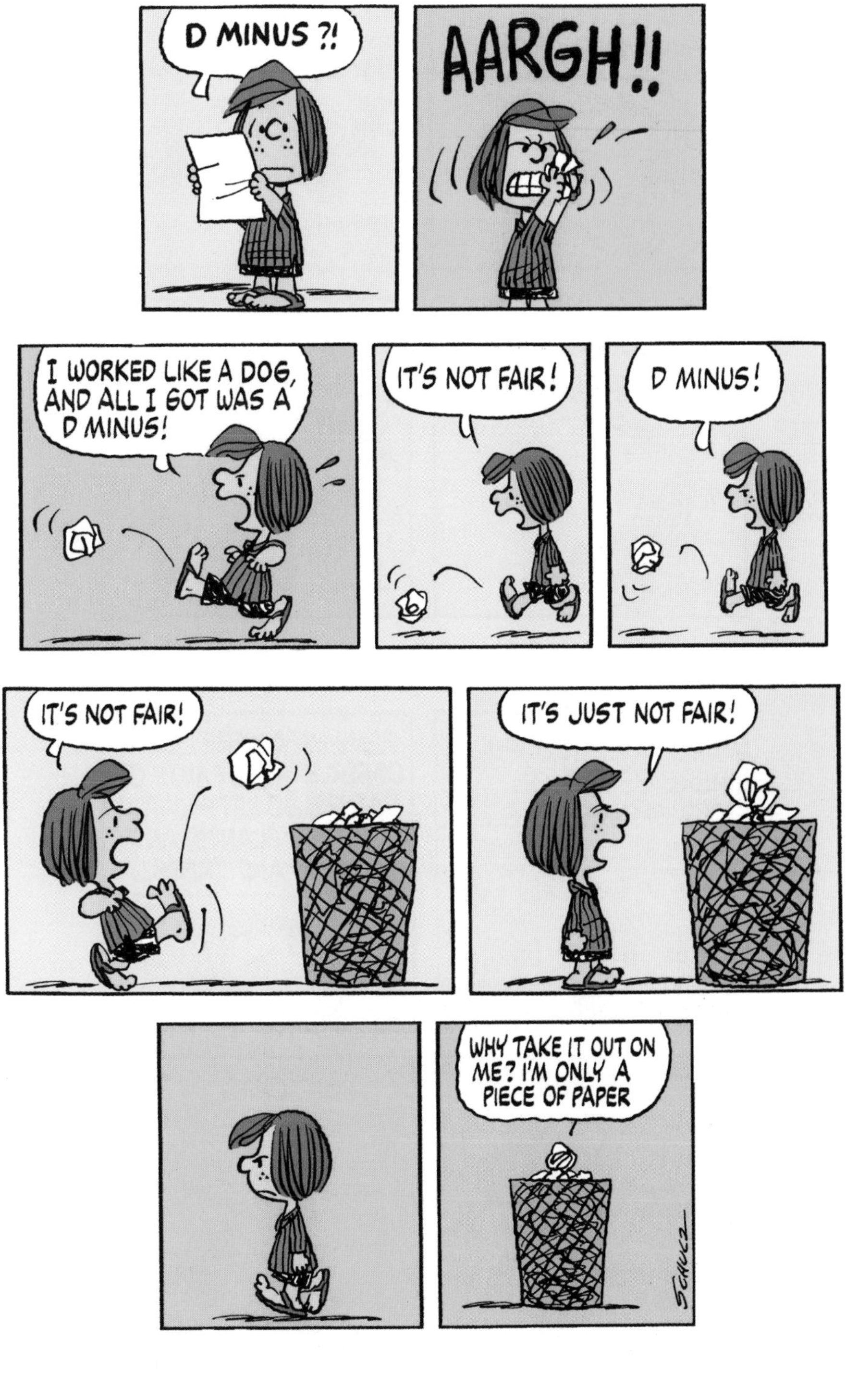
D MINUS ?!
AARGH!!
I WORKED LIKE A DOG, AND ALL I GOT WAS A D MINUS!
IT'S NOT FAIR!
D MINUS!
IT'S NOT FAIR!
IT'S JUST NOT FAIR!
WHY TAKE IT OUT ON ME? I'M ONLY A PIECE OF PAPER
SCHULZ

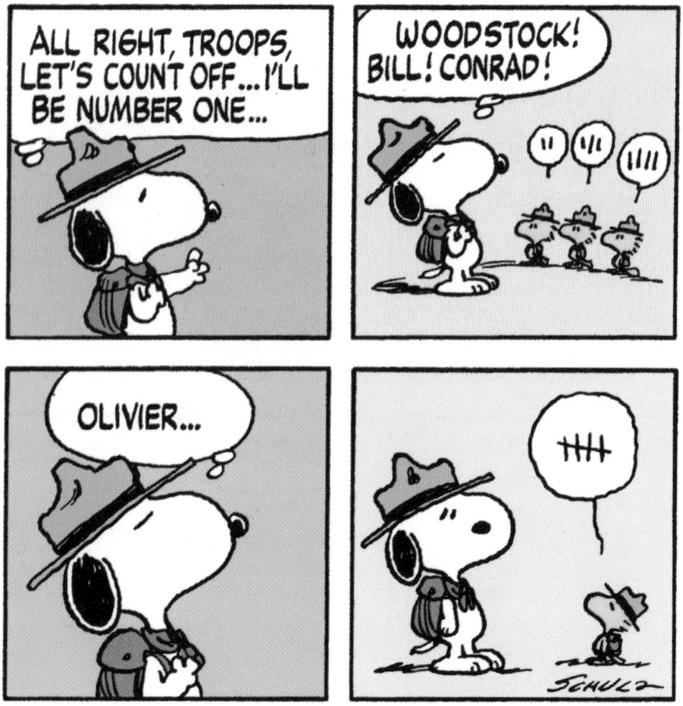
ALL RIGHT, TROOPS, LET'S COUNT OFF... I'LL BE NUMBER ONE...
WOODSTOCK! BILL! CONRAD!
OLIVIER...
SCHULZ

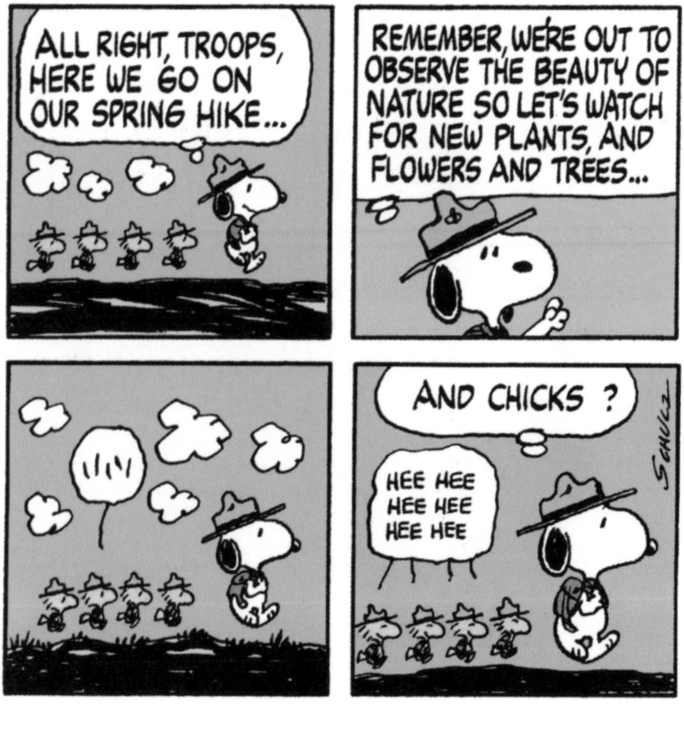
ALL RIGHT, TROOPS, HERE WE GO ON OUR SPRING HIKE...
REMEMBER, WE'RE OUT TO OBSERVE THE BEAUTY OF NATURE SO LET'S WATCH FOR NEW PLANTS, AND FLOWERS AND TREES...
AND CHICKS ?
HEE HEE HEE HEE HEE HEE
SCHULZ

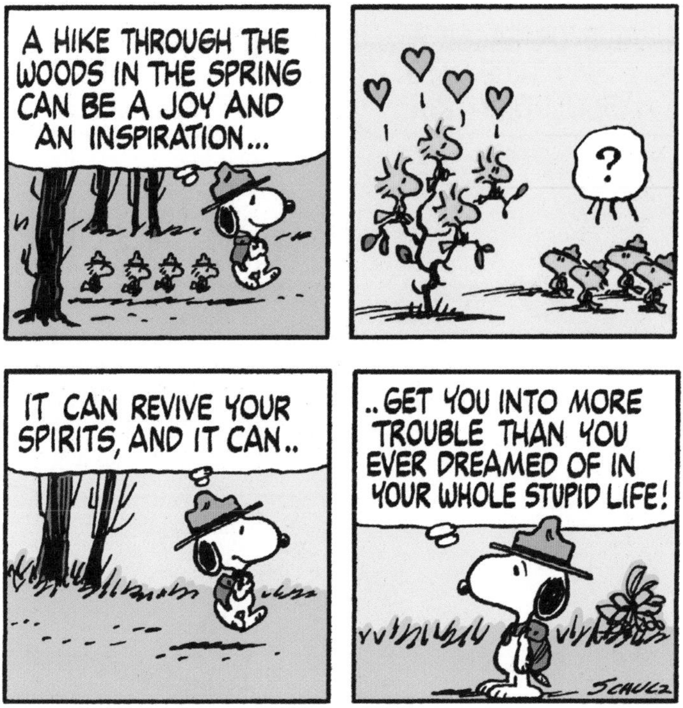
A HIKE THROUGH THE WOODS IN THE SPRING CAN BE A JOY AND AN INSPIRATION...
?
IT CAN REVIVE YOUR SPIRITS, AND IT CAN..
..GET YOU INTO MORE TROUBLE THAN YOU EVER DREAMED OF IN YOUR WHOLE STUPID LIFE!

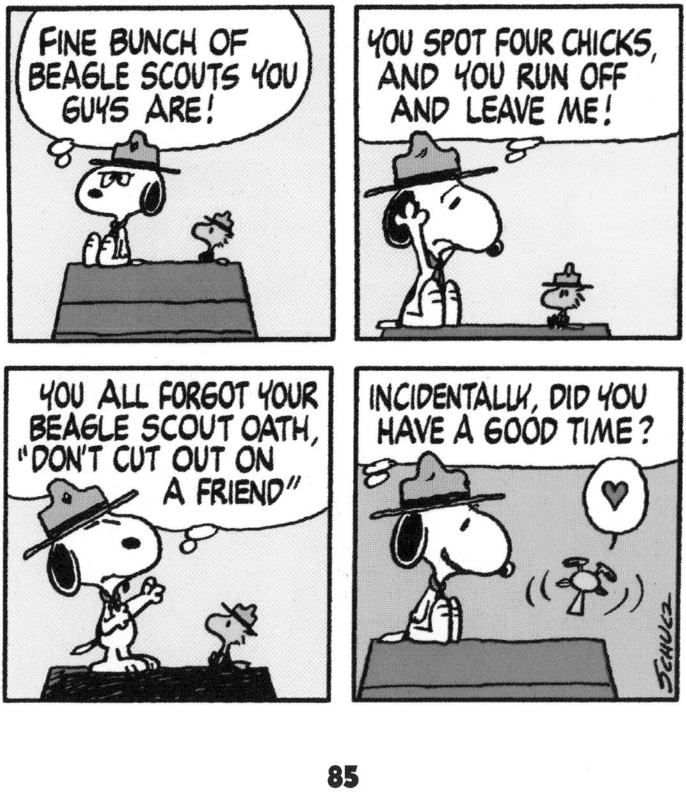
FINE BUNCH OF BEAGLE SCOUTS YOU GUYS ARE!
YOU SPOT FOUR CHICKS, AND YOU RUN OFF AND LEAVE ME!
YOU ALL FORGOT YOUR BEAGLE SCOUT OATH, "DON'T CUT OUT ON A FRIEND"
INCIDENTALLY, DID YOU HAVE A GOOD TIME?

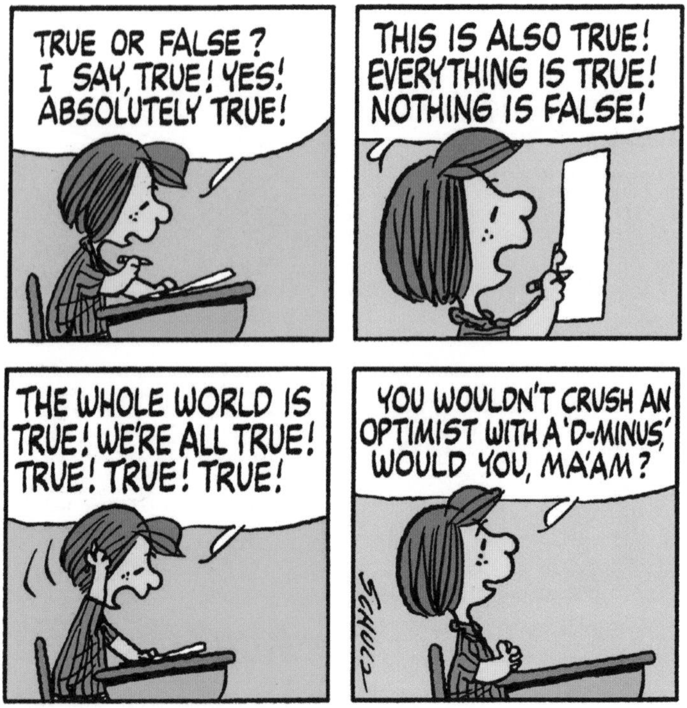
TRUE OR FALSE? I SAY, TRUE! YES! ABSOLUTELY TRUE!
THIS IS ALSO TRUE! EVERYTHING IS TRUE! NOTHING IS FALSE!
THE WHOLE WORLD IS TRUE! WE'RE ALL TRUE! TRUE! TRUE! TRUE!
YOU WOULDN'T CRUSH AN OPTIMIST WITH A 'D-MINUS,' WOULD YOU, MA'AM?
SCHULZ

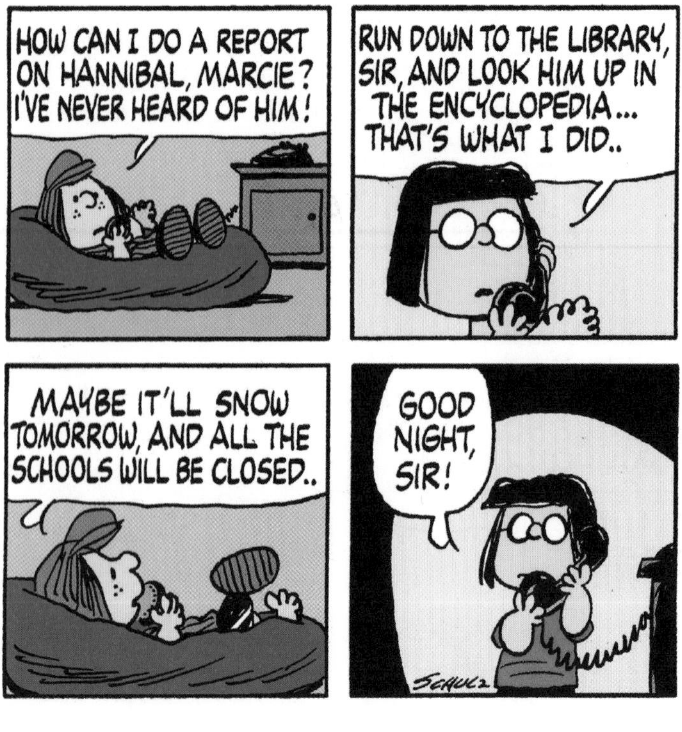
HOW CAN I DO A REPORT ON HANNIBAL, MARCIE? I'VE NEVER HEARD OF HIM!
RUN DOWN TO THE LIBRARY, SIR, AND LOOK HIM UP IN THE ENCYCLOPEDIA... THAT'S WHAT I DID..
MAYBE IT'LL SNOW TOMORROW, AND ALL THE SCHOOLS WILL BE CLOSED..
GOOD NIGHT, SIR!
SCHULZ

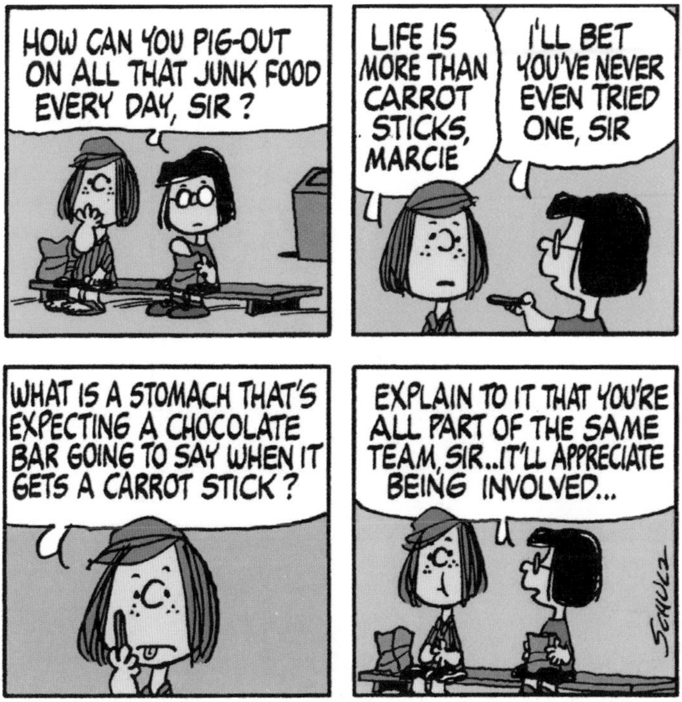
HOW CAN YOU PIG-OUT ON ALL THAT JUNK FOOD EVERY DAY, SIR?
LIFE IS MORE THAN CARROT STICKS, MARCIE
I'LL BET YOU'VE NEVER EVEN TRIED ONE, SIR
WHAT IS A STOMACH THAT'S EXPECTING A CHOCOLATE BAR GOING TO SAY WHEN IT GETS A CARROT STICK?
EXPLAIN TO IT THAT YOU'RE ALL PART OF THE SAME TEAM, SIR..IT'LL APPRECIATE BEING INVOLVED...
SCHULZ

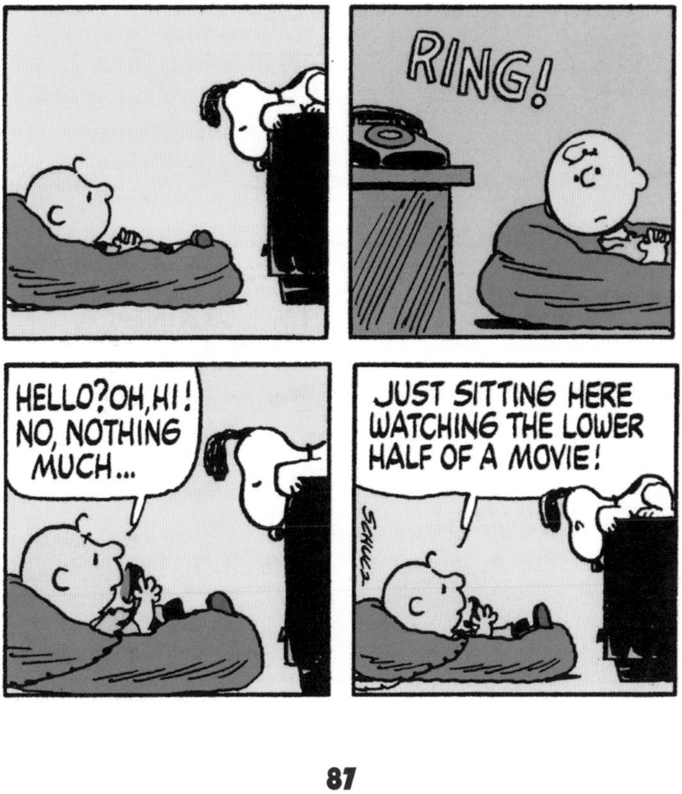
RING!
HELLO? OH, HI! NO, NOTHING MUCH...
JUST SITTING HERE WATCHING THE LOWER HALF OF A MOVIE!
SCHULZ

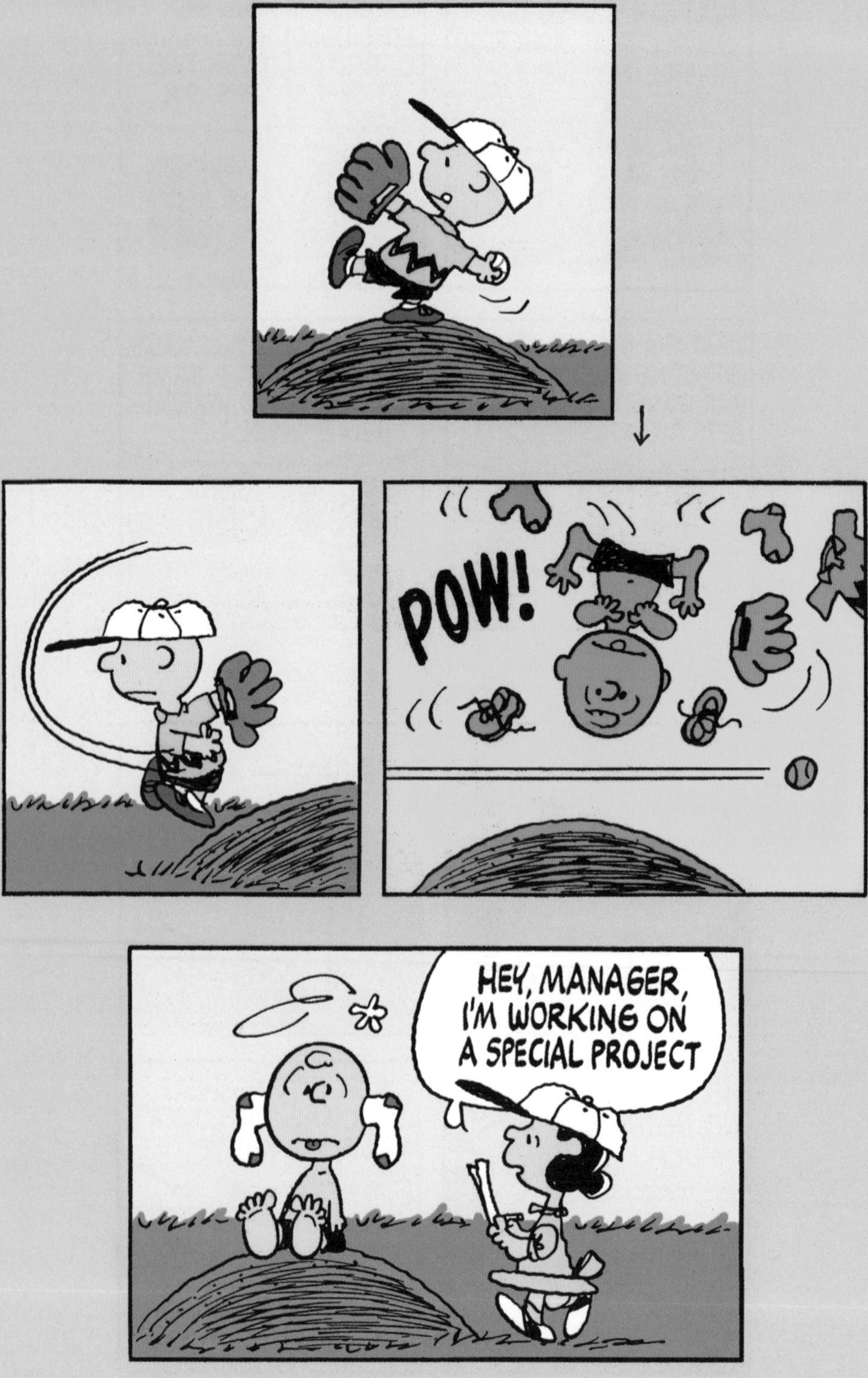
POW!
HEY, MANAGER, I'M WORKING ON A SPECIAL PROJECT

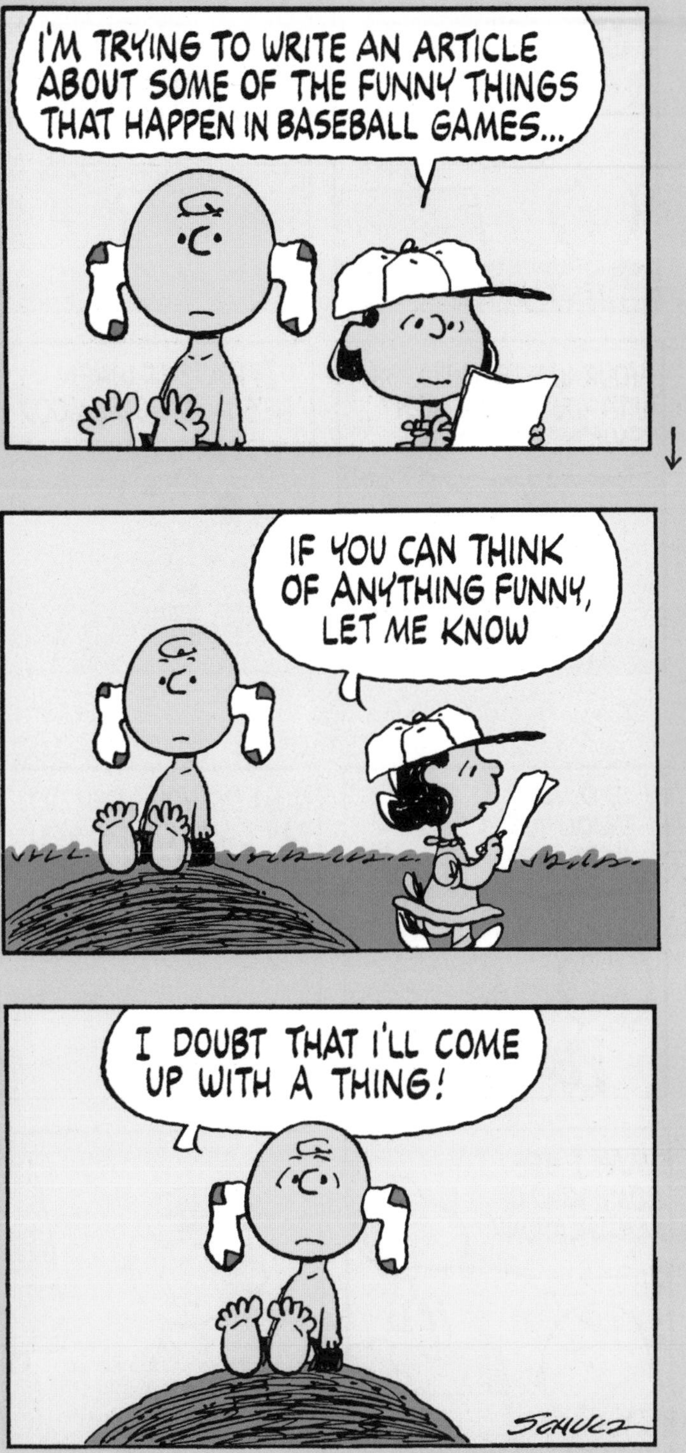
I'M TRYING TO WRITE AN ARTICLE ABOUT SOME OF THE FUNNY THINGS THAT HAPPEN IN BASEBALL GAMES...
IF YOU CAN THINK OF ANYTHING FUNNY, LET ME KNOW
I DOUBT THAT I'LL COME UP WITH A THING!
SCHULZ

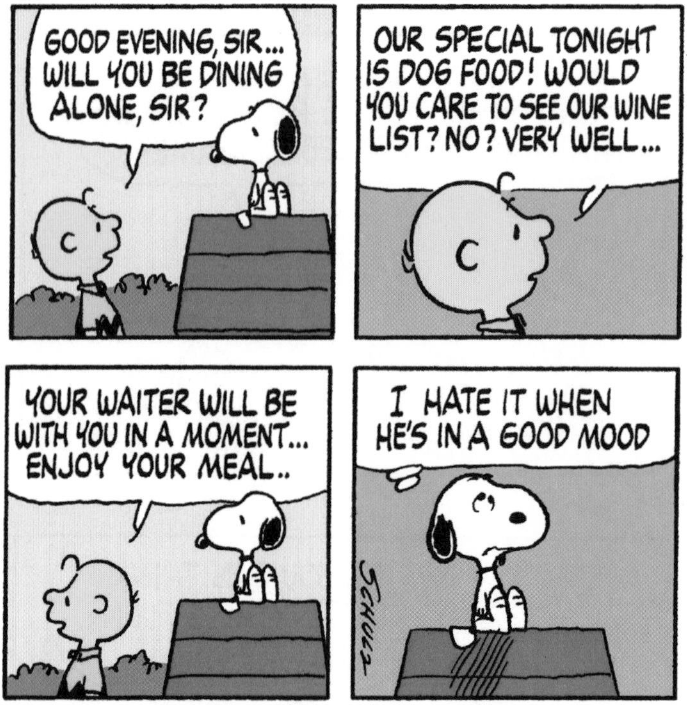
GOOD EVENING, SIR... WILL YOU BE DINING ALONE, SIR?
OUR SPECIAL TONIGHT IS DOG FOOD! WOULD YOU CARE TO SEE OUR WINE LIST? NO? VERY WELL...
YOUR WAITER WILL BE WITH YOU IN A MOMENT... ENJOY YOUR MEAL..
I HATE IT WHEN HE'S IN A GOOD MOOD

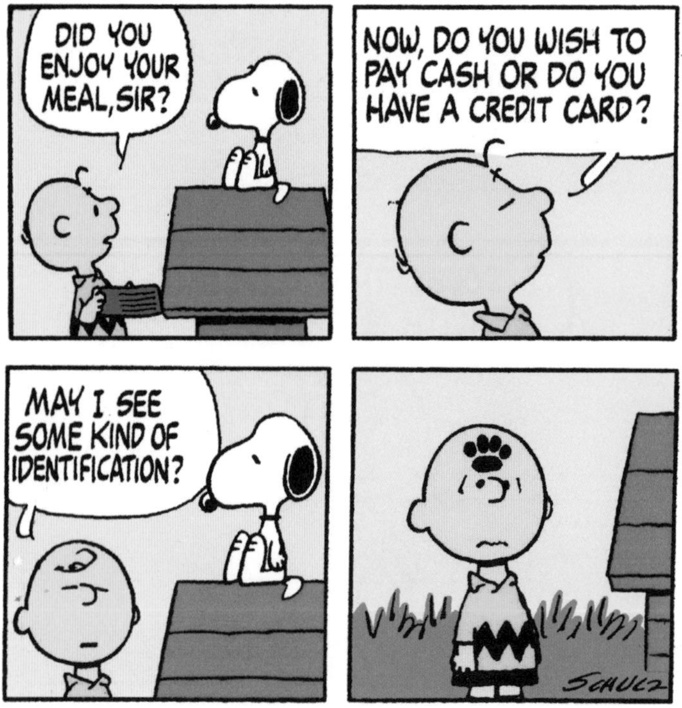
DID YOU ENJOY YOUR MEAL, SIR?
NOW, DO YOU WISH TO PAY CASH OR DO YOU HAVE A CREDIT CARD?
MAY I SEE SOME KIND OF IDENTIFICATION?

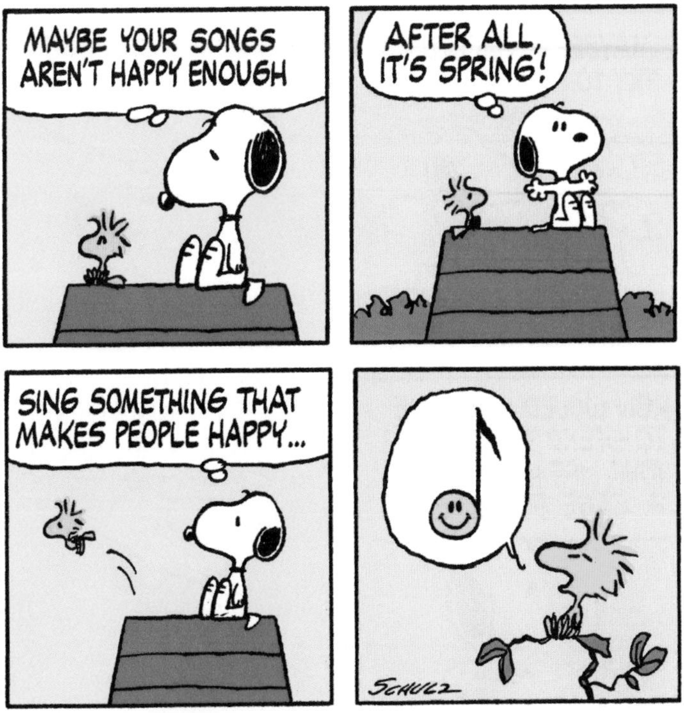
MAYBE YOUR SONGS AREN'T HAPPY ENOUGH
AFTER ALL, IT'S SPRING!
SING SOMETHING THAT MAKES PEOPLE HAPPY...
SCHULZ

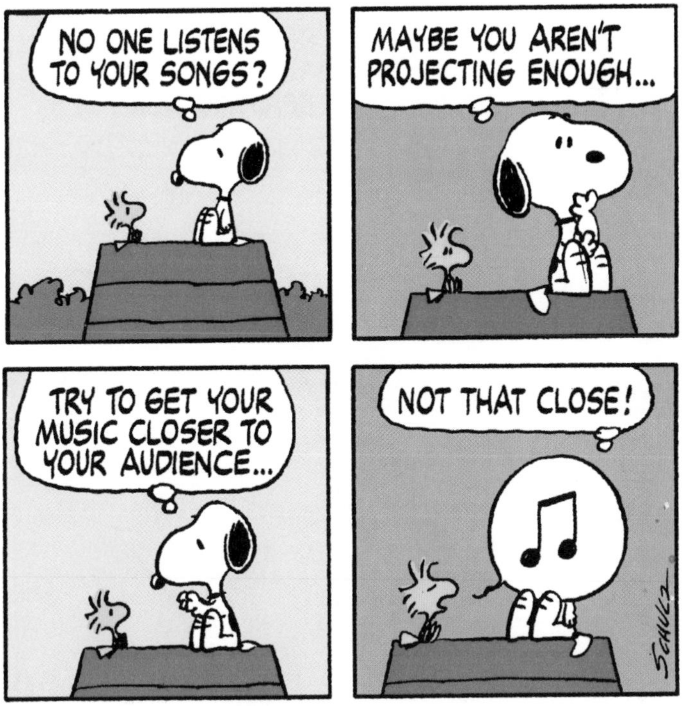
NO ONE LISTENS TO YOUR SONGS?
MAYBE YOU AREN'T PROJECTING ENOUGH...
TRY TO GET YOUR MUSIC CLOSER TO YOUR AUDIENCE...
NOT THAT CLOSE!
SCHULZ

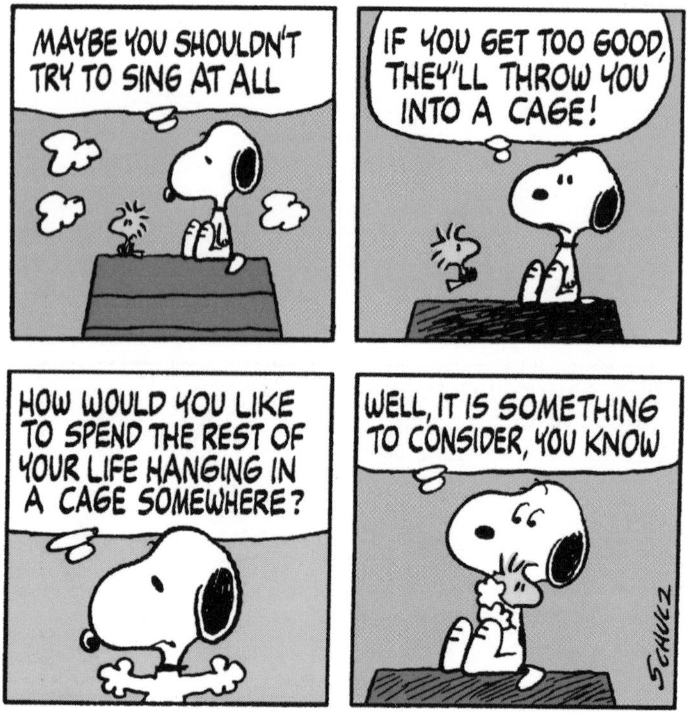
MAYBE YOU SHOULDN'T TRY TO SING AT ALL
IF YOU GET TOO GOOD, THEY'LL THROW YOU INTO A CAGE!
HOW WOULD YOU LIKE TO SPEND THE REST OF YOUR LIFE HANGING IN A CAGE SOMEWHERE?
WELL, IT IS SOMETHING TO CONSIDER, YOU KNOW
SCHULZ

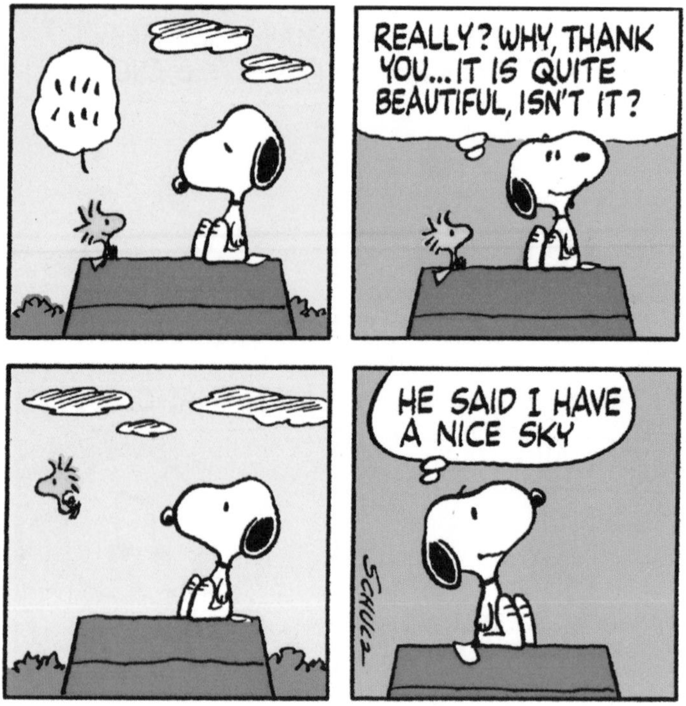
REALLY? WHY, THANK YOU... IT IS QUITE BEAUTIFUL, ISN'T IT?
HE SAID I HAVE A NICE SKY
SCHULZ

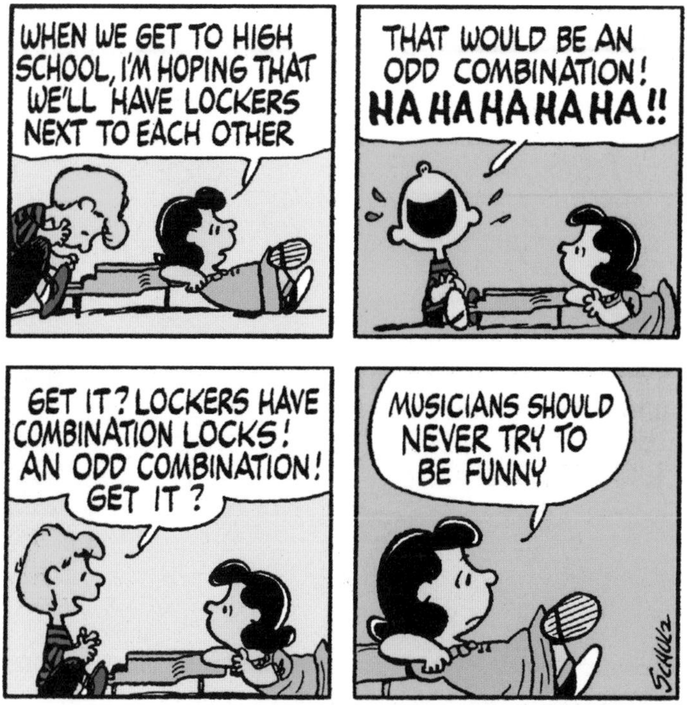
WHEN WE GET TO HIGH SCHOOL, I'M HOPING THAT WE'LL HAVE LOCKERS NEXT TO EACH OTHER
THAT WOULD BE AN ODD COMBINATION! HA HA HA HA HA!!
GET IT? LOCKERS HAVE COMBINATION LOCKS! AN ODD COMBINATION! GET IT?
MUSICIANS SHOULD NEVER TRY TO BE FUNNY

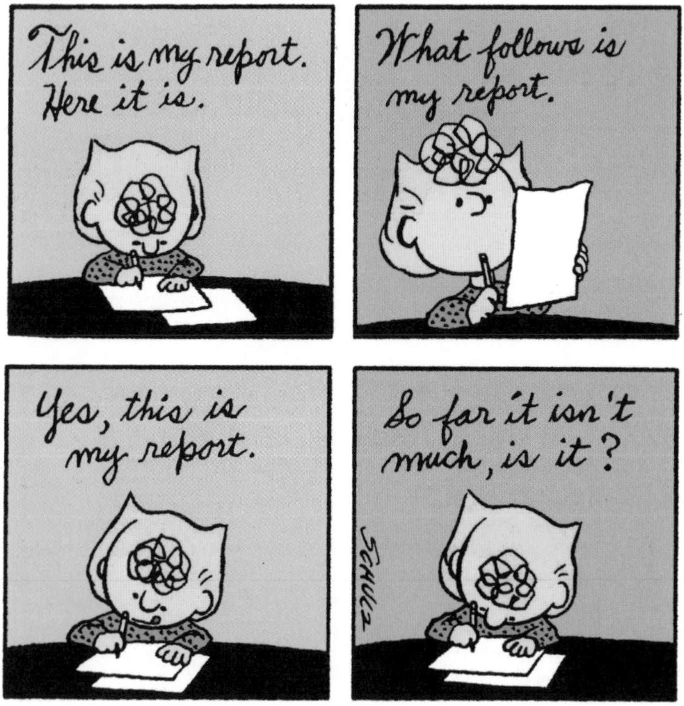
This is my report. Here it is.
What follows is my report.
Yes, this is my report.
So far it isn't much, is it?

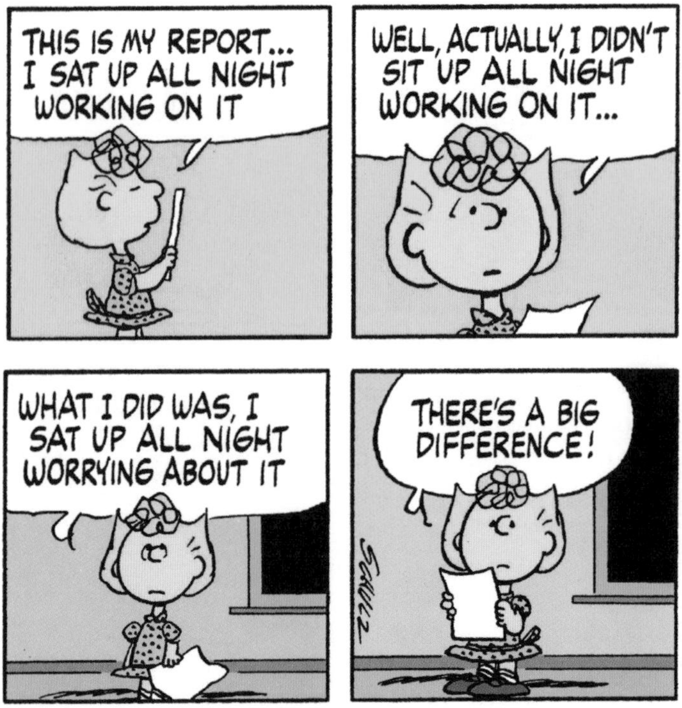
THIS IS MY REPORT... I SAT UP ALL NIGHT WORKING ON IT
WELL, ACTUALLY, I DIDN'T SIT UP ALL NIGHT WORKING ON IT...
WHAT I DID WAS, I SAT UP ALL NIGHT WORRYING ABOUT IT
THERE'S A BIG DIFFERENCE!
SCHULZ

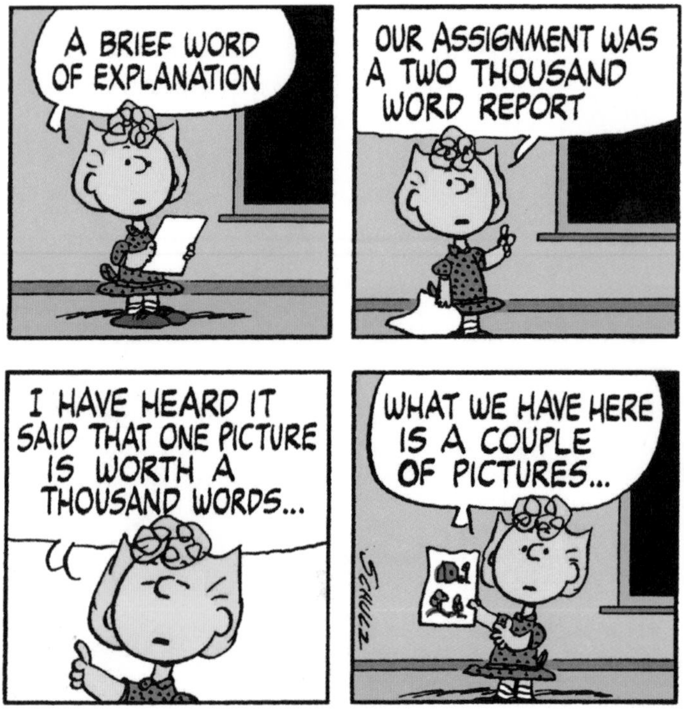
A BRIEF WORD OF EXPLANATION
OUR ASSIGNMENT WAS A TWO THOUSAND WORD REPORT
I HAVE HEARD IT SAID THAT ONE PICTURE IS WORTH A THOUSAND WORDS...
WHAT WE HAVE HERE IS A COUPLE OF PICTURES...
SCHULZ

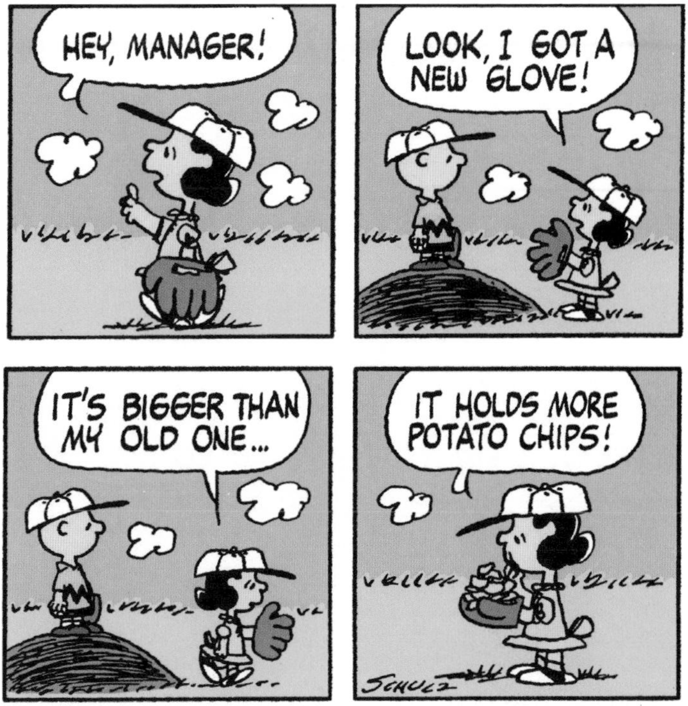
HEY, MANAGER!
LOOK, I GOT A NEW GLOVE!
IT'S BIGGER THAN MY OLD ONE...
IT HOLDS MORE POTATO CHIPS!
SCHULZ

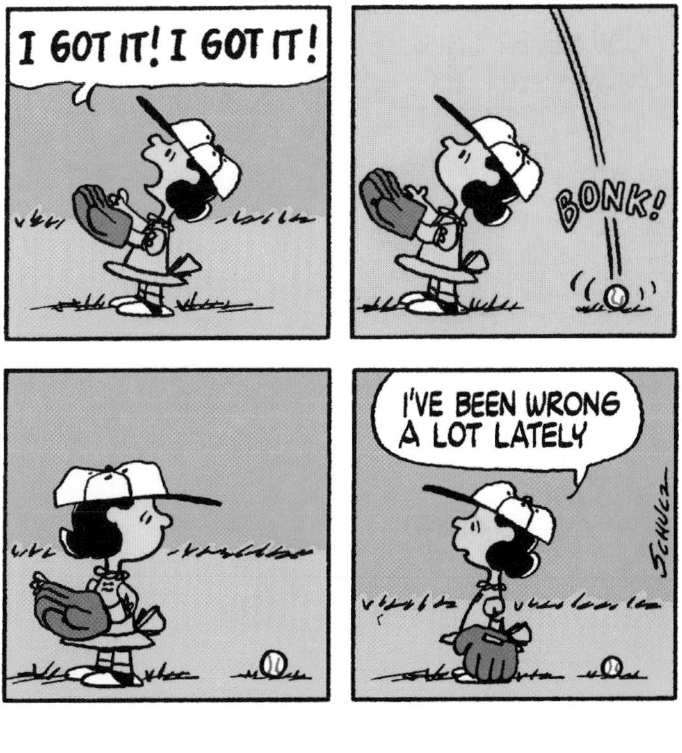
I GOT IT! I GOT IT!
BONK!
I'VE BEEN WRONG A LOT LATELY
SCHULZ

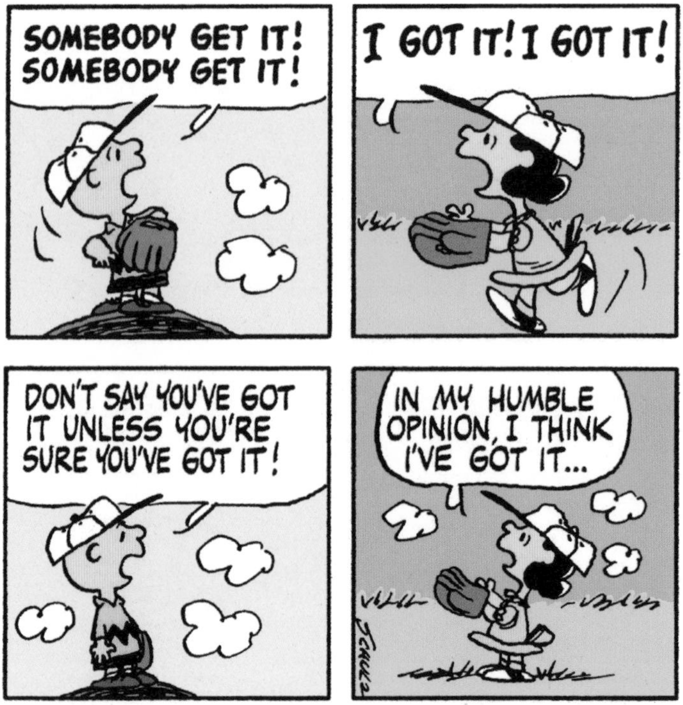
SOMEBODY GET IT! SOMEBODY GET IT!
I GOT IT! I GOT IT!
DON'T SAY YOU'VE GOT IT UNLESS YOU'RE SURE YOU'VE GOT IT!
IN MY HUMBLE OPINION, I THINK I'VE GOT IT...
SCHULZ

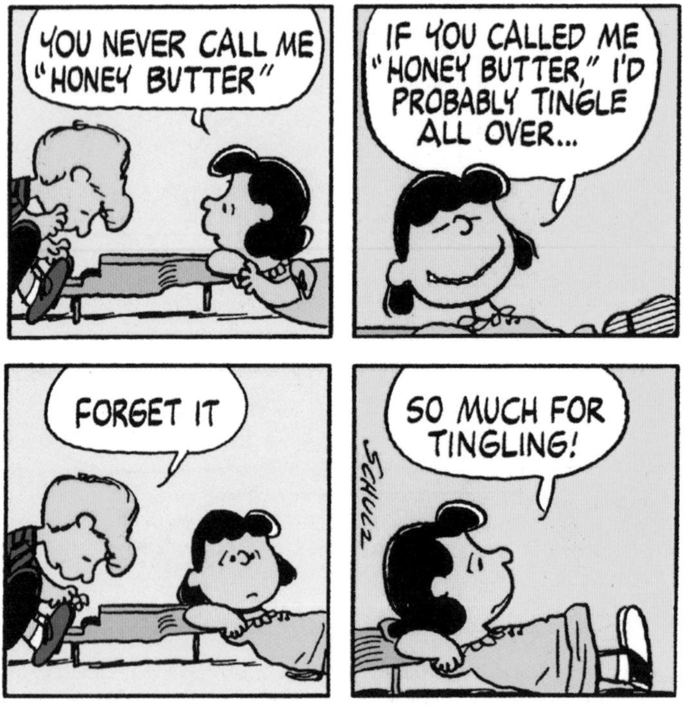
YOU NEVER CALL ME "HONEY BUTTER"
IF YOU CALLED ME "HONEY BUTTER," I'D PROBABLY TINGLE ALL OVER...
FORGET IT
SO MUCH FOR TINGLING!
SCHULZ

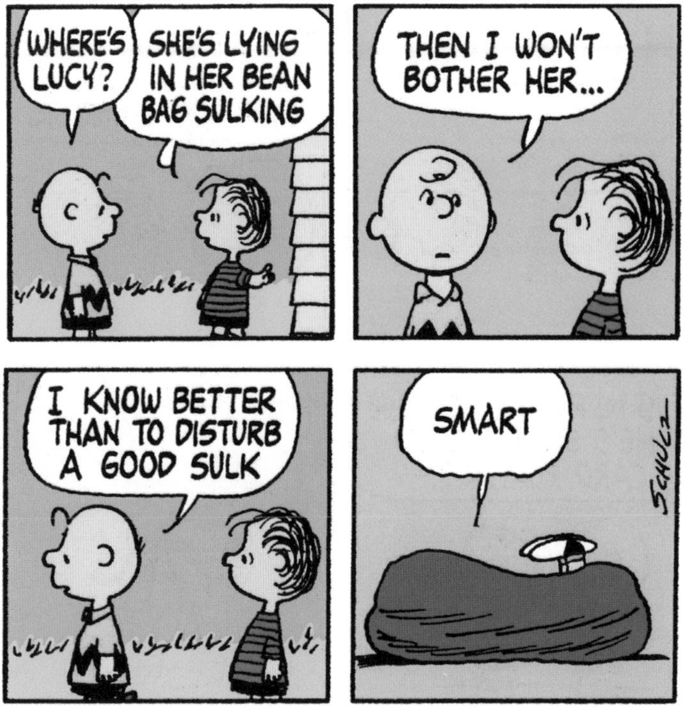
WHERE'S LUCY?
SHE'S LYING IN HER BEAN BAG SULKING
THEN I WON'T BOTHER HER...
I KNOW BETTER THAN TO DISTURB A GOOD SULK
SMART

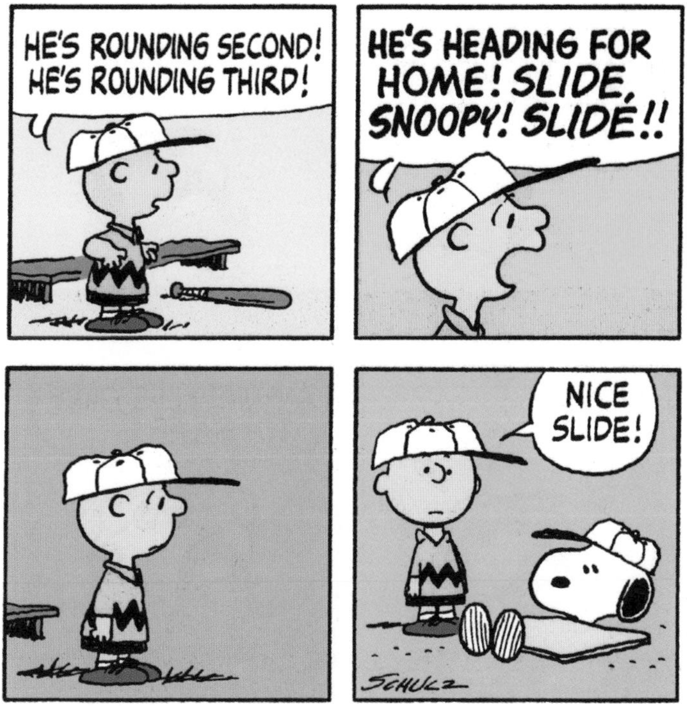
HE'S ROUNDING SECOND! HE'S ROUNDING THIRD!
HE'S HEADING FOR HOME! SLIDE, SNOOPY! SLIDE!!
NICE SLIDE!

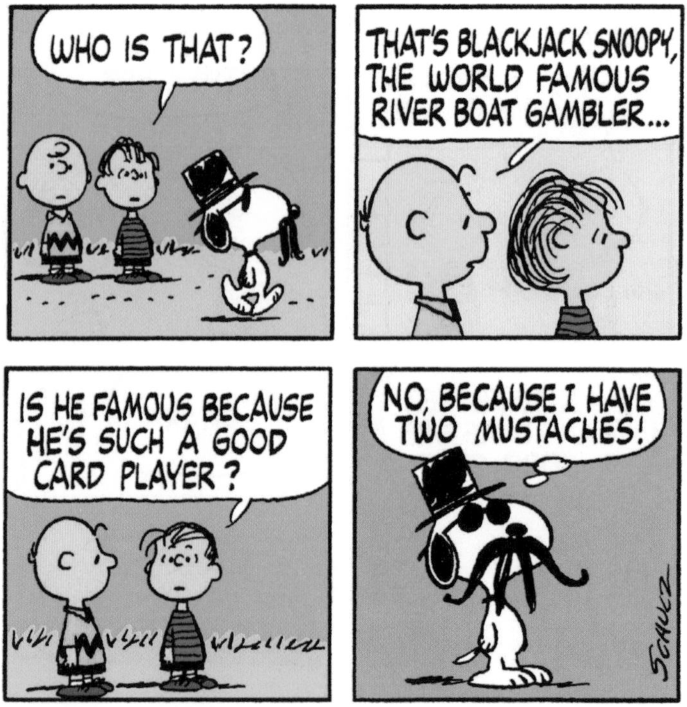
WHO IS THAT?
THAT'S BLACKJACK SNOOPY, THE WORLD FAMOUS RIVER BOAT GAMBLER...
IS HE FAMOUS BECAUSE HE'S SUCH A GOOD CARD PLAYER?
NO, BECAUSE I HAVE TWO MUSTACHES!
SCHULZ

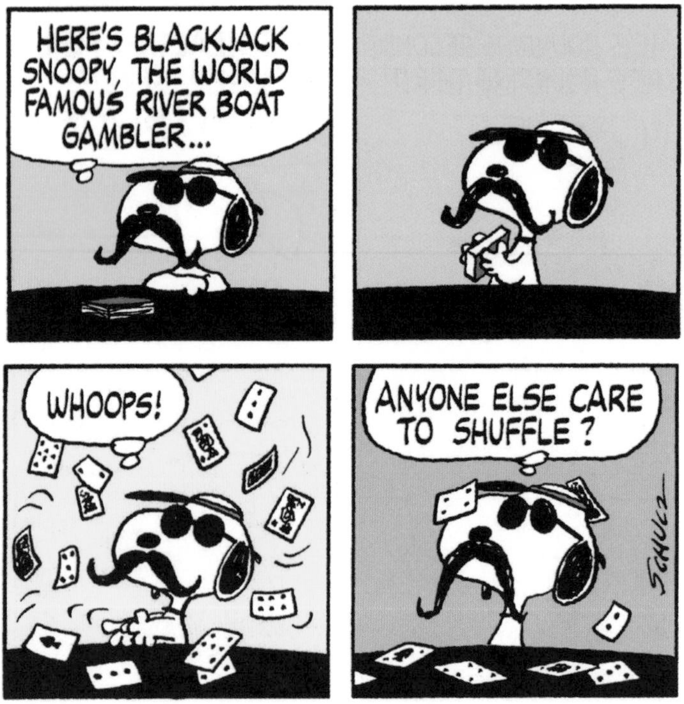
HERE'S BLACKJACK SNOOPY, THE WORLD FAMOUS RIVER BOAT GAMBLER...
WHOOPS!
ANYONE ELSE CARE TO SHUFFLE?
SCHULZ

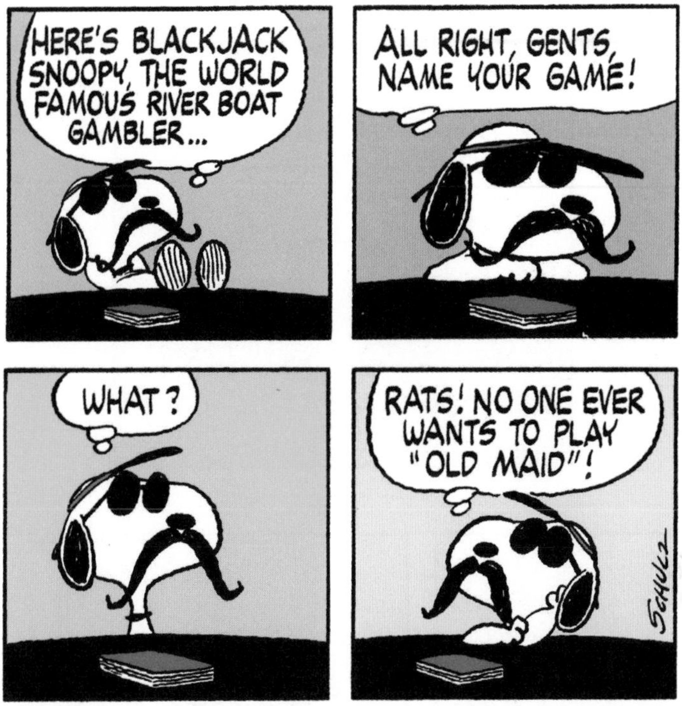
HERE'S BLACKJACK SNOOPY, THE WORLD FAMOUS RIVER BOAT GAMBLER...
ALL RIGHT, GENTS, NAME YOUR GAME!
WHAT?
RATS! NO ONE EVER WANTS TO PLAY "OLD MAID"!
SCHULZ

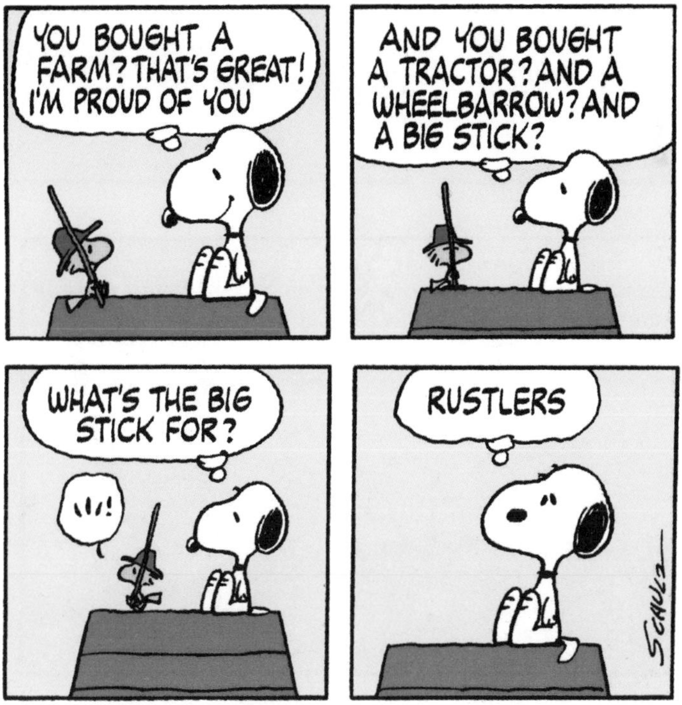
YOU BOUGHT A FARM? THAT'S GREAT! I'M PROUD OF YOU
AND YOU BOUGHT A TRACTOR? AND A WHEELBARROW? AND A BIG STICK?
WHAT'S THE BIG STICK FOR?
RUSTLERS
SCHULZ

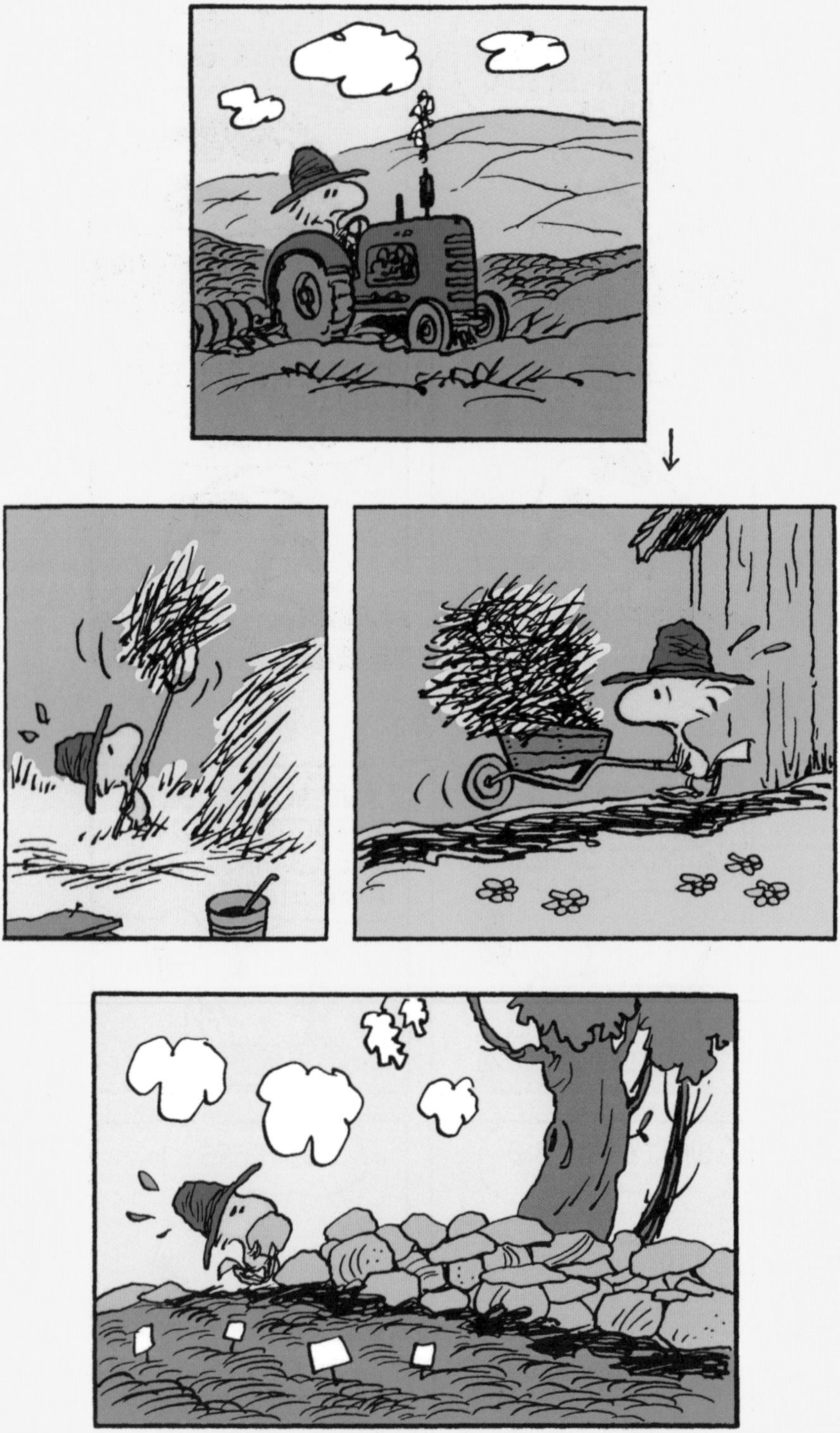

YOU LOOK EXHAUSTED! RUNNING A FARM IS HARD WORK
WELL, OKAY...
I DON'T MIND HELPING OUT ON A FRIEND'S FARM ONCE IN A WHILE...
BUT I HATE BEING THE SCARECROW!
SCHULZ

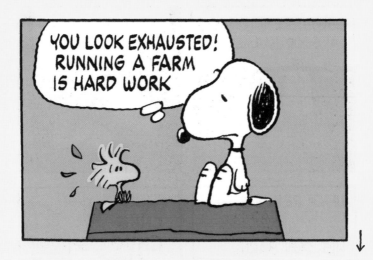

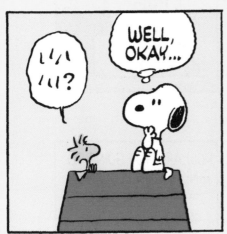

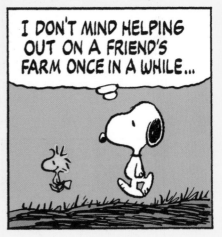

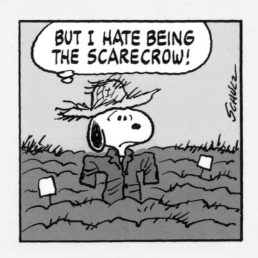

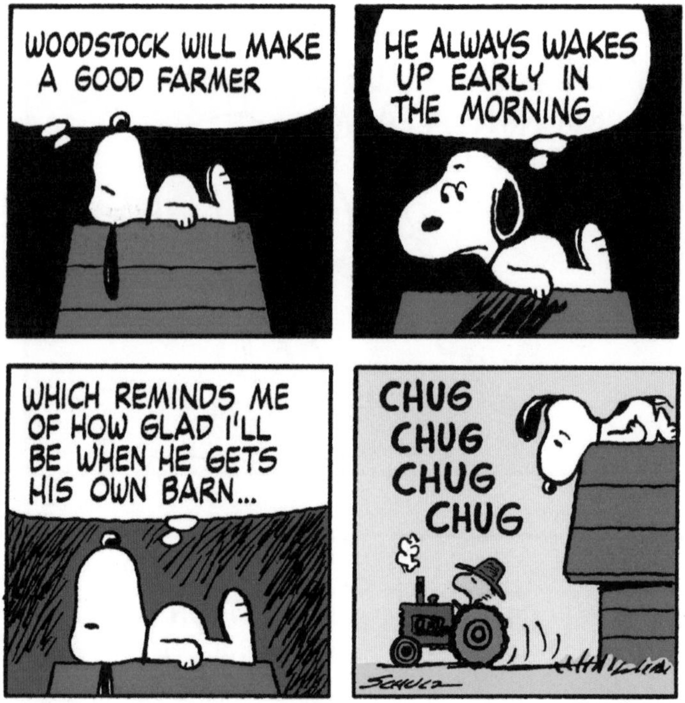
WOODSTOCK WILL MAKE A GOOD FARMER
HE ALWAYS WAKES UP EARLY IN THE MORNING
WHICH REMINDS ME OF HOW GLAD I'LL BE WHEN HE GETS HIS OWN BARN...
CHUG CHUG CHUG CHUG

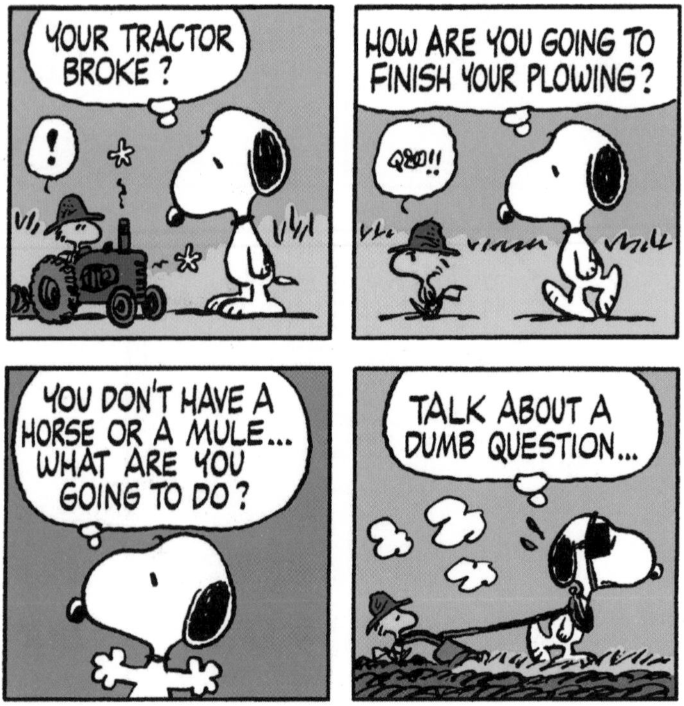
YOUR TRACTOR BROKE ?
!
HOW ARE YOU GOING TO FINISH YOUR PLOWING ?
YOU DON'T HAVE A HORSE OR A MULE... WHAT ARE YOU GOING TO DO ?
TALK ABOUT A DUMB QUESTION...

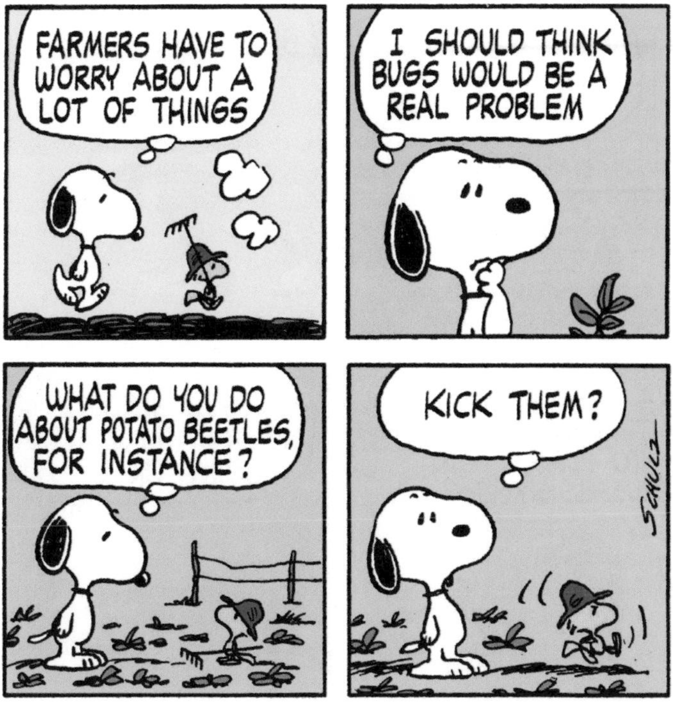
FARMERS HAVE TO WORRY ABOUT A LOT OF THINGS
I SHOULD THINK BUGS WOULD BE A REAL PROBLEM
WHAT DO YOU DO ABOUT POTATO BEETLES, FOR INSTANCE?
KICK THEM?
SCHULZ

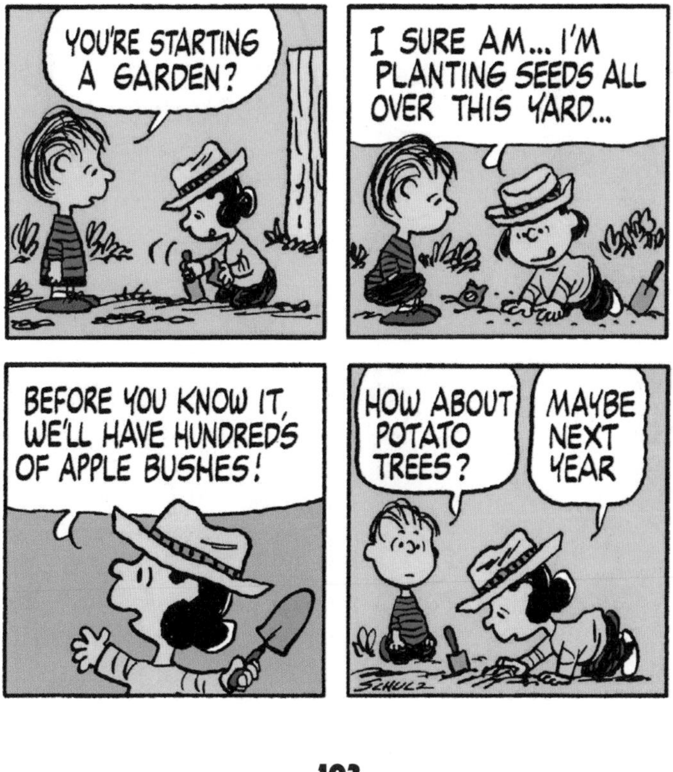
YOU'RE STARTING A GARDEN?
I SURE AM... I'M PLANTING SEEDS ALL OVER THIS YARD...
BEFORE YOU KNOW IT, WE'LL HAVE HUNDREDS OF APPLE BUSHES!
HOW ABOUT POTATO TREES?
MAYBE NEXT YEAR
SCHULZ

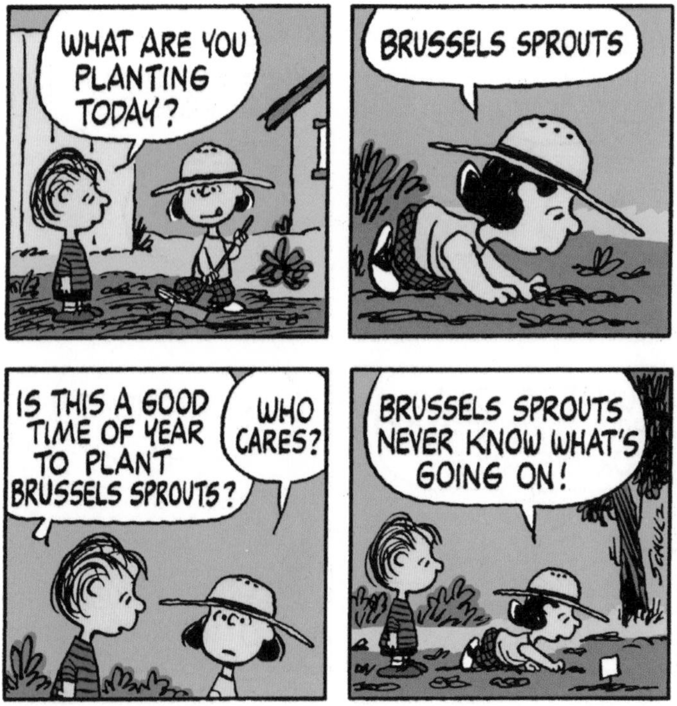
WHAT ARE YOU PLANTING TODAY?
BRUSSELS SPROUTS
IS THIS A GOOD TIME OF YEAR TO PLANT BRUSSELS SPROUTS?
WHO CARES?
BRUSSELS SPROUTS NEVER KNOW WHAT'S GOING ON!
SCHULZ

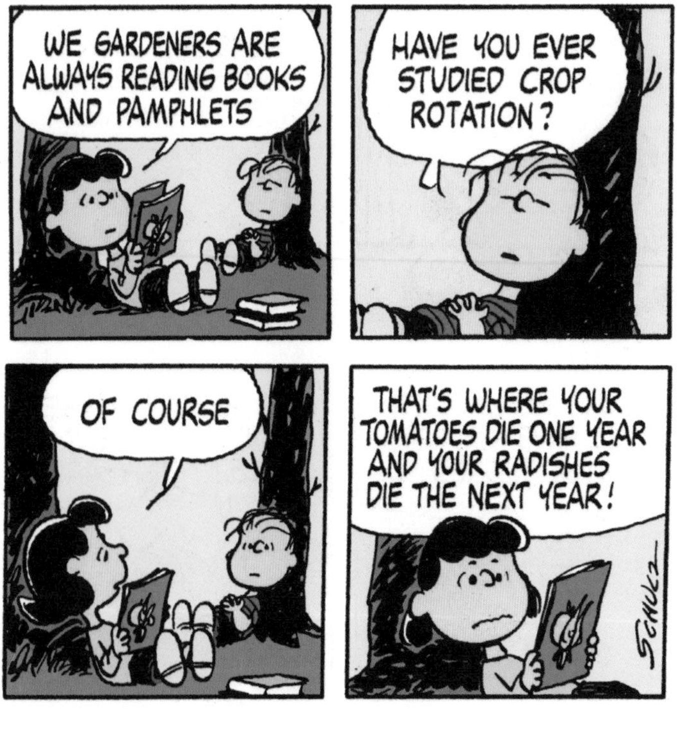
WE GARDENERS ARE ALWAYS READING BOOKS AND PAMPHLETS
HAVE YOU EVER STUDIED CROP ROTATION?
OF COURSE
THAT'S WHERE YOUR TOMATOES DIE ONE YEAR AND YOUR RADISHES DIE THE NEXT YEAR!
SCHULZ

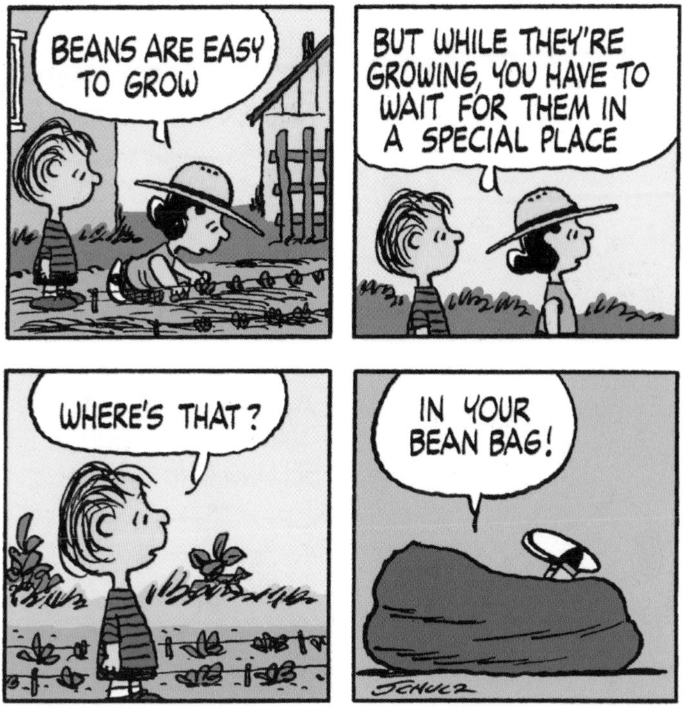
BEANS ARE EASY TO GROW
BUT WHILE THEY'RE GROWING, YOU HAVE TO WAIT FOR THEM IN A SPECIAL PLACE
WHERE'S THAT?
IN YOUR BEAN BAG!
SCHULZ

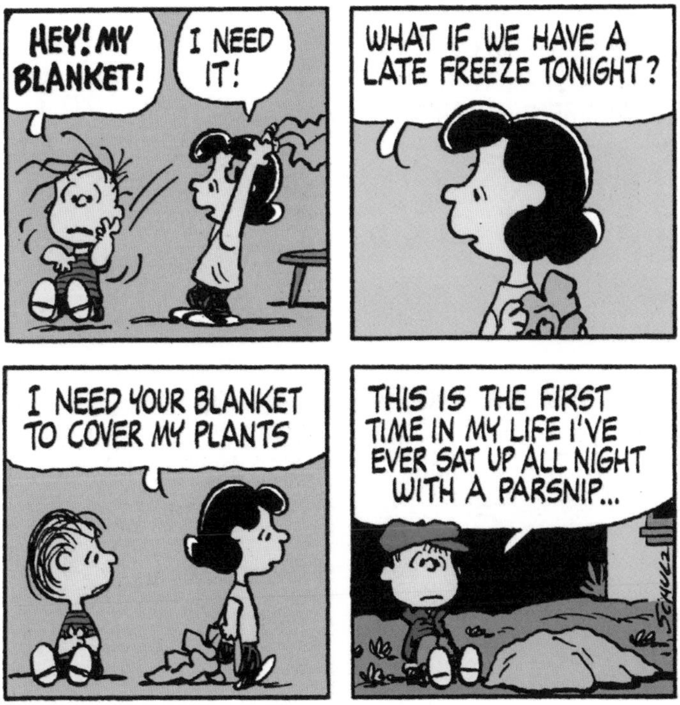
HEY! MY BLANKET!
I NEED IT!
WHAT IF WE HAVE A LATE FREEZE TONIGHT?
I NEED YOUR BLANKET TO COVER MY PLANTS
THIS IS THE FIRST TIME IN MY LIFE I'VE EVER SAT UP ALL NIGHT WITH A PARSNIP...
SCHULZ

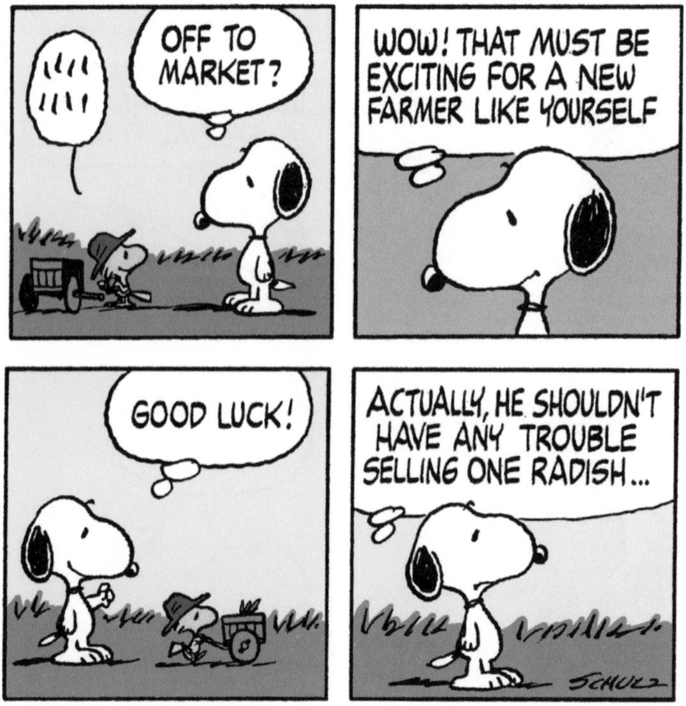
OFF TO MARKET?
WOW! THAT MUST BE EXCITING FOR A NEW FARMER LIKE YOURSELF
GOOD LUCK!
ACTUALLY, HE SHOULDN'T HAVE ANY TROUBLE SELLING ONE RADISH...

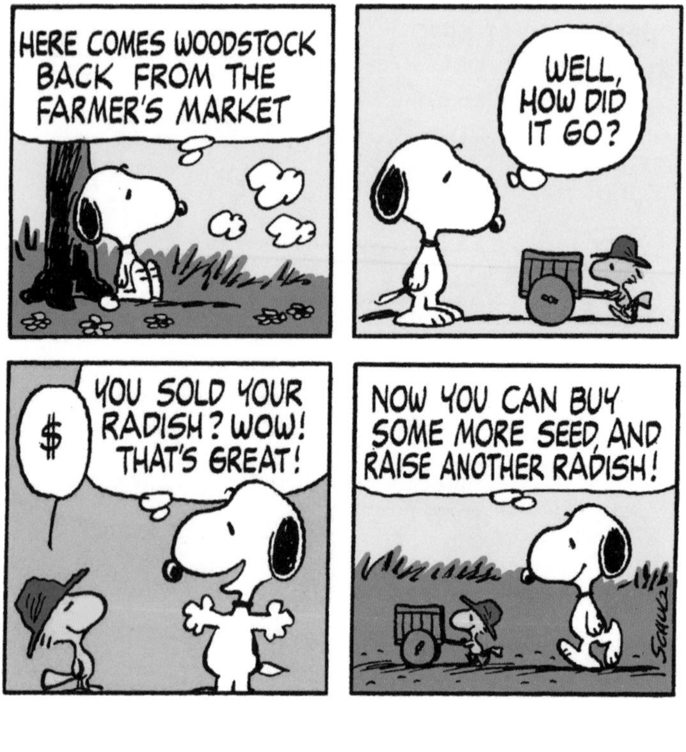
HERE COMES WOODSTOCK BACK FROM THE FARMER'S MARKET
WELL, HOW DID IT GO?
$
YOU SOLD YOUR RADISH? WOW! THAT'S GREAT!
NOW YOU CAN BUY SOME MORE SEED, AND RAISE ANOTHER RADISH!

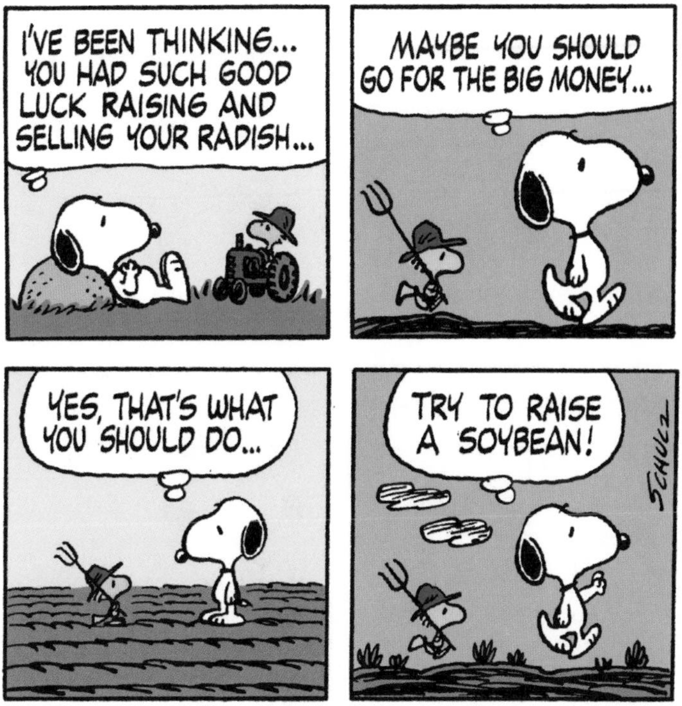
I'VE BEEN THINKING... YOU HAD SUCH GOOD LUCK RAISING AND SELLING YOUR RADISH...
MAYBE YOU SHOULD GO FOR THE BIG MONEY...
YES, THAT'S WHAT YOU SHOULD DO...
TRY TO RAISE A SOYBEAN!
SCHULZ

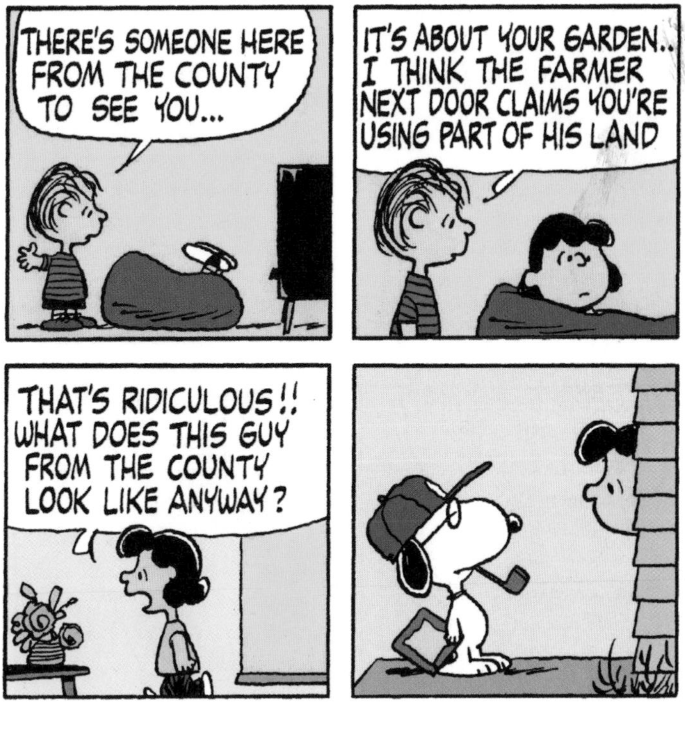
THERE'S SOMEONE HERE FROM THE COUNTY TO SEE YOU...
IT'S ABOUT YOUR GARDEN.. I THINK THE FARMER NEXT DOOR CLAIMS YOU'RE USING PART OF HIS LAND
THAT'S RIDICULOUS!! WHAT DOES THIS GUY FROM THE COUNTY LOOK LIKE ANYWAY?

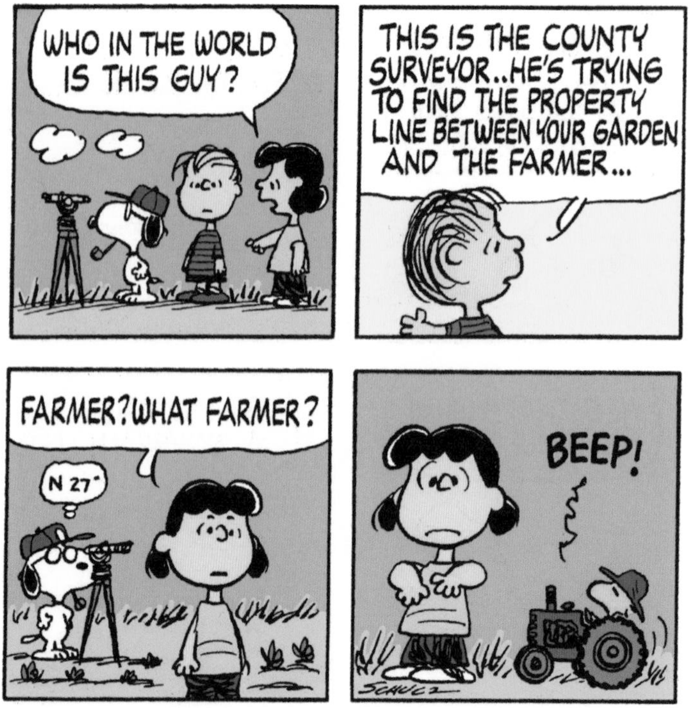
WHO IN THE WORLD IS THIS GUY?
THIS IS THE COUNTY SURVEYOR..HE'S TRYING TO FIND THE PROPERTY LINE BETWEEN YOUR GARDEN AND THE FARMER...
FARMER? WHAT FARMER?
N 27°
BEEP!
SCHULZ

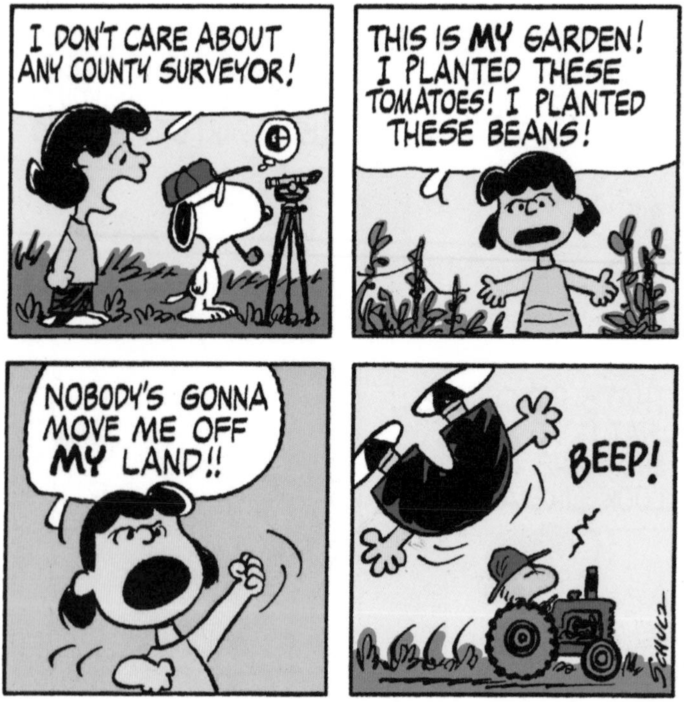
I DON'T CARE ABOUT ANY COUNTY SURVEYOR!
THIS IS MY GARDEN! I PLANTED THESE TOMATOES! I PLANTED THESE BEANS!
NOBODY'S GONNA MOVE ME OFF MY LAND!!
BEEP!
SCHULZ

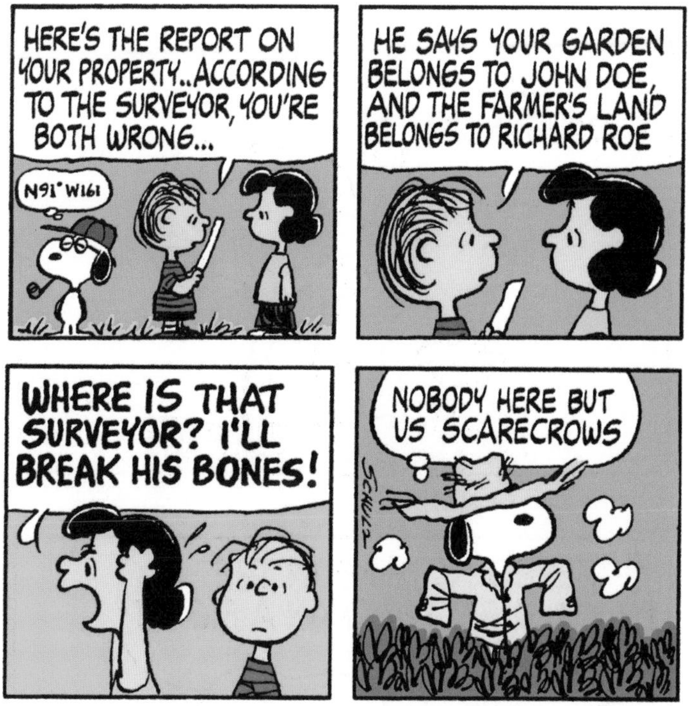
HERE'S THE REPORT ON YOUR PROPERTY..ACCORDING TO THE SURVEYOR, YOU'RE BOTH WRONG...
N91° W161
HE SAYS YOUR GARDEN BELONGS TO JOHN DOE, AND THE FARMER'S LAND BELONGS TO RICHARD ROE
WHERE IS THAT SURVEYOR? I'LL BREAK HIS BONES!
NOBODY HERE BUT US SCARECROWS
SCHULZ

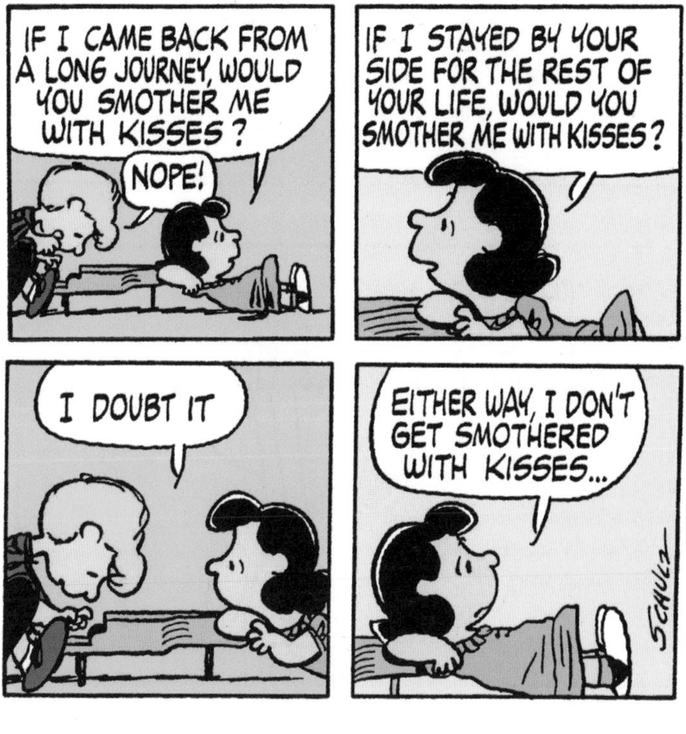
IF I CAME BACK FROM A LONG JOURNEY, WOULD YOU SMOTHER ME WITH KISSES?
NOPE!
IF I STAYED BY YOUR SIDE FOR THE REST OF YOUR LIFE, WOULD YOU SMOTHER ME WITH KISSES?
I DOUBT IT
EITHER WAY, I DON'T GET SMOTHERED WITH KISSES...
SCHULZ

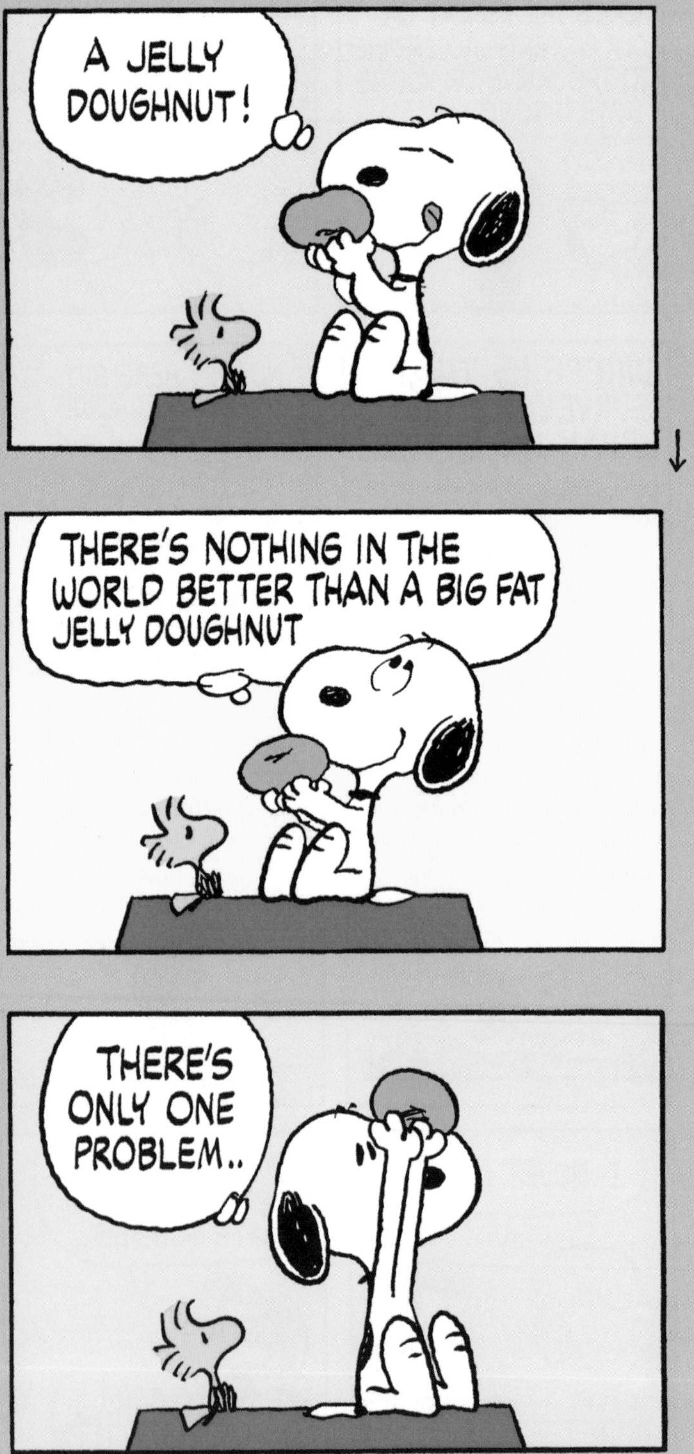
A JELLY DOUGHNUT!
THERE'S NOTHING IN THE WORLD BETTER THAN A BIG FAT JELLY DOUGHNUT
THERE'S ONLY ONE PROBLEM..

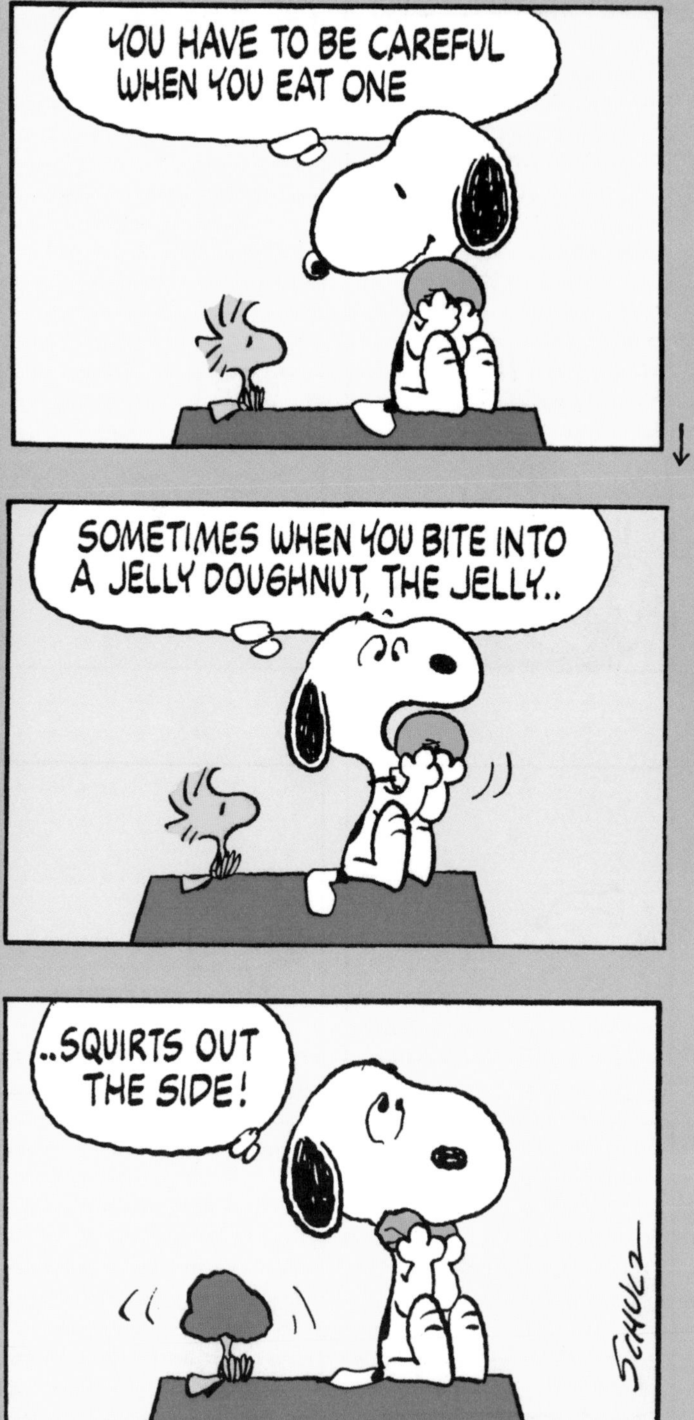
YOU HAVE TO BE CAREFUL WHEN YOU EAT ONE
SOMETIMES WHEN YOU BITE INTO A JELLY DOUGHNUT, THE JELLY..
..SQUIRTS OUT THE SIDE!
SCHULZ

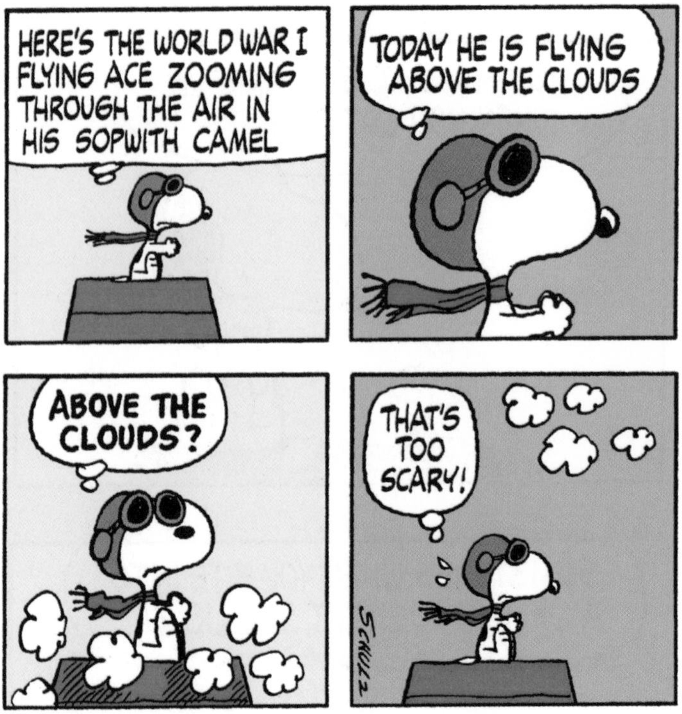
HERE'S THE WORLD WAR I FLYING ACE ZOOMING THROUGH THE AIR IN HIS SOPWITH CAMEL
TODAY HE IS FLYING ABOVE THE CLOUDS
ABOVE THE CLOUDS?
THAT'S TOO SCARY!
SCHULZ

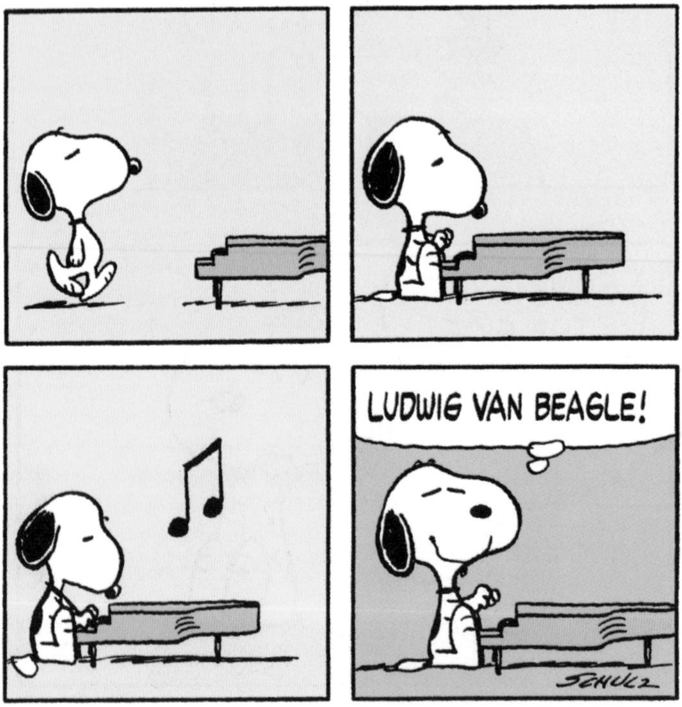
LUDWIG VAN BEAGLE!
SCHULZ

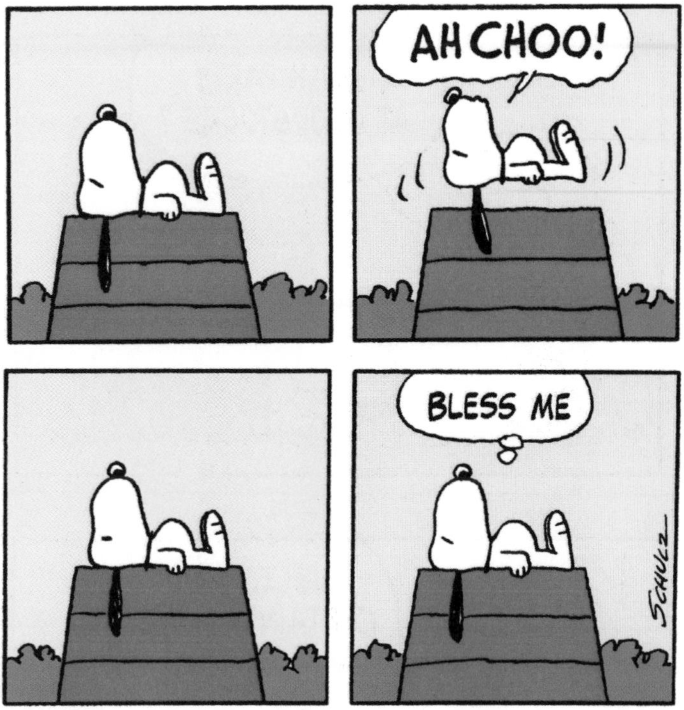
AH CHOO!
BLESS ME
SCHULZ

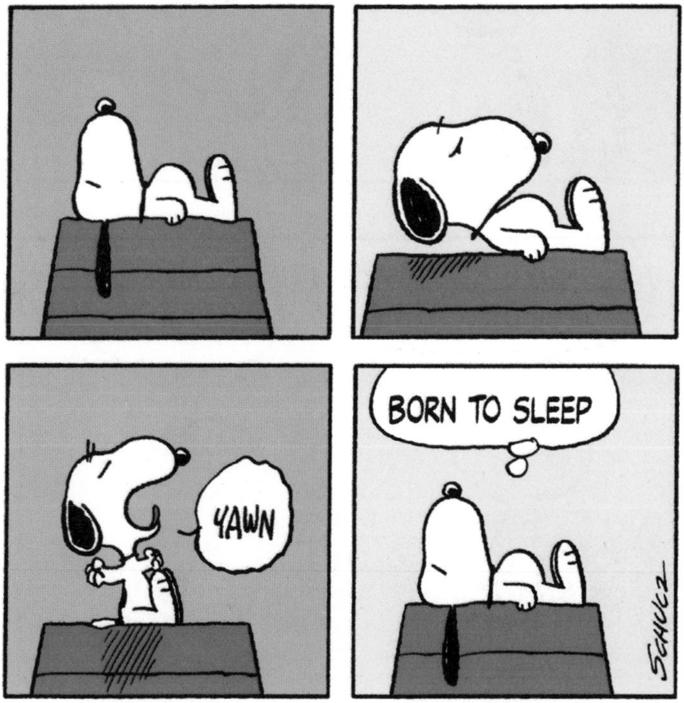
YAWN
BORN TO SLEEP
SCHULZ

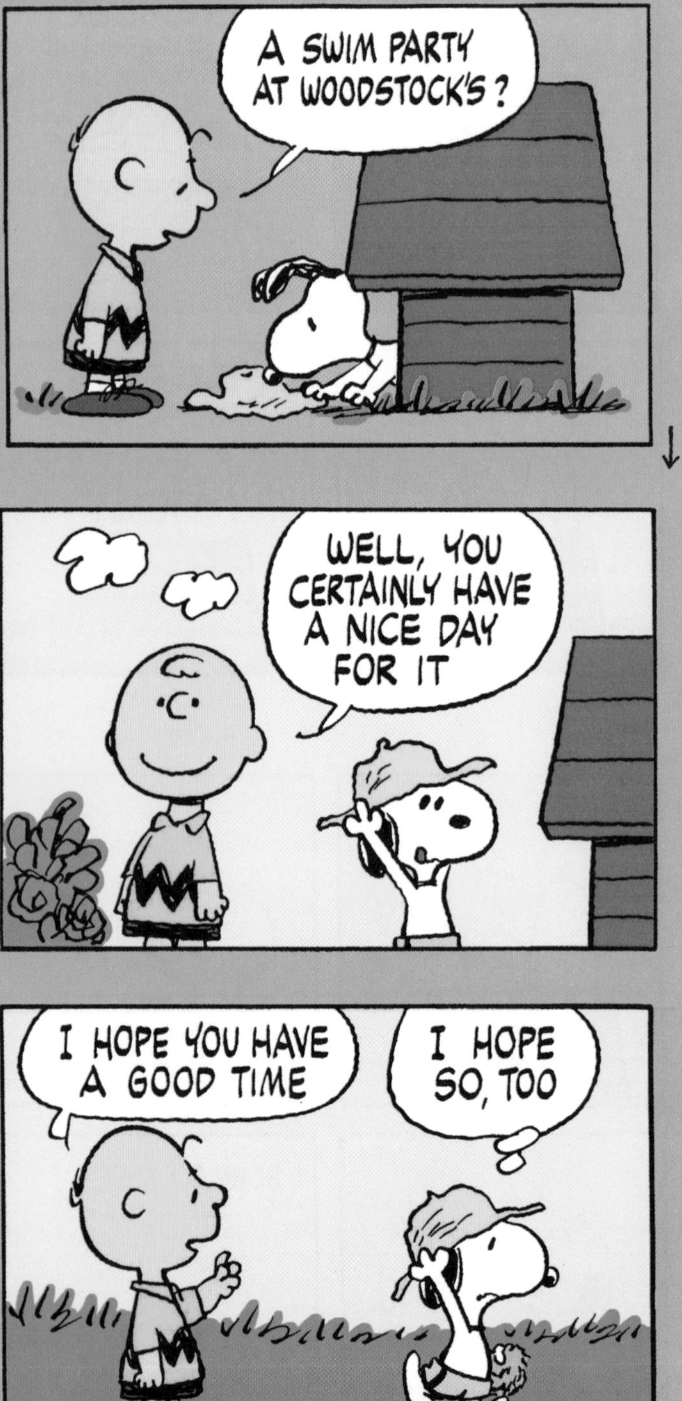
A SWIM PARTY AT WOODSTOCK'S ?
WELL, YOU CERTAINLY HAVE A NICE DAY FOR IT
I HOPE YOU HAVE A GOOD TIME
I HOPE SO, TOO

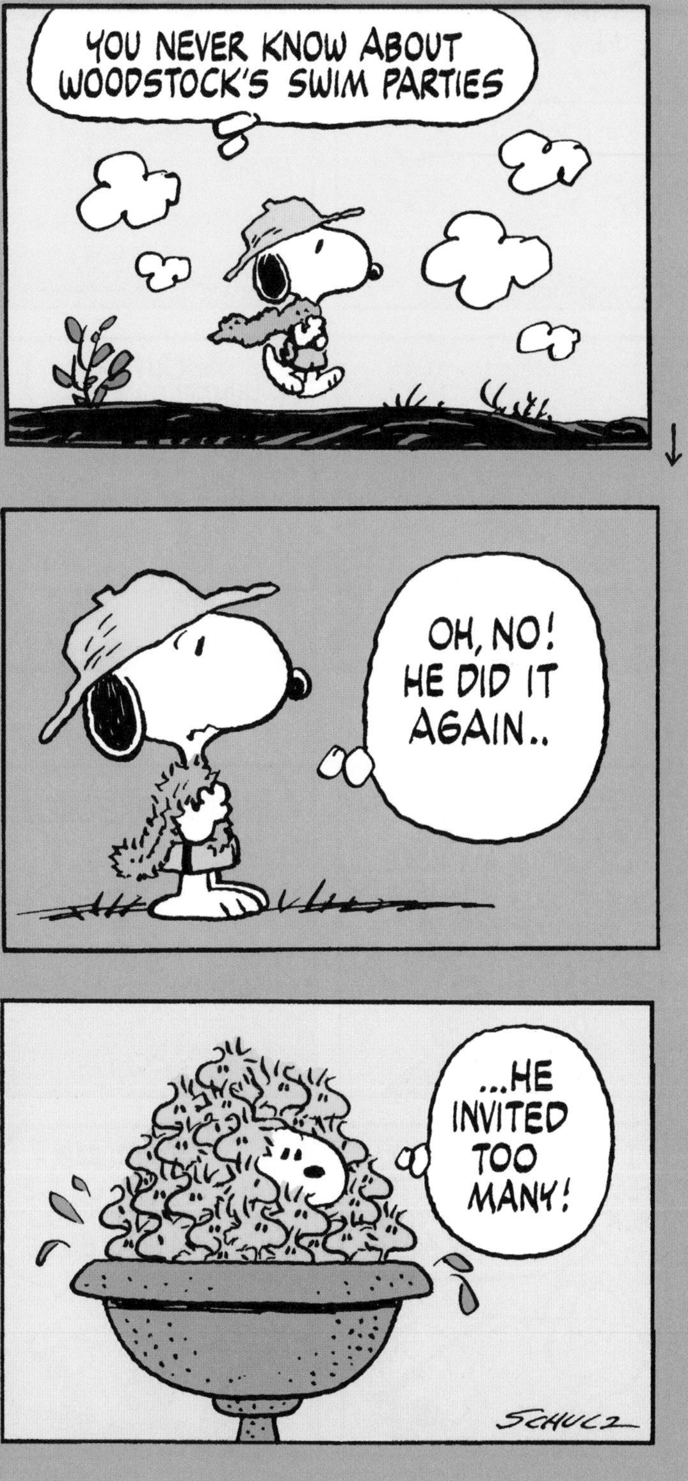
YOU NEVER KNOW ABOUT WOODSTOCK'S SWIM PARTIES
OH, NO! HE DID IT AGAIN..
...HE INVITED TOO MANY!
SCHULZ

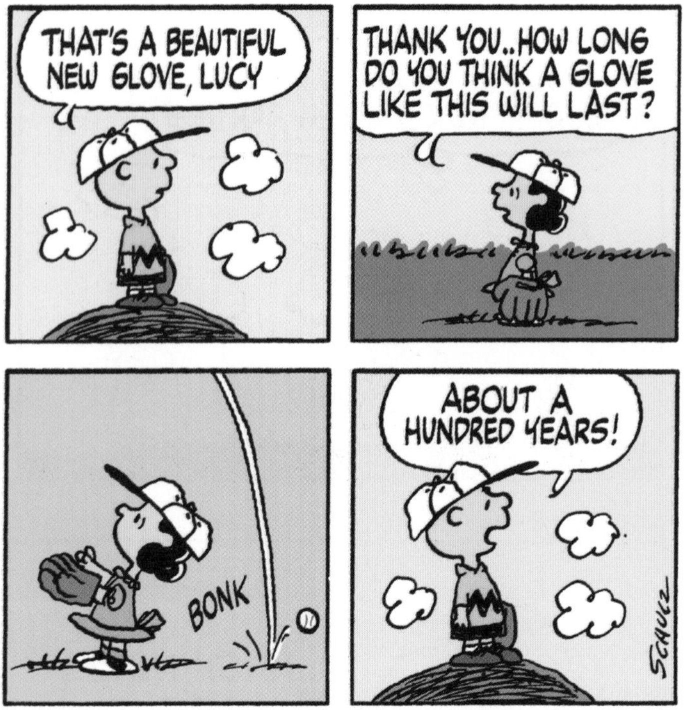
THAT'S A BEAUTIFUL NEW GLOVE, LUCY
THANK YOU..HOW LONG DO YOU THINK A GLOVE LIKE THIS WILL LAST?
BONK
ABOUT A HUNDRED YEARS!
SCHULZ

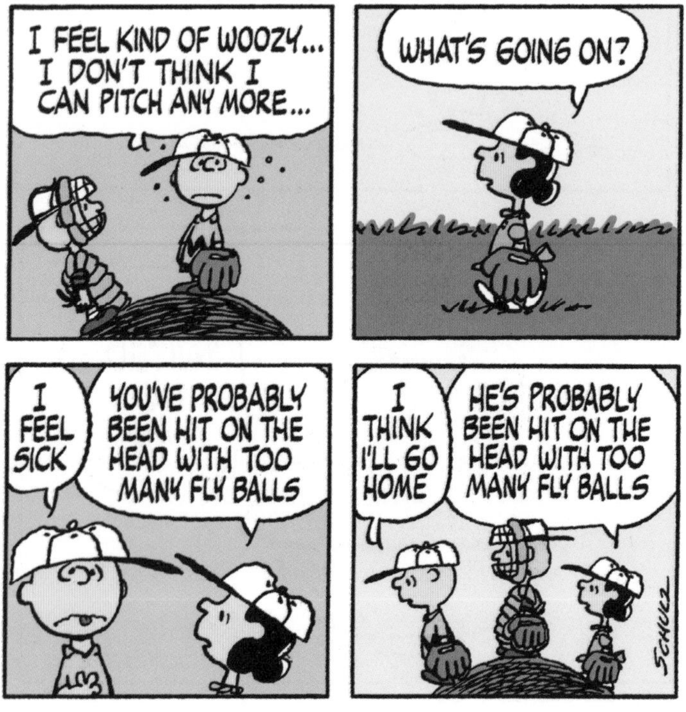
I FEEL KIND OF WOOZY... I DON'T THINK I CAN PITCH ANY MORE...
WHAT'S GOING ON?
I FEEL SICK
YOU'VE PROBABLY BEEN HIT ON THE HEAD WITH TOO MANY FLY BALLS
I THINK I'LL GO HOME
HE'S PROBABLY BEEN HIT ON THE HEAD WITH TOO MANY FLY BALLS
SCHULZ

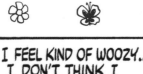

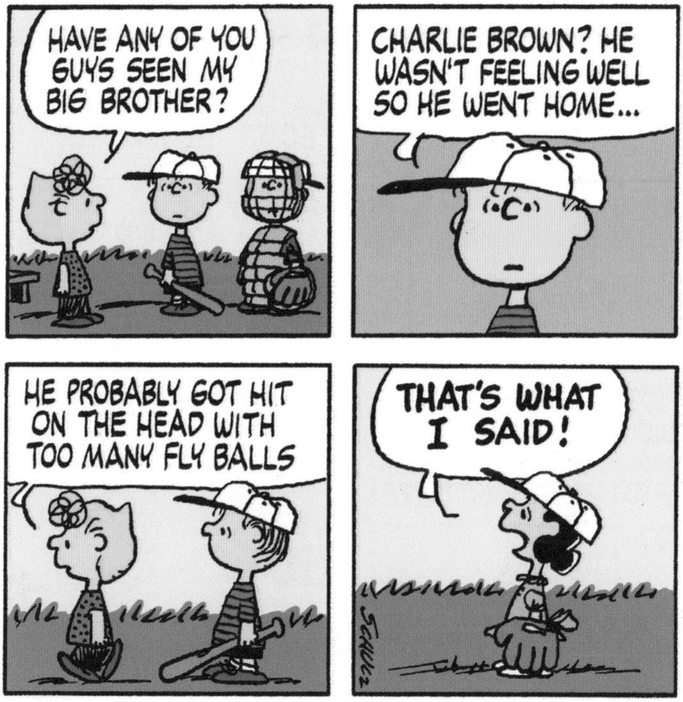
HAVE ANY OF YOU GUYS SEEN MY BIG BROTHER?
CHARLIE BROWN? HE WASN'T FEELING WELL SO HE WENT HOME...
HE PROBABLY GOT HIT ON THE HEAD WITH TOO MANY FLY BALLS
THAT'S WHAT I SAID!
SCHULZ

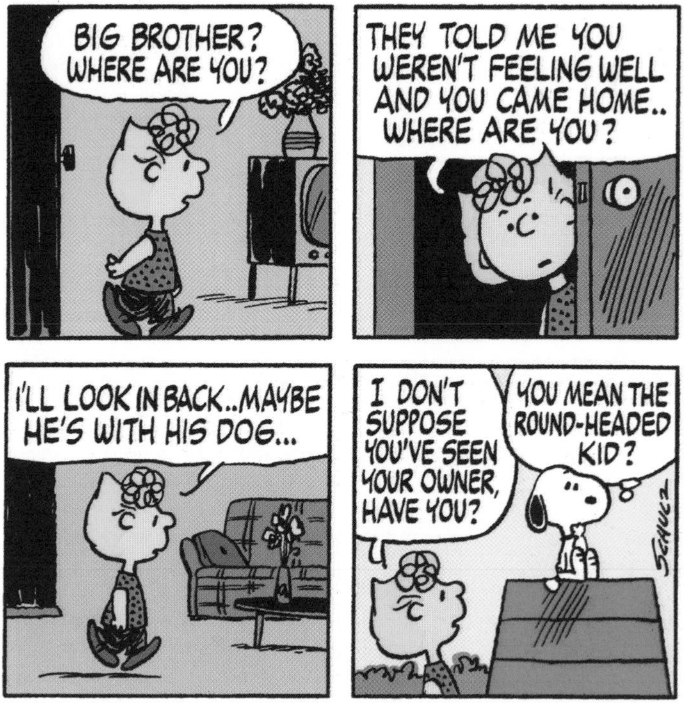
BIG BROTHER? WHERE ARE YOU?
THEY TOLD ME YOU WEREN'T FEELING WELL AND YOU CAME HOME.. WHERE ARE YOU?
I'LL LOOK IN BACK..MAYBE HE'S WITH HIS DOG...
I DON'T SUPPOSE YOU'VE SEEN YOUR OWNER, HAVE YOU?
YOU MEAN THE ROUND-HEADED KID?
SCHULZ

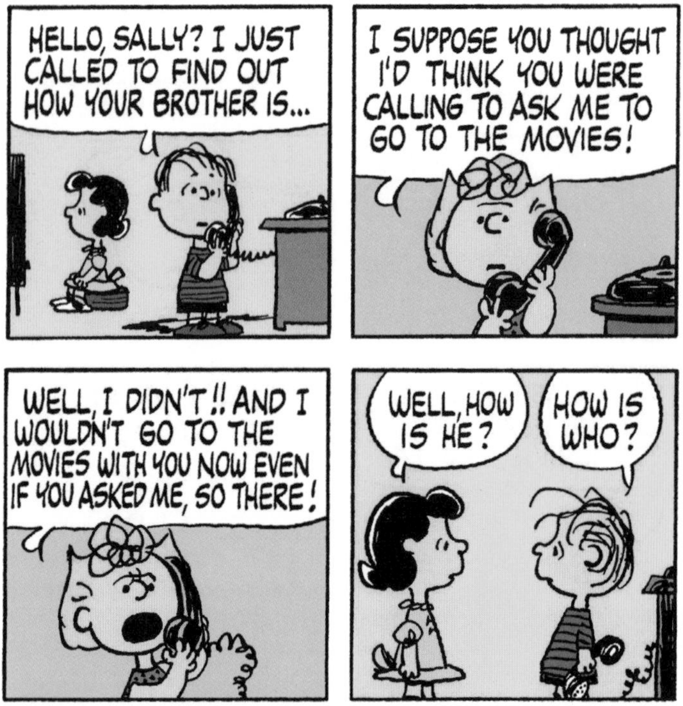
HELLO, SALLY? I JUST CALLED TO FIND OUT HOW YOUR BROTHER IS...
I SUPPOSE YOU THOUGHT I'D THINK YOU WERE CALLING TO ASK ME TO GO TO THE MOVIES!
WELL, I DIDN'T!! AND I WOULDN'T GO TO THE MOVIES WITH YOU NOW EVEN IF YOU ASKED ME, SO THERE!
WELL, HOW IS HE?
HOW IS WHO?

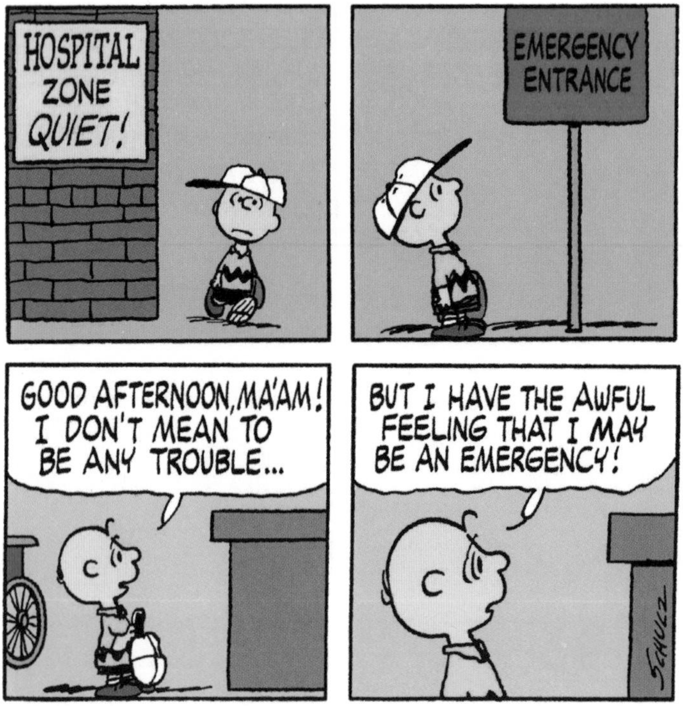
HOSPITAL ZONE QUIET!
EMERGENCY ENTRANCE
GOOD AFTERNOON, MA'AM! I DON'T MEAN TO BE ANY TROUBLE...
BUT I HAVE THE AWFUL FEELING THAT I MAY BE AN EMERGENCY!
SCHULZ

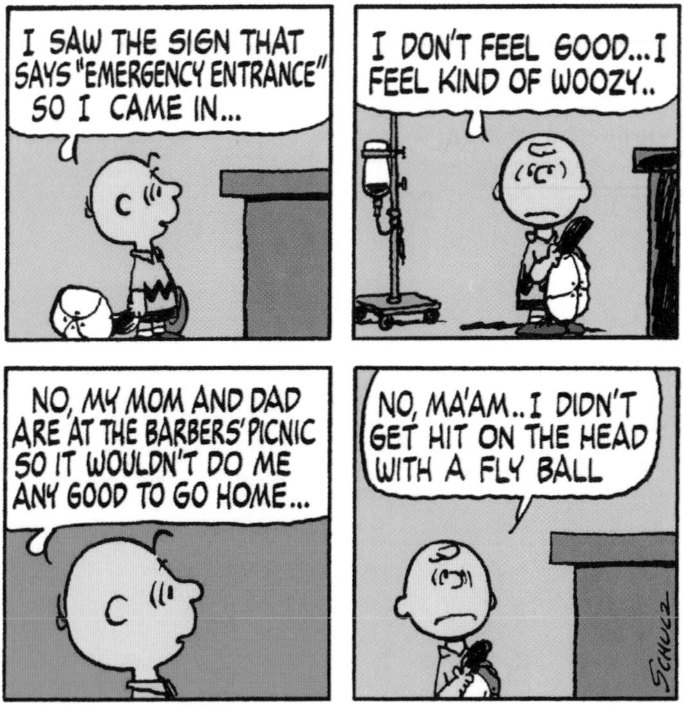
I SAW THE SIGN THAT SAYS "EMERGENCY ENTRANCE" SO I CAME IN...
I DON'T FEEL GOOD...I FEEL KIND OF WOOZY..
NO, MY MOM AND DAD ARE AT THE BARBERS' PICNIC SO IT WOULDN'T DO ME ANY GOOD TO GO HOME...
NO, MA'AM..I DIDN'T GET HIT ON THE HEAD WITH A FLY BALL

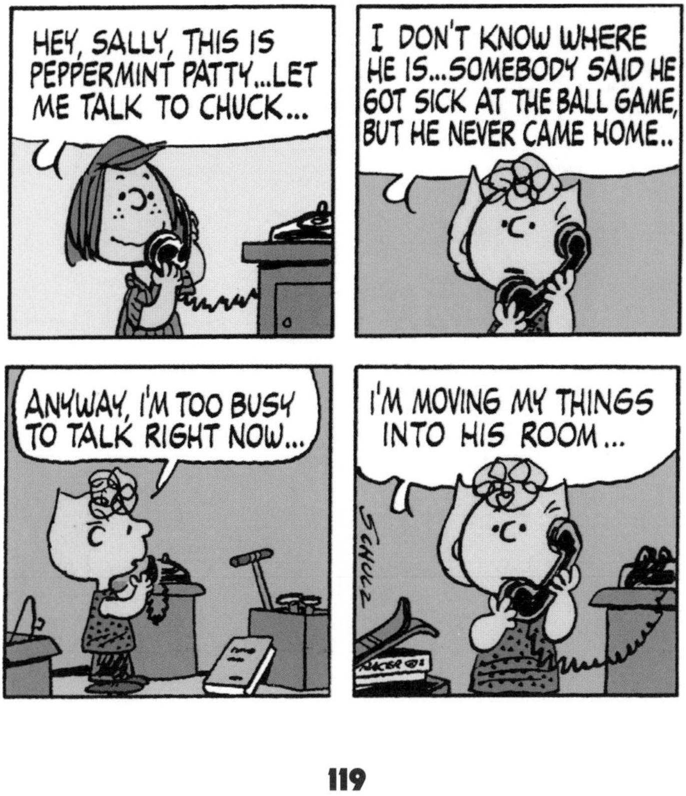
HEY, SALLY, THIS IS PEPPERMINT PATTY...LET ME TALK TO CHUCK...
I DON'T KNOW WHERE HE IS...SOMEBODY SAID HE GOT SICK AT THE BALL GAME, BUT HE NEVER CAME HOME..
ANYWAY, I'M TOO BUSY TO TALK RIGHT NOW...
I'M MOVING MY THINGS INTO HIS ROOM...

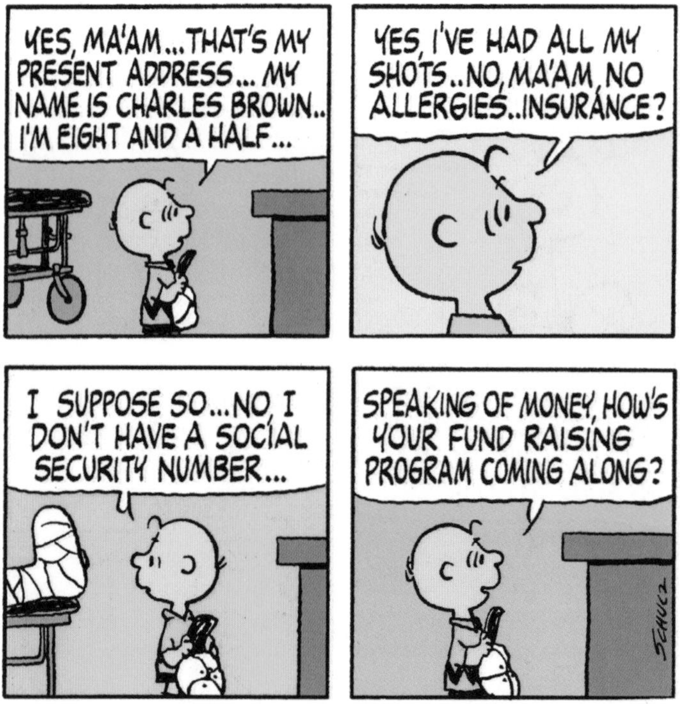
YES, MA'AM...THAT'S MY PRESENT ADDRESS... MY NAME IS CHARLES BROWN.. I'M EIGHT AND A HALF...
YES, I'VE HAD ALL MY SHOTS..NO, MA'AM, NO ALLERGIES..INSURANCE?
I SUPPOSE SO...NO, I DON'T HAVE A SOCIAL SECURITY NUMBER...
SPEAKING OF MONEY, HOW'S YOUR FUND RAISING PROGRAM COMING ALONG?
SCHULZ

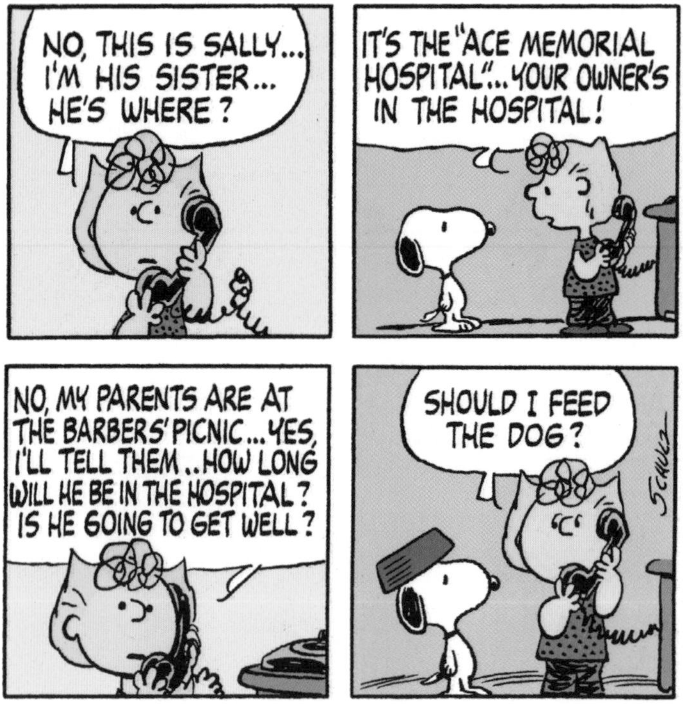
NO, THIS IS SALLY... I'M HIS SISTER... HE'S WHERE?
IT'S THE "ACE MEMORIAL HOSPITAL"...YOUR OWNER'S IN THE HOSPITAL!
NO, MY PARENTS ARE AT THE BARBERS' PICNIC...YES, I'LL TELL THEM..HOW LONG WILL HE BE IN THE HOSPITAL? IS HE GOING TO GET WELL?
SHOULD I FEED THE DOG?
SCHULZ

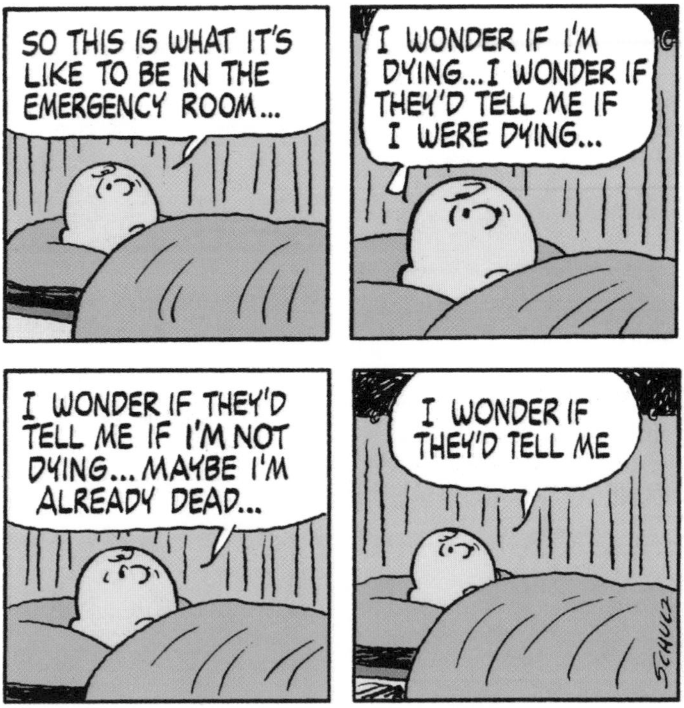
SO THIS IS WHAT IT'S LIKE TO BE IN THE EMERGENCY ROOM...
I WONDER IF I'M DYING...I WONDER IF THEY'D TELL ME IF I WERE DYING...
I WONDER IF THEY'D TELL ME IF I'M NOT DYING... MAYBE I'M ALREADY DEAD...
I WONDER IF THEY'D TELL ME
SCHULZ

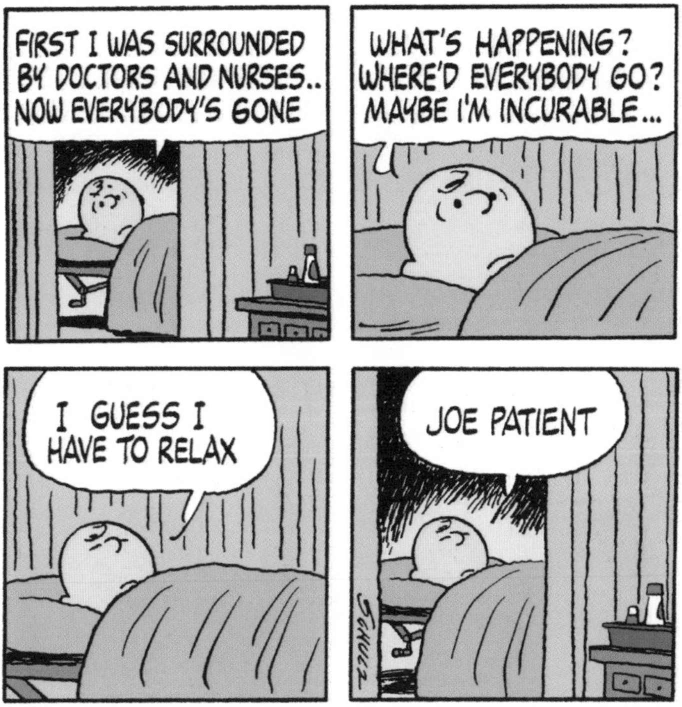
FIRST I WAS SURROUNDED BY DOCTORS AND NURSES.. NOW EVERYBODY'S GONE
WHAT'S HAPPENING? WHERE'D EVERYBODY GO? MAYBE I'M INCURABLE...
I GUESS I HAVE TO RELAX
JOE PATIENT
SCHULZ

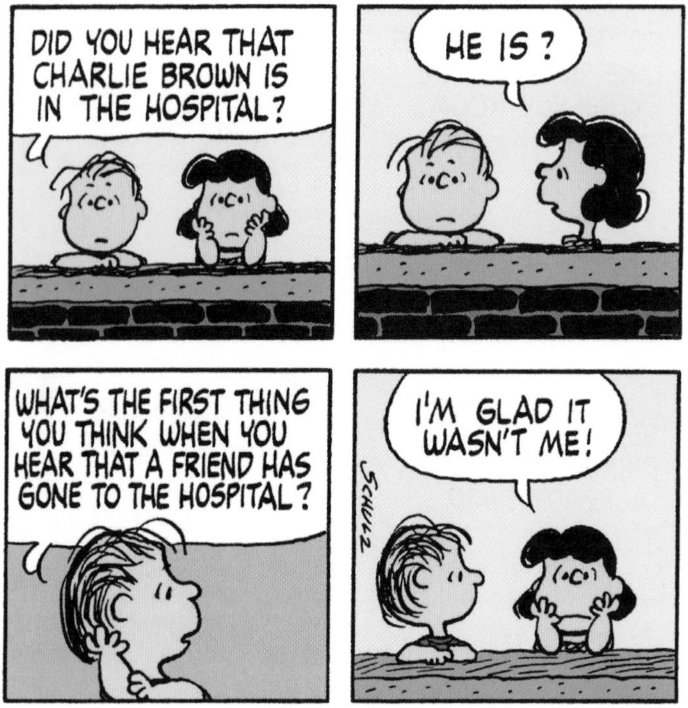
DID YOU HEAR THAT CHARLIE BROWN IS IN THE HOSPITAL?
HE IS?
WHAT'S THE FIRST THING YOU THINK WHEN YOU HEAR THAT A FRIEND HAS GONE TO THE HOSPITAL?
SCHULZ
I'M GLAD IT WASN'T ME!

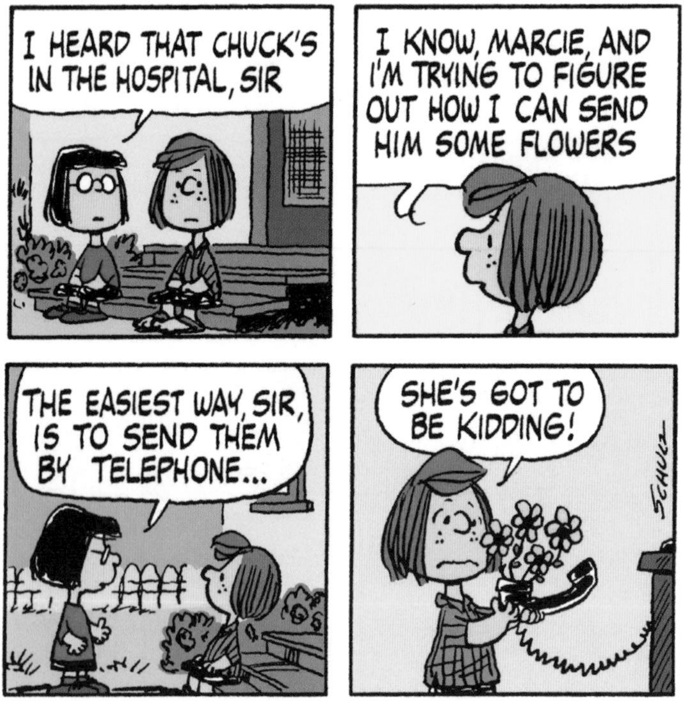
I HEARD THAT CHUCK'S IN THE HOSPITAL, SIR
I KNOW, MARCIE, AND I'M TRYING TO FIGURE OUT HOW I CAN SEND HIM SOME FLOWERS
THE EASIEST WAY, SIR, IS TO SEND THEM BY TELEPHONE...
SHE'S GOT TO BE KIDDING!
SCHULZ

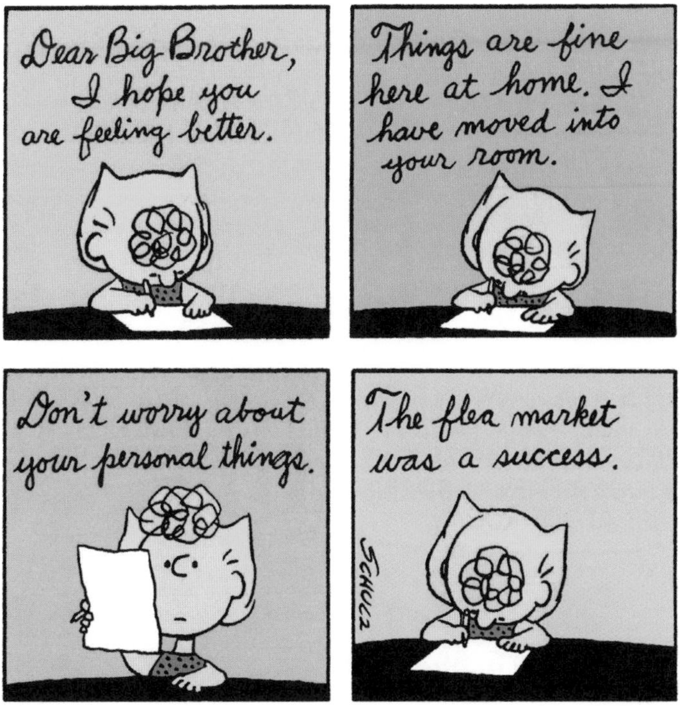
Dear Big Brother,
I hope you are feeling better.
Things are fine here at home. I have moved into your room.
Don't worry about your personal things.
The flea market was a success.
SCHULZ

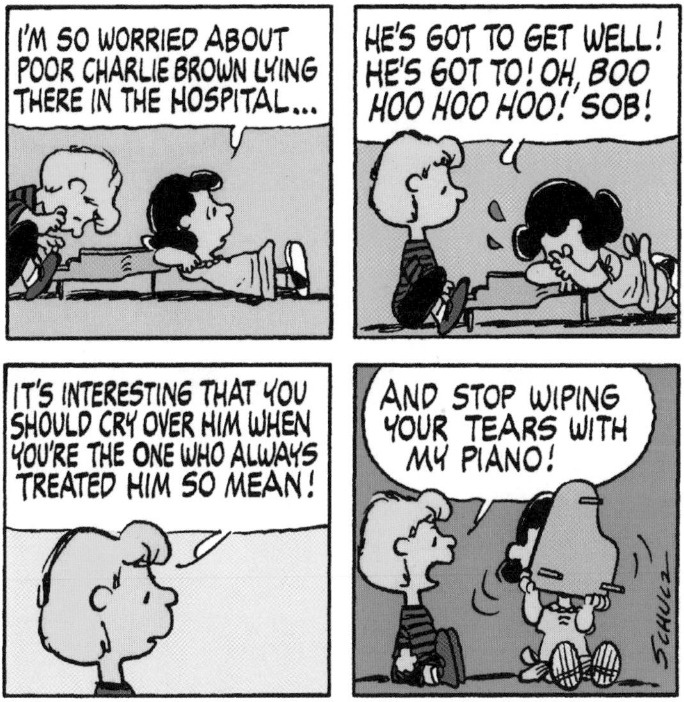
I'M SO WORRIED ABOUT POOR CHARLIE BROWN LYING THERE IN THE HOSPITAL...
HE'S GOT TO GET WELL! HE'S GOT TO! OH, BOO HOO HOO HOO! SOB!
IT'S INTERESTING THAT YOU SHOULD CRY OVER HIM WHEN YOU'RE THE ONE WHO ALWAYS TREATED HIM SO MEAN!
AND STOP WIPING YOUR TEARS WITH MY PIANO!
SCHULZ

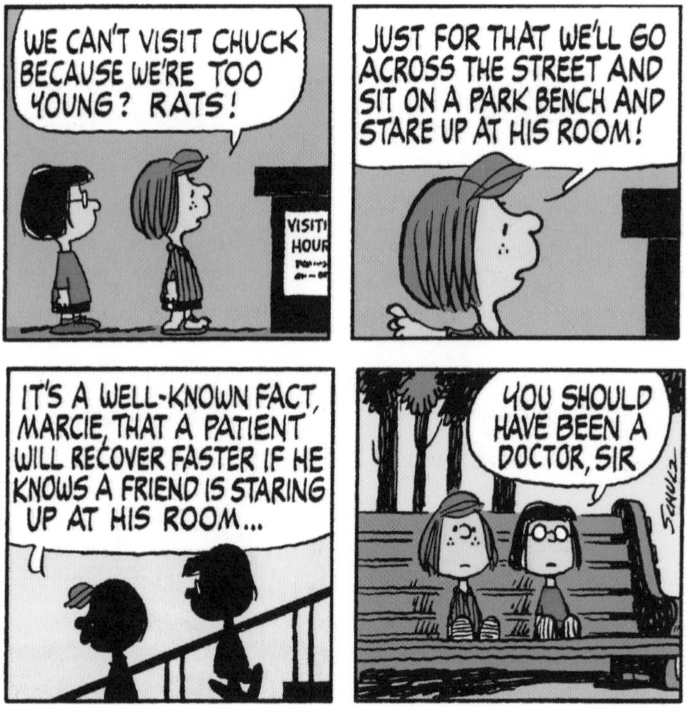
WE CAN'T VISIT CHUCK BECAUSE WE'RE TOO YOUNG? RATS!
JUST FOR THAT WE'LL GO ACROSS THE STREET AND SIT ON A PARK BENCH AND STARE UP AT HIS ROOM!
IT'S A WELL-KNOWN FACT, MARCIE, THAT A PATIENT WILL RECOVER FASTER IF HE KNOWS A FRIEND IS STARING UP AT HIS ROOM...
YOU SHOULD HAVE BEEN A DOCTOR, SIR
SCHULZ

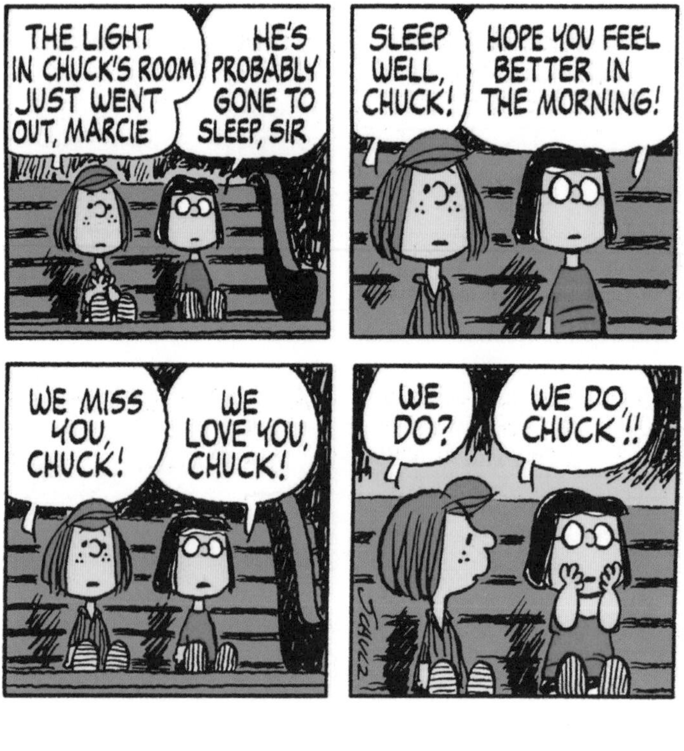
THE LIGHT IN CHUCK'S ROOM JUST WENT OUT, MARCIE
HE'S PROBABLY GONE TO SLEEP, SIR
SLEEP WELL, CHUCK!
HOPE YOU FEEL BETTER IN THE MORNING!
WE MISS YOU, CHUCK!
WE LOVE YOU, CHUCK!
WE DO?
WE DO, CHUCK!!
SCHULZ

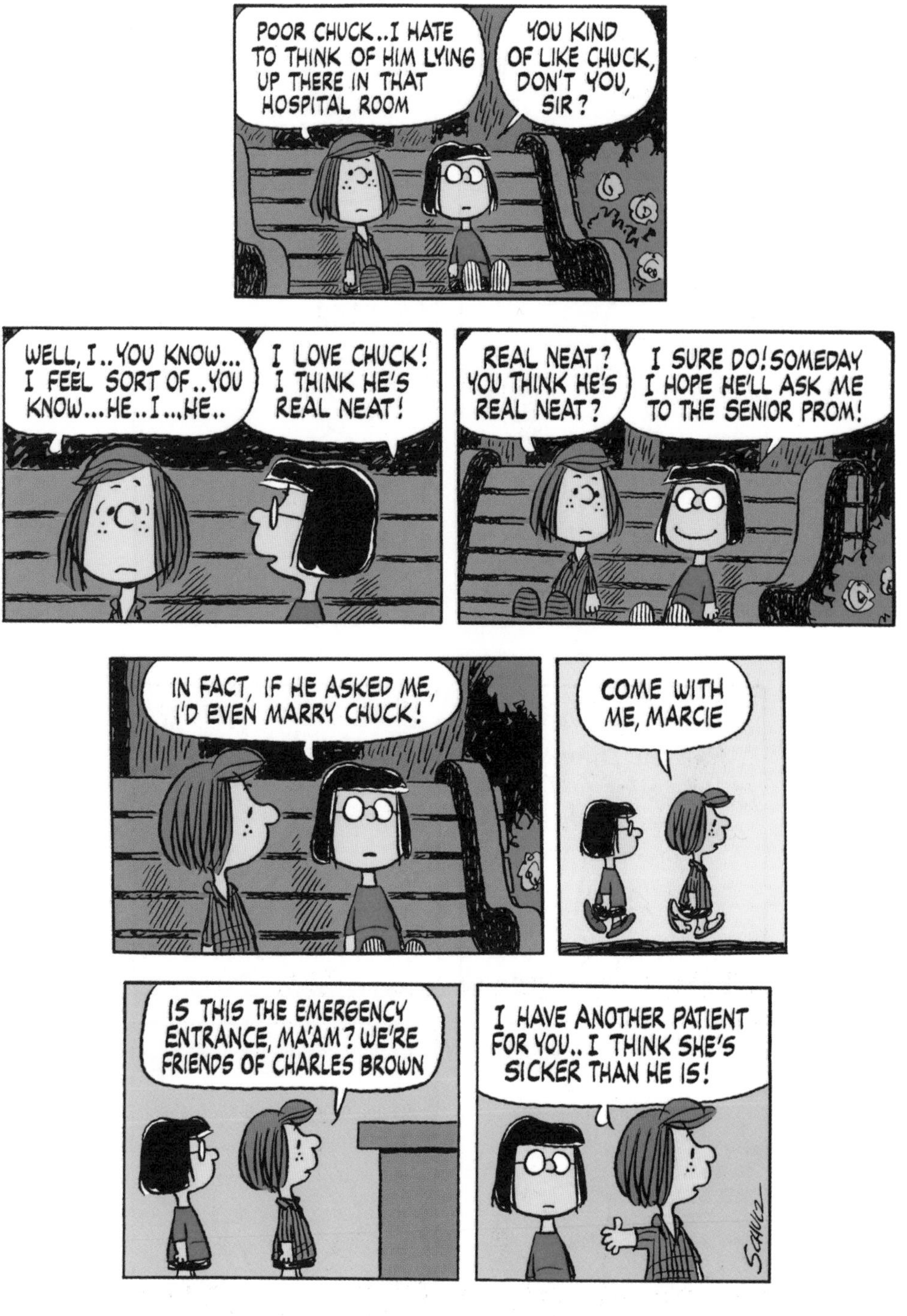
POOR CHUCK..I HATE TO THINK OF HIM LYING UP THERE IN THAT HOSPITAL ROOM
YOU KIND OF LIKE CHUCK, DON'T YOU, SIR?
WELL, I..YOU KNOW... I FEEL SORT OF..YOU KNOW...HE..I...HE..
I LOVE CHUCK! I THINK HE'S REAL NEAT!
REAL NEAT? YOU THINK HE'S REAL NEAT?
I SURE DO! SOMEDAY I HOPE HE'LL ASK ME TO THE SENIOR PROM!
IN FACT, IF HE ASKED ME, I'D EVEN MARRY CHUCK!
COME WITH ME, MARCIE
IS THIS THE EMERGENCY ENTRANCE, MA'AM? WE'RE FRIENDS OF CHARLES BROWN
I HAVE ANOTHER PATIENT FOR YOU.. I THINK SHE'S SICKER THAN HE IS!
SCHULZ

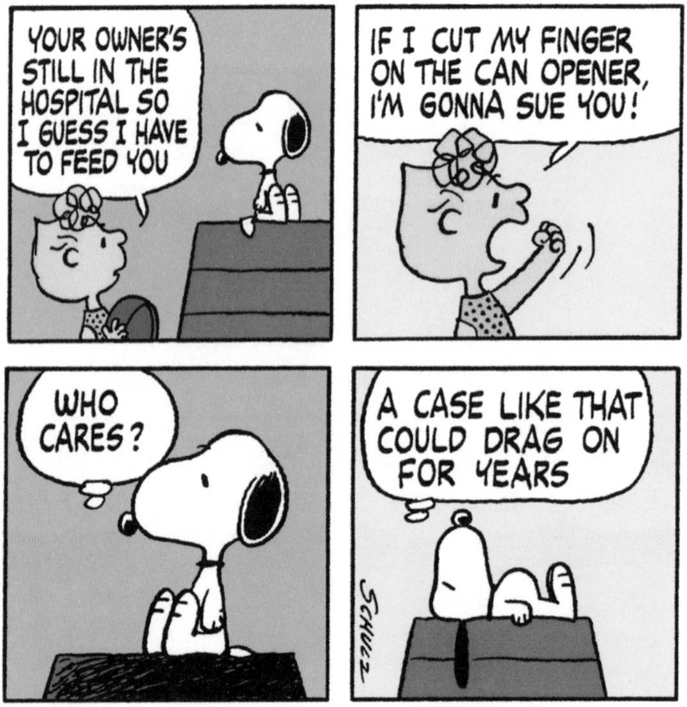
YOUR OWNER'S STILL IN THE HOSPITAL SO I GUESS I HAVE TO FEED YOU
IF I CUT MY FINGER ON THE CAN OPENER, I'M GONNA SUE YOU!
WHO CARES?
A CASE LIKE THAT COULD DRAG ON FOR YEARS
SCHULZ

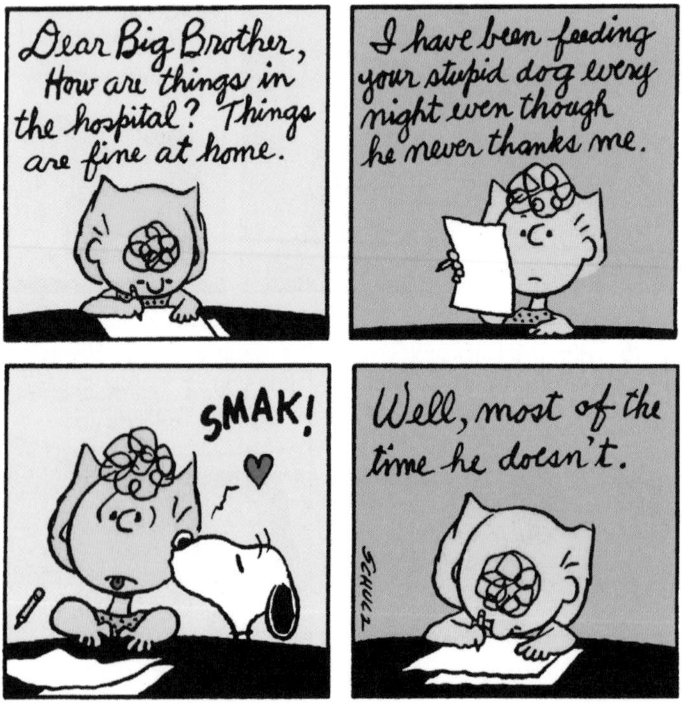
Dear Big Brother,
How are things in the hospital? Things are fine at home.
I have been feeding your stupid dog every night even though he never thanks me.
SMAK!
Well, most of the time he doesn't.
SCHULZ

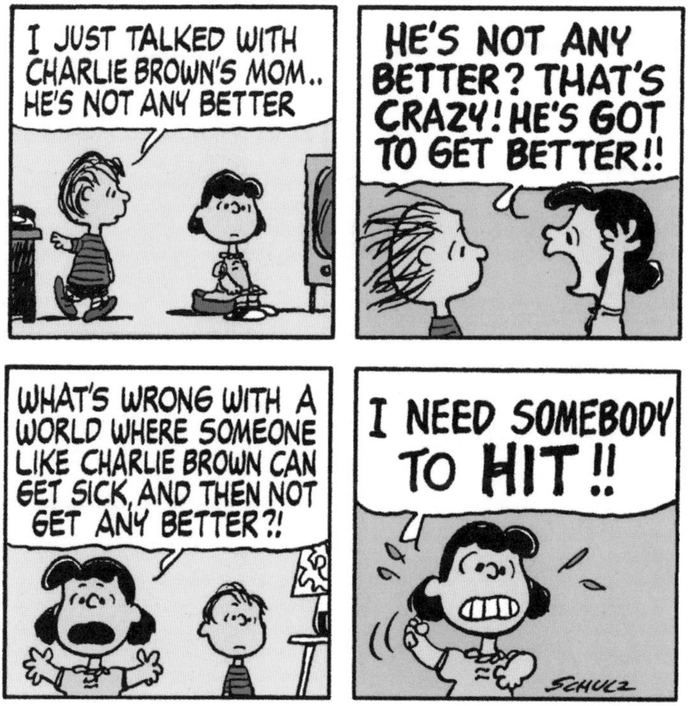
I JUST TALKED WITH CHARLIE BROWN'S MOM.. HE'S NOT ANY BETTER
HE'S NOT ANY BETTER? THAT'S CRAZY! HE'S GOT TO GET BETTER!!
WHAT'S WRONG WITH A WORLD WHERE SOMEONE LIKE CHARLIE BROWN CAN GET SICK, AND THEN NOT GET ANY BETTER?!
I NEED SOMEBODY TO HIT!!
SCHULZ

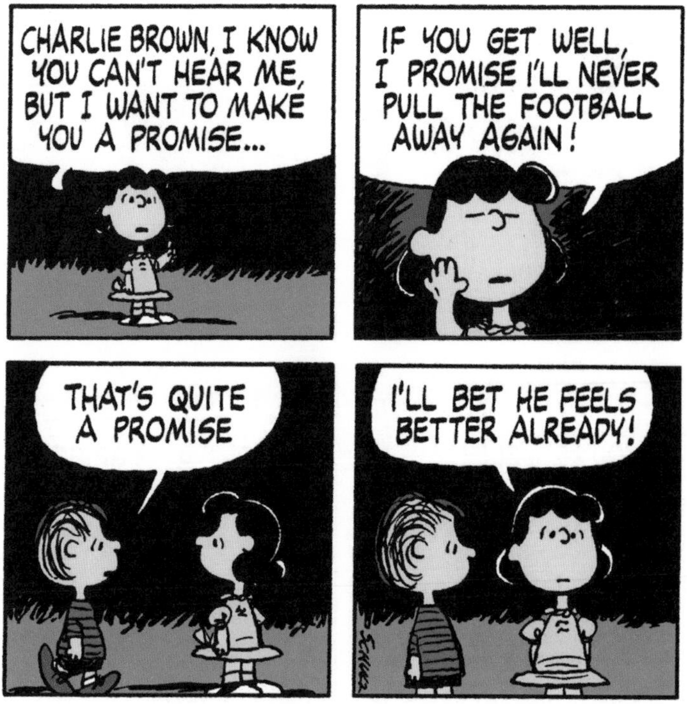
CHARLIE BROWN, I KNOW YOU CAN'T HEAR ME, BUT I WANT TO MAKE YOU A PROMISE...
IF YOU GET WELL, I PROMISE I'LL NEVER PULL THE FOOTBALL AWAY AGAIN!
THAT'S QUITE A PROMISE
I'LL BET HE FEELS BETTER ALREADY!

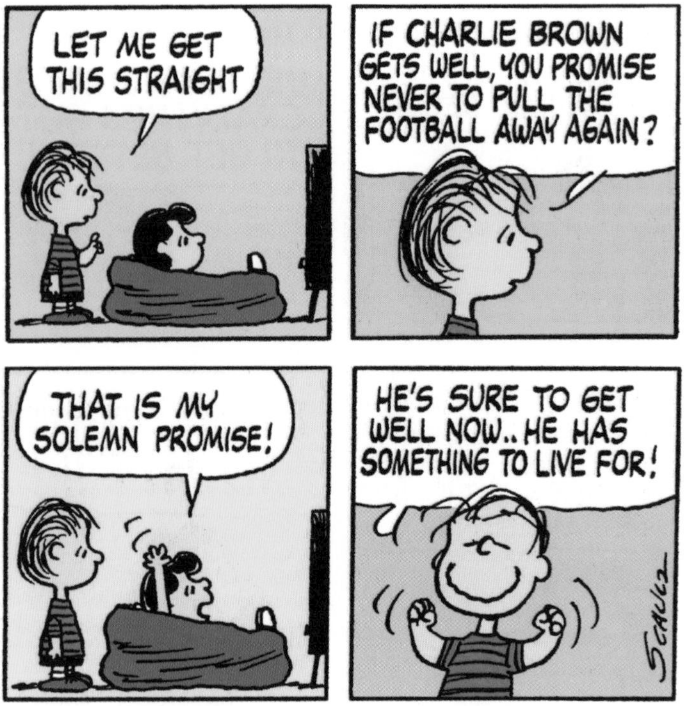
LET ME GET THIS STRAIGHT
IF CHARLIE BROWN GETS WELL, YOU PROMISE NEVER TO PULL THE FOOTBALL AWAY AGAIN?
THAT IS MY SOLEMN PROMISE!
HE'S SURE TO GET WELL NOW.. HE HAS SOMETHING TO LIVE FOR!
SCHULZ

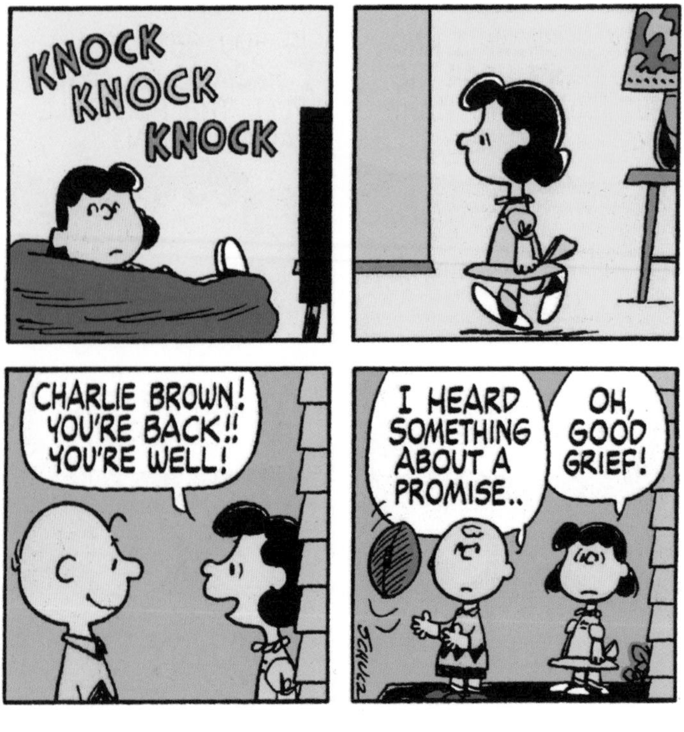
KNOCK KNOCK KNOCK
CHARLIE BROWN! YOU'RE BACK!! YOU'RE WELL!
I HEARD SOMETHING ABOUT A PROMISE..
OH, GOOD GRIEF!
SCHULZ

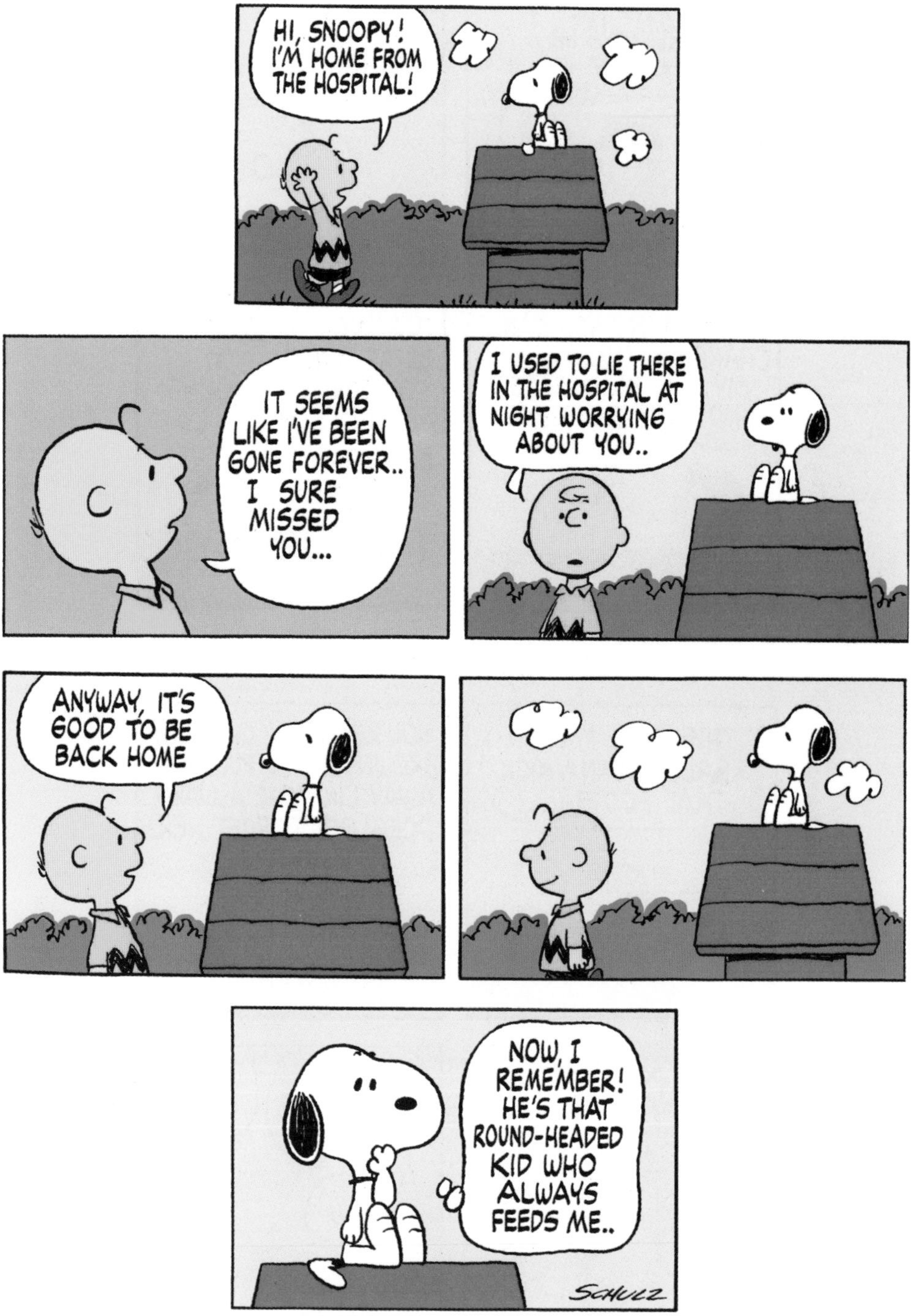
HI, SNOOPY! I'M HOME FROM THE HOSPITAL!
IT SEEMS LIKE I'VE BEEN GONE FOREVER.. I SURE MISSED YOU...
I USED TO LIE THERE IN THE HOSPITAL AT NIGHT WORRYING ABOUT YOU..
ANYWAY, IT'S GOOD TO BE BACK HOME
NOW, I REMEMBER! HE'S THAT ROUND-HEADED KID WHO ALWAYS FEEDS ME..
SCHULZ

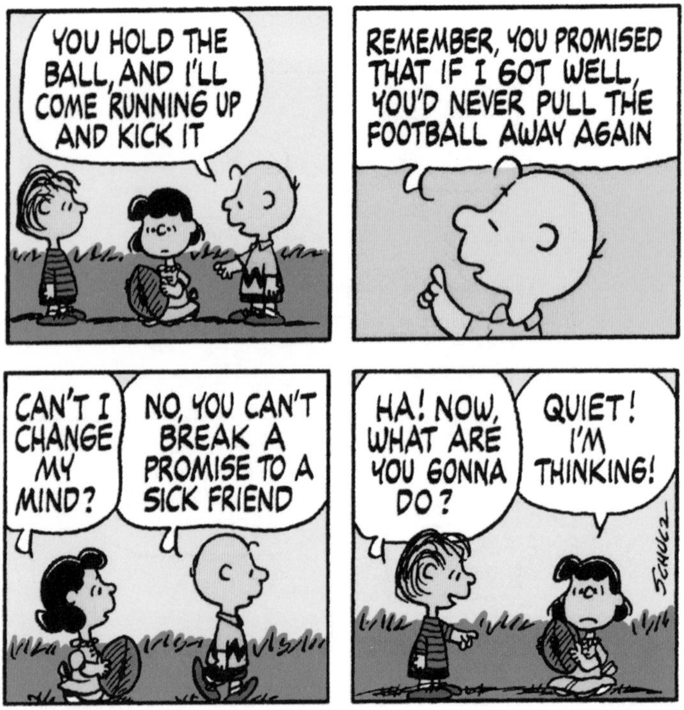
YOU HOLD THE BALL, AND I'LL COME RUNNING UP AND KICK IT
REMEMBER, YOU PROMISED THAT IF I GOT WELL, YOU'D NEVER PULL THE FOOTBALL AWAY AGAIN
CAN'T I CHANGE MY MIND?
NO, YOU CAN'T BREAK A PROMISE TO A SICK FRIEND
HA! NOW, WHAT ARE YOU GONNA DO?
QUIET! I'M THINKING!
SCHULZ

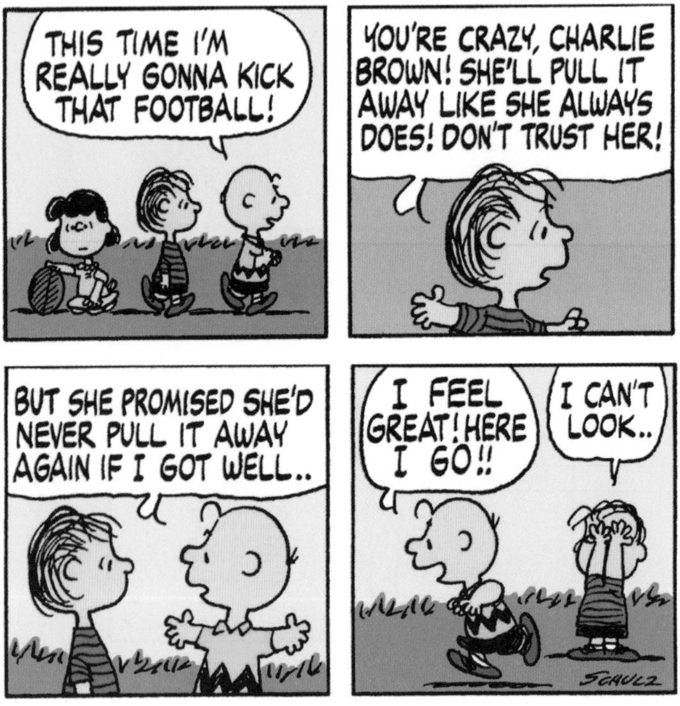
THIS TIME I'M REALLY GONNA KICK THAT FOOTBALL!
YOU'RE CRAZY, CHARLIE BROWN! SHE'LL PULL IT AWAY LIKE SHE ALWAYS DOES! DON'T TRUST HER!
BUT SHE PROMISED SHE'D NEVER PULL IT AWAY AGAIN IF I GOT WELL..
I FEEL GREAT! HERE I GO!!
I CAN'T LOOK..
SCHULZ

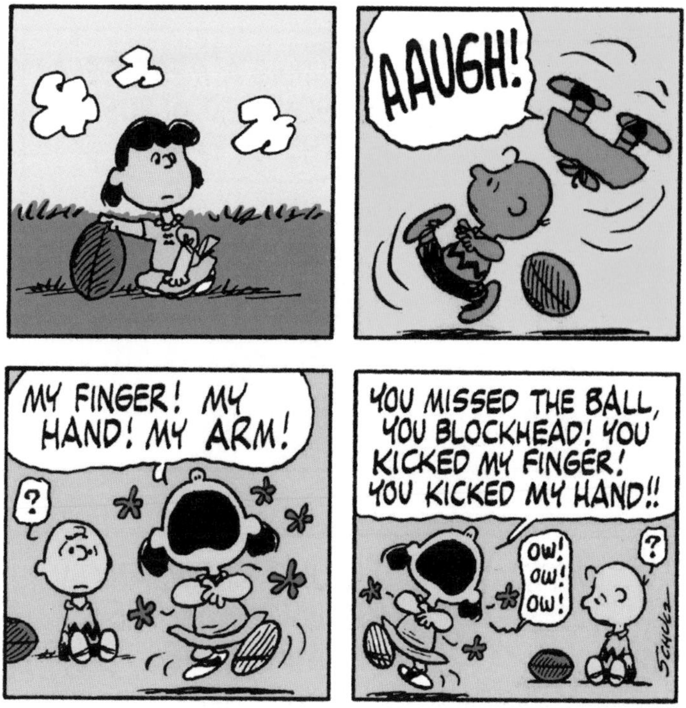
AAUGH!
MY FINGER! MY HAND! MY ARM!
?
YOU MISSED THE BALL, YOU BLOCKHEAD! YOU KICKED MY FINGER! YOU KICKED MY HAND!!
OW! OW! OW!
?
SCHULZ

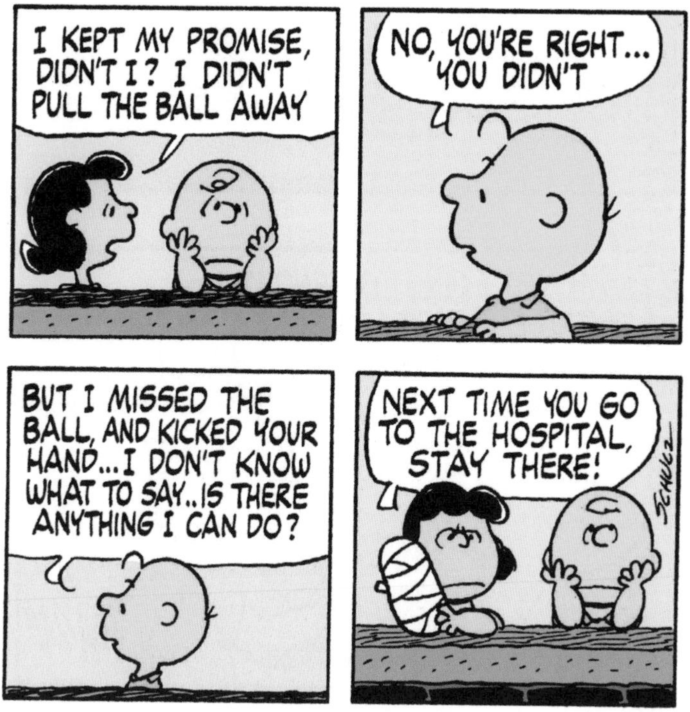
I KEPT MY PROMISE, DIDN'T I? I DIDN'T PULL THE BALL AWAY
NO, YOU'RE RIGHT... YOU DIDN'T
BUT I MISSED THE BALL, AND KICKED YOUR HAND...I DON'T KNOW WHAT TO SAY..IS THERE ANYTHING I CAN DO?
NEXT TIME YOU GO TO THE HOSPITAL, STAY THERE!
SCHULZ

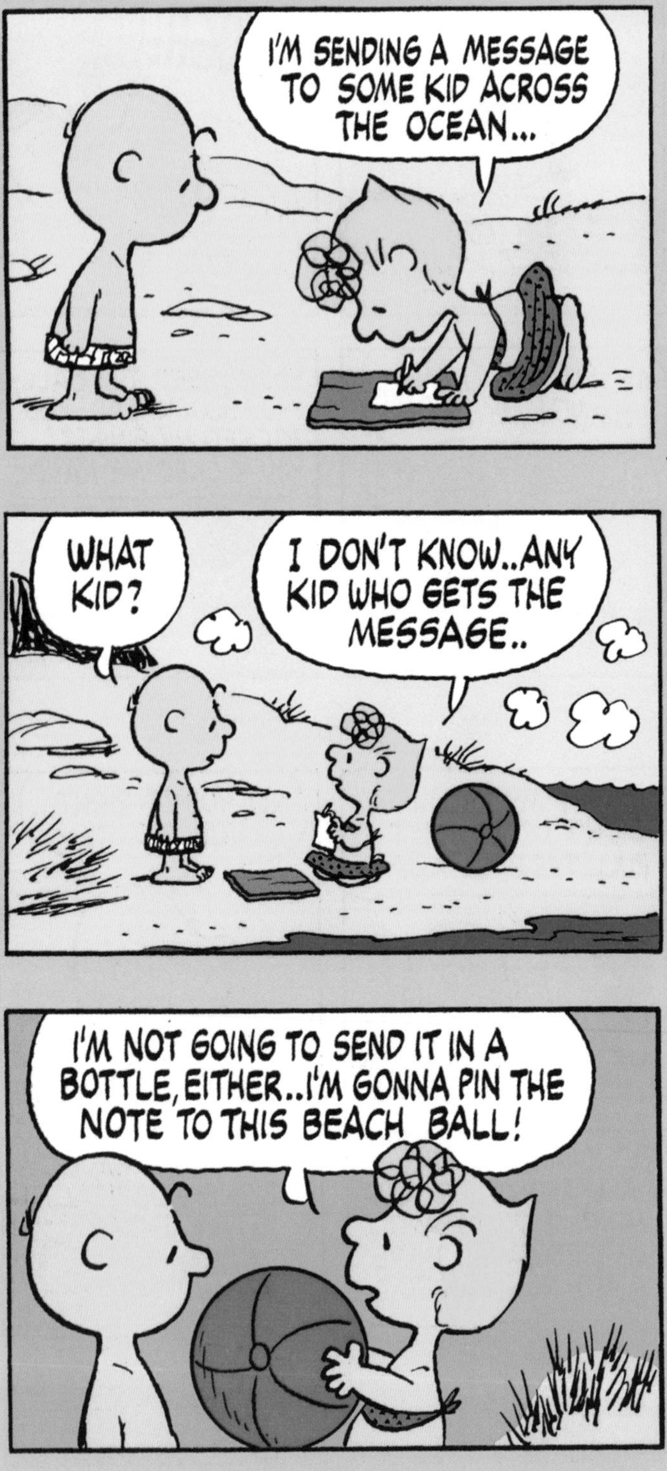
I'M SENDING A MESSAGE TO SOME KID ACROSS THE OCEAN...
WHAT KID?
I DON'T KNOW..ANY KID WHO GETS THE MESSAGE..
I'M NOT GOING TO SEND IT IN A BOTTLE, EITHER..I'M GONNA PIN THE NOTE TO THIS BEACH BALL!

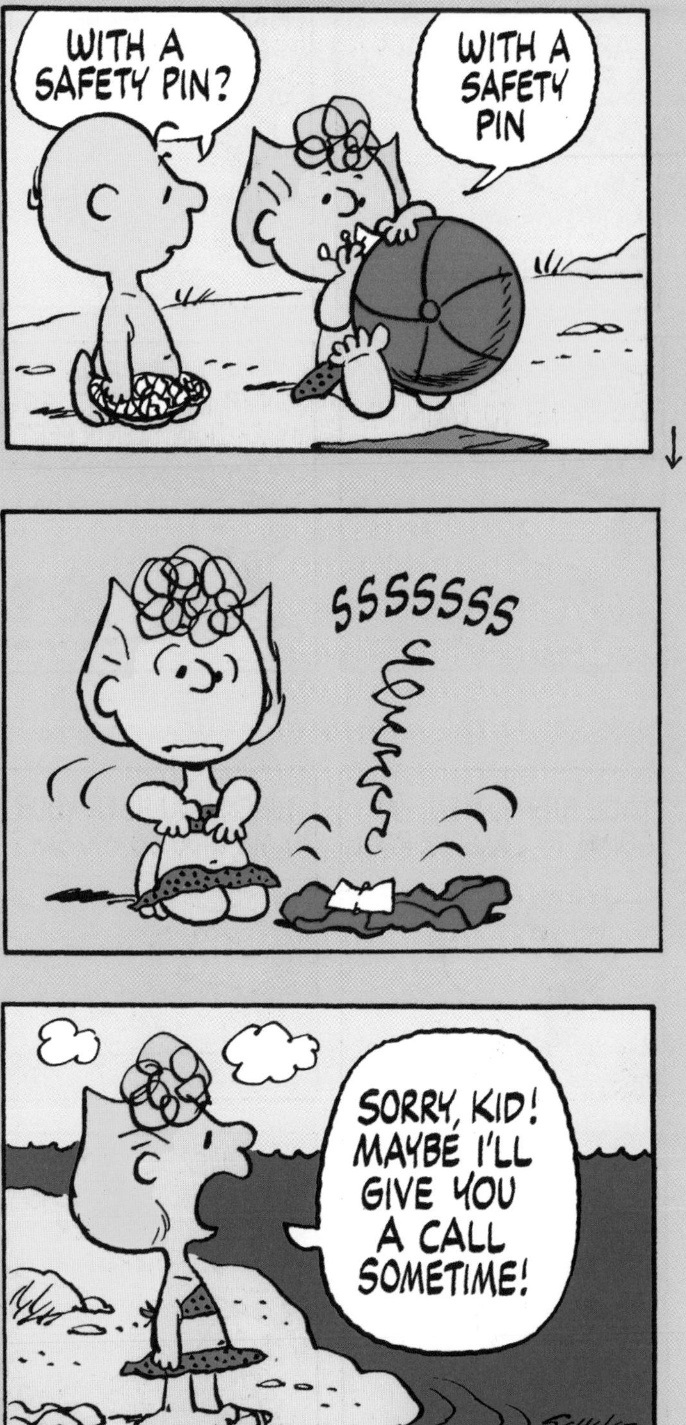
WITH A SAFETY PIN?
WITH A SAFETY PIN
SSSSSSS
SORRY, KID! MAYBE I'LL GIVE YOU A CALL SOMETIME!
SCHULZ

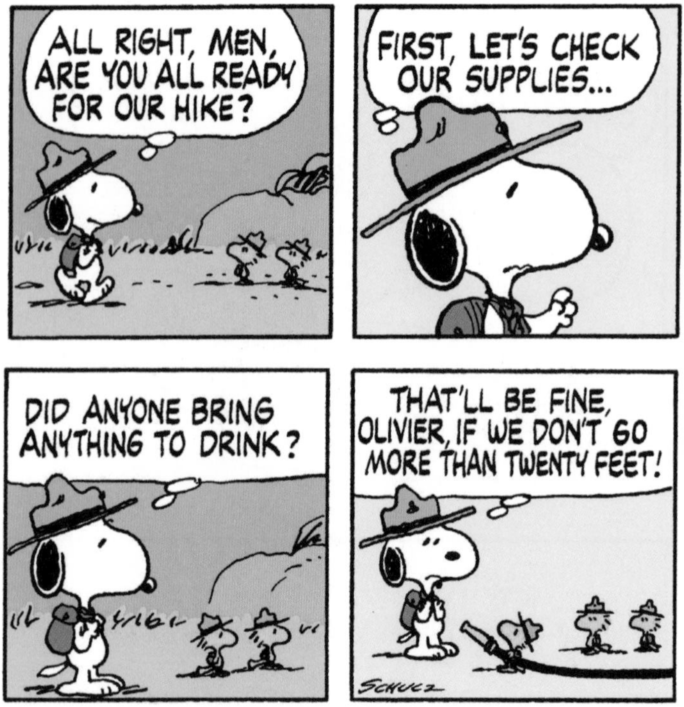
ALL RIGHT, MEN, ARE YOU ALL READY FOR OUR HIKE?
FIRST, LET'S CHECK OUR SUPPLIES...
DID ANYONE BRING ANYTHING TO DRINK?
THAT'LL BE FINE, OLIVIER, IF WE DON'T GO MORE THAN TWENTY FEET!
SCHULZ

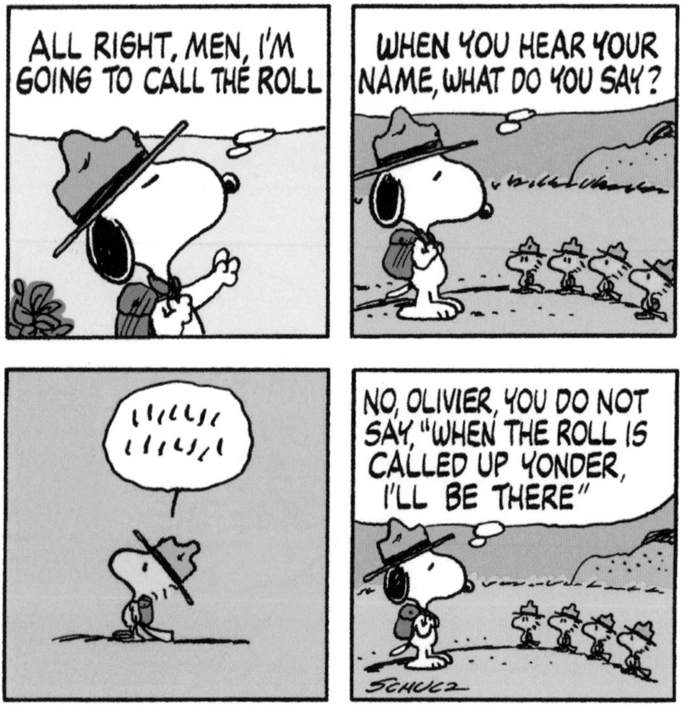
ALL RIGHT, MEN, I'M GOING TO CALL THE ROLL
WHEN YOU HEAR YOUR NAME, WHAT DO YOU SAY?
NO, OLIVIER, YOU DO NOT SAY, "WHEN THE ROLL IS CALLED UP YONDER, I'LL BE THERE"
SCHULZ

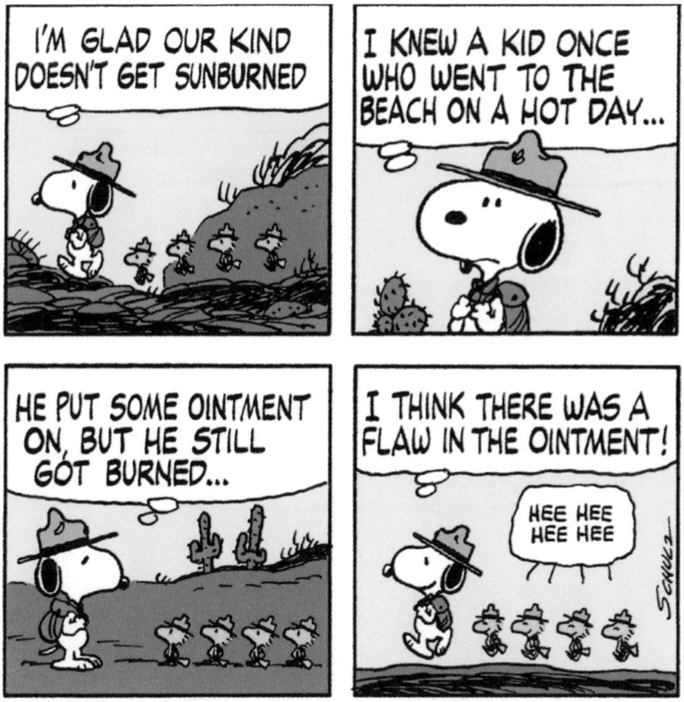
I'M GLAD OUR KIND DOESN'T GET SUNBURNED
I KNEW A KID ONCE WHO WENT TO THE BEACH ON A HOT DAY...
HE PUT SOME OINTMENT ON, BUT HE STILL GOT BURNED...
I THINK THERE WAS A FLAW IN THE OINTMENT!
HEE HEE HEE HEE
SCHULZ

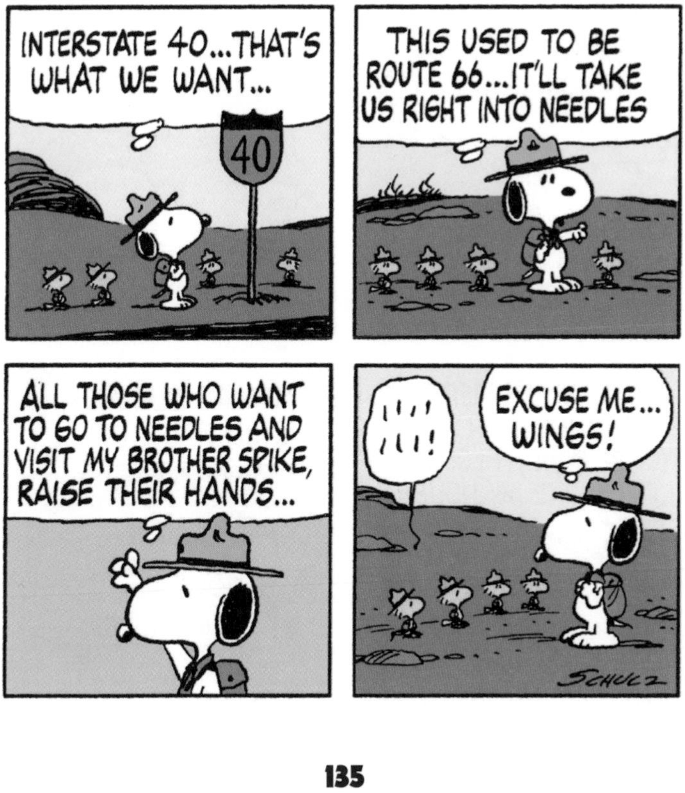
INTERSTATE 40...THAT'S WHAT WE WANT...
40
THIS USED TO BE ROUTE 66...IT'LL TAKE US RIGHT INTO NEEDLES
ALL THOSE WHO WANT TO GO TO NEEDLES AND VISIT MY BROTHER SPIKE, RAISE THEIR HANDS...
EXCUSE ME... WINGS!
SCHULZ

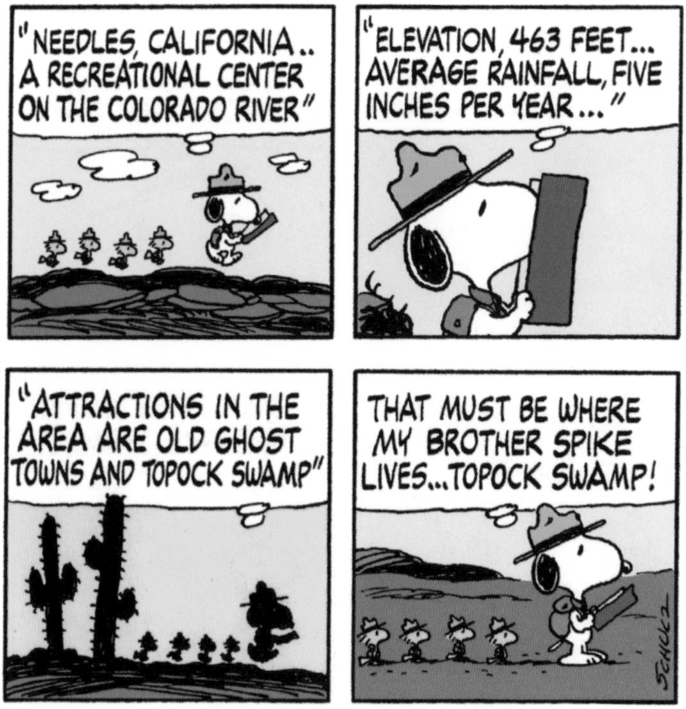
"NEEDLES, CALIFORNIA.. A RECREATIONAL CENTER ON THE COLORADO RIVER"
"ELEVATION, 463 FEET... AVERAGE RAINFALL, FIVE INCHES PER YEAR..."
"ATTRACTIONS IN THE AREA ARE OLD GHOST TOWNS AND TOPOCK SWAMP"
THAT MUST BE WHERE MY BROTHER SPIKE LIVES...TOPOCK SWAMP!

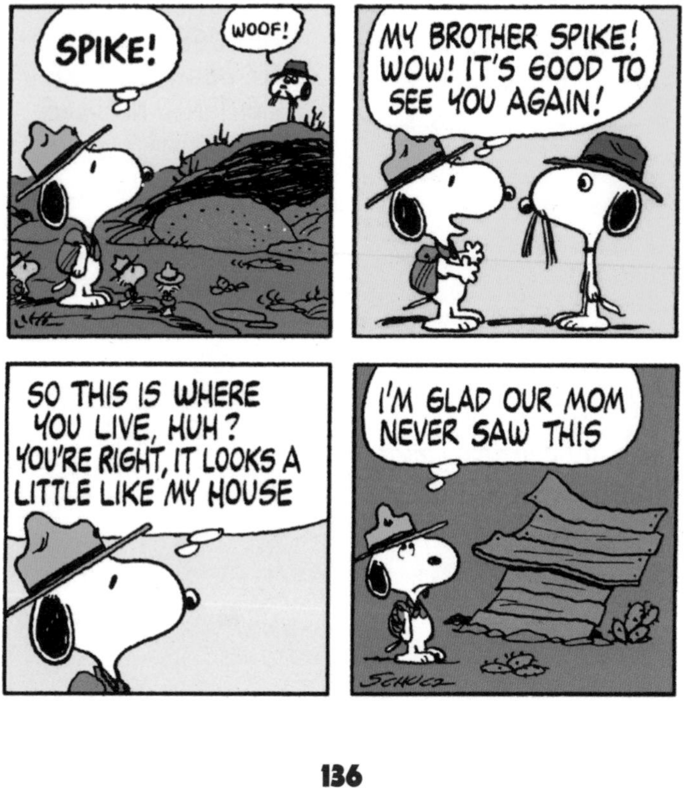
SPIKE!
WOOF!
MY BROTHER SPIKE! WOW! IT'S GOOD TO SEE YOU AGAIN!
SO THIS IS WHERE YOU LIVE, HUH? YOU'RE RIGHT, IT LOOKS A LITTLE LIKE MY HOUSE
I'M GLAD OUR MOM NEVER SAW THIS

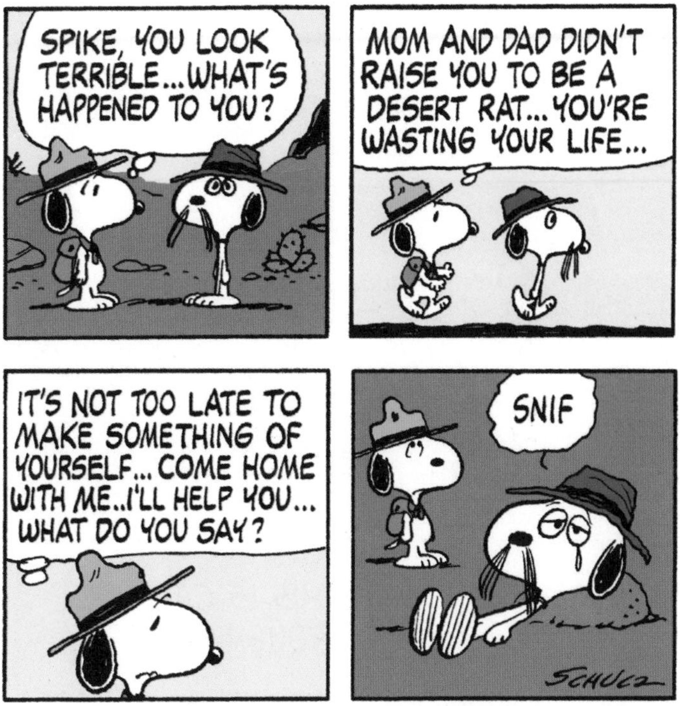
SPIKE, YOU LOOK TERRIBLE...WHAT'S HAPPENED TO YOU?
MOM AND DAD DIDN'T RAISE YOU TO BE A DESERT RAT...YOU'RE WASTING YOUR LIFE...
IT'S NOT TOO LATE TO MAKE SOMETHING OF YOURSELF...COME HOME WITH ME..I'LL HELP YOU... WHAT DO YOU SAY?
SNIF
SCHULZ

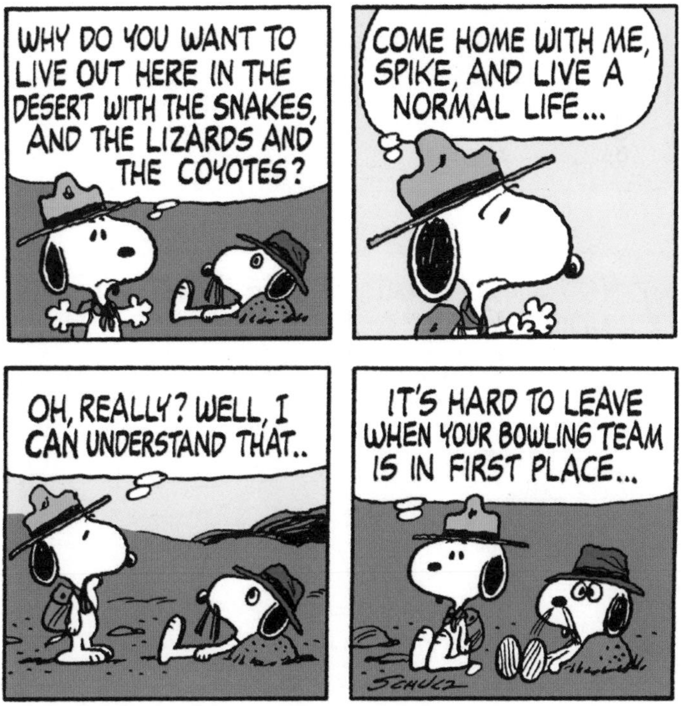
WHY DO YOU WANT TO LIVE OUT HERE IN THE DESERT WITH THE SNAKES, AND THE LIZARDS AND THE COYOTES?
COME HOME WITH ME, SPIKE, AND LIVE A NORMAL LIFE...
OH, REALLY? WELL, I CAN UNDERSTAND THAT..
IT'S HARD TO LEAVE WHEN YOUR BOWLING TEAM IS IN FIRST PLACE...
SCHULZ

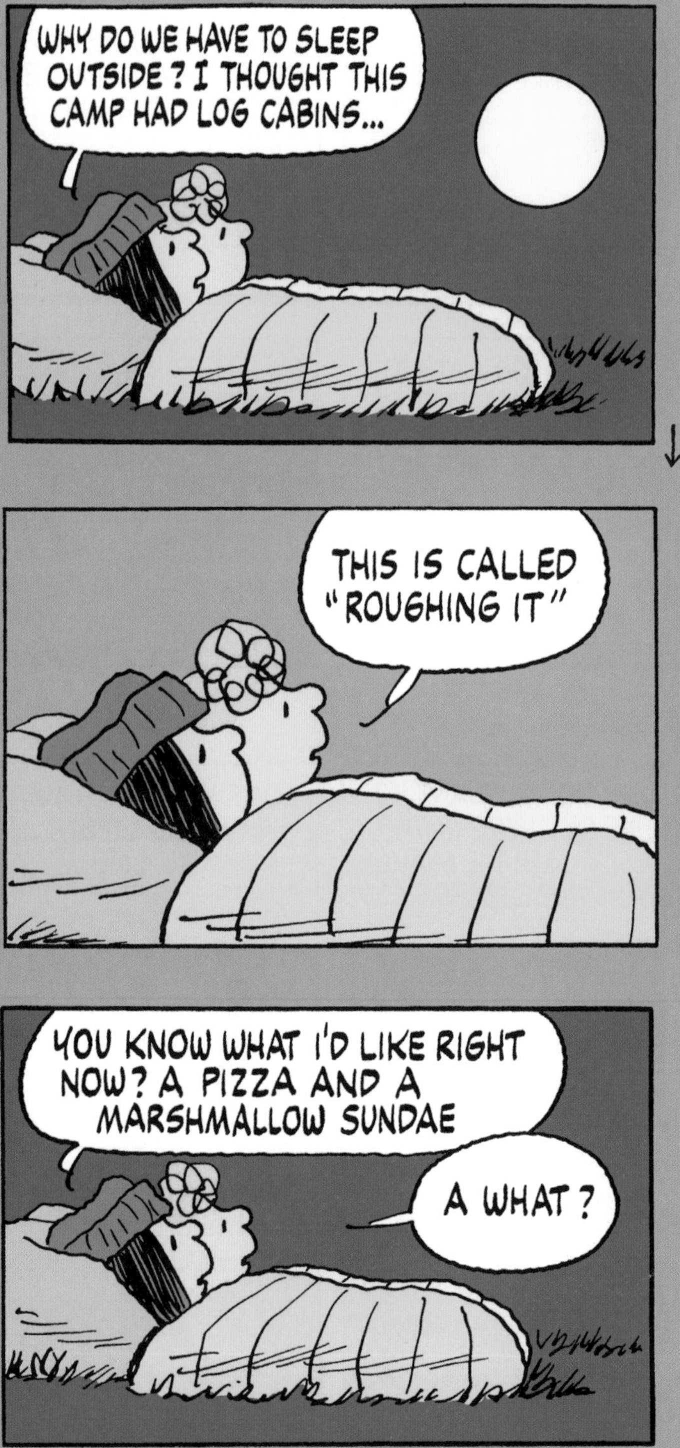
WHY DO WE HAVE TO SLEEP OUTSIDE? I THOUGHT THIS CAMP HAD LOG CABINS...
THIS IS CALLED "ROUGHING IT"
YOU KNOW WHAT I'D LIKE RIGHT NOW? A PIZZA AND A MARSHMALLOW SUNDAE
A WHAT?

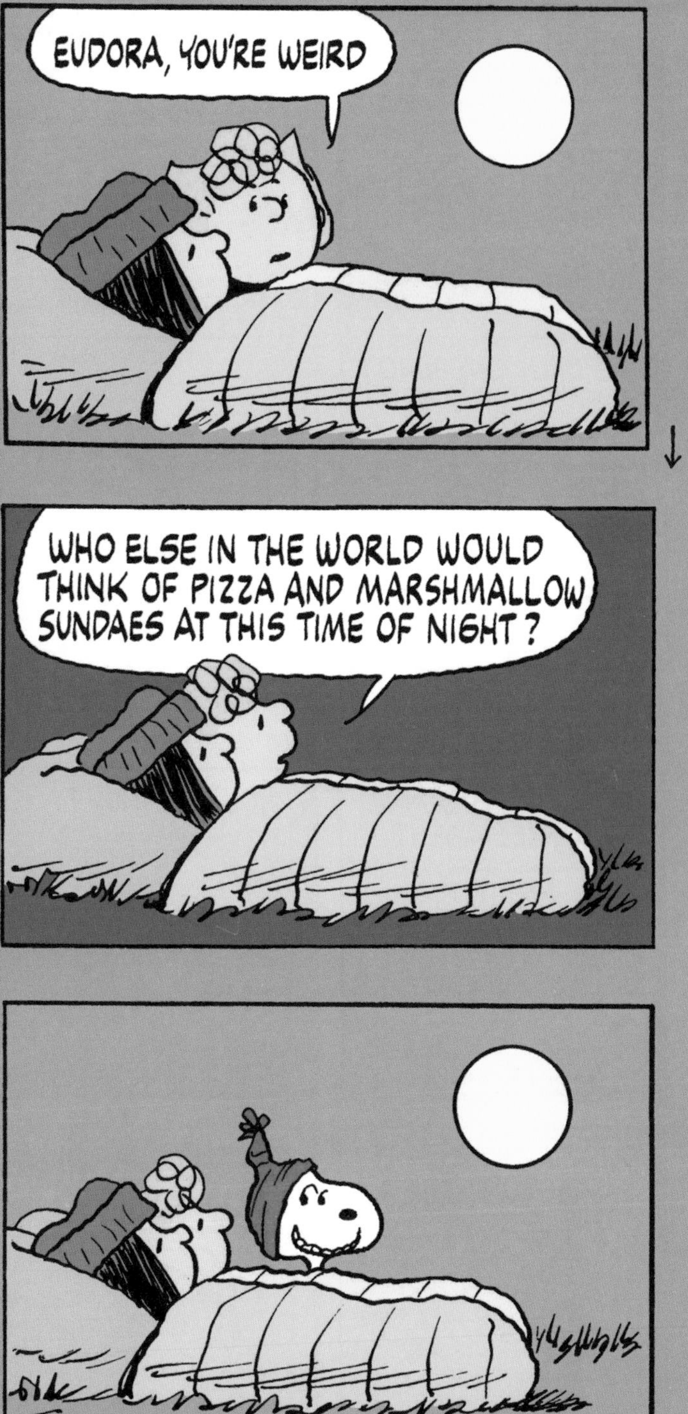
EUDORA, YOU'RE WEIRD
WHO ELSE IN THE WORLD WOULD THINK OF PIZZA AND MARSHMALLOW SUNDAES AT THIS TIME OF NIGHT?
SCHULZ

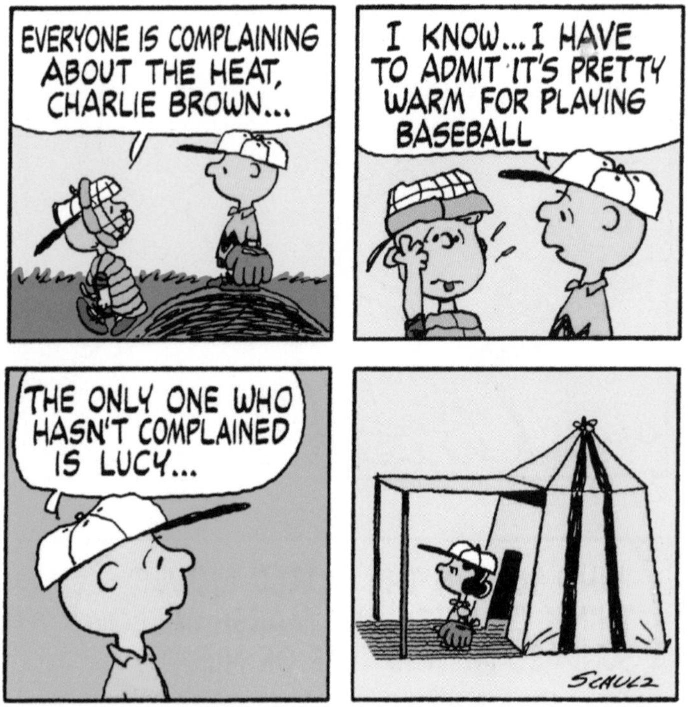
EVERYONE IS COMPLAINING ABOUT THE HEAT, CHARLIE BROWN...
I KNOW... I HAVE TO ADMIT IT'S PRETTY WARM FOR PLAYING BASEBALL
THE ONLY ONE WHO HASN'T COMPLAINED IS LUCY...

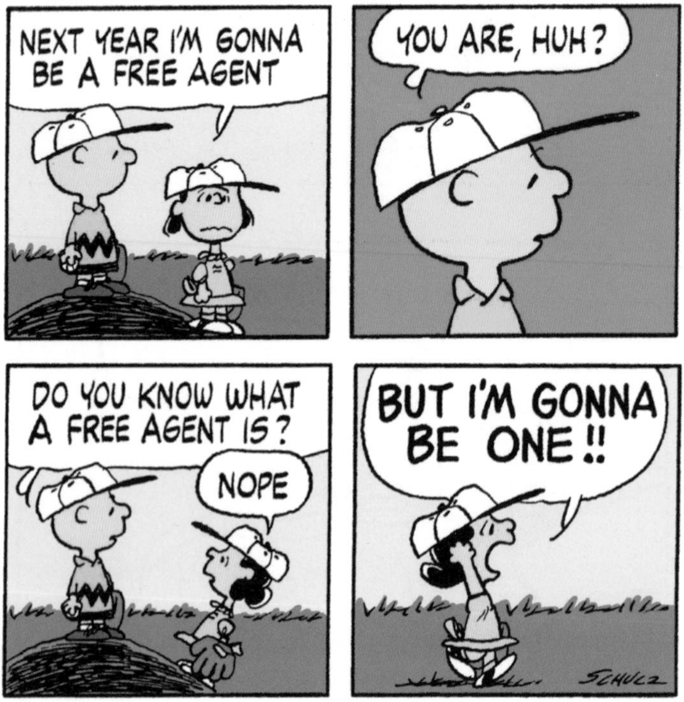
NEXT YEAR I'M GONNA BE A FREE AGENT
YOU ARE, HUH?
DO YOU KNOW WHAT A FREE AGENT IS?
NOPE
BUT I'M GONNA BE ONE!!

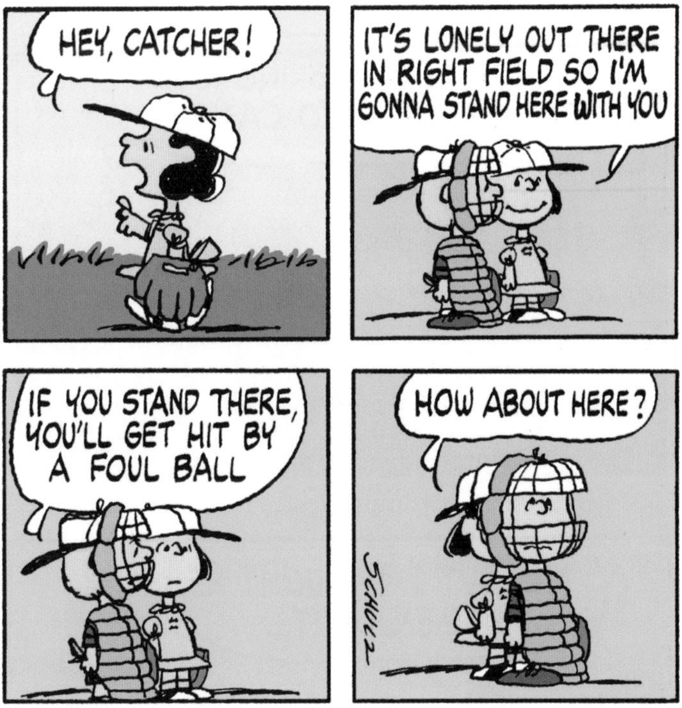
HEY, CATCHER!
IT'S LONELY OUT THERE IN RIGHT FIELD SO I'M GONNA STAND HERE WITH YOU
IF YOU STAND THERE, YOU'LL GET HIT BY A FOUL BALL
HOW ABOUT HERE?
SCHULZ

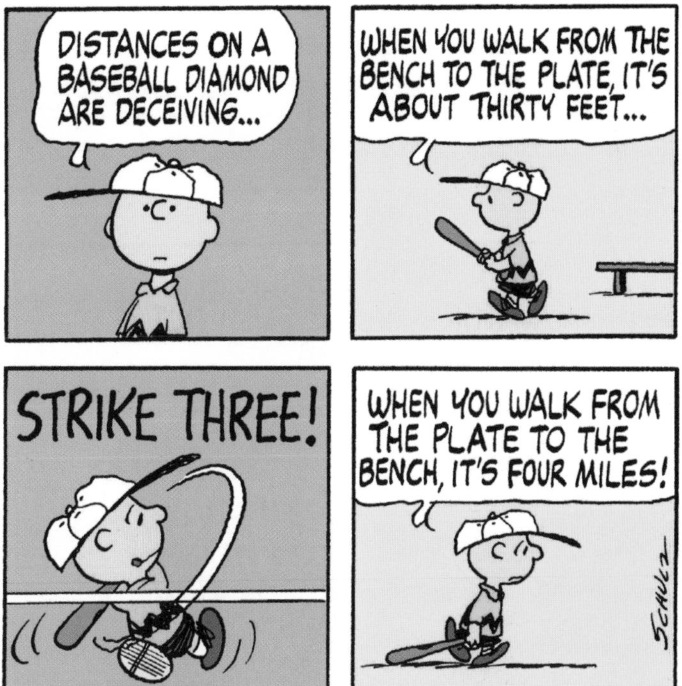
DISTANCES ON A BASEBALL DIAMOND ARE DECEIVING...
WHEN YOU WALK FROM THE BENCH TO THE PLATE, IT'S ABOUT THIRTY FEET...
STRIKE THREE!
WHEN YOU WALK FROM THE PLATE TO THE BENCH, IT'S FOUR MILES!
SCHULZ

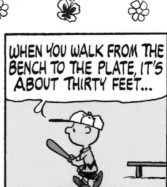

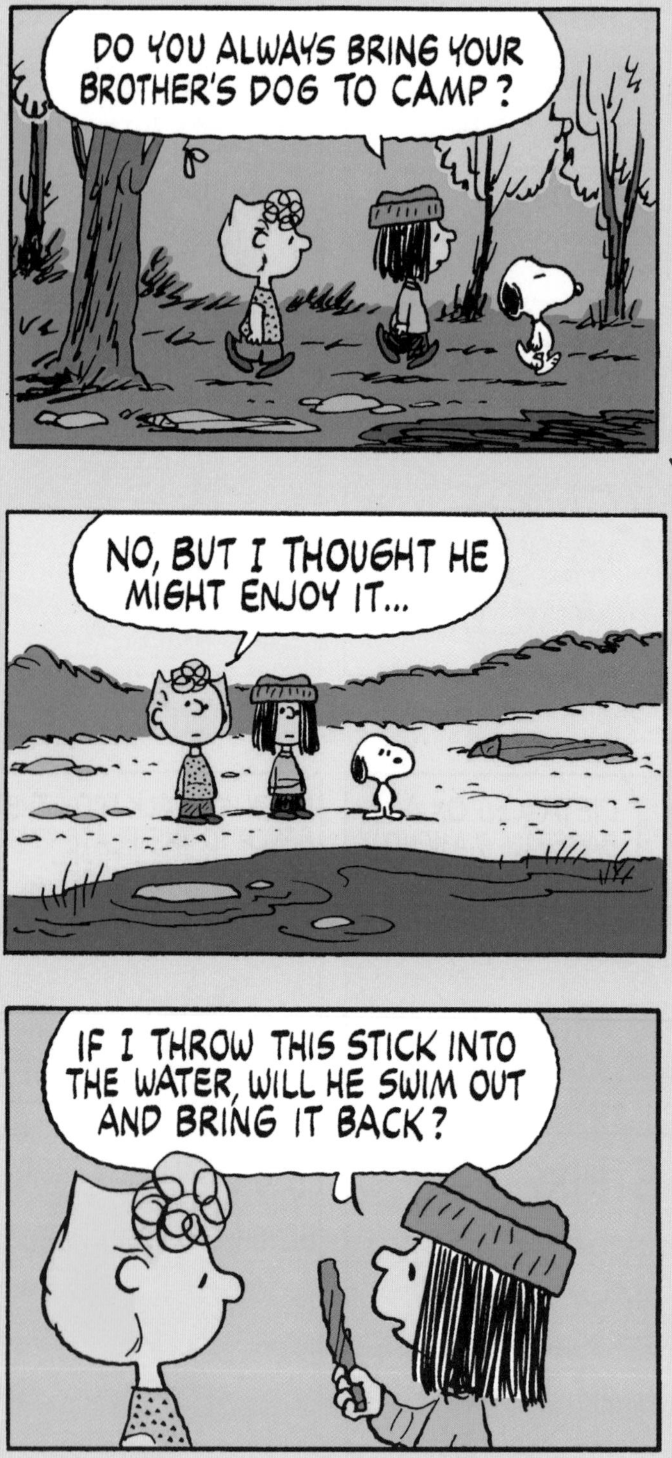
DO YOU ALWAYS BRING YOUR BROTHER'S DOG TO CAMP?
NO, BUT I THOUGHT HE MIGHT ENJOY IT...
IF I THROW THIS STICK INTO THE WATER, WILL HE SWIM OUT AND BRING IT BACK?

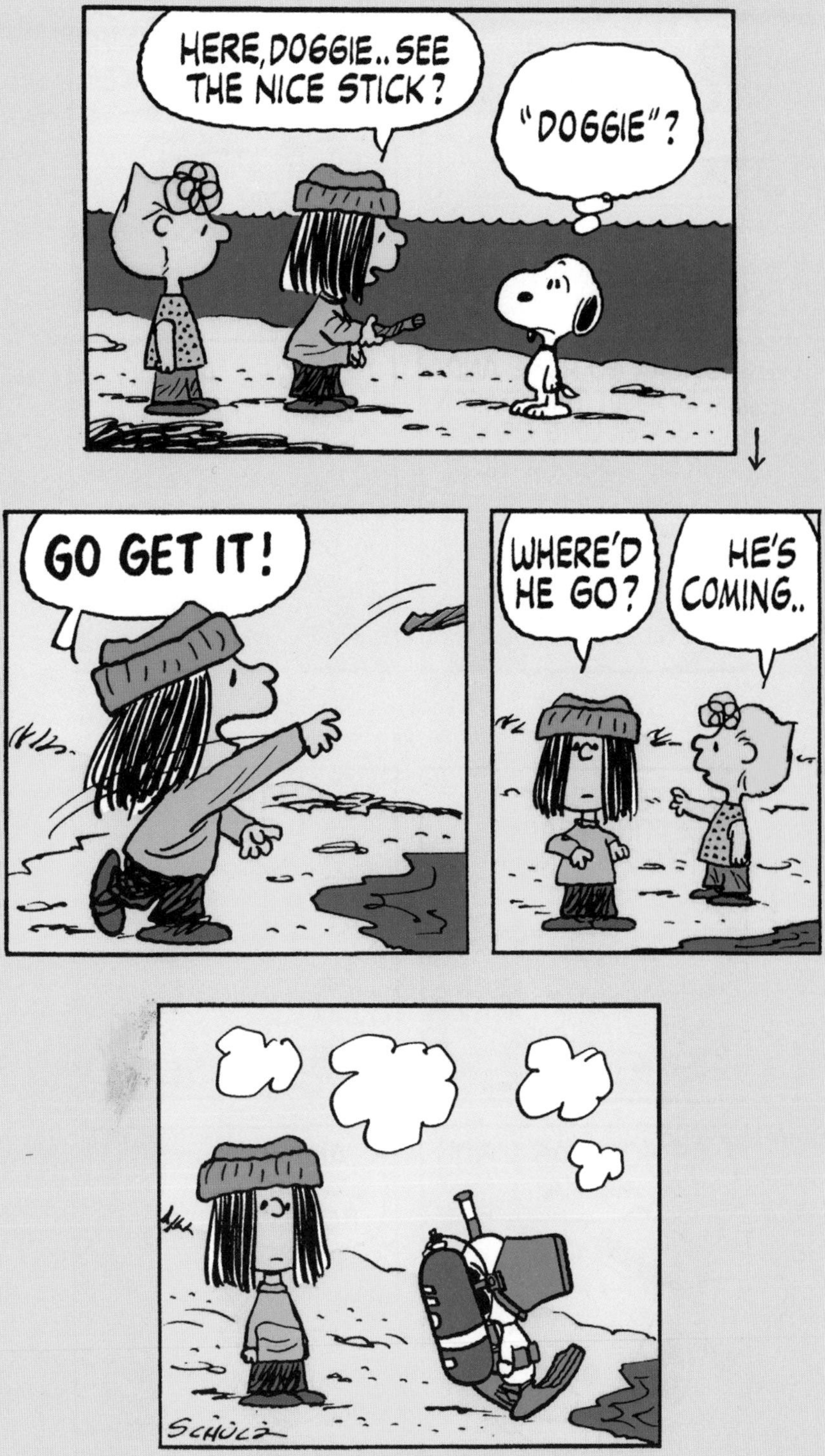
HERE, DOGGIE.. SEE THE NICE STICK?
"DOGGIE"?
GO GET IT!
WHERE'D HE GO?
HE'S COMING..
SCHULZ

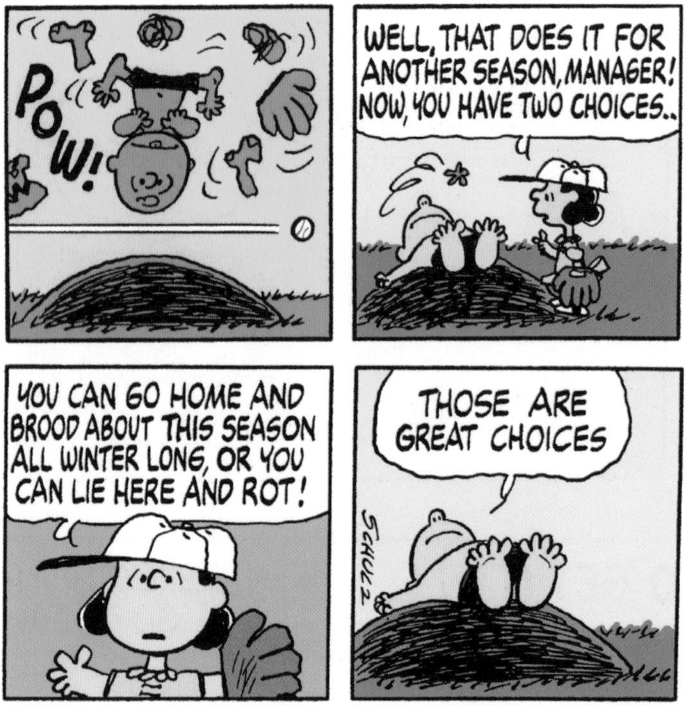
POW!
WELL, THAT DOES IT FOR ANOTHER SEASON, MANAGER! NOW, YOU HAVE TWO CHOICES..
YOU CAN GO HOME AND BROOD ABOUT THIS SEASON ALL WINTER LONG, OR YOU CAN LIE HERE AND ROT!
THOSE ARE GREAT CHOICES
SCHULZ

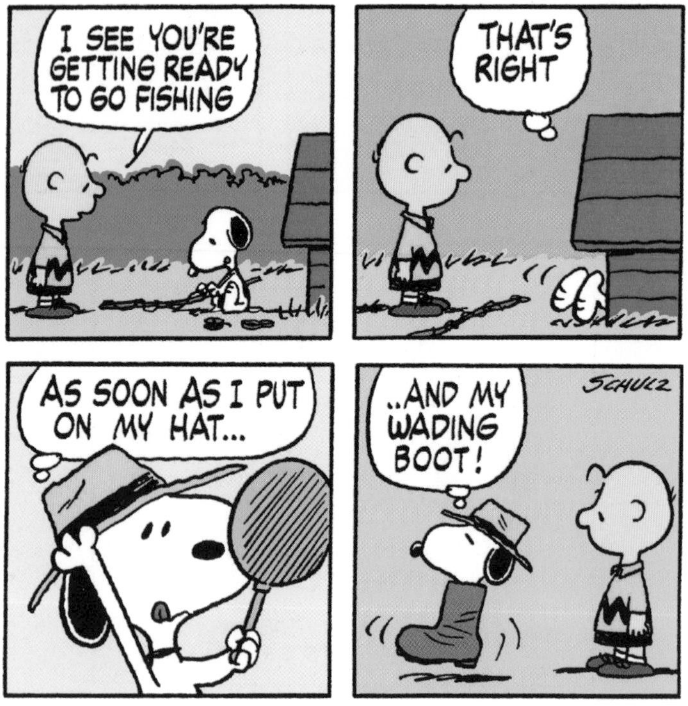
I SEE YOU'RE GETTING READY TO GO FISHING
THAT'S RIGHT
AS SOON AS I PUT ON MY HAT...
..AND MY WADING BOOT!
SCHULZ

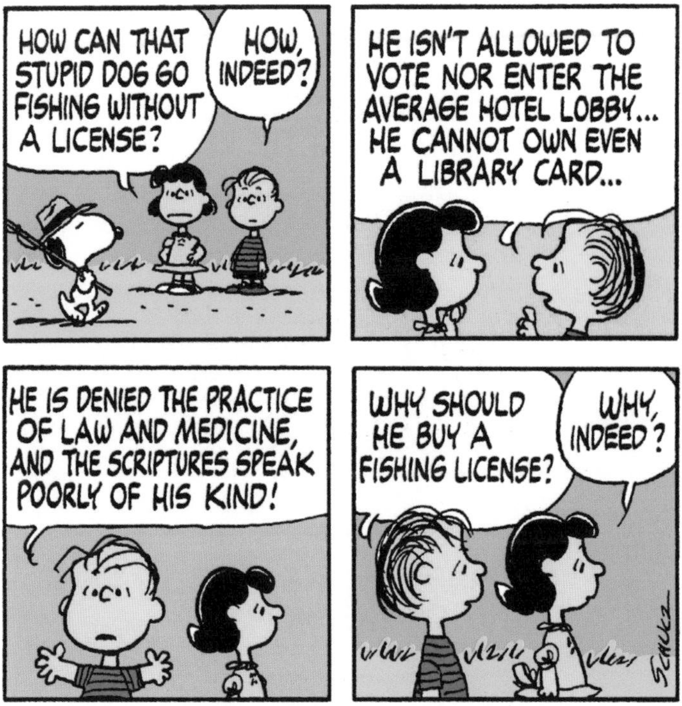
HOW CAN THAT STUPID DOG GO FISHING WITHOUT A LICENSE?
HOW, INDEED?
HE ISN'T ALLOWED TO VOTE NOR ENTER THE AVERAGE HOTEL LOBBY... HE CANNOT OWN EVEN A LIBRARY CARD...
HE IS DENIED THE PRACTICE OF LAW AND MEDICINE, AND THE SCRIPTURES SPEAK POORLY OF HIS KIND!
WHY SHOULD HE BUY A FISHING LICENSE?
WHY, INDEED?
SCHULZ

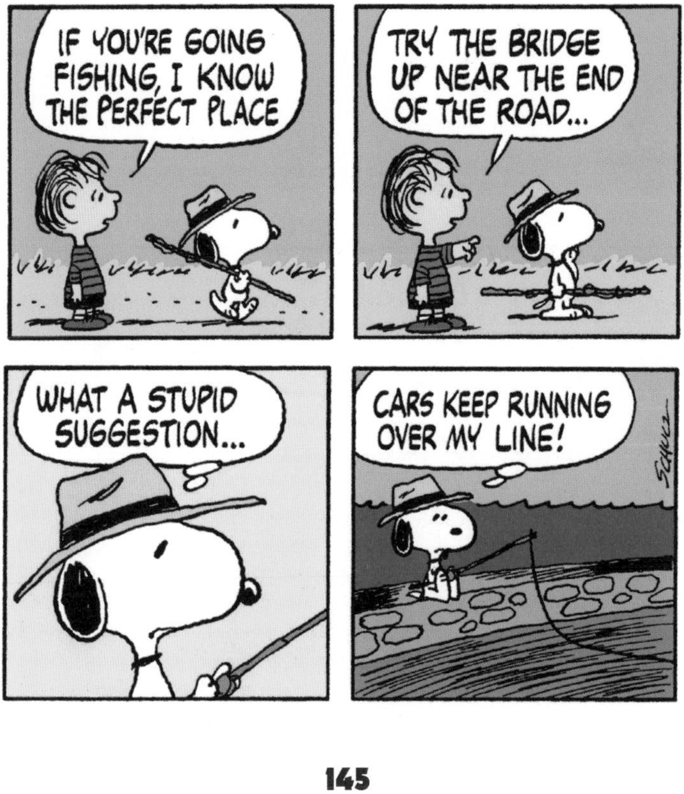
IF YOU'RE GOING FISHING, I KNOW THE PERFECT PLACE
TRY THE BRIDGE UP NEAR THE END OF THE ROAD...
WHAT A STUPID SUGGESTION...
CARS KEEP RUNNING OVER MY LINE!
SCHULZ

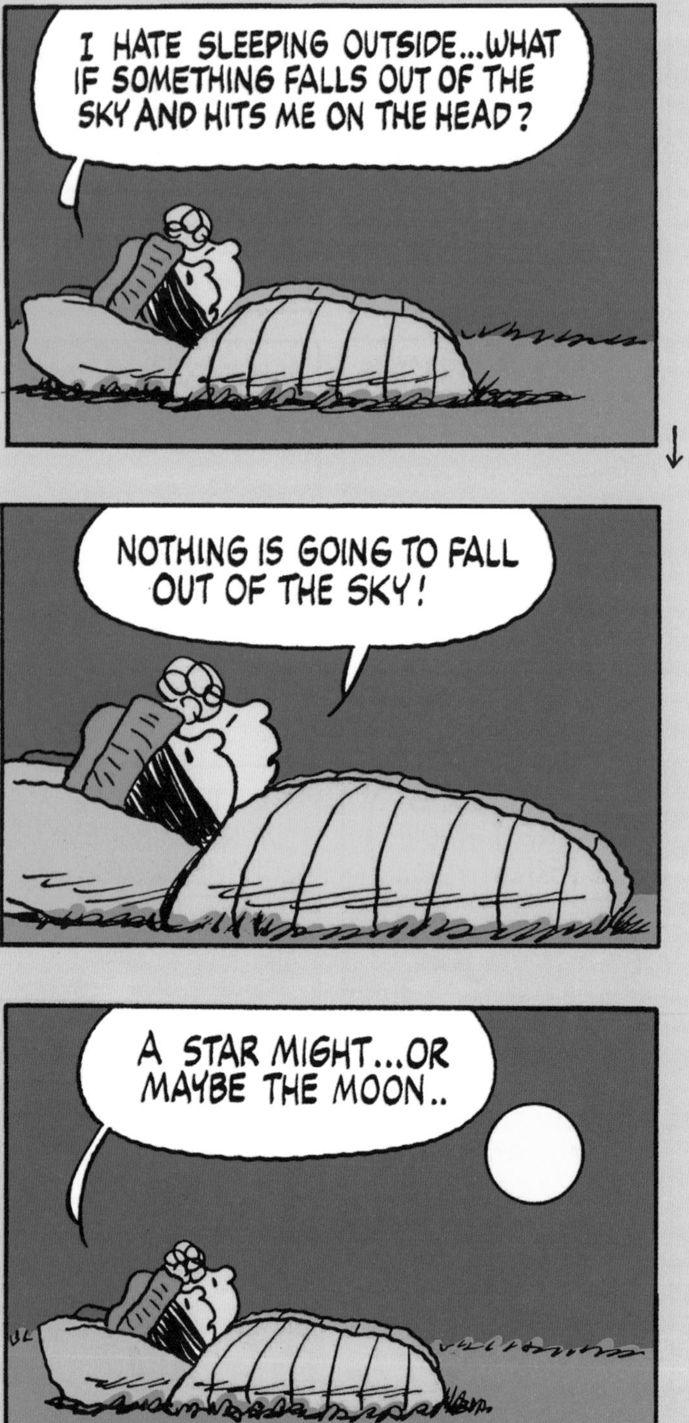
I HATE SLEEPING OUTSIDE...WHAT IF SOMETHING FALLS OUT OF THE SKY AND HITS ME ON THE HEAD?
NOTHING IS GOING TO FALL OUT OF THE SKY!
A STAR MIGHT...OR MAYBE THE MOON..

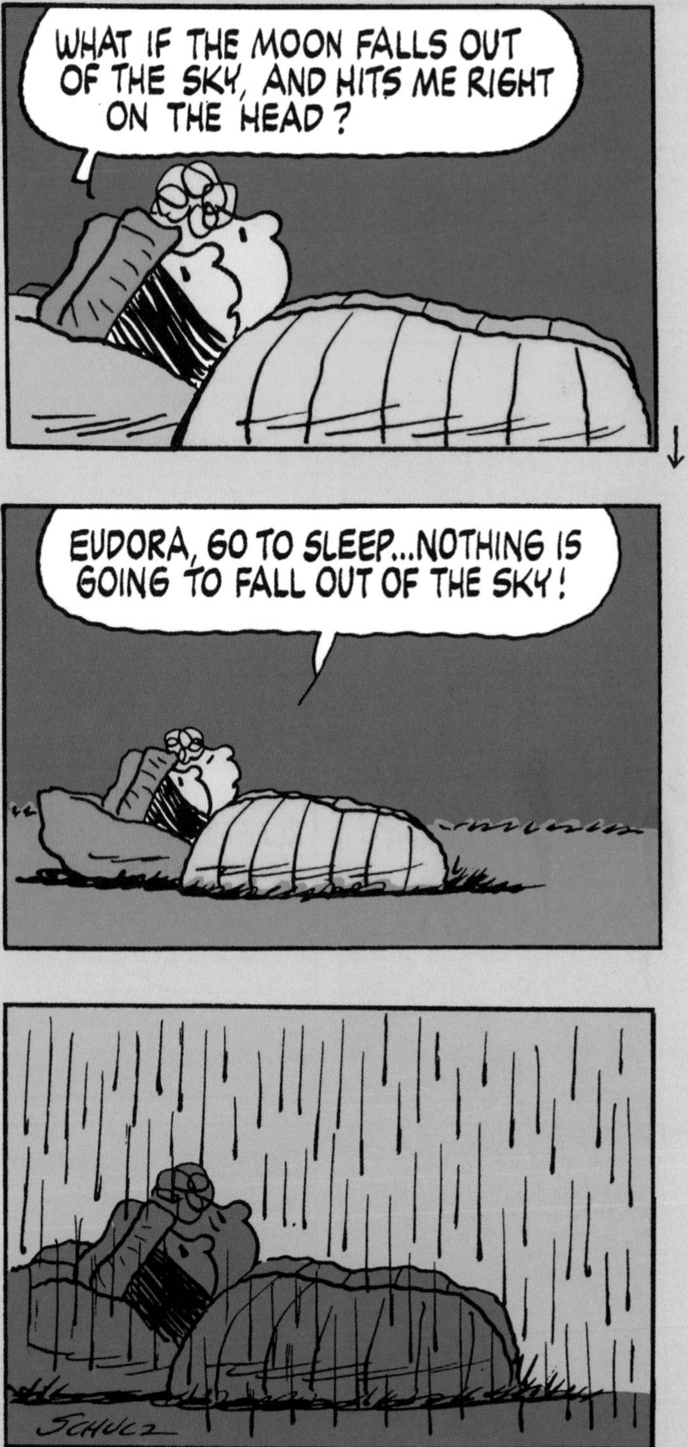
WHAT IF THE MOON FALLS OUT OF THE SKY, AND HITS ME RIGHT ON THE HEAD?
EUDORA, GO TO SLEEP...NOTHING IS GOING TO FALL OUT OF THE SKY!
SCHULZ

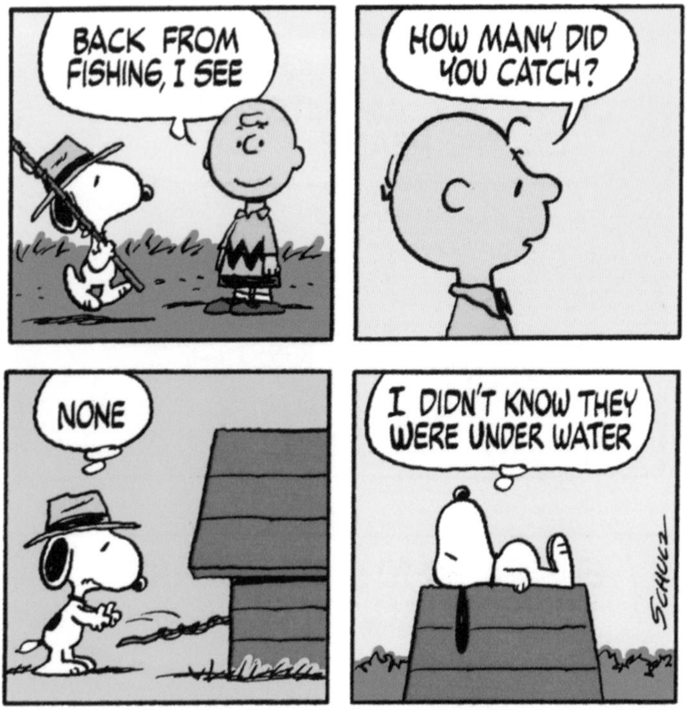
BACK FROM FISHING, I SEE
HOW MANY DID YOU CATCH?
NONE
I DIDN'T KNOW THEY WERE UNDER WATER
SCHULZ

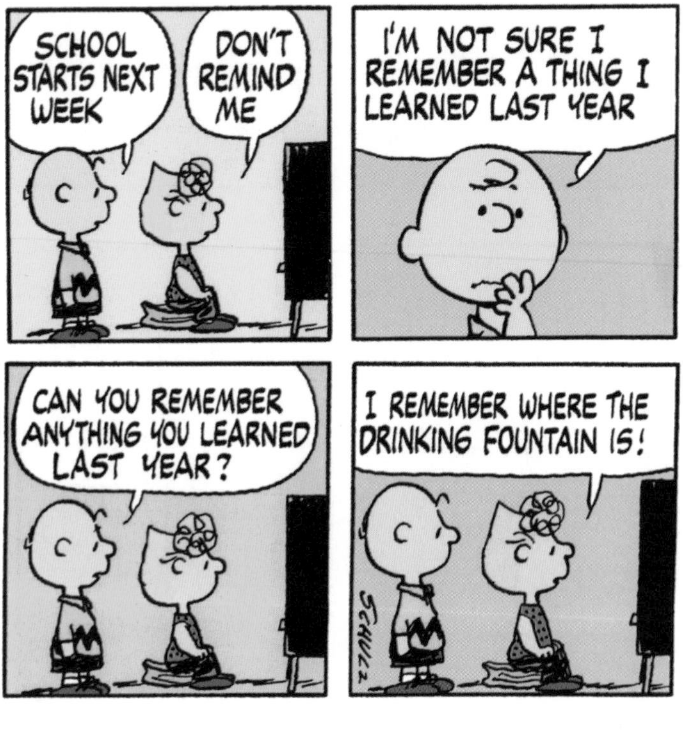
SCHOOL STARTS NEXT WEEK
DON'T REMIND ME
I'M NOT SURE I REMEMBER A THING I LEARNED LAST YEAR
CAN YOU REMEMBER ANYTHING YOU LEARNED LAST YEAR?
I REMEMBER WHERE THE DRINKING FOUNTAIN IS!
SCHULZ

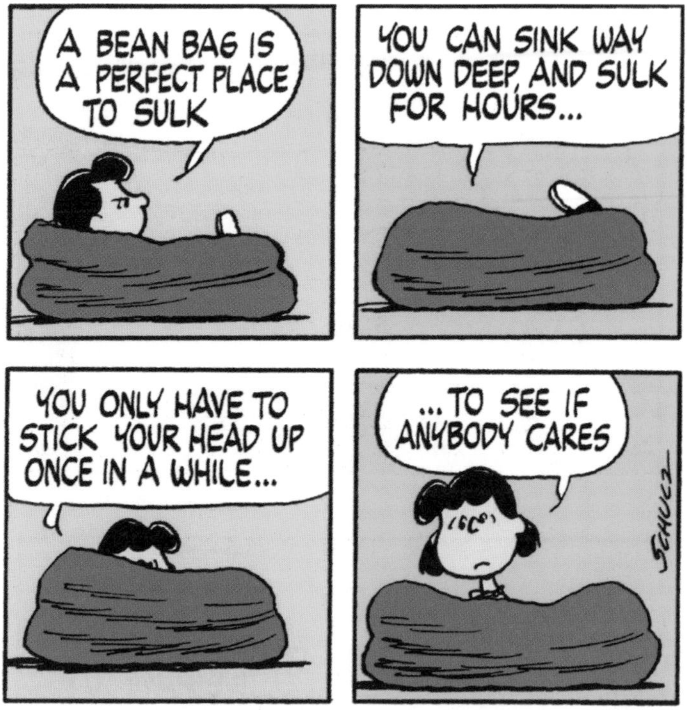
A BEAN BAG IS A PERFECT PLACE TO SULK
YOU CAN SINK WAY DOWN DEEP, AND SULK FOR HOURS...
YOU ONLY HAVE TO STICK YOUR HEAD UP ONCE IN A WHILE...
...TO SEE IF ANYBODY CARES

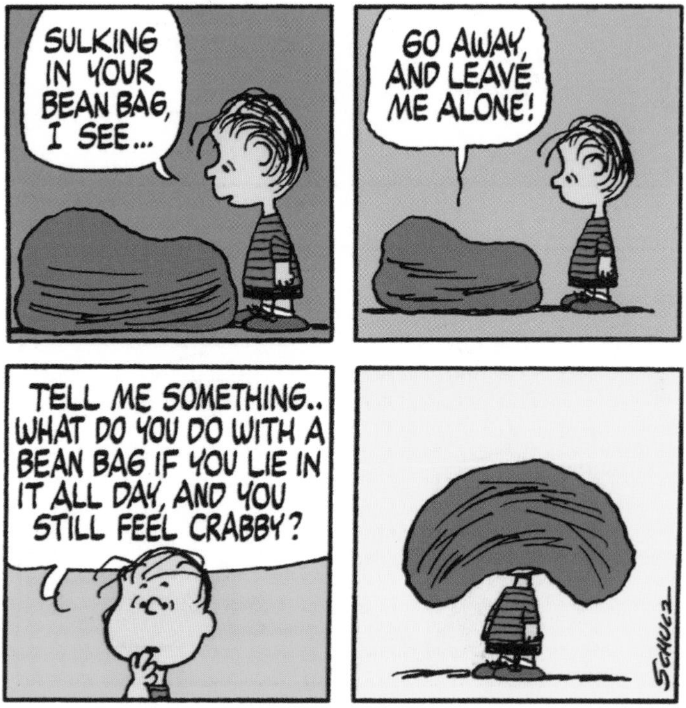
SULKING IN YOUR BEAN BAG, I SEE...
GO AWAY, AND LEAVE ME ALONE!
TELL ME SOMETHING.. WHAT DO YOU DO WITH A BEAN BAG IF YOU LIE IN IT ALL DAY, AND YOU STILL FEEL CRABBY?

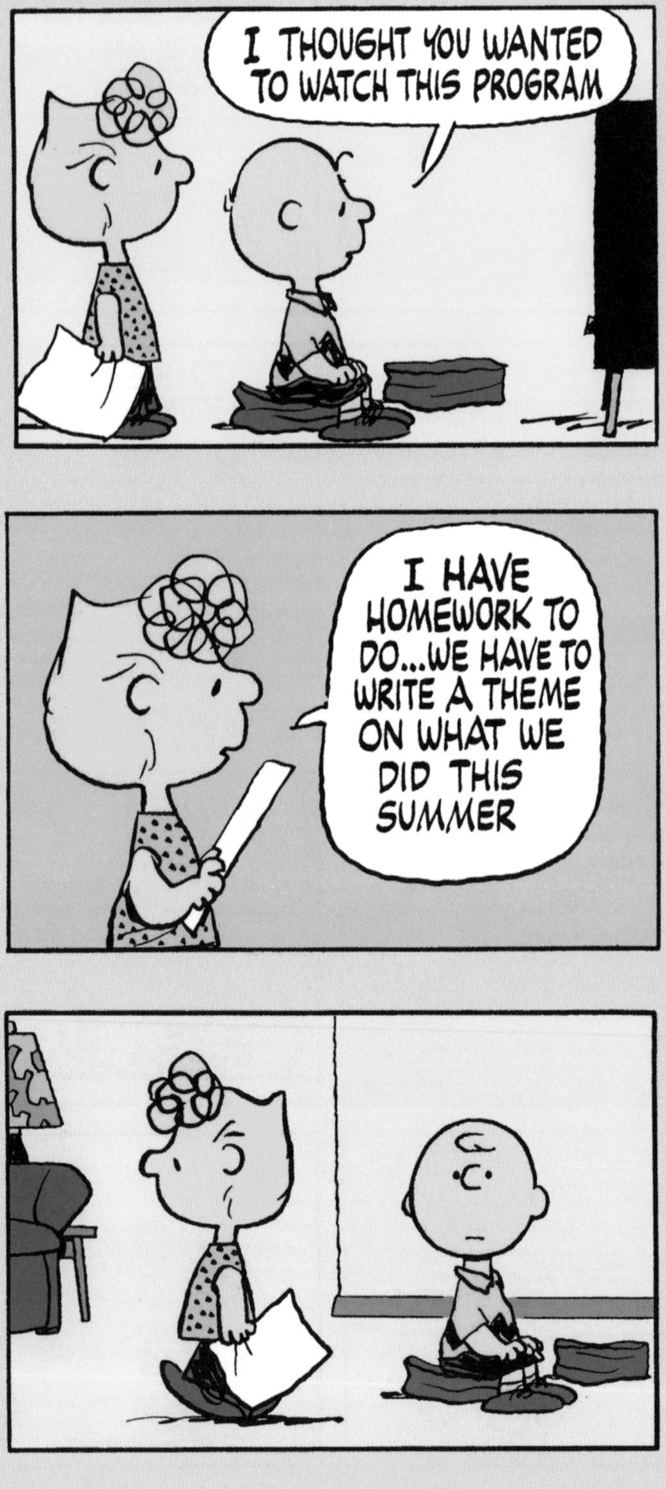
I THOUGHT YOU WANTED TO WATCH THIS PROGRAM
I HAVE HOMEWORK TO DO...WE HAVE TO WRITE A THEME ON WHAT WE DID THIS SUMMER

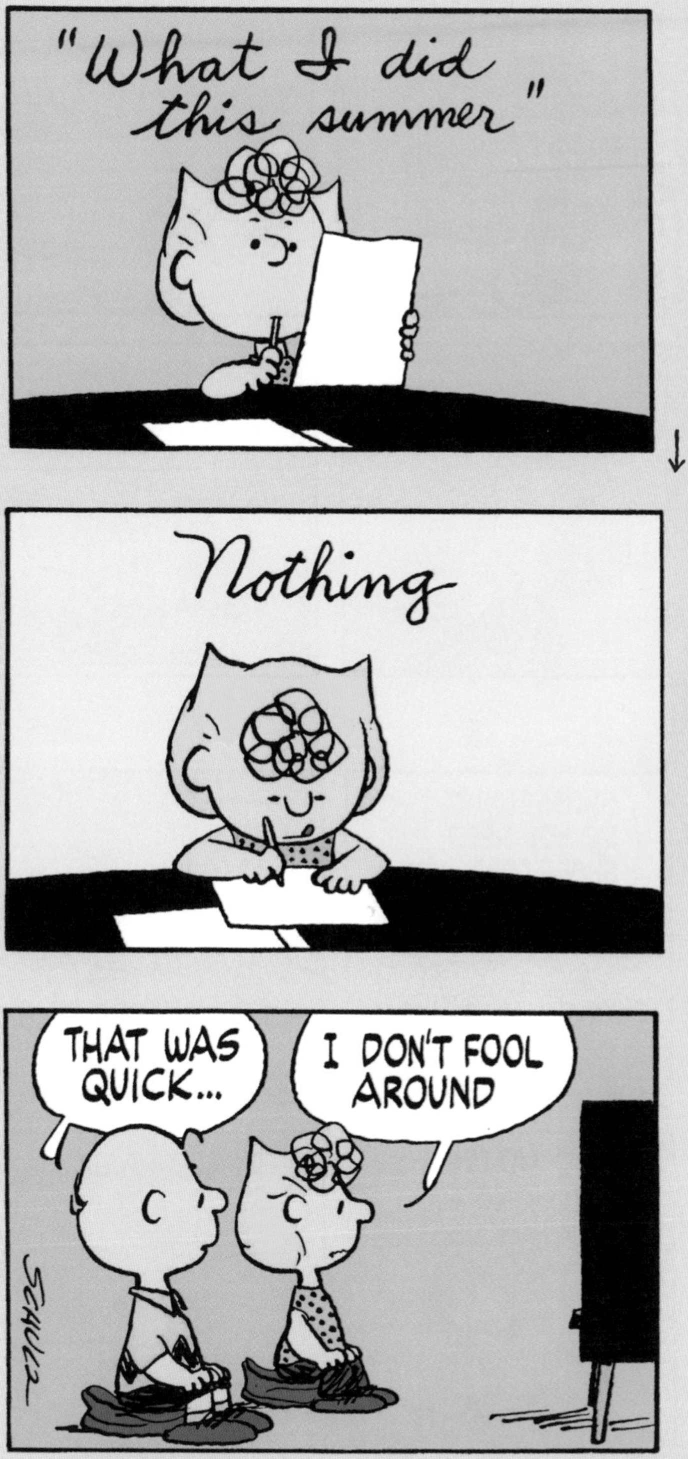
"What I did this summer"
Nothing
THAT WAS QUICK...
I DON'T FOOL AROUND
SCHULZ

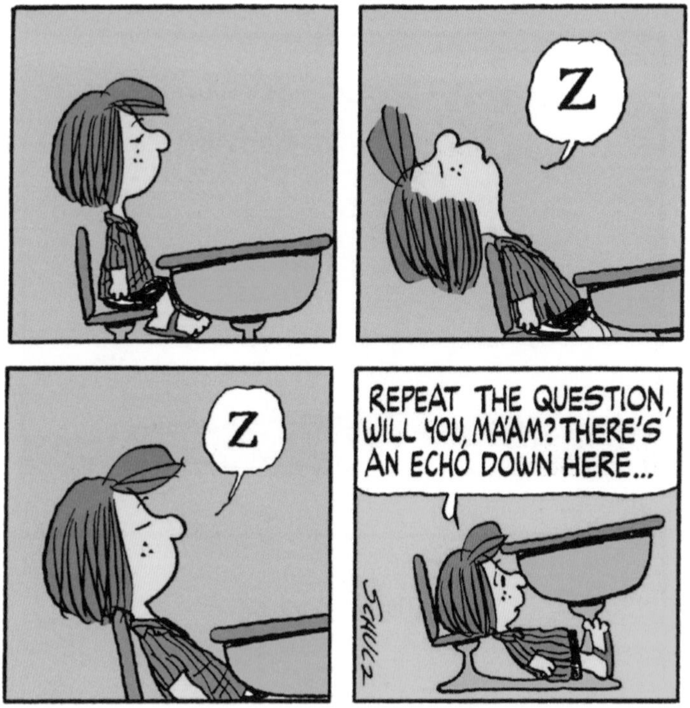
Z
Z
REPEAT THE QUESTION, WILL YOU, MA'AM? THERE'S AN ECHO DOWN HERE...
SCHULZ

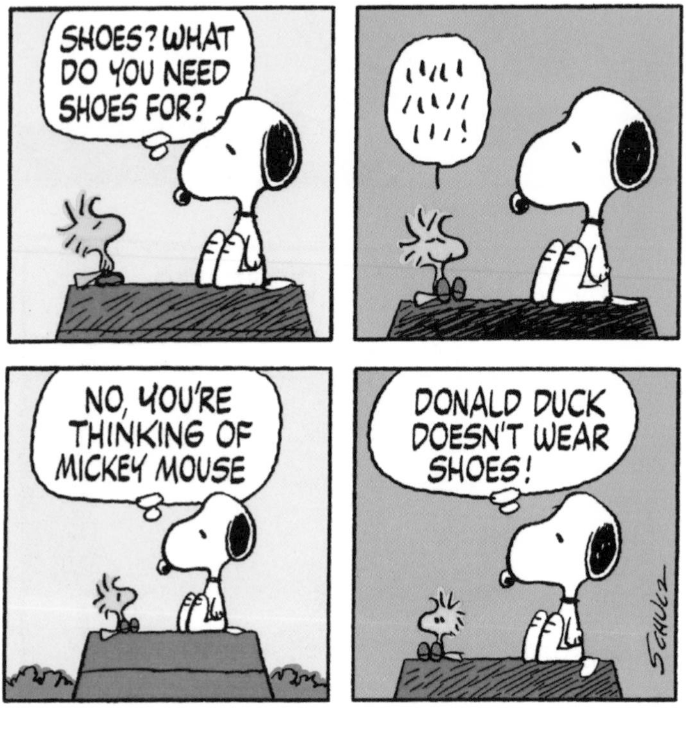
SHOES? WHAT DO YOU NEED SHOES FOR?
NO, YOU'RE THINKING OF MICKEY MOUSE
DONALD DUCK DOESN'T WEAR SHOES!
SCHULZ

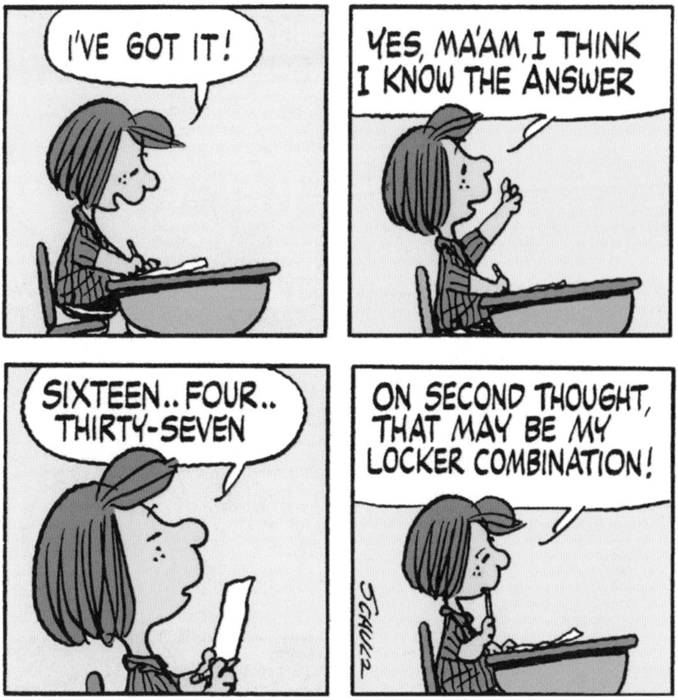
I'VE GOT IT!
YES, MA'AM, I THINK I KNOW THE ANSWER
SIXTEEN.. FOUR.. THIRTY-SEVEN
ON SECOND THOUGHT, THAT MAY BE MY LOCKER COMBINATION!
SCHULZ

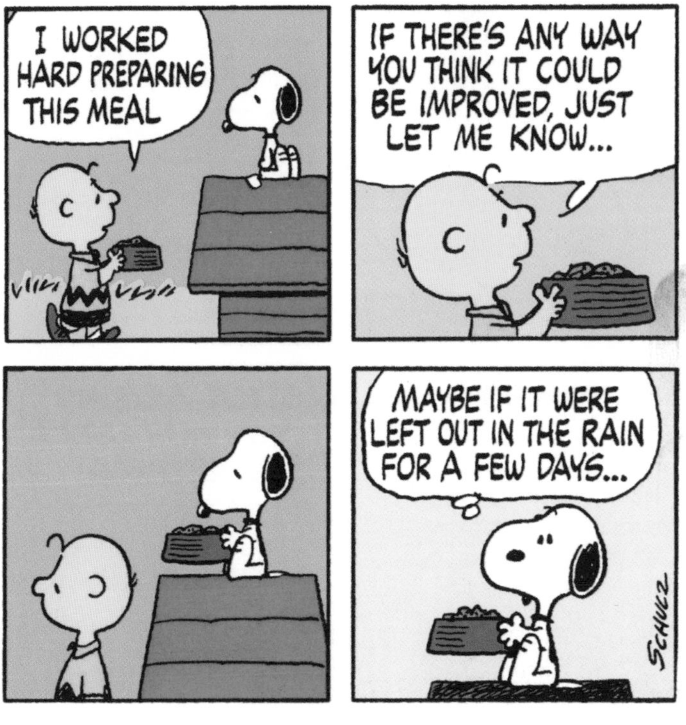
I WORKED HARD PREPARING THIS MEAL
IF THERE'S ANY WAY YOU THINK IT COULD BE IMPROVED, JUST LET ME KNOW...
MAYBE IF IT WERE LEFT OUT IN THE RAIN FOR A FEW DAYS...
SCHULZ

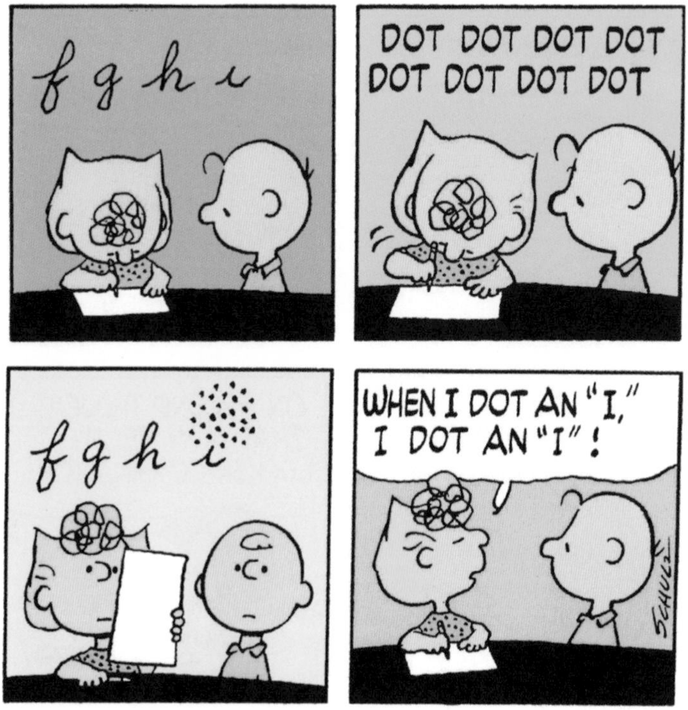
fghi
DOT DOT DOT DOT DOT DOT DOT DOT
fghi
WHEN I DOT AN "I," I DOT AN "I"!
SCHULZ

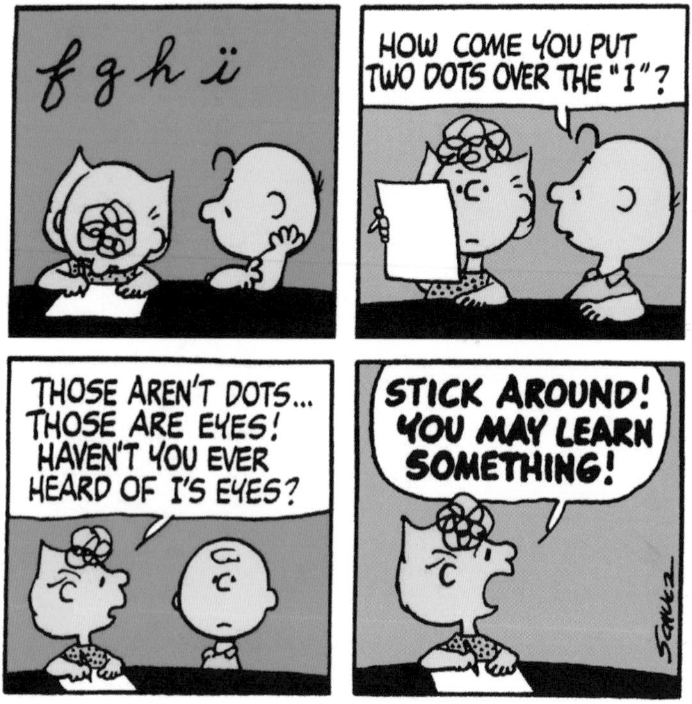
fghï
HOW COME YOU PUT TWO DOTS OVER THE "I"?
THOSE AREN'T DOTS... THOSE ARE EYES! HAVEN'T YOU EVER HEARD OF I'S EYES?
STICK AROUND! YOU MAY LEARN SOMETHING!
SCHULZ

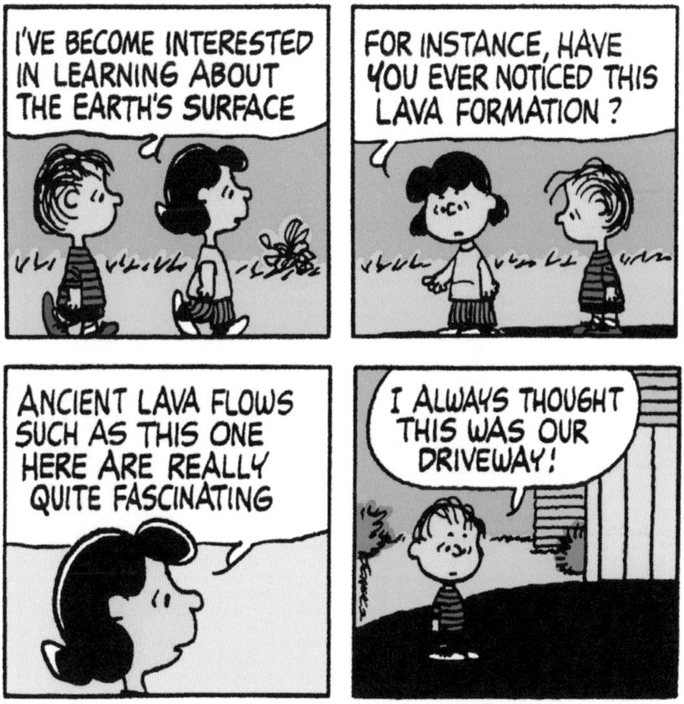
I'VE BECOME INTERESTED IN LEARNING ABOUT THE EARTH'S SURFACE
FOR INSTANCE, HAVE YOU EVER NOTICED THIS LAVA FORMATION ?
ANCIENT LAVA FLOWS SUCH AS THIS ONE HERE ARE REALLY QUITE FASCINATING
I ALWAYS THOUGHT THIS WAS OUR DRIVEWAY!

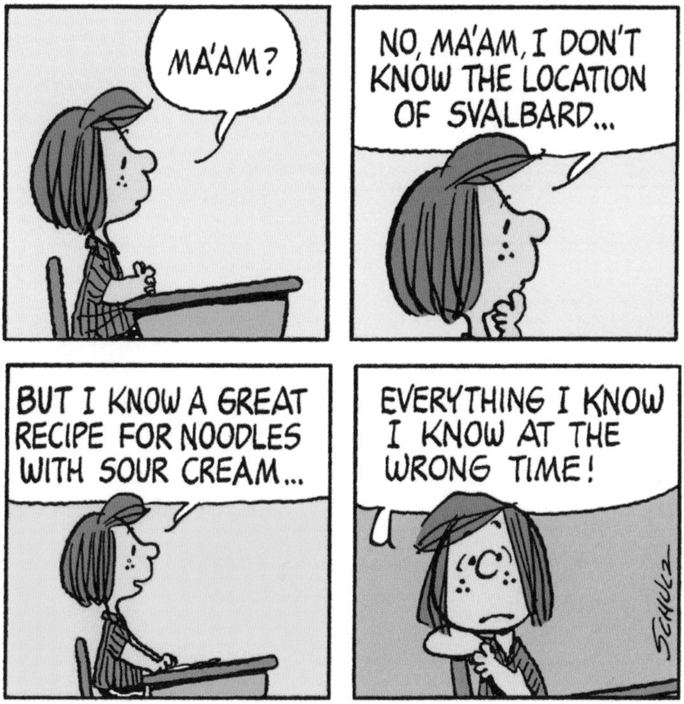
MA'AM?
NO, MA'AM, I DON'T KNOW THE LOCATION OF SVALBARD...
BUT I KNOW A GREAT RECIPE FOR NOODLES WITH SOUR CREAM...
EVERYTHING I KNOW I KNOW AT THE WRONG TIME!
SCHULZ

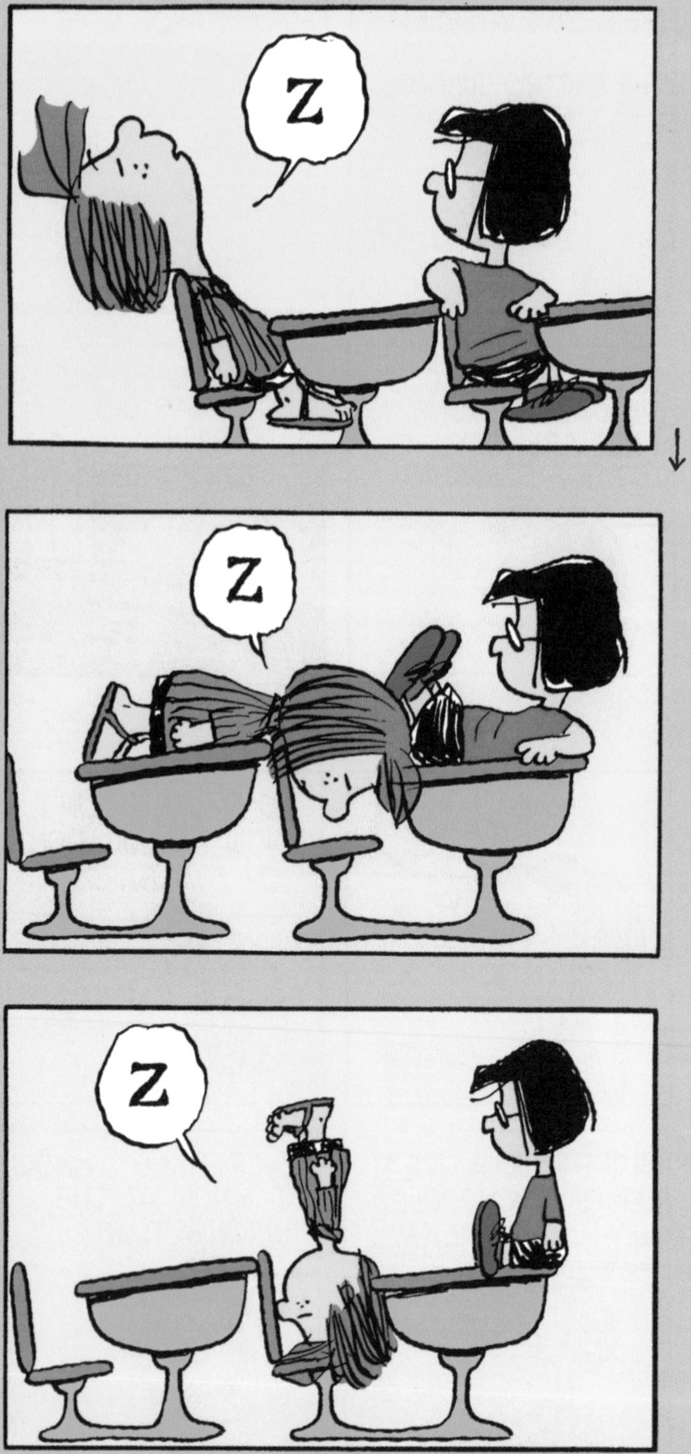
Z
Z
Z

Z
YOU'LL NEVER GET GOOD GRADES, MARCIE, IF YOU CHANGE SEATS ALL THE TIME!
SCHULZ

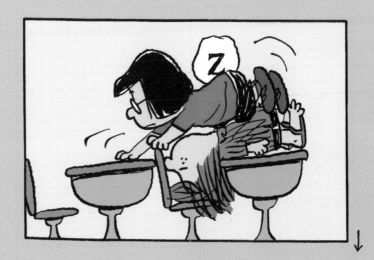

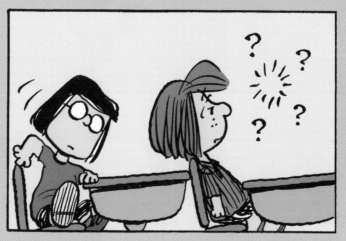

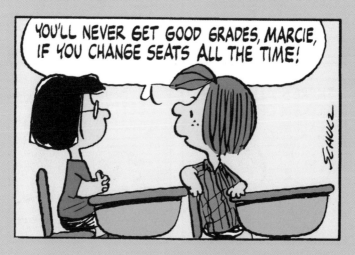

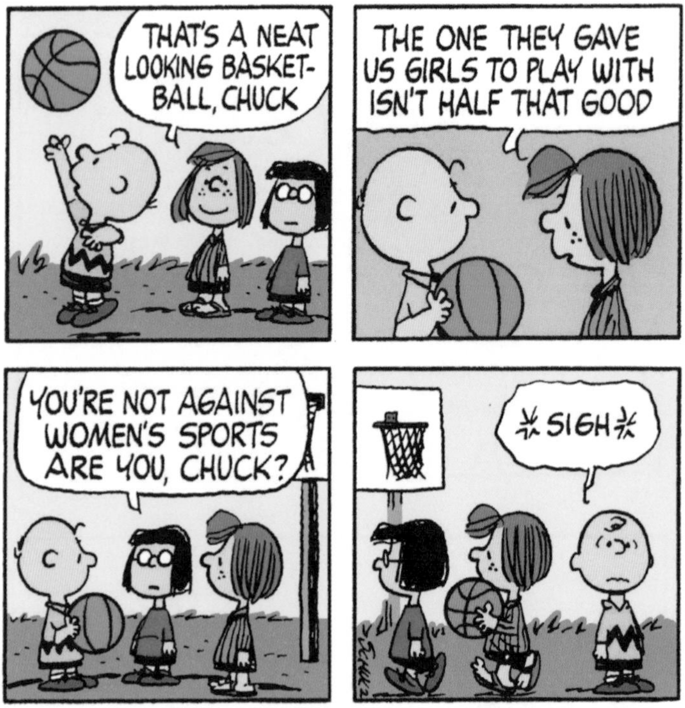
THAT'S A NEAT LOOKING BASKET-BALL, CHUCK
THE ONE THEY GAVE US GIRLS TO PLAY WITH ISN'T HALF THAT GOOD
YOU'RE NOT AGAINST WOMEN'S SPORTS ARE YOU, CHUCK?
SIGH

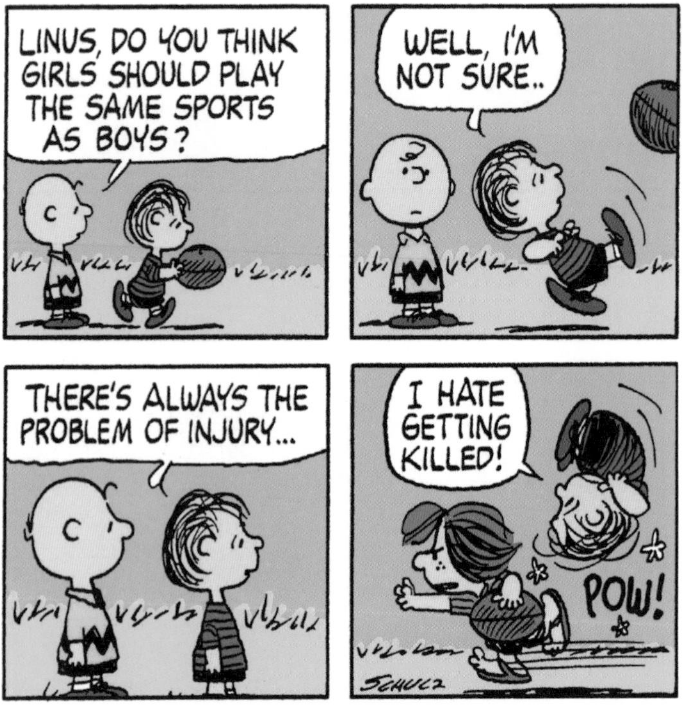
LINUS, DO YOU THINK GIRLS SHOULD PLAY THE SAME SPORTS AS BOYS?
WELL, I'M NOT SURE..
THERE'S ALWAYS THE PROBLEM OF INJURY...
I HATE GETTING KILLED!
POW!

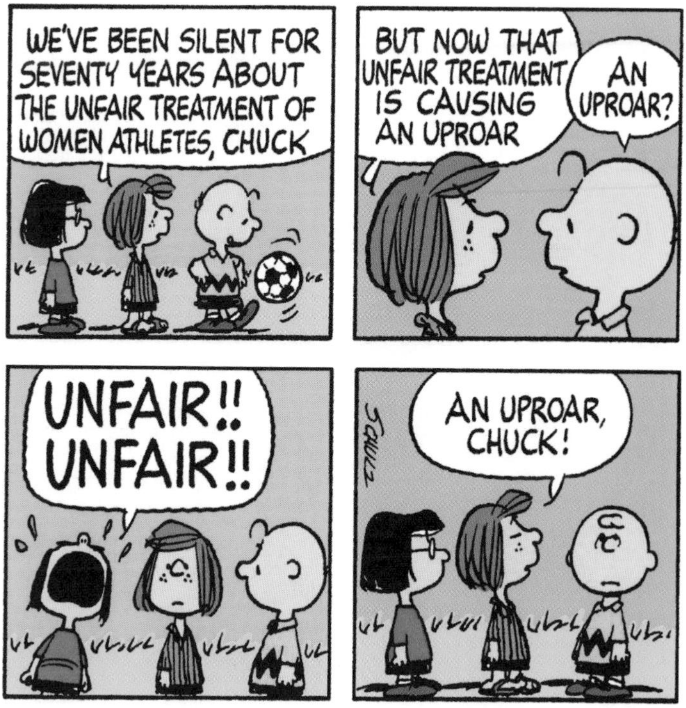
WE'VE BEEN SILENT FOR SEVENTY YEARS ABOUT THE UNFAIR TREATMENT OF WOMEN ATHLETES, CHUCK
BUT NOW THAT UNFAIR TREATMENT IS CAUSING AN UPROAR
AN UPROAR?
UNFAIR!! UNFAIR!!
AN UPROAR, CHUCK!
SCHULZ

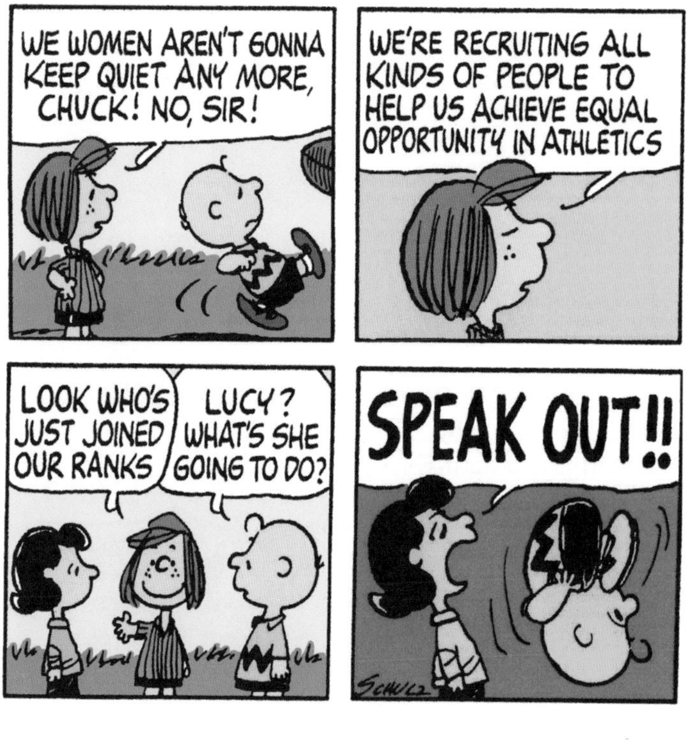
WE WOMEN AREN'T GONNA KEEP QUIET ANY MORE, CHUCK! NO, SIR!
WE'RE RECRUITING ALL KINDS OF PEOPLE TO HELP US ACHIEVE EQUAL OPPORTUNITY IN ATHLETICS
LOOK WHO'S JUST JOINED OUR RANKS
LUCY? WHAT'S SHE GOING TO DO?
SPEAK OUT!!
SCHULZ

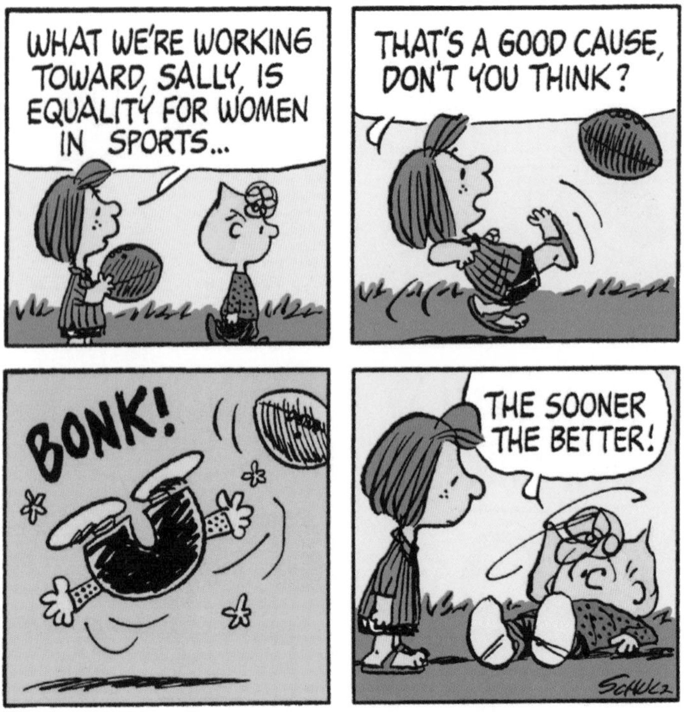
WHAT WE'RE WORKING TOWARD, SALLY, IS EQUALITY FOR WOMEN IN SPORTS...
THAT'S A GOOD CAUSE, DON'T YOU THINK?
BONK!
THE SOONER THE BETTER!

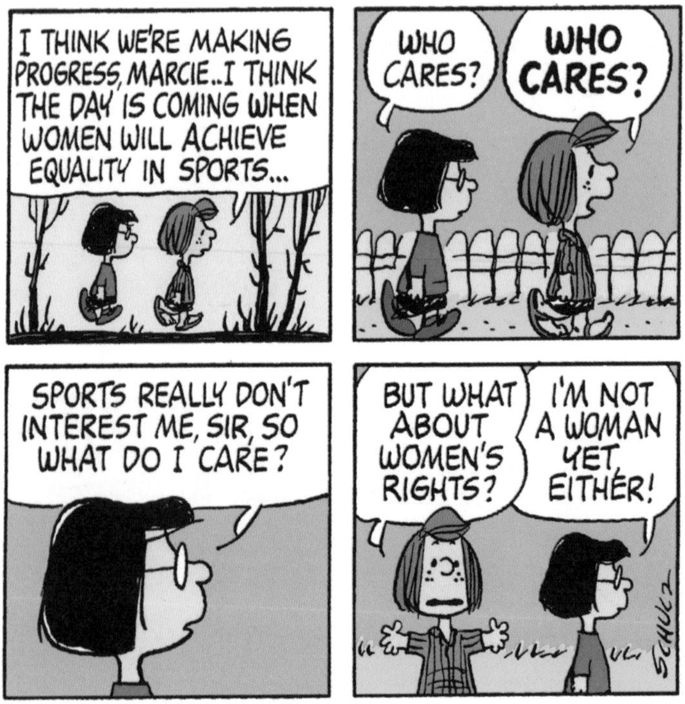
I THINK WE'RE MAKING PROGRESS, MARCIE..I THINK THE DAY IS COMING WHEN WOMEN WILL ACHIEVE EQUALITY IN SPORTS...
WHO CARES?
WHO CARES?
SPORTS REALLY DON'T INTEREST ME, SIR, SO WHAT DO I CARE?
BUT WHAT ABOUT WOMEN'S RIGHTS?
I'M NOT A WOMAN YET, EITHER!

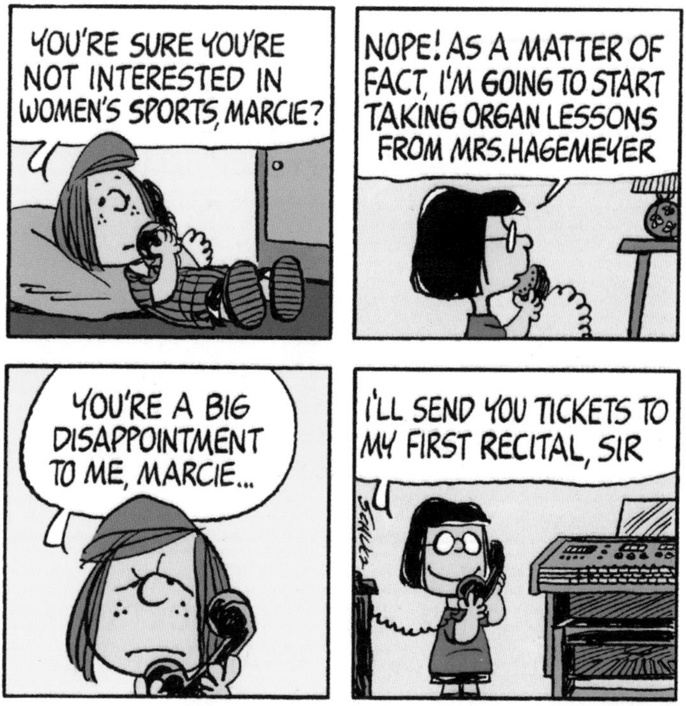
YOU'RE SURE YOU'RE NOT INTERESTED IN WOMEN'S SPORTS, MARCIE?
NOPE! AS A MATTER OF FACT, I'M GOING TO START TAKING ORGAN LESSONS FROM MRS. HAGEMEYER
YOU'RE A BIG DISAPPOINTMENT TO ME, MARCIE...
I'LL SEND YOU TICKETS TO MY FIRST RECITAL, SIR
SCHULZ

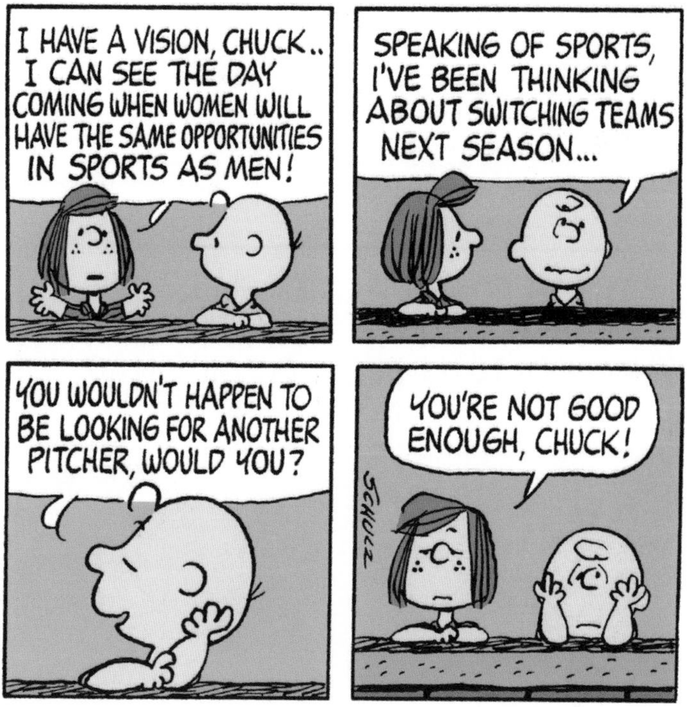
I HAVE A VISION, CHUCK.. I CAN SEE THE DAY COMING WHEN WOMEN WILL HAVE THE SAME OPPORTUNITIES IN SPORTS AS MEN!
SPEAKING OF SPORTS, I'VE BEEN THINKING ABOUT SWITCHING TEAMS NEXT SEASON...
YOU WOULDN'T HAPPEN TO BE LOOKING FOR ANOTHER PITCHER, WOULD YOU?
YOU'RE NOT GOOD ENOUGH, CHUCK!
SCHULZ

I SUPPOSE THERE COMES A TIME WHEN MOST RELATIONSHIPS SIMPLY COME TO AN END...MAYBE THAT'S HAPPENED TO US...
I GUESS IT WILL BE BETTER ALL AROUND IF WE JUST PART SORT OF FRIENDLY AND ADMIT THAT THE LOVE WE ONCE HAD IS NOW GONE...
THESE THINGS HAPPEN EVERY DAY... I GUESS WE JUST THINK IT'LL NEVER HAPPEN TO US, BUT IT DID...WE HAD OUR LOVE, BUT NOW IT'S GONE!

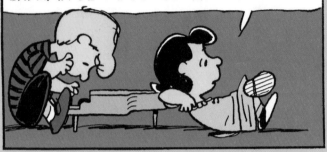

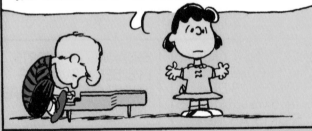

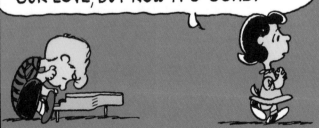

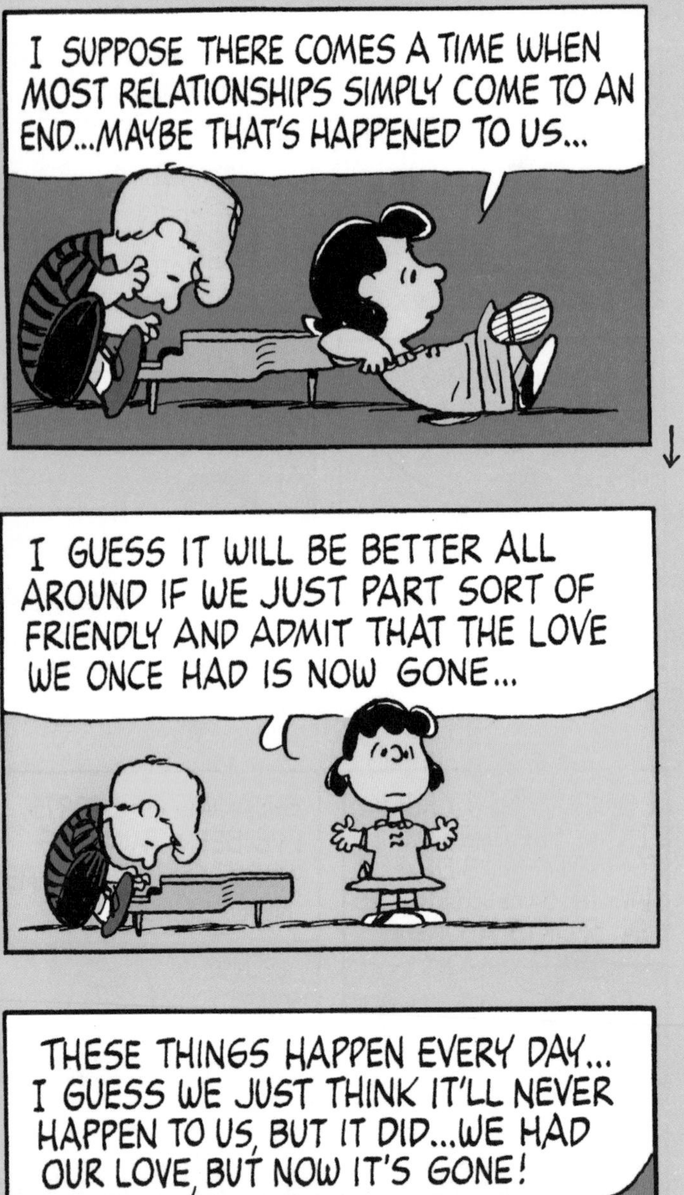

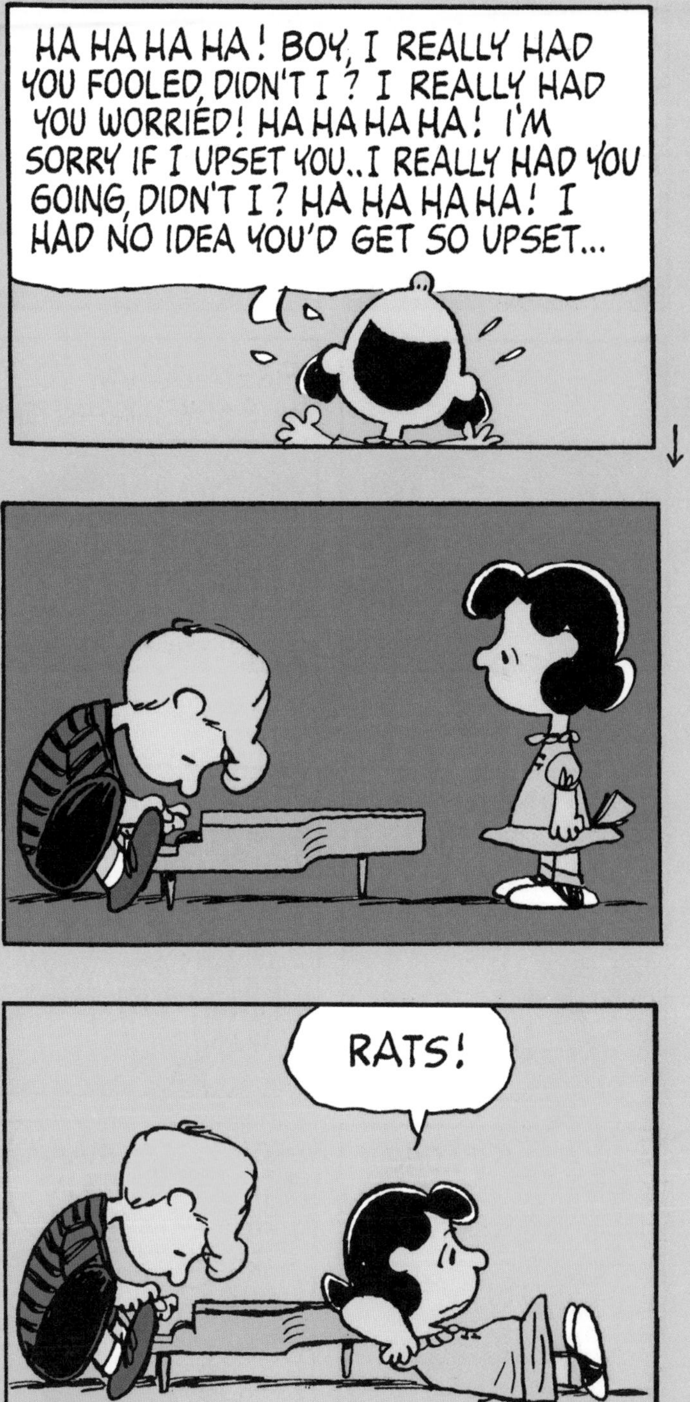
HA HA HA HA! BOY, I REALLY HAD YOU FOOLED, DIDN'T I ? I REALLY HAD YOU WORRIED! HA HA HA HA! I'M SORRY IF I UPSET YOU..I REALLY HAD YOU GOING, DIDN'T I ? HA HA HA HA! I HAD NO IDEA YOU'D GET SO UPSET...
RATS!
SCHULZ

WOMEN SHOULDN'T BE THE ONLY ONES TO CRY
MEN SHOULD REALIZE THAT IT'S ALL RIGHT FOR THEM TO CRY, TOO...
FIRST YOU HAVE TO HAVE SOMETHING HAPPEN!

TRUE? WHO KNOWS? FALSE? ONLY TIME WILL TELL...
PERHAPS... COULD BE... MAYBE..I DOUBT IT... DON'T COUNT ON IT...
MAYBE IN THE LONG RUN...IT ALL DEPENDS... WEATHER PERMITTING
SOME OF US, MA'AM, SEE EVERYTHING IN SHADES OF GRAY

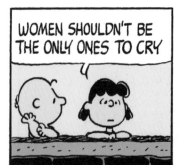

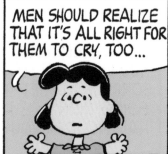

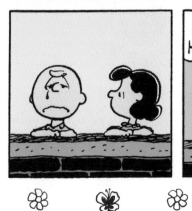

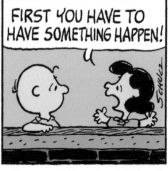

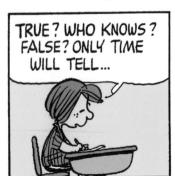

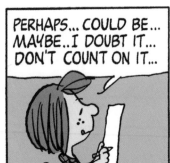

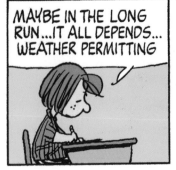

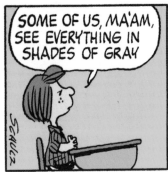

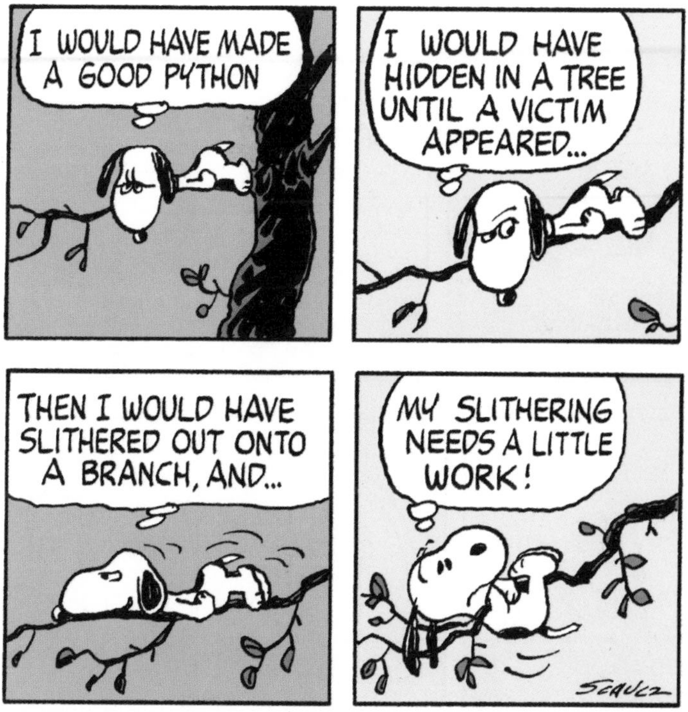
I WOULD HAVE MADE A GOOD PYTHON
I WOULD HAVE HIDDEN IN A TREE UNTIL A VICTIM APPEARED...
THEN I WOULD HAVE SLITHERED OUT ONTO A BRANCH, AND...
MY SLITHERING NEEDS A LITTLE WORK!
SCHULZ

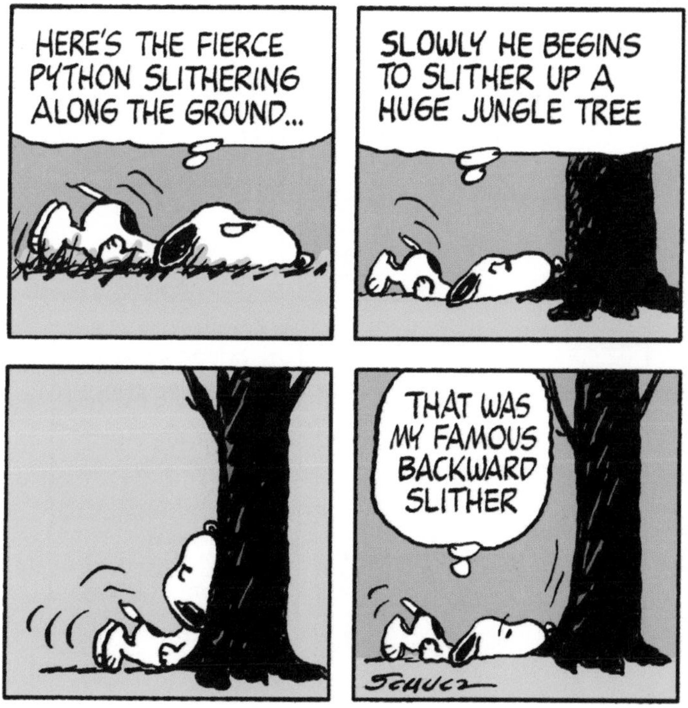
HERE'S THE FIERCE PYTHON SLITHERING ALONG THE GROUND...
SLOWLY HE BEGINS TO SLITHER UP A HUGE JUNGLE TREE
THAT WAS MY FAMOUS BACKWARD SLITHER
SCHULZ

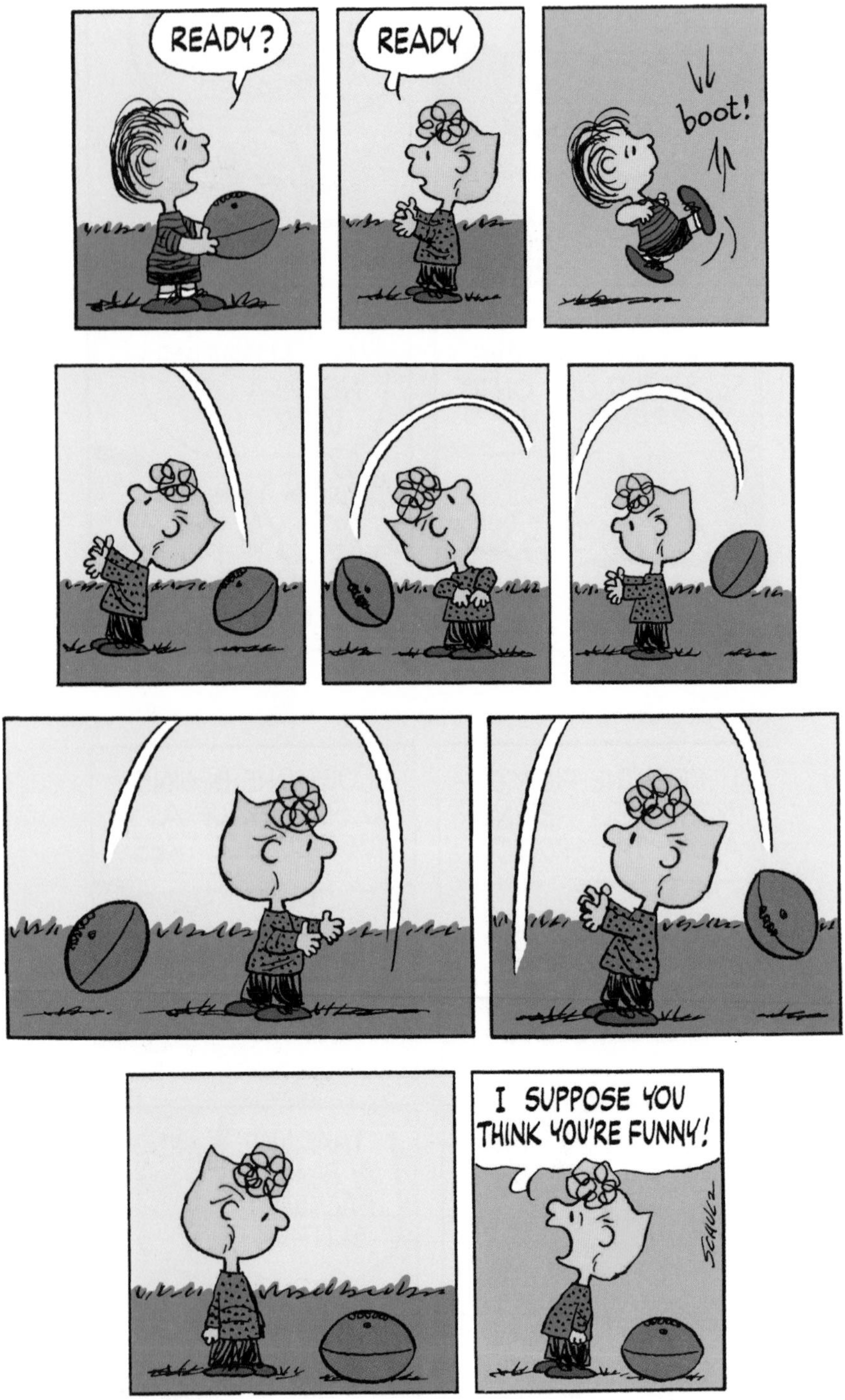
READY?
READY
boot!
I SUPPOSE YOU THINK YOU'RE FUNNY!
SCHULZ

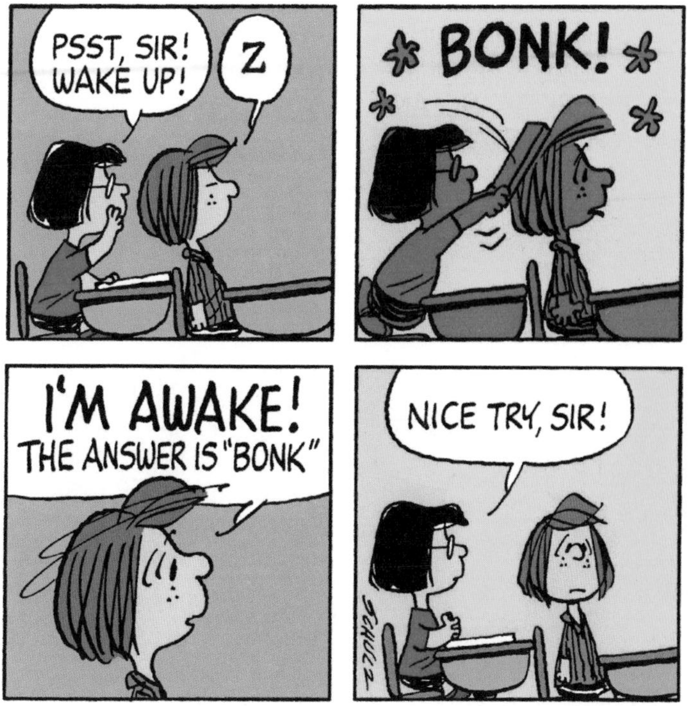
PSST, SIR! WAKE UP!
Z
BONK!
I'M AWAKE! THE ANSWER IS "BONK"
NICE TRY, SIR!
SCHULZ

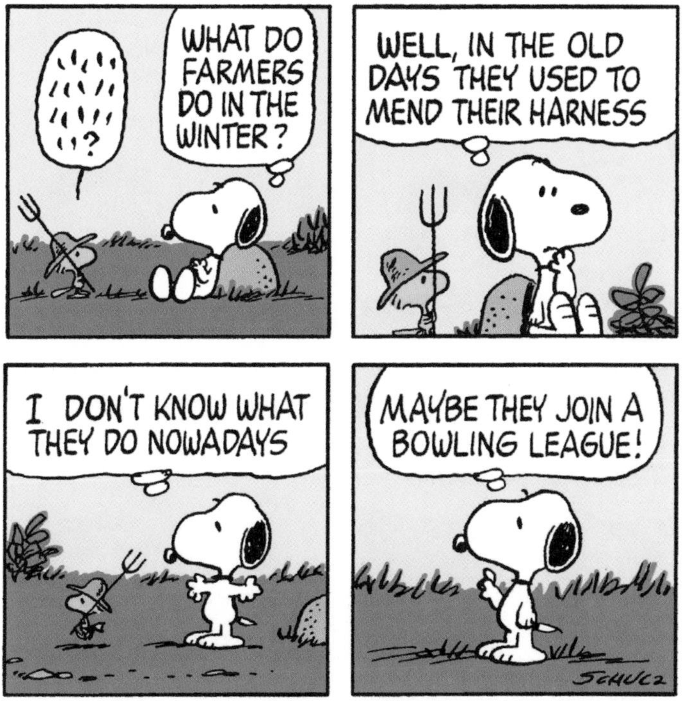
?
WHAT DO FARMERS DO IN THE WINTER?
WELL, IN THE OLD DAYS THEY USED TO MEND THEIR HARNESS
I DON'T KNOW WHAT THEY DO NOWADAYS
MAYBE THEY JOIN A BOWLING LEAGUE!
SCHULZ

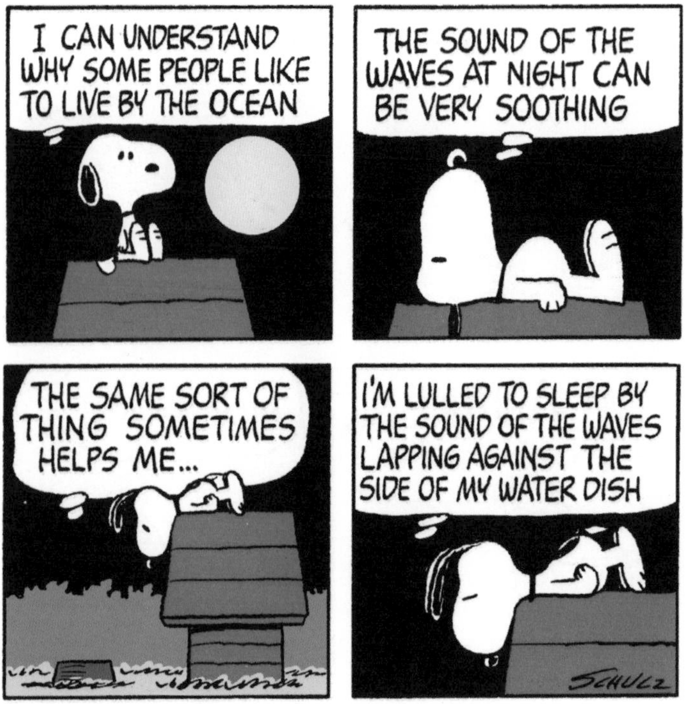
I CAN UNDERSTAND WHY SOME PEOPLE LIKE TO LIVE BY THE OCEAN
THE SOUND OF THE WAVES AT NIGHT CAN BE VERY SOOTHING
THE SAME SORT OF THING SOMETIMES HELPS ME...
I'M LULLED TO SLEEP BY THE SOUND OF THE WAVES LAPPING AGAINST THE SIDE OF MY WATER DISH
SCHULZ

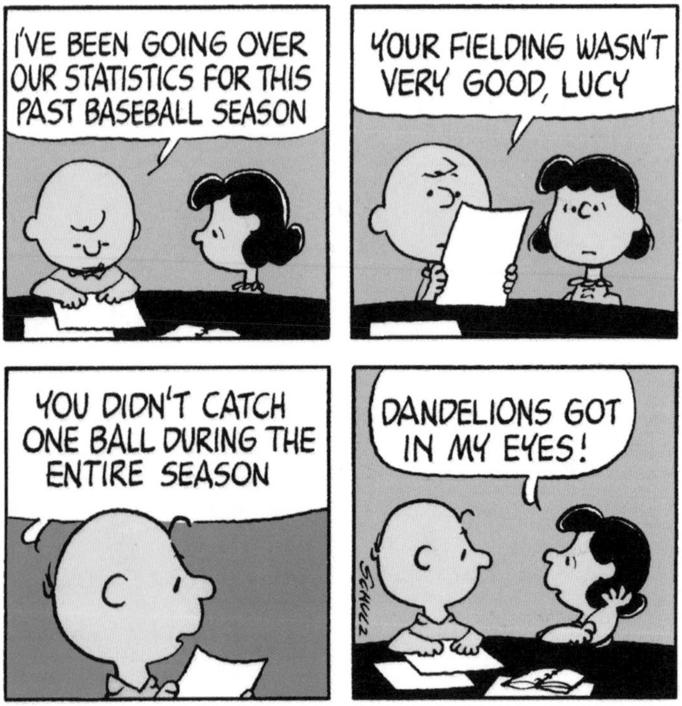
I'VE BEEN GOING OVER OUR STATISTICS FOR THIS PAST BASEBALL SEASON
YOUR FIELDING WASN'T VERY GOOD, LUCY
YOU DIDN'T CATCH ONE BALL DURING THE ENTIRE SEASON
DANDELIONS GOT IN MY EYES!
SCHULZ

MORE TO EXPLORE!

Featuring fun facts!

Charles Schulz brought his lifelong passion for sports to *Peanuts*, and from the very beginning, his female characters participated in sports of all kinds.

Schulz often used the theme of fairness in his comic strip and believed in giving everyone equal opportunity. In *Peanuts*, he created standout female athletes (and in Lucy's case, not always so outstanding) and encouraged girls' participation in sports as diverse as football and figure skating.

In this More to Explore section, we'll take a look at some of Schulz's memorable sports scenes involving Lucy, Peppermint Patty, Marcie, and the rest of the *Peanuts* gang.

Special thanks to our friends at the Charles M. Schulz Museum and Research Center in Santa Rosa, California, for letting us share this information with you!

CHARLES M. SCHULZ MUSEUM

Schulz took his support for women athletes off the funny pages and into his real life.

After Schulz met tennis great Billie Jean King in the 1970s, he threw his support behind the Women's Sports Foundation and served on their board of directors. He brought public attention to the issue of equality in women's sports with a 1979 *Peanuts* story line about Title IX, the 1972 legislation that bans gender discrimination in schools, whether in academics or athletics.

THAT'S A NICE FOOTBALL YOU HAVE THERE, LINUS
SHALL I GIVE HIM THE STATISTICS, SIR?
IN 1978, THE AVERAGE BUDGET FOR INTERCOLLEGIATE ATHLETICS FOR MEN WAS $717,000, BUT FOR WOMEN IT WAS ONLY $141,000
SIGH
SCHULZ

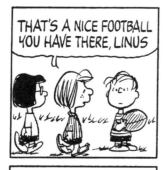

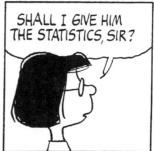

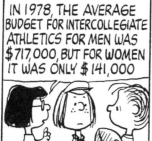

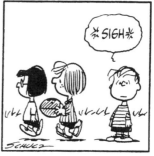

September 25, 1979

According to research compiled by the Women's Sports Foundation in 2011, participation in sports by girls and women increased by 904 percent in high schools and 456 percent at the college level since Title IX was passed in 1972.

You can read the rest of this comic strip sequence on pages 158–161 of this book!

I DIDN'T KNOW YOU COULD SKATE, SIR!
I'M REALLY INTO SPORTS, MARCIE.. IT'S MY LIFE...WHEN I GROW UP, I'M GONNA PLAY PROFESSIONAL BALL IN THE SUMMER AND SKATE IN AN ICE SHOW IN THE WINTER...
DURING THE OFF-SEASON, I'LL PROBABLY DO A LITTLE BOWLING OR POP A WHEELIE IN A MOTO-CROSS...
YOU'RE AN AMAZING PERSON, SIR
STOP CALLING ME "SIR"!
SCHULZ

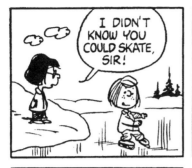

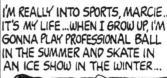

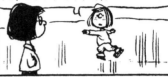

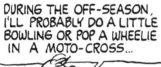

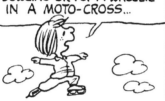

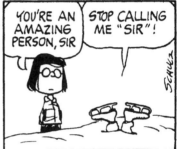

November 4, 1974

Peppermint Patty is an excellent role model for the sports-minded girl. She is also a character with whom many children growing up in single-parent households can relate. Peppermint Patty lives alone with her father. When it comes to sports, Peppermint Patty is up for just about any challenge—just don't call her "sir"!

HEY, CHUCK, HOW ABOUT A FOOTBALL GAME TOMORROW?
YOU KNOW, A REGULAR STRAIGHT AHEAD, DOWN IN THE DIRT, IN YOUR FACE, ROCK 'EM, SOCK 'EM, ANYTHING GOES, GOOD OLD FASHIONED FOOTBALL GAME!
IS THE LIBRARY OPEN TOMORROW?

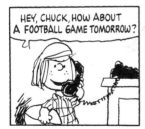

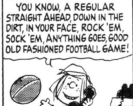

December 2, 1993

Schulz occasionally addressed social issues in *Peanuts*, finding humorous way to address relevant topics. Here he presents an encounter with a male bully, with the character Thibault provoking an uncharacteristically strong reaction from Marcie.

WHY DO YOU WEAR THOSE STUPID-LOOKING GLASSES?
GIRLS DON'T HAVE TO SEE ANYTHING! WHAT A WASTE OF MONEY SPENDING IT ON GLASSES FOR A GIRL!
YOU DON'T NEED GLASSES TO SCRUB FLOORS, DO DISHES AND MAKE BEDS!
SPEAKING OF GLASSES, MINE ARE BEGINNING TO STEAM UP!
SCHULZ

August 1, 1973

WHAT DO GIRLS WANT TO PLAY BASEBALL FOR ANYWAY?
GIRLS SHOULD LEARN THEIR PROPER PLACE
HEY! YOU'RE KICKING DIRT ON MY SHOES!
SIR, YOUR SECOND-BASEMAN HAS OFFENDED ME BEYOND ENDURANCE...CAN YOU STOP THE GAME FOR A MINUTE?
TIME OUT!
ALL RIGHT, THIBAULT, THIS IS IT!!!
SCHULZ

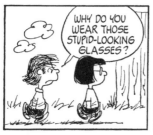

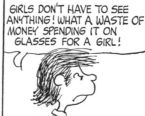

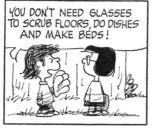

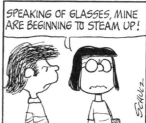

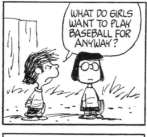

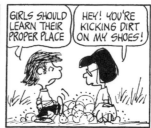

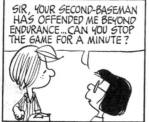

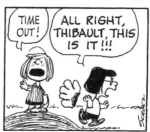

August 2, 1973

NOW, LOOK HERE, YOU CEMENT-HEADED, MALE-CHAUVINIST DUMMY...
I'M GOING TO TELL YOU SOMETHING, AND I WANT YOU TO STAND STILL AND LISTEN!
IF YOU SAY ONE WORD, I'M GOING TO BELT YOU RIGHT ACROSS THE CHOPS!
OH?
THAT WAS ONE WORD!
POW!
SCHULZ

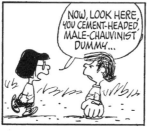

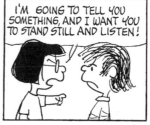

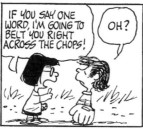

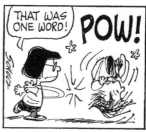

August 3, 1973

Among all the antics involving the *Peanuts* gang and sports, nothing is more iconic than Lucy's long-standing habit of holding the football for Charlie Brown, only to pull it away at the last moment. The very first such instance occurred in this Sunday *Peanuts* from way back in 1952.

PEANUTS
by
CHARLES M. SCHULZ
ALL YOU HAVE TO DO IS HOLD THE BALL, LUCY... THEN I'LL COME RUNNING UP, AND KICK IT...
I DON'T KNOW IF THIS IS SUCH A GOOD IDEA
?
!
WHOMP
I WAS AFRAID YOUR SHOES MIGHT BE DIRTY, CHARLIE BROWN... I DON'T WANT ANYONE WITH DIRTY SHOES KICKING MY NEW FOOTBALL...
DON'T EVER DO THAT AGAIN! DO YOU WANT TO KILL ME?! THIS TIME HOLD IT TIGHT!
HERE WE GO!
?
!
THUMP
I HELD IT REAL TIGHT, CHARLIE BROWN...
I'M NOT GOING TO GET UP.... I'M GOING TO LIE HERE FOR THE REST OF THE DAY...
SCHULZ

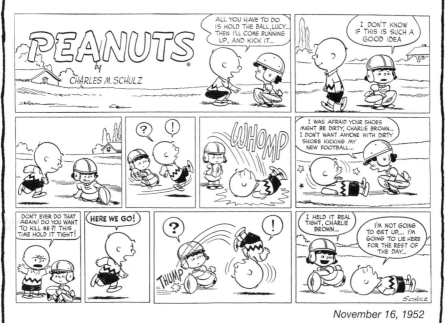

November 16, 1952

About the Charles M. Schulz Museum and Research Center

The Charles M. Schulz Museum and Research Center was designed as a tribute to the extraordinary talent of Charles M. Schulz. The Museum was created to share his legacy and genius with generations to come.

A tile mural over twenty feet high, Schulz's well-worn drawing desk, and a psychiatric booth are just some of the classics found alongside the largest collection of *Peanuts* artwork in the world. Laugh at original comic strips, explore in-depth exhibitions, watch animated *Peanuts* specials in the theater, and draw your own cartoons in the education room. The Museum features changing exhibitions, a re-creation of Schulz's studio, a life-size biographical timeline, and special programming. Learn more at schulzmuseum.org.

Andrews McMeel Publishing
a division of Andrews McMeel Universal
1130 Walnut Street, Kansas City, Missouri 64106

www.andrewsmcmeel.com

www.peanuts.com

19 20 21 22 23 SDB 10 9 8 7 6 5 4 3 2 1

ISBN: 978-1-4494-9355-4

Library of Congress Control Number: 2018949445

Made by:
Shenzhen Donnelley Printing Company Ltd.
Address and location of manufacturer:
No. 47, Wuhe Nan Road, Bantian Ind. Zone,
Shenzhen China, 518129
1st Printing—12/17/18

ATTENTION: SCHOOLS AND BUSINESSES

Andrews McMeel books are available at quantity discounts with bulk purchase for
educational, business, or sales promotional use. For information, please e-mail the
Andrews McMeel Publishing Special Sales Department:
specialsales@amuniversal.com.

Check out more *Peanuts* kids' collections from Andrews McMeel Publishing.

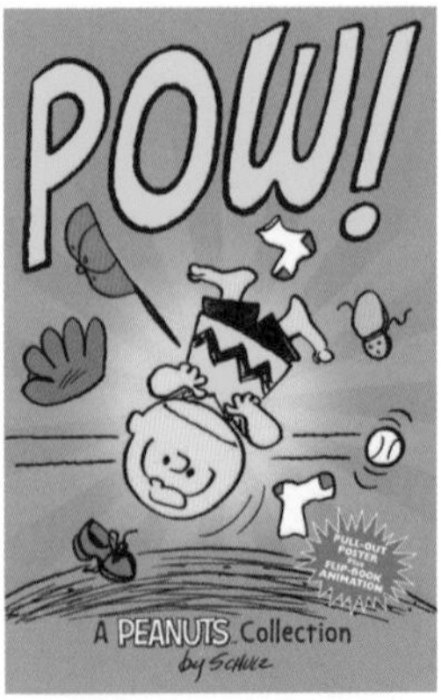
POW!
A PEANUTS Collection

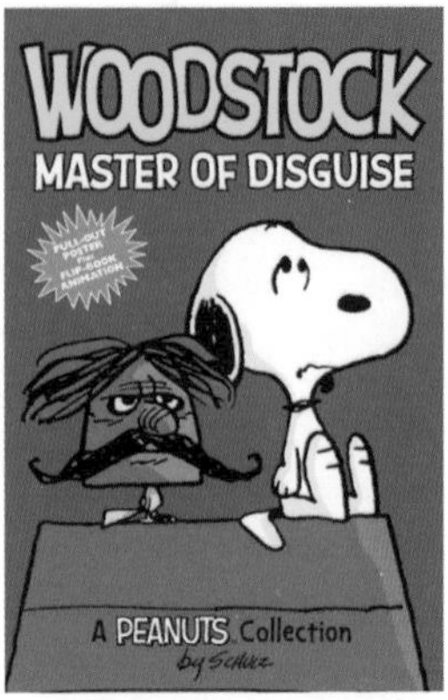
WOODSTOCK
MASTER OF DISGUISE
A PEANUTS Collection

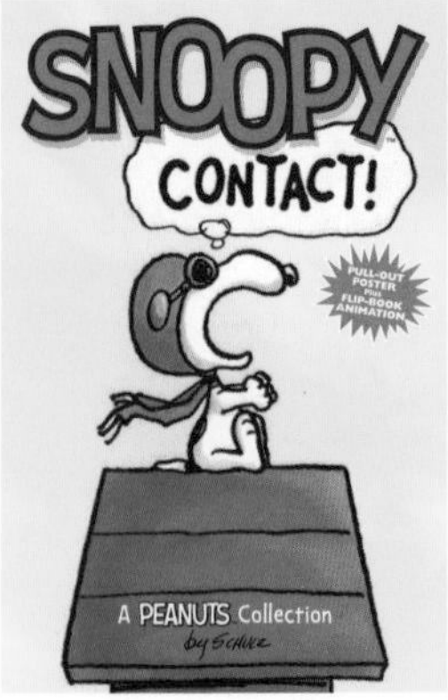
SNOOPY
CONTACT!
A PEANUTS Collection

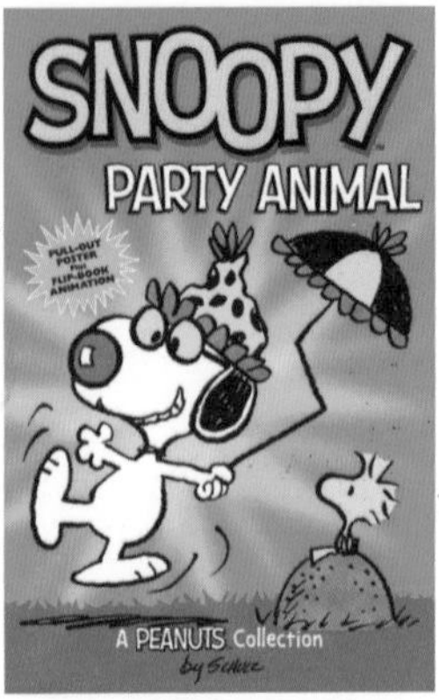
SNOOPY
PARTY ANIMAL
A PEANUTS Collection

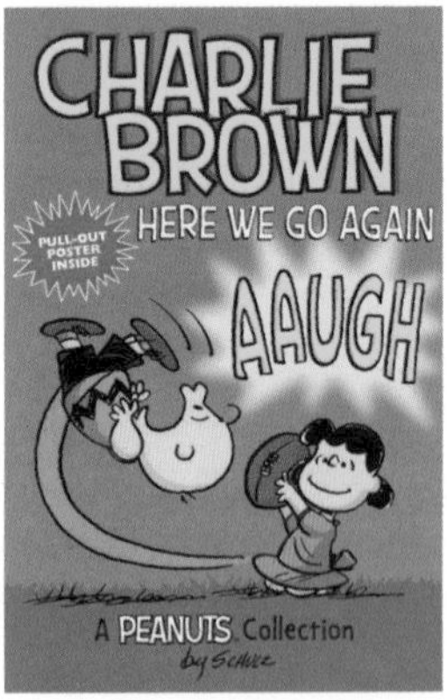
CHARLIE BROWN
HERE WE GO AGAIN
AAUGH
A PEANUTS Collection

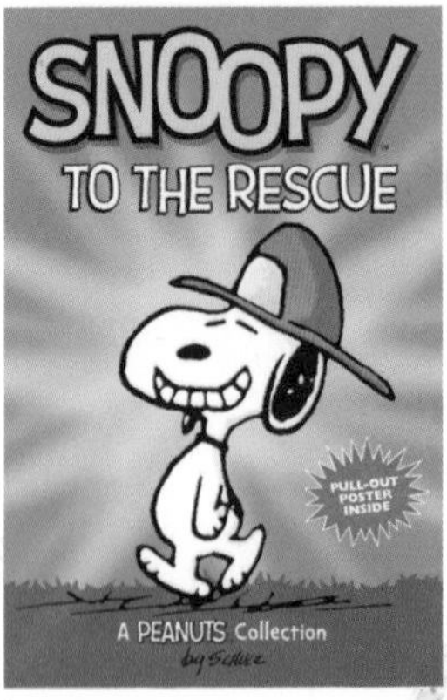
SNOOPY
TO THE RESCUE
A PEANUTS Collection

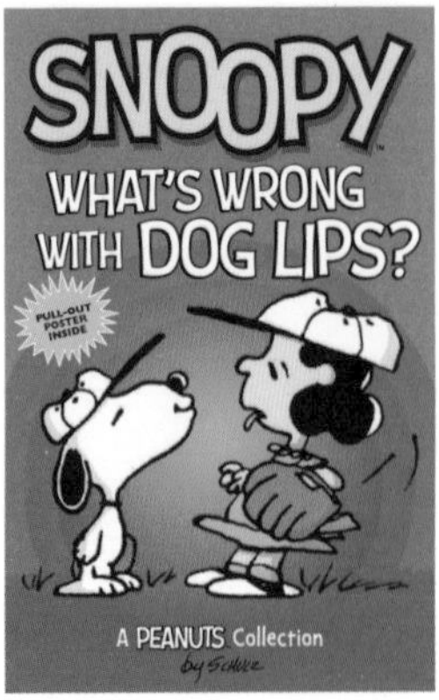
SNOOPY
WHAT'S WRONG WITH DOG LIPS?
A PEANUTS Collection

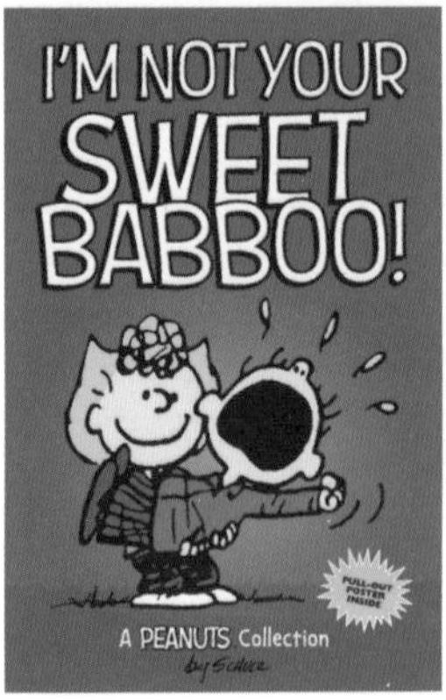
I'M NOT YOUR SWEET BABBOO!
A PEANUTS Collection

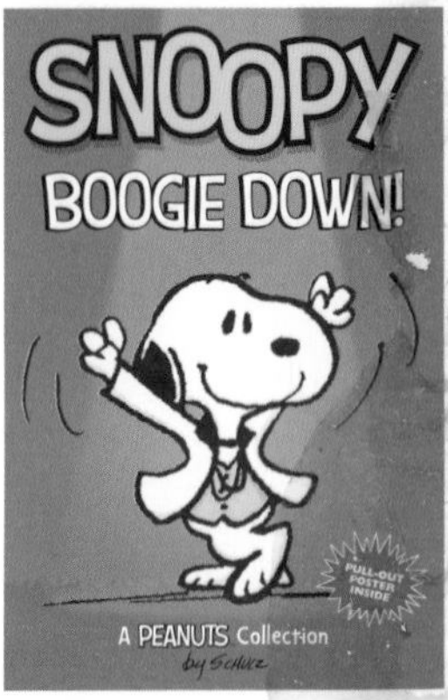
SNOOPY
BOOGIE DOWN!
A PEANUTS Collection